NICK LAIRD was born in Northern Ireland and studied at Cambridge and Harvard. He has published two novels, *Utterly Monkey* and *Glover's Mistake*, and three collections of poetry, *To a Fault*, *On Purpose* and *Go Giants*. He is the recipient of many awards for fiction and poetry, including the Betty Trask Prize, the Rooney Prize for Irish Literature, the Geoffrey Faber Memorial Prize and the Somerset Maugham Award. A Fellow of the Royal Society of Literature and a 2016 Guggenheim Fellow, he teaches in the creative writing programme at New York University.

Praise for *Modern Gods*:

'In *Modern Gods*, Nick Laird takes two experiences poles apart and unites them in gorgeous language, with the same fierce tenderness as he employs in his poetry. It's about families, tribes, peoples – and if you're a member of any of those you'll find a home both strange and familiar in this story'   DAVE EGGERS

'Laird marks himself out as a first-rate novelist, applying his virtuoso linguistic skills and acute ear for dialogue to a subject – religion – that is rarely well handled in fiction'   *Financial Times*

'Finely etched, impeccably structured, *Modern Gods* has the enduring echoes of a classic'   BBC

'*Modern Gods* has realer-than-real characters, unexpected turns of plot into unknown corners of the world, and language that finds its way through the darkest moments and states of mind to shine its clear bright light, revelatory and unforgiving. And it encompasses deep – the deepest, thorniest – questions of faith and redemption, fate and forgiveness'

MICHAEL CHABON

'[*Modern Gods*] also fulfils its duty as a corrective to our collective idiocy by reminding us what we've forgotten: at bedrock, it says, we're all just confused, lonely, yearning, terrified of death and desperate for love'

Irish Times

'An impressive, often funny, often tender novel' *Literary Review*

'Laird's overarching concern, for individuals trapped by politics and religion, carries *Modern Gods* along on a tide of vigorous compassion'

The Times

'Nick Laird's prose disseminates unease – a sure sign of originality. The aura of danger derives not so much from his theme (how religious faith is inseparable from violence) as from his sensibility: the reader feels the ever-present likelihood – the risk – of confrontation with unpalatable truths. Laird is a poet-novelist; his fictional world may be harsh and raw, but it is balanced by the imaginative habits of a poet, which always tend towards forgiveness and, indeed, towards celebration' MARTIN AMIS

'With a mere flick of description, Laird summons vast stretches of politics and history' JENNIFER EGAN, *New York Times*

'*Modern Gods* is at once remorselessly clear-eyed about human frailty in the aggregate and full of loving kindness for human beings as individuals. The taut prose reveals a poet's hand, and the dialogue a playwright's ear; Laird can nail an entire character in one acutely perceptive description, and he channels Amis in richly suggestive transitions that crystallise the truths of well-wrought scenes. Ferociously intelligent, radically contemporary, deeply affecting, stunning' MATTHEW THOMAS

'His most assured work of fiction to date ... *Modern Gods* shows him to be as equally a gifted writer of fiction as he is of poetry ... hugely enjoyable' *Sunday Times*

'Nick Laird knows a great deal about violence, physical, emotional and spiritual, and of how it eats into the lives both of survivors and perpetrators, and continues to corrode, like a slow-acting acid'

JOHN BANVILLE

MODERN GODS

NICK LAIRD

4th ESTATE • London

4th Estate
An imprint of HarperCollins*Publishers*
1 London Bridge Street
London SE1 9GF

www.4thEstate.co.uk

First published in Great Britain in 2017 by 4th Estate
First published in the United States by Viking in 2017
This 4th Estate paperback edition published in 2018

1

A catalogue record for this book is
available from the British Library

ISBN 978-0-00-825735-4

Designed by Cassandra Garruzzo

Printed and bound in Great Britain by
CPI Group (UK) Ltd, Croydon

MIX
Paper from
responsible sources
FSC™
www.fsc.org   FSC® C007454

I.M. Carol Laird
(1950–2017)

MODERN GODS

PROLOGUE

"I am a man of constant sorrow."

The microphone right up at his lips and the black Stetson tilted back, Padraig was going at it full tilt. He liked to start a capella with that long and twisted first note, just the way Ralph Stanley did.

"I've seen trouble all my days."

Around the bar the drinkers were two or three deep. Each of the snugs was occupied and the wee round tables by the dance floor were pretty much full. No one was dancing, not yet, but you could see it was about to start. When Alfie kicked in on the banjo the shoulders of a couple of women began swaying. In a matter of moments the floor would start filling up.

The lounge bar on the other side of the counter—you reached it through the side entrance—looked to be busy too. The front door banged against the high side of the first booth—some sort of scuffle broke out—and then there were two eejits in plastic Halloween masks.

"I bid farewell to old Kentucky."

One, a vampire, the other a Frankenstein's monster. The gipes. But it was Halloween soon enough and sure why not.

"The state where I was born and raised."

Padraig hooked his thumbs in his belt and did a quick two-step to the side as Alfie and Derek harmonized.

"The state where he was born and raised."

He pointed to Derek, who nodded and grinned and hit the hi-hat, then to Alfie, who closed his eyes and flicked the neck of the banjo vertical and back again.

"For six long years I been in trouble."

A car backfired outside was it? And again, and then a young fella in a hooded top standing near the fruit machine seemed to fall into the wall. The vampire had his arms straight up and at the end of them was a pistol. Frankenstein strode out fast into the middle of the dance floor and in his arms he carried a semi-automatic. A surge of bodies away from the door now, pushing across the lounge bar and much screaming. Dozens of customers were pressed up against the front of the stage. Padraig sang, *No pleasure yet . . .* and trailed off. Alfie strummed on for a couple of chords, but then he stopped too.

Frankenstein spun round and round on his heel, firing. There was a loud dull *pop-pop-pop-pop*, and a little puff of redness erupted from the side of the head of an old man seated at the bar. Down he went off his stool like the string was cut inside him. A woman sitting at a table clutched at her breast and fell into her husband. He was shaking her by the shoulders, holding her head up. A wee fella trying to get down the corridor towards the toilets stopped when a large darkness flowered on the back of his shirt.

The screaming. Jesus, the screaming.

Alfie came to life and jumped over the drums and the whole kit went toppling backwards off the stage, taking Derek with him. The gunman became a centrifugal force—all the people threw themselves outwards, away from him, against the walls of the bar, scrambling, scrabbling— against the tables, the booths—trying to get farther and farther away as he turned round and around. *Fut-fut-fut-fut* went the gun.

A young woman wearing red spectacles ducked down under her table. Two women were already under there, but four had been sitting in the alcove. Wine glasses empty and half empty all slid down now, smashing onto the floor.

The shooting stopped and a man's voice, hoarse with delight, shouted, "Trick or treat!"

Then the shooting started again. A pause and a different kind of gunshot: clipped, duller, efficient. The other man was firing now with a handgun. The vampire. Frankenstein was in the middle of the dance floor, loading the magazine on the semi-automatic. Bodies moved slowly on the ground.

Here was one moaning where the carpet met the dance floor. The vampire with the pistol fired another shot into it. The head just exploded everywhere.

Here was a man in a sports jacket curled into a ball. Here was a lady gripping the legs of a bar stool and wailing hysterically. Here was a scatter of archipelagic blood on a "Guinness Is Good for You" mirror.

Here was a man lying over his wife; more blood flowed out from under their huddled crying form in competing dark runnels across the parquet dance floor. Vampire fired at them again and *fut*, the huddle lay flat. A woman banged against the door of the ladies' toilets, but the three women inside held the door closed. "Trick or treat," the voice shouted hoarsely. "Trick or treat." The woman screamed, "Please, please, please, please," but then a very fast piece of metal entered the side of her head and she stopped.

PART 1:
SIX NOTHINGS

CHAPTER 1

"**H**ello."

"Do we need milk? Did you get the paper?"

"I got the paper."

Kenneth opened the fridge.

"We have . . . half a carton of semi-skimmed."

"There any buttermilk?"

"You making wheaten bread?"

"I was going to."

"I don't see any."

"I'll get some apple pancakes for Liz. Did the marquee people call?"

"Not yet. There's an ad I see there in the *Telegraph* magazine for trousers with elasticated waists—"

"I have elasticated-waisted trousers."

"They're very reasonable."

Judith sighed: "If I want to buy elasticated trousers, I'll just go into Cunninghams and buy elast—"

"I'm just saying these are very reasonable. They're twenty-nine ninety-nine. And they're in every color. Salmon. Mauve. What are they in Cunninghams? Twice that? Three times?"

"Why don't you order a pair for yourself?"

It was Kenneth's turn to sigh. That Kenneth was overweight was not in doubt, but if anyone needed elasticated trousers, it was Judith: the deadly, hidden growth they knew from the X-rays was now a physical presence, rising up beneath her belts, no longer hidden by cardigans, and her husband was breaking an unwritten rule by referring to it—however obliquely—first. She didn't need reminding. If she wanted to talk about it, she would talk about it.

"Did Liz call?" Judith asked, shoving the conversation on, and down the line Kenneth could hear the engine of a tractor, turning over somewhere near his wife's car, and her busy hand tapping out her impatience on the steering wheel.

"No.

"Does she expect collecting from the airport?"

"Well, she's a grown woman, I'm sure she'll let us know."

"I'll be back in five minutes," said Judith.

Kenneth paused and then offered, "I'll leave the magazine out anyway for you to see."

Judith performed the last and therefore definitive sigh of the conversation.

Kenneth plugged the phone back into the charger. The *beep beep beep* went again and he remembered why he was standing in the kitchen. He tugged the dishwasher open, feeling the ligament twinge in his elbow. No, not the dishwasher: lifeless, smelling ruinously of yesterday's fish pie. He pushed at the fridge door to check the seal was intact and saw out past the rockery a beige smear on the back lawn. He raised his readers from his nose up to his forehead, and with the other hand slid the distance glasses into place. A rabbit sat in the middle of the lawn, brazen, chewing stupidly.

Kenneth tapped on the window with his gold signet ring. Two coal tits fluttered off the bird feeder, lapped the tarmac, and re-alighted. But the rabbit did not move. Chew chew. Sniff.

He tapped the glass again. Sniff. Glance. Nothing. For a moment the "guiding best presence" he'd been working with their counselor Theresa, since September, to establish—"the mindfulness" to help steer the boat of himself through the treacherous currents of "this new life"—was utterly lost to Kenneth. He was pounding the window explosively hard with the side of his fist.

The rabbit jerked its gaze towards the house but felt that, no—on consideration it must decline. Chew chew. The base of Kenneth's palm hurt, and yet how briefly elevating it had felt to bang one thing very hard against another. "Anger," Theresa believed, "comes from feeling power-less." Well, yes. *Beep beep beep.* A sudden hunch and Kenneth rounded the table quickly to depress the fat button of the microwave; the little door popped and swung out to reveal a vaguely semenistic stain of hardened oatmeal on the frosted circular plate. But no, not the microwave. He sat on the edge of the sofa and waited. The room was silent. He stood up and waited, and the room was silent. He walked back and stood at the kitchen window and looked out and waited. *Beep beep beep.*

That sky hanging over the back hills was heavy with rain about to get falling. Sidney, his older brother, would be heading up to the cattle in an hour or so. He'd get soaked.

Beep beep beep.

In every room in the house something was dying or calling out or cry-ing to be tended to and soothed and nursed again on energy. Behind that rabbit, on the hillside in McMullens's field, the pylon, the carrier of all that energy, stood with its arms upraised like St. Kevin's, in perpetual ache, bringing the news of heat and light to all these decent bill-paying people. At the beech hedge the telegraph pole met a substantial black cable and led it down into the soil to swim through articulated tubing beneath the neat lawn and raucous flowerbeds, a few potato drills by the bitumen fence, the three bent-backed apple trees, and the tarmac and newly var-nished decking, before it surfaced at the back door to surge through the rubberized wires in the wall, slalom the fuse box circuits, and arrive in his house to power this fucking beeping he still could not locate.

There was a rumble of the cattle grid and a second later Judith's Volvo swung round the back of the house. The bunny upped and scarpered across the grass into the beech hedge, and the finality of the movement—the way the coppery leaves gulped down the little marshmallow tail—pleased Kenneth. He liked it best when problems disappeared themselves. He thought of Liz, his eldest, sloping towards him across twenty-five years, down in the hollow of Faulkner's back field, retrieving a rabbit

Kenneth had just shot. The wee lass's lanky arm straight out, the coney hanging by the ears, urine still trickling from it. He remembered how his daughter had turned away from the thing, her mouth closed tight and her face concentrated upon not showing any emotion at all. He'd shot it through the hindquarters, the bullet entering from the back, and as Liz walked along little bits of white fluff came off the tail like a dandelion clock unseeding.

He put the kettle on and pressed his fingertips against it until they started to hurt with the heat. It was what? Eleven o'clock? A quarter past. He felt sleepy and heavy, like he might tip forward onto the counter. He tried it slightly, letting his stomach press against its beveled edge. The New Truth Mission calendar hung on a nail by the window, a little black child grinning out at him from Africa, delighted to receive some wispy shaving of Kenneth's eight pound monthly direct debit. The child had a perfectly round head, and perfectly round eyes with perfectly round pupils, black circles in white circles in a black circle . . .

Judith was back now, she was just outside, she would come through the door and events would happen, life would move forward. A starling hung upside down on the feeder, mutilating with a wild flurry of pecks the fat ball he'd put out after breakfast. They went so quick. He'd bought twenty of them in Poundland only a couple of weeks ago. The door of the Volvo banged shut. The sky above the Sperrins was like a sheet of lead, cutting him off from all sources of energy—the sun's heat, the sun's light. He was trying to put off the thought that in two days there would be 112 drunk people in his garden, no doubt trampling over his newly planted flowerbeds.

The next beep entered his left ear a millisecond earlier than the right, and with a small grunt of triumph he realized it must be the tumble dryer. It sat atop the washing machine in the little porch by the back door. He pressed the button with the symbol of the key and the porthole clicked open; Kenneth pulled out the clothes in tangled clumps and let them fall in the plastic basket by his feet. They gave off warmth and a lilac smell and Kenneth felt his mood shift slightly upwards. The optimism of a load of freshly tumbled clothes. He could see his morning spreading benignly out before him. A bit of telly, one of the auction shows. A cappuccino. A piece of shortbread. But then as he lifted the basket, *beep beep beep*. It came from behind him, from the tumbler again.

Seeing the pixelated Judith looming through the back door, fiddling with keys, he said loudly, "But this is only ridiculous!"

He had the basket in his arms and was stepping through to the kitchen when she got the back door open. He could see immediately that something was not right by the look on her face, that his own morning trials were about to be subsumed by something much larger, but he kept going and set the basket on the table, and was already back in his armchair by the time she'd hung up her coat and come in. Maybe if he didn't look at her, maybe if he kept his focus to the orange-skinned fool on the TV pricing antiques, whatever was coming would not arrive.

Judith unpacked the bags and put the shopping away, letting the cupboards slap shut, Kenneth noted, with scant regard for the hinges.

He kept on staring at the TV, but on the far left of his vision he could still see her, trying to arrange scarlet tulips in a Belleek vase so that a bent-necked one stayed straight in the middle of the bunch. It flopped forward, and again. The rain that had been threatening for the last hour started. Big drops exploding on the roof of the car. The patio spotted, mottled, in a moment darkened uniformly.

"I don't know why I ever buy these. They never last. Honest to God the petals are already coming off this . . ."

Something in her voice—some new alarm, some warning—made him turn to her. He softened as he always did at the sight of sadness and stood up in his new, tentative way, and went to her. She was sobbing now and fell into him, and held him while he repeated—although he knew the answer—"What's wrong, what's wrong? Whatever's wrong now?"

CHAPTER 2

The moment the students filed out of the classroom, Liz felt humiliated. She could never entirely shake the suspicion that they had been laughing at her moments before she entered, and then at best they seemed indifferent and at worst contemptuous through the long three hours that followed. The ideal of teaching was surely to produce something like a gravitational effect when one walked into the room. She'd certainly had dons like that: dry, thickly draped women with hair in retentive buns; or Professor Paulson himself, who would walk up the lecture hall to a silence that gathered and gathered until only the sound of his footsteps ascending to the podium were heard. But lately Liz found herself forced to the conclusion that she was of a different stripe, the kind of teacher who talks fast because she's not entirely sure of her facts, directs questions to the logorrheics to waste time, and forgets her grading, or forgets to do it, and whose lesson plan is three lines long and most weeks consists of reading out chapters of her own far-from-finished book. She couldn't get her act together. Although the classroom engendered panic, it was never quite enough to spur her into useful action. Now she closed the door behind the last shuffling backpack, fell into one of their empty seats, and at once opened her Gmail, looking for relief, distraction, and read: LIZ: URGENT DISASTER which seemed an accurate if brutal definition.

Liz, darling, it's Margo—

It's been so long! Too long!
I still think back to the Myth project with such affection and such pride

and I've been hoping to work with you again for the longest time. I heard
you were teaching in America so I hope this e-mail finds you happy and
well and ensconced in life stateside. But not *too* happy and not *too*
well! Because I need your help!

A somebody called Charlotte Taylor-Anderson had been lined up to present
The Latest of the Gods—a documentary about a religious movement in New
Ulster, an island off the coast of Papua New Guinea, for *The State of Grace*,
a special season on religion the BBC were doing—but this Taylor-Anderson
had just broken her back on an artificial ski slope in Perthshire. Margo had
an experienced cameraman lined up who'd done an Attenborough series, the
permits were in place, but she lacked a presenter. They were meant to shoot
next week. Would Liz consider stepping in?

Several PDFs were attached, including a newspaper clipping from the
Sydney Morning Herald, "A New God in New Ulster," written by Stan
Merriman. Liz skimmed the article. A cargo cult prophet named Belef had
started a movement called the Story, which merged some of the local religions with Christianity, and threw in a bit of political independence. The
missionaries were all stirred up. The most surprising thing seemed to be
that Belef was a woman.

Could she do this? She'd have to go back to the apartment and get hiking gear and waterproofs, more contact lenses, a couple of books—maybe
William James's *The Varieties of Religious Experience*, and there was
that Peter Lawrence one on cargo cults. She opened Google Earth and
called up New Ulster. Curved like a scimitar. Entirely green. A chaos of
peaks and valleys. When she tried to zoom in, none of it, not an inch,
appeared to be mapped.

The excitement propelled her effortlessly along, all the way home, until
she reached the front door of her own studio. She knocked, got no answer,
and began to look for her keys. She jiggled away the loyalty key rings for
various pharmacies, opened the door, and look, there was a man she
didn't know standing in her kitchenette. He wore a green T-shirt that had
the words "Some Crappy Band" printed on it, purple underpants, and one

red sock—the other foot was bare and long toed and dirty looking. Clearly not a burglar. It occurred to Liz that she had for once occasioned something like a sudden atmospheric change—her presence used up all available oxygen. Atlantic, her useless dog, butted at her shins and whined. Joel was also standing—also wearing a T-shirt and pants—on the far side of the bed, breathless, saying, "Liz, hi, I didn't—this is Jeff."

"Okay."

Liz said it very slowly, testing the weight of the word on the room. Nobody replied. Joel was for some reason on the verge of smirking. She turned towards Some Crappy Band.

"Hello."

"How's it going?"

The man in the kitchenette spoke with no embarrassment or shame. Really quite cheerful, considering the situation he now found himself in. There was some disjunct going on here. Tall and freckled and milky-skinned with light brown eyes, somehow even more Joel's opposite than she was, gender aside. A farm boy with that fleshy softness. Innocent as butter. And a dark wet coin on the front of his purple briefs.

Joel said, "Weren't you going straight to Newark?"

There was no need to answer this, but she found herself doing so: "I got an e-mail. I've been asked to present a TV show . . . in Papua New Guinea."

Joel was nodding foolishly.

"Amazing," he whispered across the bed.

Atlantic butted and pawed at Liz's knees.

The man said, "A TV show? Cool. Very cool. And very cool of you to let Joel crash here."

"Oh. Well. I am nothing if not cool."

What was she saying? She felt her fury being ousted by some kind of ironic pose. And there was an inconvenient pressing in her bladder that was now a matter of some urgency. In her tiny bathroom, only a rattan door separated her from the rest of the studio, she turned on the tap to camouflage the sound of her ablutions. But now she couldn't hear them.

Were they whispering? She stopped the tap, and waited. Nothing. She turned it on again.

Crap Band. She'd seen him before, at the SoulCycle class a few weeks ago. He'd worn a green, deep-cut sleeveless vest and sat on the other side of Joel. When Joel dropped his water bottle Crap Band picked it up. It was Liz's first time and she had not returned. But Joel now went every other day to hear Madison shout, "The body does what the mind tells it"—which had never been Liz's experience. She sat on the toilet and gripped the edge of the basin in front, pissed while staring dumbly at her hands, the way Atlantic pissed, as if it were happening to somebody else. Like the end of this relationship. Apparently unfolding right now, though it somehow felt like it was happening to somebody else.

She'd first met Joel in the lobby of the Standard hotel. A young Asian man sat eating by himself nearby, facing a wall. He wore a black tie and a white shirt, and she'd realized he worked here and was on his break. Widely spaced eyes and a tiny bud-mouth, grinning intensely at her. Then he was not there—then materialized again from behind a very tall black woman in a silver lamé body suit. He was coming towards her, weaving between tables. Shorter than she might reasonably have hoped for but proportionate. Ran a hand through his fringe and squared his shoulders, which endeared. She'd studied the melt of ice in her glass and swirled the blunted cubes around with the straw. Here, here he was. The most marvelous cheekbones and thin mocking eyes.

"You've really got to stop staring at me," he had said.

All delightful. But beginnings always are. They tell you nothing. It's the end of the affair that brings the real information.

Washing her hands, delaying reentry, she looked at herself in the mirror above the sink. She made herself bare her teeth like a monkey, then dried her hands on the towel and walked back into the crime scene.

Jeff put his hand out and Liz shook it meekly, not meeting his eye. He'd pulled on a pair of unclean denim dungarees that were a few inches too short, and now he punched his way into a frayed plaid shirt and began buttoning it up.

"Good to meet you finally. Joel talks a lot about—"

"Jeff," Liz repeated dumbly, setting her bag down on the chair.

"That's right. Jeff."

"This is my flat," she said, as if that were news.

"Hey, you know," said Jeff, spreading his arms. "I'm sorry if any of this is awkward for you."

Three mason jars were standing on the kitchen counter—one green, one purple, one yellow—and each held some kind of fetal-looking object.

"They're mine," Jeff said, following her gaze. "So, I pickle? Pretty much every vegetable you can think of, really. It's a hobby. . . . I brought a few jars over for Joel."

Liz turned her full attention to Jeff, and looked into his brown eyes. Too late he understood that he shouldn't keep mentioning Joel's name. It poked up out of his speech like a swear word. They both looked at the name's owner; at some point he had climbed back into bed and there was a definite sense of bemusement coming off him. He was wearing her Montclair T-shirt, and it was on inside out.

Joel said, "I'm sorry about this, Jeff—"

"You're apologizing to *him*? Really?"

"Can we do this later?"

"Oh, I think we need to do this now."

"These things happen," Joel said. "We agreed monogamy was . . . not for us. You said that you—Liz!"

She had decided to kick over the chair on which she'd hung her tote, but her foot got entangled in the strap and she stumbled slightly, had to hop. Enormous lovely Jeff steadied her with a hand to the shoulder, which Liz shrugged off. She had an urge to rip something up, but the only thing she could see was some junk mail on the oven. She lifted it but saw now it was a bill from Con Ed and they were a massive pain to contact and she set it down again. Jeff the pickler left a minute later, having silently wrapped his three jars in hessian sacks and placed them in an old blue Pan Am bowling ball bag. Joel finally found the decency to look unhappy, and Liz righted the chair and sat in it and stared at him.

_____

Eleven minutes later Joel set his holdall and three plastic bags by the door, and sat down on the edge of the bed, facing her. He placed his fingertips together and, as if admitting something, sighed and said, "I hate to think you're unhappy. That I've made you unhappy."

Liz felt her own silence working on him as punishment, and she kept it up and stared at him. Was it the fact it was a man? Did that make it better or worse? The morning after they'd first fucked, which was the morning after they'd first met, she and Joel had gone for coffee at the Moonlight Diner a block down from her apartment. Peaceably hungover, him back in his waiter's uniform, they'd studied their respective magazines and Joel had ordered eggs—no yolks—and mentioned, offhand, that his last relationship had been with a man.

She'd just sipped her green tea and smiled and said, "In this economy you got to diversify."

How brave, the new world. She slid the menu between the salt and pepper shakers and went back to Shouts & Murmurs, feeling the fond glow of her progressive nature.

After two months of very casual dating, Joel's sublease in Astoria expired and he asked her could he stay at hers for a week. Some cocaine had been taken and she'd readily agreed. That was three weeks ago.

But they were having fun. She liked him being around.

But now it was not fun, and now she did not like him.

Why was one thing always followed by the other? Why did no emotion hang around for very long?

"Did you fuck him or was he fucking you?"

Joel looked disappointed in her.

This was almost enjoyable. Bring on the heteronorms. Bring on the suits and ties. These kids were too free. They were having way too much fun. Bring back standards, family values and monogamy and chaperones, modesty, lowered hemlines, the death penalty. These kids with their Tinder, their Grindr, their 3nder, their constant fucking. It was too much.

Joel was nine years younger and it occurred to Liz that the difference in their races, in their nationalities, in their sexes, was irrelevant. It was really a question of where you sat in relation to time. Did she have more in common with a thirty-four-year-old anywhere in the world than with this twenty-five-year-old in front of her? Was it self-sabotage? Did she want to get married? Did she want to have children? Did she want what she was supposed to? Sometimes. Sometimes she really thought she did. But mostly she did not.

Atlantic was scratching against the cupboard under the sink, where her food was kept. Pointless fucking dog. What were you doing while this was going on? Sleeping? Watching?

Joel was sorry she'd reacted like this.

Liz was sorry he was such a total cock.

Joel was sorry she was so consistently uptight and hadn't she discussed this with her therapist?

Liz was sorry he thought it was fine to behave like such an entitled asshole.

Joel was sorry she was so limited and bourgeois and prejudicial and narrow-minded.

Liz was sorry he was such an unbelievable fucking cock.

The door shut behind him and she sat and stared at it and felt herself collapse in stages, like a marquee.

She was picking bits of wax out of Atty's ears and rubbing them into her sock when her phone beeped. Alison. Amazing. One of her sister's gifts—perhaps her sister's only gift—was to contact people at their weakest, lowest, most humiliated point. Across oceans, across time zones—no doubt across light years and galaxies and the expanding unfathomable distances of deep space—Alison could smell it. The inimicable scent of sibling disaster. She was getting married—for the second time, admittedly—but still, Liz was getting nothing, was getting shafted, left alone again. . . . She stuffed the phone in a crevice of the duvet nest she had constructed. It was silent for a few seconds then buzzed again. She willed herself to draw it out.

Flight on time? All OK? looking 4ward to catching up x

———————

The sun had sunk out of sight, but the glass sides of the skyscrapers down-town gave back its old lion face. A diffuse ruddy light fell on the upper stories of the brick edifice of London Terrace. Liz tightened the left strap of her rucksack and considered her circumstances. No boyfriend meant no dog sitter.

There were no cabs. She needed to take Atlantic to her cousin Marcus's flat, if he'd take her, and then head straight to Newark. Even if the fuss Marcus caused about Atlantic was tedious—setting a tea towel on his lap before the dog sat on him, ostentatiously picking the yellow hairs off his black sofa and dropping them into the toilet bowl—there was no one else.

She flicked through her phone. Who was Jason? Who was Lesley? Who was Nicky P? Man or woman? Friend or foe? Atlantic's charms were far from legendary. She scrolled back to MARCUS and hovered her thumb above the name. Atlantic was giving something an exploratory chew. Liz crouched and pulled an Almond Joy wrapper from her slippery and unre-sisting teeth. She texted Marcus—BIG DOG FUCKUP: ANY CHANCE YOU COULD TAKE FOR A FEW DAYS? RIGHT NOW?—and walked north for a block before Marcus replied. He was in Hong Kong and it was 6:00 a.m. in the morning. He hoped that nothing was wrong and that she was doing OK—the kind of text that is like a plea to end the matter there. Liz took off the rucksack and sat on it on the corner of Twenty-fifth and Tenth. It happened like this. You were fine you were fine you were fine, and then you fell apart.

CHAPTER 3

The problem with zopiclone was it launched you into the ocean of sleep handily enough, but subsequently it tossed you up on the beach of 3:11 a.m., wide awake, spectacularly marooned. You came to with a jolt, alert, your mind already mid-churn.

So here we are again, the Voice said to Judith. *Just you and me. Us two. Us twosome. Us all alonesome. Us gruesome duo. How do you do, so?*

The vast hulk of Kenneth beside her whistled serenely, steadily steaming across his own deep.

The Voice said, *You know, you never should have bought a memory foam mattress. It makes you so hot. Like lying in a slice of white bread. And you can never admit this now, of course, since it was your idea to buy it. Not just your idea. Your* insistence. *Nothing else would do. Oh no.*

The blinds were still black but would start edging closer soon to gray, then a kind of gray-green, then forest green, deciduous green, the green of well-fed grass, of grass that grows on graves.

It was impossible not to imagine the worst at 3:11 a.m.

What did Theresa say?

Allow the feeling in, experience it, and let it go again. Let it move on. Let it float past.

The Voice said, *Do you think little Michael will remember you? Sure, how could he? What age will he be when you go? You'll be a kind of misty presence in his memory, at best, and maybe video or pictures will remind him, maybe. But you won't be reading books to him, you won't be watching him at football matches, you won't be seeing him put on gang shows with the scouts . . .*

The Voice would not shut up. It would not be outwitted or shouted down. You could not threaten it or bargain with it. The Voice just talked and talked, recounting the things that must be done, the things that never would be, mixing the probable and the possible, the hopeless and the endless and the pointless . . . The mind leapt from rock to rock. The only way to escape it was to get up and go into the kitchen and make the mind do what the body told it. Read a book or make some wheaten bread or pay the bills. Clean the grouting in the upstairs bathroom. Which is what she had intended to start on this afternoon and might as well tackle now. Why not.

She put her feet on the cold floor and the Voice said, *Slippers, Judith, you'll catch your death. Ha.*

The Voice had a sense of humor, of course, and yet it was not funny. You could not call it funny. Kenneth was doing his best. She was doing her best. Everyone was trying hard to do their best but so what? To what end? You went through the day doing your utmost and smiling and telling everyone you were fine really you were coping and then the night came and you lay down and in the darkness were gripped by the million hands of terror. *So,* said the Voice, *I said how are we doing?*

Not great, Judith replied. *I've been better.*

You have, said the Voice. *Oh, you surely have.*

She crept up the stairs. This had been the "kids' toilet" until her son Spencer moved out it must be almost eight years now. Overnight Judith began calling it "the guest bathroom," which Kenneth found "a bit affected." But as usual he misunderstood. It had taken a conscious effort to rechristen it, and it was a deliberate overwriting, part of her efforts to keep abreast of time, not fall behind it. Time snuck up on you and she'd seen some of her friends—Carol Thomson, Betty Moore—keep their children's rooms like little shrines when they went off to their universities or jobs. She was not going to be one to wallow. As the clock moved on, so did she. It felt important—morally important—not to be caught in past attitudes. Not to be hung up on it, on what happened, on the museum of the family. There was an obligation to live your life forward. She told anyone who'd listen that she wasn't going to be one of those grandmothers obsessed with their grandkids, looking after them every week and talking of nothing else. But then of course Isobel was born and this was exactly what happened.

Now that Isobel, Alison's daughter, stayed with them all the time, in the little box room called "Izzy's room," the bathroom too had reverted to its old name, its first name.

Judith tugged on the light and the extractor fan ticked awake, too loud. It wouldn't rouse Kenneth unless she plucked it from the wall and dropped it on his head, but its whirring was too loud for the night. There was no place for the mechanized in this darkness pulled up like a coverlet over the fields and the woods and Ballinderry River, over the garden and the hillside beyond it, its gorse and bare rocks and tussocks, and over the house, the middle one of three on the lane, that she stood in now, breathing very lightly. She tugged the bulb off and stepped into the guest room, turned on the bedside lamp and carried it to the bathroom, setting it on the lowered lid of the toilet. The plastic Tesco's bag full of bath toys in the sink she moved to the low shelf of the wicker unit. She ran the hot tap and used her fingernails to clean Izzy's hardened red toothpaste off the smooth enamel.

Things, being things, always wore out. They wore down. They got dirty and needed cleaning. They wanted bleaching. Over the years, the grouting in the shower had turned from white to this mouse gray. She needed to spray it first, really, with a peroxide-based cleaner, and then leave it for half an hour. It would need to be scrubbed fairly gently not to take the grouting off. Wire wool would be too harsh. A nailbrush. Even a toothbrush.

She opened the cupboard under the sink. Cleaning products were always named to make it sound like cleaning took no time at all. In a jiff. In a flash. Everyone was so concerned with time. So worried about spending it the right way. And how much more pressing was it now. Life-limited. The phrase Dr. Boyers used. The limited life. But wasn't everyone's?

She spritzed the grouting until all the tiles ran with little foamy rivulets, and the chemical smell nauseated her. When she opened the window the night air came in like a cold hand on her neck. There was a smell of cut grass, manure. She'd leave the liquid to soak for a while, and go and have a look at the attic. It would need to be cleared at some point.

She found herself sitting on the bed in the guest room, staring into the deep-pile carpet, a striped affair of red and cream, and then at the curtains, a heavy red damask.

Liz had said, after her first night in here after it was decorated, that she'd felt like she was sleeping inside someone's womb. Now what slept in Judith's womb was monstrous. Awful.

Hello, the Voice said. *Are you referring to me?*

Of course it could be beaten. It was unlikely, very unlikely, but who knows what could happen? Who knows what miracles science might yet come up with?

People would say to her sometimes there are good things about getting a diagnosis, and she would smile and say, "Oh yes," and think, *How dare you*. But it was true that the fact of the thing had freed her, for a bit. She'd moved into the center of their lives, hers and Ken's, and found herself appreciated—like an ornament gathering dust in the back of a cabinet unexpectedly appraised at some fantastic value, and brought out to the light of the mantelpiece. But here too the dust alighted.

Four years, two months, and seventeen days ago she'd noticed that she couldn't close the button of her good navy slacks. She had carried three children and now this lump. It could be benign, a benign cyst. Why not? What was the point in mentioning it to Kenneth? He had enough going on. He was making a good recovery from his surgery, and his speech was pretty good, considering the way it had been six months before. It was a Saturday night and she didn't sleep well at all, even after several G&Ts. The next day she'd made a roast chicken for lunch and Ken's brother Sidney came round, and told them in his halting way a long story about

Lynn's horse being stolen from a field outside Markethill and her friend
Sean buying said horse back from a man in a pub in Dundalk, but she was
too distracted to follow all the details, and when she tried to lift the bowls
of trifle before Kenneth and Sidney had finished eating, her husband
looked at her like she had two heads and said, "What's got into you?"

I don't know, she wanted to scream. *I don't know what's got into me
or how it got there or how to get it out.* But instead she smiled and said,
"Och, I didn't sleep last night. I'm dead tired."

The following Monday morning at 8:30 a.m. she stood at the back
door of the clinic at the Westland Road waiting for someone to arrive and
open up. Once inside, Judith did what she was told. It was a relief to follow instructions, to enter a system and just sit and look at a poster telling
people—especially old people and children, who were apparently particularly at risk—to get flu shots, and just to sit and wait and wait and sit and
know that the process, whatever it turned out to be, had started. A relief
it was to pass the problem of herself to other people. They would sort it.
They would know. They would do what they could.

The attic was accessed by a half-sized door—an Alice-in-wunnerland
door, Izzy called it—in the wall of the small bedroom. Judith stooped and
entered and tugged the light pull. Even with her slippers and terry-cloth
dressing gown, the coldness felt cautionary. She was still too warm-blooded
to be standing here among lifeless junk, the abandoned clothes and pictures and games and books. Heaped in the corners, hanging from makeshift rafters, filling cardboard boxes and shelves and plastic-lidded stacked
bins, the grave goods. A foot away from her head, a spider, her host,
shinned down its twisting filament and twirled and reconsidered and
hauled itself back up.

Look at all this crap, she thought. *Look at all this* crap.

All the many hundred accumulated products of marriage and children.
They could open a Museum of Late-Twentieth-Century Life. The History
of Board Games, of Soft Toys, of Side Lamps, of Winter Coats. Maybe

Isobel and Michael would want some of it. But she never showed any interest in making things, Isobel. Judith couldn't get her to touch the Lego or jigsaws. She was all about dolls. Girls liked things with faces; no matter what the feminists thought, it was true.

She pulled out a broad hanger from which a maroon suit bag hung. A transparent window in the bag revealed thick brown fur. It was so heavy. When they'd gotten engaged over a bag of chips in Morans' Café on Lower Merrion, Kenneth had said they would have four children, a house with a river that ran through the grounds, where he could fish—and she would have a fur coat. They'd managed three children. That took ten years. The coat took twelve . . . Life was both slower and faster than you expected. You saved up and worked towards . . . Must have been 1982. They were living in the wee Iveagh estate up in Prehen on the Waterside in Londonderry and she was working in the City Shirt Factory, in Personnel. Kenneth traveled for a while from Dublin and then got a job with Kennedy Collins estate agency, which had just opened a branch in Derry, up at the diamond.

She unzipped the bag and a great rush of soft fur escaped from the plastic. She ran her hand down it, and static made the fur twitch as if it were alive.

She found herself reluctant to try it on. It was a different Judith who'd worn it. She smoothed a hand down the collar of the coat, with the nap and then against it. It looked dark brown this way, then black the other. It all depended. She thought of pushing her face into it for a second but didn't. Mink? It was mink, wasn't it? What was mink? Like an otter? More ferocious. Like a ferret. How many minks? You got a coat like this from ten, twelve animals, she thought, checking the pockets automatically. Nothing.

The things they'd done in this coat! She slipped it on and sunk her hands into the pockets lined with satin. She gave a little curtsy for no reason, and noticed in the corner another rail of clothes balanced between a rafter and the housing for the water tank. She hadn't looked at those in years. Among the trench coats and sheepskin jackets and leather skirts, she came to a plastic bag on a wooden hanger, filled with exercise books. She worked the bag off the metal hook of the hanger and pulled out the tired orange and blue exercise books.

Liz Donnelly. P.4 English. P.4 Geography. P.4 Maths. P.4 History.

Judith opened the English book to a story written by the eight-year-old Liz from the point of view of the town of Ballyglass. Such imagination!

Each step round the chimney took her further into the past. Boxes of their own wedding presents from forty-two years ago were stacked here, and boxes of books and crockery from Kenneth's parents' house in Ballyshannon. There was too much of it. It overwhelmed. She moved back into the lit part of the attic, pushed with her slippered foot a plastic crate of old candles and Christmas decorations under the eaves, making a passable trail from the door to the chimney stack. The bookshelf leaning against it held all the books in the house. Molly Keane's *Good Behaviour*. Frank O'Connor's *The Cornet Player Who Betrayed Ireland*. Dick Francis. That was Kenneth's, and unread. Jeffrey Archer. He turned out to be a shyster, didn't he? His poor wife. What were those boxes? Oh, the Hummel plates—they'd bought one a year for the first twenty years of their marriage. History of Hummel Plates, circa 1972 to 1994.

It hadn't been easy. God knows. They'd fought and fought. She'd moved out once, moved into the flat above the agency for a night, and taken one of the girls with her. He was a terrible thorny old bastard sometimes, no doubt about that. Things you think you'll always love you don't. You really don't. She'd wanted a nice home with nice things. On the farm there was never enough of anything. Except for work. There was enough of that.

She didn't want the children to have to go through the boxes—she'd done it with her own mother's things, few though they were. All her mother's clothes had fitted in two bin bags. She found she was hugging herself now, hugging her fur-coated body. She wanted to sift her life through her fingers, to weigh the thing and not find it wanting. To find that everything was worth it in the end.

Liz would be home in nine hours—eight. She must remember to cut some hydrangea from the garden and set a vase of it in her room. She lifted Liz's exercise book and tugged off the attic light. Back in the guest room she sat on the bed and read:

As towns go, I'm not the best looking. My spine is one big wide street running along for over a mile, dead straight. I have shops all down me and you can tell how well the shop owner did a hundred years ago by the highnesses of the building. I sit at the foot of a mountain, Slieve Gallion, which wears its white cap in winter and in summer time is brown. I was born in 1645 as a marketplace, a meeting place for all the peeple to come and buy and sell vegtables and animals, cows and pigs and horses. I was burnt down and built bak up, and burnt down and built back up. My name is also An Corr Crea, from the Irish for Boundry Hill.

There has been a lot of fighting. Everybody wants me. My MPs have been UNions and Shin Fein—the people who walk all over me are both Protesants and Roman Catholics. There are the same amounts of people of both kinds. I have nearly ten thousand people living on me like little nits in my hair.

My synbol is made up from the synbol of the county and three fish. The synbol of the county is the red hand and it comes from the story of when Ulster had no proper ruler. The men agreed that a boat race would happen and who's hand was first to touch the shore of Ireland, would be the owner of the place. Many boats were in the race and a man called O'Neill saw that he was losing so he got a sword and chop off his hand and lifted it and threw it and it reached the shore first. O'Neill was made the king and he lives at Tullyhog fort outside the town near Christine's house.

The family Donnelly live in the south part of me, on the Lissan road. They are a happy family and there are five of them. Mummy and Daddy and Liz and Alison and little baby Spencer. The mummy makes rice krispy buns and cherry scones. The Daddy sells houses to people who need places to live. Alison and Spencer are OK.

My businnesses are to make cement out at the Cement works and to make sausages at the Bacon Factory. Sometimes out in the playgground of the primary school you hear the pigs squealing in the factory as they're being brought in or put down. They cut their throats, but quick so it doesn't hurt. And sometimes there is a bad smell from the factory sweet and rotten both.

CHAPTER 4

She was in no doubt at all; she could handle this. The embarrassment inside her had been turned way down—it still burned merrily and brightly like a gas ring left on, but it was bearable. She could bear it. It had not been a serious enterprise. She knew that. And there had been precedents. There were incidents pertaining, sure. The party in Brooklyn Heights where she had walked into the kitchen and "a good friend" had been hugging Joel from behind. Little folds of time. You can quicken memory and scatter it and thread the incidents together.

She felt a bubble of new anger rising through her and reached for her phone, then put it down again, sat back against the plastic seat, and concentrated on the view as her train rattled through the industrial edgelands of Newark. Concrete grandeur, a thin scrim of light rain. Unaccomplished graffiti on abandoned railcars. She looked at the phone. She wanted very much to be able to hurt him, and she realized that one of the things bothering her about this was that she wasn't sure she could. She decided to send the text: You broke my heart. Inadequate, self-harming, momentarily satisfying. Nor did it feel remotely true even as she typed it, but what with the renewed steady movement of the car, and the rain, and the dilapidated splendor of New Jersey's manufacturing heritage, she tried to think herself into a space where it might be true, and stared out the window, and for a moment thought she might cry again, if she kept still and stared hard enough at the particulars of night coming on.

Her phone vibrated, but once more it was her sister. Lovely weather here today. Izzy outside on bike all day! We looking forward to seeing you. You sort car hire OK?

Liz's family had downsized their role in her life since she left home, of course, but not in the way she'd expected. They were like a village she had once lived in that had been shrunk down to miniature. The relationships didn't loosen to old friendships; they contracted over the years, but retained all the same angles and shapes, the same functions of shame and despair and joy. It was like a scale model she lived in—and it still functioned. The little train ran, the signs swung outside the little shops, tiny people went from room to room, turning on and off the lights. Interacting with her family was like entering the village as an adult—outsized, and trying to crawl under the arches and bridges and flyovers, trying not to put one's size-fives in the miniscule flowerbeds.

She spoke to her family every other day or so. *Is this healthy?* That was one of Joel's lines. *Is this healthy?* Possibly, she'd reply. It's possibly healthy.

She texted Alison back: Didn't hire car yet. Any chance of a lift? Why you still up?

The reply came after a minute.

Up when M's up. He's feeding, mostly screaming. I'm giving him a bottle and watching Downton Abbey with earphones. I'll get Stephen to pick you up. I have a final dress fitting. They messed up the zip.

Liz considered for a second, and replied:

Awful show! Btw just came home to boyfriend in bed with someone. Not feeling too chipper tbh.

She knew the phone would ring. She watched the display light up with ALLY HOME, and considered whether this conversation would make her feel better or worse. Liz always felt like the black sheep; her mother and father and brother and sister were their own club, and Liz was invariably outside the circle. But there was nothing more rewarding, in some lights, than a conversation with her sister. If Liz were a plaintiff in the court of some anecdote, Alison would quickly side with her and adopt on her behalf the prosecutor's wrath. She was loyal as a pit bull, but then you don't want a pit bull in the house, ideally. In phone conversations Alison would frequently crown a line offered by her elder sister with a stinging, cryptic, catchall phrase: *Well, that's typical of you.* Or: *You're never going to grow up, are you?* And once, astonishingly: *That's what you get for crying wolf your whole life.*

She pressed the TALK key.

At once her sister's tone, accelerated but contained, suggested she could somehow take control of this situation and fix it up nicely. She could see her three thousand miles away, drooly fat infant slumped across one shoulder, the phone wedged between the other and her ear, her blue eyes shining with the ecstatic confirmation of someone else's pain.

She said, "I can't understand how he could do that to someone."

The beast Despair prowled behind the chemical stockade her two Xanax had erected. Liz's real self could see it perfectly well in the distance, waiting for the barriers to come down, waiting to enter Lizville, ransack it, raze it to the ground.

Liz replied and Alison said, "I mean do it to you, obviously. I don't understand how anyone could do that to another person."

An inability to comprehend the bloody obvious—Alison often expressed this to Liz. Was it real or an act? It was the easiest thing in the world to understand how someone might have sex with someone else. It was the easiest thing because it was pretty much the only thing, the one reliable force in the world, universal human gravitation. Every scandal was confirmation of it. It made everyone act crazy, risk their jobs and lives and families . . . Oh, someone might pretend—or really have—an interest in, say, sailing or the opera or growing cabbages. But there, beneath it all, was the thing happening, every fleshy particle in the universe attracting every other one. . . . Now and at all times, nearby, very close, people were being pulled towards each other. Bodies tending towards other bodies.

Someone was entering, someone was getting entered. Liz loved and hated the sex hum of cities, manifested in a million tiny glances and gestures, in its streets, its cafés, its libraries. It kept everything electric. Alison, mother of two, had had sex presumably at least twice, though she always spoke of it as something distant or alien or beyond her. Or at least she always did to Liz. And now, as Liz, against her better judgment, tried to sketch the details—replacing Alison's assumed gender pronoun with the correct one—she found herself cut off midsentence, like a student who has given the wrong answer.

"No, no, no, I don't want to hear all that. Bad enough he was ten years younger. And gay, as it turns out. Okay, whatever. Bi," said Alison over her sister's barks of protest. "Nine years younger. You want to split hairs? Sometimes I think you want to be unhappy."

There it came. The great expected wash of tiredness ran across her. She leaned forward and rested her head against the cool leather of the seat in front. Her body relaxed into sadness and she swallowed hard. She wasn't going to start crying again. She leaned down and tickled Atty's head as Alison continued, warming to the theme of Liz's general fecklessness:

"You haven't seen Izzy in what? Nine months? Ach, you won't believe the change in her. She's up to my chest now. She was just moved up in her reading group. And sure Michael was tiny. Oh, we're so excited. Izzy hasn't talked of anything else all week. And there's Stephen! You'll get to meet Stephen!"

Two hours later and they were up, away, climbing. The lights in the cabin dimmed and she put the bag on her knees and covered both it and herself with the staticky polyester blanket. Atty popped her head up and panted and panted and finally calmed down, as Liz let her rest her muzzle in her hand. The Ambien that Yahoo Answers had advised her to give the dog kicked in, and Atty fell deeply asleep for the entire flight while Liz periodically worried that she'd killed her. She marked her student essays on mate choice and marriage finance with mostly random tics all the way through their two double-spaced pages, and wrote "Excellent!" at the end.

> *Goodbye Shirlita Goddard, she thought, and your repellent*
> *staccato laugh.*
> *Goodbye Hector Martinez and your outsized silly quiff.*
> *Goodbye Steve. Steve Something. Yellow polo shirt, psoriasis.*

Repeatedly she slid her hand into the bag and placed her fingertips on the dog's chest and felt the little reassuring tom-tom of its effort.

CHAPTER 5

When you found yourself hissing at your baby to shut up, to please for God's sake just shut up for a bit, it was important to set said baby down delicately in his cot and leave the room. That was Rule Number One in Alison's Big Book of Parenting. It was true that nothing gave her more joy than to look in Michael's huge cornflower-blue eyes, which even now at 3 a.m.—especially now—radiated curiosity and attention, and to stroke his smooth fat cheeks, and feel his whole life force settle itself as she held him to her and pressed his small hard skull against her chest. But who wants to feel joy at this time of night? She wanted to feel sleep, to feel nothing, to be unconscious for eight or nine blissful hours. She had left him to cry for twenty-three minutes and then given in and got up again. Exactly the opposite of what you're meant to do. Maybe if she'd waited twenty-four minutes he might have stopped. This was the infinite puzzle of parenting: You never could know for sure what might have been avoided, what inevitable. The crying wasn't even the worst of it; he interspersed that with a kind of porcine grunting that intensified and lessened and intensified again, as if he were working out with tiny baby dumbbells.

Rule Number Two: Carry concealer. Apply it each morning in natural light to the deep shadow rings under your eyes.

Number Three. What would number three be? Not to run out of Baileys Irish Cream.

Number Four was not to feel guilty about feeding your baby formula or rusks, or your toddler fish fingers or an Easter egg, or letting them watch telly or do any of the necessary activities that other parents—other mothers—tried to make you feel guilty about. The one-upmanship of the whole thing had to be ignored.

Rule Five was to make yourself laugh madly when one of your wee bairns boked on your black party dress just before you left the house for your bimonthly night out, or when one of them wet the bed, or when Izzy tugged the eight-inch purple vibrator the girls had given you on your hen night out from under the bed and started smacking it against her cheek.

Maybe you made rules in your head because there was no other way to feel in control. You had to keep churning the events of your life and try to skim some sense from them. It all slipped through your fingers otherwise. And what was "it"? Time. Children ate time. Before, days moved at a walking pace, routine and predictable. You could liken time to some natural state or process, a backdrop to events, not an event in itself. But once Isobel came, and now Michael, time itself changed. The minutes hardened into objects that could be counted and traded like money, and she always came up short.

At Izzy's birthday party last week in the café at the leisure center, as she was planting the four pink candles in the cake shaped like a football, which was the only children's cake left in Tesco's and would just have to do, it struck Alison that she was going to be sticking candles in cakes every year for at least the next eighteen, which would take her up to the age of fifty, and the conclusion made her sit back for a second on the edge of a radiator. Judith was slicing open a packet of paper plates with a pearlescent fingernail and Alison had managed to turn to her and say, "Can you believe that Izzy's four?"

"It just gets quicker and quicker," her mum had replied, smiling her wisest, most insufferable smile.

Michael's breathing regulated and Alison inched forward to the edge of the tub chair. Slowly, slowly she stood up. He raised his head and she began swaying in their nightly slow dance. He gave a curt, liquidy burp, hot on her ear, and then settled his cheek into her shoulder.

Even as she was telling Liz how excited they all were to see her, she felt a protective wariness. She didn't mind Liz with the kids—when she actually saw them, she was great with them—but she didn't particularly want her sister to meet her soon-to-be second husband. And Liz's presence introduced a stress to the household that was paralyzing. Kenneth and Liz had not actually come to blows since school—but the needling and riling that Liz considered normal made everyone around her tense. Liz was the star of the family, and her mother's clear favorite. She was so sure she had the answer to everything. But she just had different questions. Normal people, real people, who had to get up and go to work and come home and make dinner, found answers enough in the repetition, in the dull, rough ceremony of cooking, and bathing the kids, and reading three stories, and downing a large glass of chenin blanc, and turning off the television, and double-locking the door, and heading up to bed, amen.

Educated to the nth degree—but so what? To what purpose? Liz knew a lot about some things, sure, but nothing about how to live. She was one of life's tenants—she rented: flats, people, cars. Trying them out, using them up, breaking them down, moving along. Liz was older, twenty-one months older, but as soon as Alison could speak she'd adopted the responsible role. Had Liz got money? Had she got tissues? Had she remembered her packed lunch? Alison could never have told her, of course, but it was clear as day that Liz would never become an adult till she had children of her own—climbing over her, lying on her, needing her at three in the morning. And not until she became a solid fact in someone else's life would she start to understand her own parents. She still had the world-view of a child. She faced upwards. She hadn't yet forgiven Kenneth and Judith—not that there was so much to forgive. Alison knew that Liz pitied her, still stuck in Ballyglass, still stuck with their parents, the business, but in turn Alison pitied her right back, pitied her harder, longer, louder.

The laptop was still showing *Downton Abbey* on the wicker stool, and she closed it and exited the room, shutting Michael's door softly. Typical Liz to be snobby about a TV show she didn't even watch. How could it be offensive? It wasn't as if it didn't show the servants to be just as wise and just as confused as the masters. Just that everybody knew their place back then. They weren't lost in wanting more. Now everyone thought they deserved to have everything at every moment. She was a great fan of the individual, her sister, while hating any actual person she ever had to meet. Liz liked the concept of people but not the reality. That's why she couldn't hold onto a boyfriend. Alison stood for a moment on the landing. A soft, repetitive clicking that took her a second to identify as the tap dripping into the bath. It had started again. How amplified a sound became at night. She'd mention it to Stephen.

This was the umpteenth time he'd stayed overnight, but only the third or fourth time he'd done it with the kids here and not at Judith and Kenneth's. You couldn't say the evening hadn't gone well. She'd made a proper roast chicken dinner and Stephen lit the fire. The kids were pretty good, and after dinner, when she bathed them among the ducks and frogs and foam letters that Isobel still refused to spell her name with, he'd slid Bill's old red toolbox out from between the turf basket and the coal scuttle under the stairs and fixed the loose shelf beneath the sink. Back when Bill was around, she'd have nagged him for weeks, and he'd have botched it anyway, if he ever did it. But Stephen would be a different kind of husband: He could do stuff. He'd be a great dad, and Isobel and Mickey would soon think of him as the only father they'd ever had. She hadn't heard from Bill in almost two years. Stephen was far from perfect, God knows, what with his sullenness, his gift for switching off, leaving the room but not through the door or the window. Stephen, Stephen, Earth calling Stephen, and he'd turn back towards her and smile a little shyly.

The kids went down easy and they shared a second bottle of Tesco's finest Italian red, and watched TV and cuddled on the sofa. Upstairs, in bed, they did it twice, once quickly and then, twenty minutes later, again but slowly. She didn't come but she wasn't far off the second time. She wore a new nightie from M&S, a classy white satin thing, and he liked it, or said he liked it.

She looked in now to check on Isobel. Her daughter's darling head was pressed against the wall, the hair covering her face entirely so that for a second she couldn't tell which direction she was facing. One bare foot came out from under her Tinkerbell duvet. She gave a little moan and shifted her legs, taking a step. What went on in her head? When she came home from school now she was silent about it, just said it was "good."

Alison knew already the inner life of her daughter, at four years old, had closed up to her, was newly zoned and fortified and she couldn't visit. She might tell Isobel her life was one long carousel ride of being fed and entertained and washed and soothed, but she'd seen her daughter nervous, embarrassed, tense. You can't protect them from everything.

Everyone sleeping, Alison felt like a ghost wandering the house, benevolent, visiting the much loved, the much missed. She put an ear to Michael's door, but it was silent. In her own bedroom Stephen lay splayed across the duvet, his white T-shirt riding up his narrow back, revealing the scatter of a few moles. At the nape of his neck the hair whorled in such a way that it came down into a perfect point. She slipped in under the duvet and felt his warmth and the lovely new security of a breathing human body in her bed. And then he spoke, surprising her.

"Was Michael all right?"

"Yeah. Just wanted a cuddle."

There was a long pause, and just when she thought he'd gone back to sleep, he spoke again.

"Wouldn't mind one of those myself."

He turned towards her and draped one of his skinny arms across her waist. A few minutes later, Michael started again. Stephen and her lay perfectly still. Michael grew louder, the pitch rising and rising until he was wailing in utter despair. He started making a hacking, sobbing sound. She set a hand gently on Stephen's chest and whispered, "I'm going to leave him. He needs to learn to settle—"

Stephen's whole body jerked awake and backwards in a panic, as if she'd flicked a switch. It was intent on repelling her, hell-bent on defending himself—the side of one hand caught her on the cheek, the other grabbed her by the throat hard.

Something awful possessed him. His eyes stayed closed and she screamed and tried to pry his fingers from her neck. He raised his leg and kneed her in the thigh. Then he was looking at her but his eyes were strange and hard and far away and he was shouting, "Fuckoff, fuckoff" in a voice high pitched and different, sharp with fear. Then it was over—but what had it been? She was crying and hitting at him and he hugged her as she tried to pull away. "It's me, it's me," he kept saying, "I'm sorry I'm sorry. I was dreaming. I was dreaming. I'm sorry."

Ten minutes later she sat in the empty bath, her knees pulled up. Stephen passed her a bag of frozen sweetcorn from the freezer and wrapped it in a tea towel. She held it now to her eye.

"Go on back to bed, you. There's no point in us both being up."

Stephen perched on the toilet lid and sighed repeatedly, as if he were the one thumped in the face. She couldn't bring herself to look at him. It wasn't that she thought he'd done it on purpose. He'd have been out on his ear with the door banging his heels if she'd thought that. It was not deliberate, and that was the point, wasn't it? But another point, another really very pressing point, was that it hurt.

"Go on, really. I'm fine. Go back to bed."

"I am so sorr—"

"Honestly, it's fine."

She didn't want to hear it but he kept on.

"Well, it's not fine."

"No."

"I was just—it was an accident. We'll have to get separate beds if we get married."

She looked up and he was trying to smile. She nodded.

"*If* we get married? You haven't left yourself much time to pull out."

"Sure, it would only take a minute." He was grinning, knowing that the worst of it was over now; she was coming round.

"You planning on standing me up at the altar?"

"Course not," he said, but then widened his eyes and nodded.

"Stephen!"

He shook his head.

"Not funny. What were you dreaming?"

"For the life of me I can't even remember. I think I thought I was being attacked. You know sometimes how you can't even tell where you are or what's happening . . ."

She didn't.

Stephen stood up and sighed again and said I'm sorry again and finally left.

The frozen sweetcorn were still too cold on her hand, even wrapped in a tea towel. There was a hook by the bathroom door behind her and she reached up and pulled a purple towel off it and down onto her.

The towel knocked off his wash bag and she lifted it back onto the side of the bath. It rattled and she opened it. Just to see. A bottle of diazepam—they were tranquilizers, weren't they?—and one of zopiclone. And one of paroxetine. What did they do? And why did they all have parts of the labels, where his name should have been, ripped off? She'd ask him about the tablets in the morning. Or maybe google the names to see. In the eight months she'd known him, she'd never once seen him sick.

She got back into bed. Stephen, dead to the world, gave a low intermittent wheeze. A few minutes later she opened her eyes and there stood a miniature person staring at her a few feet from the bed, naked but for Cinderella underpants. She lifted her side of the covers and Isobel climbed in, pressing her warm back against Alison's body.

"Can I ask you something? Are witches real?"

"No, honey. Go to sleep."

"Are goblins real?"

"Shush."

"Are they?"

"No."

"Are dragons real?"

"No. Go to sleep."

"Are robbers real?"

"No. Sort of. But no one's going to rob us."

"Are bad men real?"

"Honey, *please*."

"Are bad men real?"

"Sleep!"

A rustle and sigh. Another rustle. The tempo of her breath loosening and loosening.

(i) Patrick Creighton, 19

The smell was on his clothes, on his hands, in his hair. He'd washed before he left the plant, but it hung around, that metallic taint. Maybe it was the iron in all the animal blood. He liked to go and spend a good long while at the silver trough scrubbing his hands and under his nails before punching out; it was not, in fact, allowed, but who cared. Of course Morrison had noticed, in the locker room announcing in his wee high voice that standard practice was everyone clocked off *before* washing up, all the while staring directly at him, but he'd just looked right back and through him. Later, in their red boilersuits and white wellies and hairnets, he'd stood beside him at the urinals. Morrison kept on sighing and sighing as if he might start up with the weeping. The man was a fucken freak show. It was creepy.

He wound down the car window. Someone was spreading slurry out the Ardrum Road. Pearl Jam came on Downtown and he turned it up. *You're still alive, she said. Oh, and do I deserve to be?. . .* There would be some crack had tonight. The Cotton Mountain Boys were booked so there'd be a big crowd in. There was a point in having two jobs, as he'd explained to Gerry at lunchtime. You didn't get a motorbike given to you. You couldn't win one or steal one or build one from fucken twigs. You had to just buy it, and by Christmas he'd have eighteen hundred quid in the Ulster Bank, which would be enough to get a Suzuki RGV250, probably from late '88 or early '89.

He parked outside the house and went down to the yard, fed the dogs, then went in and had his own tea of a gammon and a half, a couple of eggs, some boiled potatoes. His sister Majella was in fine form; she'd sold three engagement rings in two hours and Francie Lennon had told her she was in line for a proper bonus. She kept winding him up about

Veronica, who she said he should really think about asking out. What was wrong with him? She was a pretty girl, and it wasn't like he had them queuing up outside his fucken bedroom door. A little later, in the shower, he made his list. The bad: this weird raised redness round the mole on his thigh, and the length of the fence he had to bitumen tomorrow down by McAleer's. The good: Portrush with the boys next Saturday night, and Damon's uncle having that caravan they were going to crash in on the site behind Kelly's nightclub. The crack would be mighty altogether. Altogether mighty. It would be something else again. And it also meant skipping Mass on Sunday. Oh, he could handle that!

He got to the bar before Hugh turned up. It was unreal why Hugh insisted on him arriving at 6:30 p.m., when he himself never bothered showing up till a quarter to seven. If he wanted him to open up he would, he would be happy to, but he was fed up to the back teeth with sitting out in the car, watching an empty Tayto's crisp bag scraping across the tarmac, waiting on Hugh to show his fucken face.

Two of the barrels needed changing, which meant Seamus D hadn't bothered closing up properly. Plus, the drip trays in the lounge bar hadn't been washed out. It was best just to get on with it. Stickiness. Stickiness here by the Tennant's mats. Stickiness here on the top of the mixers fridge. Lazy fuckers. He rolled a barrel of Tennant's in from the store, then a barrel of Murphy's. The band was to arrive at 7:30 p.m., and Hugh was mucking around with the lights for the stage. He flicked on the tap for the Tennant's and heard the air whistling out, and then a low gurgle, and caught the splutter of foam with a pint glass.

The Cotton Mountain Boys—Derek and Padraig and Alfie—had a combined age of two hundred and something, and they offset their different plaid lumberjack shirts with the same black leather waistcoats and bootlace ties. It was slow starting off, but around 8:00 p.m. or so a whole pile of customers arrived at once, and by 8:15 p.m. the place was packed. The Boys were doing "The Gambler" and the chorus had been gradually taken up by the customers, so when they got to "You got to know when to hold 'em, know when to fold 'em" for the third time, the whole place joined in and you could feel it go through your body, the sound of it. Then they started on the one about the man who's constantly sorry or something and Derek's voice cut through the pub like a hot knife. The man could still hold a note, no doubt. Paddy was reaching up for a few empties on top of the quiz machine when it started, the shouting, and that sound like firecrackers. He felt a sharp pain in his shoulder and looked down to see the sleeve of his blue shirt gone dark with wet.

CHAPTER 6

It must be him. Short and severe with his hand held out. Unimpressive, Liz thought. Blotchy stonewashed jeans and a black fleece. She shook the hand and immediately afterwards swung the bag round on her shoulder and unzipped it, but a small dog did not poke its head out. She put her fingers in and stroked the skull until Atlantic gave a thin disgruntled moan and her squirrelly head arose, eyes half shut. Stephen, startled, laughed and cupped Atty's head in his hands. Tattoos on his wrists. A gold signet ring.

"Hello, och, who have we here?"

Liz set the bag down and the dog hopped neatly out. Stretched her front legs, her back. When Stephen tried to pet her from above, she pushed her soft nose up into his fingers, pulled back, and looked at him a little formally, then gave the fingers a confirming swipe with her pink clean tongue.

"They let you take him on the plane?"

"Sort of."

As the dog began olfactory investigations of the column they stood beside, Stephen gave a little grimace of pain.

"He's not about to piss on that, is he?"

"It's a she. We should head outside."

Liz looked at his profile as they tramped down the corridor to the exit. The small sharp nose that reached from his small round face seemed permanently primed for smelling something foul in the atmosphere. There was a slight anxious squint to his whole aspect and an awful softness in the large brown eyes. Some neediness or base want. Alison always had a weakness for weakness. But Liz had nothing against him. That was the phrase she held up in her mind for Stephen. *I have nothing against you. You seem fine. Your fingernails are short and clean. You wear an analog watch with a white face and a black leather strap. You seem like hundreds of men I might walk past: shrunken, tired, aligned to some faction that has suffered defeat.*

For his part Stephen noticed the sandals, the black nail varnish on the toes. It was none of his business. And he had nothing against her, no, nothing against her. Bit trendy, no doubt. And a bit smart in herself, definitely. And from all those stories Alison had told him, a bit of a loose cannon. But she was his fiancée's sister, and would be treated well by him. He hadn't expected the dog. And that rucksack had seen better days—as had she.

The light of Ulster traveled not by particle or wave but by indirection, hint, and rumor. A kind of light of no-light, emanating from a sun so swathed in clouds it was impossible to tell where it lurked in the sky.

As they drove, Liz stared dully out the window. This hour was the strangest. The car functioned like a decompression chamber, adjusting the body to the new density surrounding it, to the element of Ireland. The rain that came in off three thousand miles of ocean left the land so verdant, so lush, that the light reflecting back into the sky took on aspects of the greenness, a deep virescent tinge. It was not raining, but it had been, and the land they drove through was waterlogged. One low field outside Antrim had a pair of swans riding across it as if on rails, cutting metallic wakes. This filter of light made the scenery seem a kind of memory, already heavy with nostalgia. She thought of the peeled, bare light of New York, its blues and yellows, its arctic sharpness and human geometries. Here the day was softened, dampened, deepened. The light was timeless— in the sense that midmorning might be midafternoon. Ten a.m. in May could be five p.m. in late November.

"Great you were able to come back for the wedding."

"Aren't I the good sister?"

"Ah now you're both good."

Liz hadn't meant it as a comparison but now that he'd taken it that way, she didn't much like his response. It gave him too much of a role in their lives. Who did he think he was? Who did he think *she* was?

"Everyone's good in their own way," she replied. Which seemed petty, so she added solemnly, "Alison's one of the best, really. She's there with Mum and Dad at all times."

"Your dad seems a bit better."

"That's good . . . How're you getting on with all of them?"

"Good. No, good, I think."

When Kenneth's first stroke occurred four years ago, Liz had intended to fly back to Dublin to see him but had, in the end, skyped instead. There was not enough time before the heart surgery and she had no money, and was just starting her teaching load for the term, and no one could have expected her to drop everything. She sent him an e-card with a gif of a tree frog in a fez singing "I hope you're feeling better, better, better" to a jazzy little break beat. He underwent quadruple-bypass surgery, and she came home three months later for a long weekend. If he got his words wrong sometimes, if he moved with stiff languorous gestures, as if he were underwater, still he seemed all right, or mostly all right.

Her father's health was common ground and a safe area, but neither Stephen nor Liz could be bothered to pursue it. Kenneth himself never mentioned it, and if Liz asked him on the phone how he was doing she received a brusque, offended "Fine," as if she'd questioned his sanity or his professional credentials.

"You want a fag?"

Obviously the answer to this query from Stephen should be no, but Liz felt that she was feeling, realistically, about as shitty as possible. Why not double down?

Home was like climbing into a suit that was made of your own body, and it looked like you, and it smelled like you, and it moved its hand when you told it to, but it wasn't you, not now.

She flicked the finished fag out the window and closed her eyes and sleep overtook her. She woke on the dual carriageway into Ballyglass when her head bumped against the glass. There was Charlie McCord's old petrol station, abandoned, the pumps chained and padlocked.

"Sorry I was out that whole time."

"No bother. Good for you."

"Did I miss anything?"

"Your wee dog snores."

"She does, yeah."

As they turned down Westland Road a woman in a plum-colored ski jacket and an orange bobble hat was hanging washing out on a rotary line.

"She won't be cold."

"She will not."

There was a pause and Stephen felt himself about to tell Liz something but stopped. He hadn't thought of the house for a long time—it was that rotary line that did it. A neat enough wee bungalow on a few acres, pebbledashed, brown trim, with two concrete cockerels on the gate posts he could still see raising their necks about to crow—and a rotary line in the garden. When he was a lad of ten they'd left Londonderry to move there, just outside Limavady. He'd loved that house. Surrounded by animals: doltish sheep, cows, rabbits, sticklebacks in the wee stream and birds, always birds, in the trees trilling out their notes, flittering about. The rotary was in the garden by the side of the house, where it could be seen from the road, and his mother, with that indefatigable air she had, would hoist the plastic basket of washing outside and peg up the damp things for him and his siblings, the wee socks for their wee feet. But not his father's shirts. His father's shirts were dried in the bathroom, over the bath, though the question of why did not even occur to him until his mother picked him up one Monday evening from Scouts in Dungiven and asked him, with a queer edge in her voice, what had happened at school today.

"Nothing, nothing really."

They were stopped by traffic lights at the courthouse, the huge stockade of barbed wire and guard posts and searchlights.

She said, "Do you tell people what Daddy does?"

"What do you mean?"

"What he does for a living?"

"He's a policeman."

"He's a policeman, yes. But when people ask you, you should say he works for the council."

"Is Daddy OK?"

"Some bad men attacked the police station today, honey. But your daddy's OK."

He wanted to ask if someone was not OK, if someone would never be OK again, but he found that he couldn't, that he was too scared to hear any more, and he sat in silence, his forehead pressed on the cold glass. Overhead there were a million stars; the dark branches of the trees sifted and released them. If there was a god, why was his purpose not to stop this?

After a few minutes, as the road unfurled under the headlights, as they sped through the fields and hedges, his mother said, "You're a good boy, Stephen."

Maybe everything led back to this exchange. Some small initial tilt in direction will cause, over time, a great distance to arise between the intended destination and the actual one. Certainly for days afterwards, it seemed to Stephen like someone had taken a kind of universal remote to his life and turned up the brightness and contrast, making everything sharp-edged and garish and strange. But his father was OK, until a few years later he wasn't. Thirteen when his father was killed, shot twenty-six times by two men hiding in a ditch. There are clean deaths and messy deaths and this was the latter. Closed coffin.

The milk lorry was attempting to reverse. The sun had come out and the truck's huge silver container tank caught the light. Stephen flicked down the visor and his license fell out, hitting the gear stick and landing in Liz's footwell.

"Oh sorry. Here, I'll stick it back up here."

Liz lifted the license. The black-and-white photo showed Stephen with a side parting and a blank, slightly idiotic expression.

"You've a bit more hair there."

"Aye a lot more. Here."

He reached over sharply and lifted it out of her hands, but not before she saw his name was printed on the pink plastic card as McLean, Andrew. He slipped it back into the sun visor and flipped it up.

"Andrew?" she said involuntarily.

"Oh that. It was my father's name, but they always called me Stephen."

"Oh."

Here was the sign announcing **YOU ARE LEAVING COUNTY LONDONDERRY**— though since a republican had blacked out the **LONDON**, and a loyalist had come along and erased with blue paint the **DERRY**, and finally some misanthrope or reasonable man at the end of his tether had whitewashed the **O** and **Y**, and all of **LEAVING** except for the **A**—the sign now cheerfully explained that:

YOU ARE A C UNT

The unofficial but more typical greeting was the next sign, which had been there as long as Liz could remember, painted in foot-high letters in a mock Gothic font on the side of the gospel hall:

The wages of sin are death: but the gift of God is eternal life.

Romans 6:23

This was a place of voices, they jostled and contested with one another—a small hard town with one long road leading to a mountain—but even now the sight of sunlight shifting on those distant slopes of bog and rock and gorse made Liz's heart give a little shiver in her chest. They drove past the agency—Liz could see her father's receptionist, Trish, standing behind the desk in a white blouse looking into her phone—then through Monrush, smoke rising straight up from a few chimneys on the council houses. And here another voice spoke—a new sign, roughly lettered in red, white, and blue on a sheet of plywood nailed to a telephone pole:

In Texas murder gets you the electric chair. In Magherafelt you get chair of the council.

She gestured up through the windscreen at the sign.

"What's that about?"

"Oh, that Shinner Declan Keogh. The one who escaped from the Maze. It's out of date now anyways."

"How come?"

"Well, he's now replaced wee Kieran Smith as our 'local representative' for Stormont. You know Kieran's the new MP?"

"That's right."

Liz did not know, and when Liz did not know something she had found that "That's right" was a usefully ambiguous formulation to reply with, particularly in the classroom. But that was in New York.

In Northern Ireland, Stephen said, "What's right?"

"About the new MP."

"Yeah . . . I just said it was. Oh they look after their own. McGuinness handed it on to Smith, and the Unionist was a fella called Barrett. Now Barrett's father was a caretaker at Springhill. Smith was the main suspect in his killing, they say."

"I heard that."

There was a long pause. Stephen shifted into third. They passed the new estates—dozens and dozens of white blocky constructions littering Morgan's Hill; they'd been erected quickly in the years of madness and entitlement when everyone could buy everything and did. The houses had something childish and optimistic about them as they strained for a little grandeur; flanking each primary-colored front door were thick fluted Doric columns.

"I'll say this. It's all one sided in any case. There's no consultancies coming our way."

Our way? She wound the window down a few inches and let cool air into the car. There was the lancing smell of slurry. Our way. Our way or the highway. Press-ganged back into the caste, no questions asked. Impossible not to be picked for a side. If you tried to sit on the fence, you came to real-ize that you couldn't move, not an inch, for you would topple off and land on one side or the other, covered in bullshit. The north was thesis and an-tithesis, but no synthesis. It would outlast us all. There was no way round it. What was the word? There was a French word. *Uncontournable*. There was no getting round it. *For sufferance is the badge of all our tribe.*

At university she wrote her master's dissertation on the special kinship groups of Ulster. Her home province was a nightmare of disorder in which she tried to find an order. She became an anthropologist, she told herself and others, because her childhood in that province, state, statelet, made her search for reason in the most unreasonable of places. The work she loved—Lévi-Strauss, Bourdieu, even Foucault—shared the desire to tease new meaning from habituated reality. For how could you live here and not be sad? It was absurd: You didn't "believe" in something if you were born into it. You ac-cepted it, you acquiesced, you submitted, you lost—and you gave up the chance to become yourself, to come to conclusions of your own. *One must be very naive or dishonest to imagine that men choose their beliefs indepen-dently of their situation.*

"A mess. A complete mess. And that crowd at Stormont, sure they couldn't organize a piss up in a brewery."

She pressed the tip of her index finger against the side of the pad of her thumb, shaping from her hand a triangle. She made the other match it, touched the tips of the fingers and thumbs to each other. Were there other triangles in a world of circles and squares? Was everyone a triangle pretending to square-hood or circledom? Who was Andrew McLean? The triangle, the circle, the square? Her hands looked like a mask. She wanted to ask him but didn't. *I therefore claim to show, not how men think in myths, but how myths oper-ate in men's minds without their being aware of the fact.*

"True enough."

They were through the roundabout.

She was almost home and then she was.

And here on the doorstep were her parents: her mother—elegant in black slacks and a caramel cashmere sweater—watering the dripping hang-ing baskets; and behind her Kenneth, directing, grayer and frailer and smaller than in the memory but now waving with both hands, and pleased to see his daughter. She could see that clearly now, the real pleasure that she brought to them both just by being in their world, at least at first.

As she hugged her mother, Stephen carried her rucksack into the hallway and her father commented on the rain holding off. Then he looked down and said, "Now what in God's name is that?"

The dog was jumping up at her knees. She stooped and picked her up.

"Atlantic. You remember me telling you about the dog?"

"I do, yes. I didn't know you were bringing it over."

"Her."

Atlantic gave Liz's ear an explorative lick and Kenneth grimaced.

"I found her on a subway platform."

Judith said to Stephen, "Will you sit and have a cup of tea? Or coffee? We have a new machine."

"I really should fly on, actually. I have to be in Tandragee by twelve." Stephen felt the little extra silence Judith greeted this with, and said, "Maybe a quick coffee."

"It's very good of you to go and pick this one up," Judith continued, to Stephen, who did not disguise in his face the fact that he thought it was good of him too.

"Well, Alison's off to a fitting there for the dress, isn't she, and I know you guys have enough to be getting on with."

"I think we're almost there," Judith said.

Kenneth frowned. "I don't see why your brother couldn't have—"

"I didn't ask Spencer," Liz cut him off. "I mean I texted him and left him a message, but sure he never got back to me."

Stephen looked from Liz to her father. Already a gloom of mutual resentment was setting in on both their faces.

"The garden looks very well," Stephen offered, but the thought of the garden only reminded Kenneth of the tent that was destined to destroy his lawn.

"The marquee people were supposed to come tomorrow morning to put it up, but now they say they can't come till the afternoon."

"It'll be fine," Judith said, throwing Liz a glance. "It'll all be fine."

CHAPTER 7

Liz lugged her rucksack up the stairs, and set it on the bed beside one of her old exercise books. She flicked through it and felt a great rush of sadness. There was such pathos in childish handwriting, especially one's own. Time had this terrible habit of creeping up and pistol-whipping you on the back of the head. She unzipped her suitcase and decided she couldn't be bothered to unpack yet. She emptied her pockets of her passport and coins and gum on the vanity unit, where her mother had set a little vase with a head of blue hydrangea from the garden. Behind the vase, propped against the mirror, was a neat row of eight copies of her own book—all signed by her—which Kenneth kept there in case he ever found anyone else to give it to. She lifted the books and set them in the bottom of the built-in wardrobe.

After she received her PhD from King's College, London, Liz had entered "her slump," as the family referred to it: two years of trying to get her thesis on Lévi-Strauss accepted by academic publishers, and being rejected for dozens of research fellowships and junior teaching positions, and working in a bar in Clapham, and smoking a great deal of weed. One lunchtime, having woken at noon, she stood in the kitchen, waiting for the kettle to boil, and noticed the letter on the table, a smear of raspberry jam on its corner. Aberystwyth University Press was keen to meet and talk about the thesis, meaning they were interested in bringing it out, and the very next day, a Friday, she traveled at ludicrous expense on two trains and a rail-replacement bus service to see their publisher, Owen Hughes, who was, it turned out, a Lévi-Strauss expert himself. He disagreed about aspects of Liz's characterization of Lévi-Strauss's relationship to art, had met Claude, more than once, and had come away with many subtly self-flattering anecdotes from these encounters. Liz perched in a low leather club seat and felt herself sliding lower and lower and lower, until it seemed she looked up at the desk from several feet beneath it. The interview concluded with Liz being asked whether she'd be capable of writing a short guide to either quantum physics or dogs, which was the kind of thing that sold at the moment, and her replying no, not really, no.

For the next month Liz got up and sat in her pajamas and watched daytime television, smoked more weed, and read only magazines, and on a drizzling Wednesday morning woke up knowing instinctively what she had to do. She caught the 34 bus to the Victorian library on Brixton Hill, walked between the rows of computers where recent immigrants typed up their CVs, and found the self-help section. She photocopied the chapter pages and indices of every book that didn't look obviously stupid or crazy. She found an empty carrel, set up her laptop, and started a spreadsheet in which she collated the main recurring topics, and typed in what Lévi-Strauss had to say about them. And that was the genesis of *The Use of Myth: How Lévi-Strauss Can Help Us All Live a Little Better.* Whenever she couldn't find anything relevant in the actual work, she just extrapolated from the circumstances of his life, and soon she had a seventy-thousand-word manuscript that told the story of Lévi-Strauss's life and work and pontificated cleverly, or cleverly enough, on the usual topics of love, marriage, infidelity, work, ambition, children, parents . . .

It found a small but respectable publisher, Hawksmoor, within a few weeks. The advance was a modest two thousand pounds, but after a series of interviews, the book began to sell quite well. When it was taken as a Radio 4 Book of the Week, sales accelerated and they went to a fifth reprint. A week after that, the publisher forwarded an e-mail from a producer called Henry Barfoot who was interested in possibly making it a program for BBC Four. Was Liz interested in presenting?

Having taken a few months to write and rewrite, and a few weeks to shoot, and one tortuous day to add voice-over to, when it was finally broadcast at 10:00 p.m. on a Wednesday evening the *Times* heralded the hour-long show, *The Use of Myth*, as "fairly informative," the *Guardian* trumpeted it as "standard BBC Four fare," and the *Telegraph* lauded Liz's presenting as "adequate, if a little stiff." Judith had half of Ballyglass watching and was in tears on the message she left on Liz's answerphone, telling her how proud she was. She'd even coaxed Kenneth into leaving a bluff "Well done."

She had been writing the follow-up—attempting to do the same with Margaret Mead—for the last seven years. The book seemed to expand in every direction as she got more and more and also less and less interested in her, reading volume after volume of published work, then diaries and letters, and taking notes and underlining and stockpiling the timeline with anecdote and incident. The work had grown monstrous. She'd stopped actually putting words on the virtual page when the word count had hit 321,123, though her reasons for halting there were random and inscrutable to herself and seemed to be based solely on the palindromic, magical nature of the figure. That had happened several months ago, as she sat marking essays in the Moonlight Diner on Tenth Avenue. Now just seeing the file on her desktop gave her a singular feeling of dull terror. She was currently managing to look at the manuscript for a few minutes every couple of days before getting bored, or panicking, or getting bored of panicking. She'd follow the thread of her inattention through a maze of hyperlinks, and two hours later would know slightly more about, say, Hawking or fracking or twerking.

Alison's voice came up from below. She was describing something as *just completely pointless* to her parents. Liz went down and met her younger sister at the bottom of the stairs, where they hugged and then pulled back and thought to themselves how old the other one appeared.

"You look great!" Liz said.

"I do not," Alison countered with a wince. "I've been dieting for the wedding, but sure I've only lost seven pounds—"

"That's not bad."

"That short haircut really suits you—" Alison said.

"Och, it's an old woman's cut."

"And you've lost weight."

"Not on purpose."

"Don't sicken me."

"How was your dress fitting? All ready to go?"

"Sandra'd put the zip on upside down. Can you believe it? It's sorted now. I'm not paying her to fix it."

Liz followed her into the kitchen.

"Is this new?"

Liz ran her finger along the top of the dining table. Alison nodded and whispered to her, "It wouldn't be to my taste, but I can see why it's nice."

Kenneth's voice arose from the armchair. "No one's asking you to sit at it."

Alison made a face at her sister. "Nothing's changed." She raised her voice: "I'm just saying it's very dark, for my taste. For a kitchen."

"Is it mahogany?" Liz asked.

"Yes, and extendable," Kenneth's voice announced.

Home was where you could spend an hour discussing any fixture or fitting or real estate question. Judith tended to praise, Alison to criticize, Kenneth to lament—the mysteries of planning permission or building regulations, the fad for Artex, the difficulty of removing stone cladding. Bay windows, rockeries, conservatories, the exotica of PVC apexes and dado rails and pelmets and the correct way to edge a lawn or instruct a repossession. They talked about crawlspaces and conversions. A rumor of subsidence or dry rot came among them with the same frisson that another family might have felt upon encountering reports of embezzlement or incest. Any house or flat or shop that entered the Mid-Ulster market fell squarely in their purview and their remit. They knew who'd built it, who'd lived in it, why it was to be sold, what they were asking, what they were hoping, what they would accept.

They talked like this because they talked in code of what they loved—not this particular extendable dining room table in mahogany but Ballyglass, continuity, sitting in judgment on one's neighbors, and being granted membership of a family by way of all hating the same thing.

"How are the kids?"

"Mickey's in the car. Come out with me now and we'll wake him. Stephen said you slept the whole way."

"I didn't mean to . . . I was just—I hadn't slept all night."

"But did you like him?"

"I really did. We had a good chat, I mean, when I wasn't dozing."

"He doesn't drink, you know, not really."

Liz smiled sadly at this preemptive defense. The next thing she said as kindly as possible, though it didn't stop the collapse of her sister's face.

"Have you heard from Bill?"

"Nothing. I send photos to his mother but sure she hardly replies. I have to pinch myself to remember: These are his children! Imagine doing that."

Atlantic padded dolefully into the kitchen doorway and stood there like she brought bad news from the front. Liz felt grateful; it saved them both from the painful act of conceiving Bill's interior life.

She'd met her first husband, Bill, when the office was broken into and her parents were in Connemara for the weekend. Sergeant Bill Williams. It was a Protestant joke, that name: William, son of William, inheritor of sash and stick and puritanical despair. He was not handsome, but he had a nice clean freckled face and innocent blue eyes. Nor was he funny exactly, but he tried hard to be funny, and she liked that. She was twenty-six years old and absolutely ready to fall hopelessly in love. When he took her to Paris for the weekend, they stayed in a little hotel called Select near the Sorbonne, the bellboy departed, untipped, and they'd fallen on each other with an animal hunger surprising to her. But it seemed to have used up all the desire in one go. That night they'd gone out and Bill drank two bottles of the restaurant's house white, almost by himself, and fell asleep immediately, not touching her. And that was her first clue. Didn't stop her marrying him, but also meant she wasn't entirely surprised by what followed. He was never physically abusive, but when he drank he said the most awful things, and it took it out of you, being told you were a whore, a fat slut, a moron, a useless fucking bitch. She started to apologize all the time, for nothing, and to everyone. If she dared mention his drinking he had a list of responses ready, usually referring to his "stress." And did he tell her to stop stuffing chocolate down her throat? She met her future in his

mother, Edna, who ran the grocery shop in Comber while Norman, Bill's
father, drank the takings. Edna had learned to refuse the world's over-
tures, its silly promises, had the hardened air of the continually disappointed.

Soon enough it was a nightly thing. Collapsed by ten p.m. in the arm-
chair. Even so, initially she managed to hide his drinking from her family
pretty well. Then the first Christmas came, and with it the family lunch at
Judith and Ken's. They'd all sat down when Alison remembered the gravy.
As she hoisted herself up to get it—she was six months pregnant with
Isabel—and edged past Bill, he stuck a Christmas cracker out at her.

"I'll do that when I'm back."

"Just pull it," Bill sighed.

She could see the danger of the moment, and part of her wanted it all
to go wrong. She wanted him exposed to her family. She wanted them to
know the truth of it. He continued to push the cracker at the curve of her
stomach and she ignored it.

"Ah, just pull it now, pull the cracker, you fat cunt," Bill muttered, and
grabbed her arm.

Across the linen tablecloth and pale candles and silver reindeer napkin
rings, Judith lowered her head into her hands. Spencer jumped up. All of
him shivering with tension under his shirt. Part of Alison detached from
the scene; that part was very interested in how all this would play out.

Bill worked out a laugh as Kenneth slowly got to his feet and said,
"Perhaps you should go upstairs, to Ali's old room, and take a nap."

The note in her father's voice meant business. Spencer's eyes shone
with a defeated fury. Bill stared drunkenly ahead of him into the bowl of
homemade cranberry sauce and then lazily turned to Kenneth, grinned
wolfishly, and asked, "Why don't *you* go and have a lie down, oul fella,
before I put ye on yer fucking back?"

Spencer was on him. Two chairs were knocked over. Although Bill had
a few inches' advantage, Spencer got him in a full nelson headlock and
dragged him out onto the porch. It ended with Spencer banging Bill's head
against the doorframe.

Bill joined the AA group that met in the community center off the

Dungarvan Road. She did what she could. She poured bottles down the sink. She told him she loved him and wanted to help him. He avoided the old crowd from the station and didn't go to the pub after work. They began attending her parents' Presbyterian church out at Killyclogher. She could feel him trying, really trying, the constant effort coming off him like a buzzing. He was stretched and tense as a balloon, always on the cusp of losing it. It was necessary to devise stratagems. Each night she made dessert, she ran him a bath, she checked the listings to try to ensure there was some sport or a documentary or an action flick for him to watch. She bought a thousand-piece jigsaw of *The Last Supper* in Toymaster and started it on the dining room table, called it their project. They spent a single evening with their heads engrossed in it, so close they were almost touching, and she thought, as she sometimes thought, that this could work. The next night he wouldn't look at it. Called it boring and stupid, and asked what the fuck was the point of a jigsaw. You put it together and then you pulled it apart. Like a marriage, she thought. She spent two weeks sitting at the table for an hour or two here and there, and hadn't even half of it filled in. There was the entire sky still to do. She looked in the blank, unhelpful face of Jesus (out of the whole picture, he was the only one looking at the viewer) and swept the whole lot into a bin bag.

It amazed her now how long it took her. It was a Friday night and she was washing up after dinner, watching the sun sinking between the town's twin spires—Catholic and Protestant—and she thought, *This isn't going to get any better.* She'd taken a pregnancy test at school that afternoon—according to her diary her period was three weeks late—and the little cross of St. Andrew surfaced in the stick's window, a blue crucifixion. Felt nothing. Not happy, not sad. Nothing. She taught the rest of the day in a daze of nothingness, smiling at the children, but absent inside. Now she looked at her own daughter—soft-limbed, big-eyed, spellbound in her high chair in front of the telly, but no longer a baby, surely only a few months away from the consciousness of what it meant when your daddy passed out in an armchair. She peeled off the rubber gloves, lifted the child to halfhearted protestations, went upstairs, started packing.

Four months after she moved back home, Kenneth had another, minor, stroke, and Alison took early maternity leave and entered—little by little, toe by toe—the family business. Showing a home here, making a phone call there. Spencer had been working in Donnelly's Estate Agents for years, but if he objected to her coming in, he never said anything directly, and Alison discovered she was good at it, at selling homes. She'd grown up with the lexicon of estate agency as her first language. Convenience. Location. Good bones. Character piece. Low maintenance. High yield. In recent years the property TV shows had added to her stock of ready-made phrases—wow factor, curb appeal, forever home, ticking the boxes—but it always felt a little ridiculous using them. She did, though. Her direct, judgmental manner worked on people; they wanted to agree with her, and if Alison made sure prospective buyers noted certain things, they were less likely to focus on certain other things, like the smell of the downstairs bathroom or the rising damp in the garage. She swept into a room and took control, opened blinds and cupboards, pointed out the overwhelming economic benefits of an electric shower or a multi-fuel stove or the lagging on a boiler. One wet cold morning in September—as she told the recently widowed Lily Burns to think of herself sitting out here on the patio, in the suntrap made by the fence and the back wall of the kitchen, reading a book and having a glass of wine or a cup of tea—it occurred to her that if she had a gift for presenting things not as they are, but as they really should be, well, that was only to be expected of someone who'd lived with an alcoholic for as long as she had.

CHAPTER 8

Liz was sleeping off her jet lag. Kenneth had gone to Ray Mullens's funeral and Judith and Alison stood alone in the kitchen. Alison turned the carousel display of coffee capsules for the new machine, while Judith winced at her daughter's neck: "He must be a very heavy sleeper."

"Oh, he woke up almost immediately. Do you want cold water in this?"

"Just a splash. Is it just the neck?"

"He kneed my thigh and there's a bruise but it's nothing. Did you see the doctor yet about your bloods?"

"Next Wednesday."

"How's the tummy been? There's more milk powder in a tub in the bag, but he shouldn't need it."

"Not bad at all. I'll give him a biscuit later."

Judith took the bottle out of Alison's hand, and bent down to put her face in Michael's. He sat still strapped in his car seat on the living room floor, asleep.

"Oh, I know what my little boy needs, don't I?"

As Alison stood up, Judith touched her arm.

"It's not like Bill again, is it? He wouldn't hurt you, would he?"

"Stephen wouldn't hurt a fly!"

Alison waited for her mother to say, "It's not flies I'm worried about," accompanied by a steady imploring gaze that Alison would avoid meeting. But nothing happened, her mother moved away, and to cement her victory, Alison cheerfully lifted a millionaire's shortcake and took a bite from it. She knew Judith thought her younger daughter had a history of making bad choices. But Judith herself hadn't made many better ones. She'd married the first man who came along, and if they were still together that was part indolence and part convention. Whereas Alison had faced up and taken hard decisions and was in many ways a braver woman than her mother. No one could deny that. She'd risked things for love! She'd suffered! All of this she intimated by the brusque way she buttoned up the second and third buttons of her lemon-colored wool coat. Her mother walked past her, opened the fridge door, and rearranged various Tupperware containers.

"If you see your brother remind him he said he was coming for his dinner."

"I wasn't going to call into the office. I was just going to pick Isobel up."

"Well, no rush. We're going to be very happy here. Aren't we?"

"Well, maybe I'll call in at the church and check on the flowers. Just text me if you need anything, or if Mickey's playing up."

How Alison could christen her grandson with a lovely strong name like Michael—the name of an archangel no less—and then call him Mickey as if he were a gangster or a cartoon mouse was just beyond her. At times it seemed to Judith that her daughter held her in permanent contempt, and little decisions like these were designed purely to rile her. She knew it was irrational and unfair, but she felt it.

Kenneth came in from the funeral, plucked the tweed trilby from his head, and unwound the scarf delicately. It hurt today to lift his arms too high. Shrugging off his coat was taking some time, and Judith slipped behind him and began guiding one arm out of its sleeve. He pulled away.

"I can do it my*self*."

"Just trying to—"

"But it's not helpful. You're getting in the way. I need to be able—"

"Calm down."

Judith stepped back and lifted the wheaten loaf out of the bread bin. For over forty years of marriage, telling her husband to calm down was the closest Judith came to a daily mantra. Depending on the way the phrase was

accented, the two words could mean almost anything—endearment, warning, threat. This "calm down" meant nothing in itself, but was designed to
cut Kenneth off in his monologue; if it was allowed to continue, the trickle
would turn to a torrent and carry him away into the kind of black despair
it could take hours to dissipate. He had a remarkable gift for misery. The
next step was to change the subject quickly, which Judith duly did.

"Big funeral? Do you want tea? A slice of wheaten?"

"I'll have tea, yes. No bread. Not that many. A hundred maybe."

She was surprised by how long it had taken to get used to watching this
big bear of a man adapt himself to simple situations. To see him do such
simple things with such tremulous care and physical trepidation. His eyes
expressing fear, his fingers fiddling with a zipper. It was like the element
he lived in had changed, had once been air and now was water, and the
entire choreography of daily life had to be relearned. It was necessary to
familiarize yourself with the actions of brushing your teeth, to study the
order of the movements of getting into a car. It had been four years since
the first stroke and heart surgery, but everything was still heavier, denser.
For Kenneth, everything was a potential source of hurt.

Now he looked at her abdomen, at the hurt hiding in there, and asked,
"You tell the kids?"

"I'll tell them after the wedding. Sure, I'm not going to spoil everyone's day."

"Did you speak to Dr. Boyers?"

"I left a message."

"You OK?"

"I'm all right."

Kenneth watched her set the kettle on its base, the spout facing inward.
When she went to the cupboard for cups, he adjusted it so it faced
outwards, to let the steam vent away from the underside of the cupboards.
She noticed and he watched her jaw perceptibly tighten with anger. It was
not about cupboards and steam; it was about authority and submission, or
men and women, or simply the ways of Kenneth and the ways of Judith.
And so marriage goes, thought Judith. Everything becomes a sign and
symbol of something else.

———————

By four o'clock, Liz was awake and Alison had returned, though there was still no sign of Spencer.

In the living room Kenneth's eyes were trained on yet another antiquing show on the TV, but in deference to the gathering of his daughters on the sofa, he voluntarily muted it.

"Mickey is a wee dote. God, those eyes."

On cue, Michael appeared from the hallway, carrying a plastic dustpan in one hand and Kenneth's tartan slipper in the other. Judith trailed behind, staring amorously at his blond curls.

"Cute, isn't he? When he's not screaming the house down."

"Shooooooooos!" Michael tunefully declaimed, and handed his mother the slipper.

"The thing with Stephen is," Alison said, "he's very family orientated."

"Is he from a big family?"

"It's terrible actually. There was a brother in England but he's dead now. Cancer. And his parents died years ago. He's on his own. But he loves family, he's so good with the kids."

Liz played along, though she did not see why her sister was so set on selling her life to her, as if without the approval of others she could hardly bear to live it. Then it occurred to her that it was perhaps a mark of how unsure Alison was about the marriage if she was seeking even Liz's affirmation.

In Liz's eyes, her younger sister had always been much closer to Judith and Kenneth than she was, and if their parents didn't always applaud Alison's choices, there was no doubt she was the daughter they understood. After all, she stayed behind while Liz had upped and left. She shared their setting—the restaurants, doctors, local news, TV shows, all the cast and daily apparatus of their life—and Alison had the Donnelly gift of reducing something complex to a clichéd phrase, and saying it over and over, singing it almost. She had the same strange numerous compartments of expectation and orthodoxy, growing predictably outraged—like Kenneth—because a Christmas card was not returned, or a neighbor's lawn was left to get too long, or the tip was automatically added to a bill.

If, occasionally, Judith liked to complain on the phone to Liz about Alison, it was with the understanding that Liz would not offer her own criticisms of her sister but simply listen and agree. Whatever competition there had been for their parents' affection, Liz was certain that she'd withdrawn, honorably, from it, having accepted defeat. During the years when their parents had argued continually—when Spencer was a toddler—Judith had moved out for a night, to the flat above the estate agency, and so little did she trust Liz not to fight with Kenneth, and to look after Spencer, who was hysterical and wouldn't leave his father, that she took Liz with her, entrusting Alison with her little brother's care. Alison was the steady one, the responsible daughter.

Her father lifted a cork-lined, laminated coaster from the stack on the little table by his chair and lobbed it at Liz for the coffee she had in her hand. It landed on the sofa and she ignored it.

"Oh, dear," Judith said, straightening up from looking in the cupboard under the sink, holding a can of Brasso and a cloth. "It's so sad when a family just disappears."

Everyone murmured in agreement. It was indeed awful when a family disappeared, though it did make your own look much more solid.

After Liz had helped her mother tidy the bathrooms, and put out fresh towels, and organize the glasses in the utility room, and clear various surfaces for the caterer to set her wares on, they found they had everything done, suddenly, at least until the caterers and marquee people started turning up the next day, and Judith announced she was "going to have a wee nap."

"Does she often go and lie down during the day?"

Liz had never, as far as she could remember, known her mother to go to bed during the day. She'd rarely seen her sit down. Sometimes, in the late evening—after the dinner was served and the dishwasher loaded and the pots and pans washed and dried, and every surface cleared and wiped down, and the laundry done, and the piles of ironing completed—she might perch for a half hour before bed on the arm of a chair, watching TV distractedly, offering everyone tea or traybakes, always threatening to jump up again. Occasionally she'd sit properly, draw her legs up under herself, and read a paper from the rack by Kenneth's chair—the *Belfast Telegraph* or the *Mid-Ulster Mail*—scanning it for people she knew. Sometimes she'd be working on a fat novel that one of the girls—her group of sixty-something female friends—had recommended, and would read steadily while Kenneth flicked the channels between football and golf and the news. But mostly she was vertical, industrious, quick.

"I think she's tired," Kenneth replied, not looking up from the quiz show.

"Has she been getting tired a lot?" Liz pushed on.

"None of us are getting younger. You want up here? You want up?"

Kenneth had been feeding Atlantic scraps from his ham sandwich, and Atlantic had found—what all dogs want—a brand-new god to worship. She stood now on her back legs, resting her front paws on the side of Kenneth's armchair, her long foxy head propped on the little fanned paws. Animals sometimes seemed the only remaining recipients of Kenneth's affection. Five or six years ago, home for Christmas, she'd been sitting reading in the conservatory and looked up to see him through the glass door, alone, wiping away a tear. Kenneth was sobbing, actually sobbing, as an Australian vet in *Animal Hospital* put down a black Labrador, whose big dumb beautiful eyes looked up at the vet and then were stilled. Her father, she realized suddenly—and wondered why she hadn't put it in these terms before—was seriously depressed. In the intervening years, the evidence accumulated for this point of view. Several times she had tried to broach the topic with him, but he would not have it. She watched Atlantic lick his paw as her father looked at the dog with more pure affection than she could ever remember him showing his children.

"Where'd you say you got this beast then?"

He was rubbing Atty's head.

"On a subway platform. She'd been abandoned."

"Manky-looking thing."

"She's a sweetheart."

"You get it injections?"

"All of them."

"What about fleas?"

"She doesn't have them."

Despite himself, her father was grinning at the dog.

Liz knew Kenneth's objections were only in principle. He had a sentimentalist's adoration for all large-eyed mammals, excepting humans. Animals didn't try to negotiate a lower percentage on commission, or let a leak in a boiler cause a ceiling to collapse, or fall behind on their rent. You knew where you stood with a dog, and where you stood was on a pedestal. Kenneth let Atlantic jump up onto his lap.

"How's the teaching?"

"Fine, fine, I had a promising class this year really. One or two who'll—"

"I see your man Dan Andrews is doing very well."

Dan Andrews was a TV historian. He'd been in the year above Liz at Edinburgh, where his most famous action had been to fellate a future cabinet minister in the corridor of one of the residency halls.

"Oh yes?"

"He does a very good one on Tuesday nights. About the Tudors. It must be his fifth or sixth TV show."

"Must be. Which reminds me."

Her father un-muted the telly.

"I meant to tell you I'm off on Sunday to Papua New Guinea to make a TV show."

Before anyone could reply, Liz left the room, like a boxer landing a knockout punch and striding from the ring.

The Donnelly home had broadband, technically, though in practice it was unbearably slow. Over the years Liz and Alison and Spencer had each spent several hours on the phone to British Telecom complaining, rebooting, inserting various adaptors and splitters, but it was still not feasible to download photographs. At least, not feasible in human time. In geological time, maybe, or if you experienced the world as an oak tree did. Still, Liz was making a determined effort. As she waited for the system to boot up, she propelled herself slowly in a circle in the office chair with her right foot, taking in the study.

Alison in graduation gear from Stranmillis—her head tipped slightly forward in embarrassment, though there was pride in her glance. Her blond hair had been permed to an awkward frizz, and she wore a touch too much blue eye shadow. One of Liz in the same getup, staring defiantly at the camera—her short brown hair hardly coming out from under the mortarboard. In lieu of a graduation photo for Spencer, there was one of him on the eighteenth hole of Killyreagh golf course handing over, on behalf of the estate agency, an outsized check to Cancer Research.

If you met the sisters you'd have no reason to think that Alison and Liz shared the same parents. One so fair and blue eyed and one so dark with eyes so brown that in certain lights they were almost black. But then Spencer arrived and made sense of the gene pool; he grew up with Liz's dark complexion and Alison's blue eyes, and both his sisters doted on him. Had it made him a little infantile? A little protected? Even in photographs you could see he had always been loved—his broad physique, his ready smile. He was at home in the world, convinced of his place in it.

Kenneth had three desks in the study, none of them for studying. They were mostly covered with prizes for various charitable lotteries and raffles he was running for Rotary, the golf club, and the Save the Children Coffee Morning. The computer screen began filling up with e-mails. There was nothing from Joel. And a great deal of bumpf. She opened the e-mail from Margo—LIZ: URGENT DISASTER—and began the tortuous process of downloading the PDFs.

On the wall beside the photographs of the three Donnelly siblings was a framed map of the world. Liz located the huge island of PNG, and next to it New Britain, an archipelagic scatter, a broken grin in the gridded blue, small and very far away from Old Britain, and from New York. She stood up and looked closer. Here was New Ireland, and here, below it, was the little curved splinter of New Ulster.

She found herself thinking of that moment when one steps from the lip of an aircraft onto the top of the steps, and the tropical heat hits you, remaking you. She wanted that, to be remade.

Half an hour later, Liz sank down onto the sofa and began ostentatiously leafing through her stack of printouts.

"So. A TV show," Kenneth said, not lowering his paper, and using the abstracted, bored, and slightly hostile tone he reserved for his nearest and dearest.

"Shoooooooooooos," Michael half sang, trekking past, pulling Atlantic by her collar. "Shoooooooooos. Shoooooooos."

"For a BBC special season on God: *The State of Grace*. Our bit's about the world's newest religion."

Liz tried not to sound excited.

"Oh, darling, that's wonderful," said Judith. She leaned against the Corian breakfast bar, fluently peeling an apple for Michael with a paring knife. A springy green ribbon grew below it. Isobel stood in the conservatory, tapping away on her wooden phone. The windows were open and the faint gargling of a distant tractor could be heard in the moments when the racket from the TV quietened. It had been nine months since Liz had sat on this sofa, in this room, and now it felt like all that time had collapsed into a few seconds.

"Very good," Kenneth said, lowering the *Daily Telegraph* but maintaining partial cover.

"And you have to leave on Sunday?" asked Alison, without looking up. She was rearranging the wedding seating plan on an A2 piece of paper at the kitchen table.

"I'm not going to miss anything. I mean, I'll still be in the wedding."

Alison gave a sniff that suggested that while Liz's response was technically true, it was—at the very least—morally suspect.

"We're going to an island called New Ulster."

"*New* Ulster?" her mother asked, and Kenneth nodded impatiently, as if that were the place they'd just been discussing moments before.

"It's off the coast of Papua New Guinea."

"Down under," Kenneth said. "You could go see your cousins in

Sydney. Margaret Kingston, your grandfather's sister's daughter—her husband has a paper processing site."

"Yeah, I think it's several hours on a plane to Australia, even from there, and the schedule's pretty packed," Liz said.

"Just a suggestion." The paper resumed its full eclipse.

"Will you do it?" Alison asked, though Liz felt she had already made perfectly clear that she would. She plumped herself down beside Liz, and snatched Michael up from the rug, where he was pushing a small blue Lego brick into Atlantic's ear canal.

"Yes, I want to, it's a very interesting subject. There's a woman over there who's started a new 'cult,' I suppose you'd call it—"

"It's not dangerous, is it?"

"No. I mean, there's malaria. And food poisoning."

"A lot of violence in these places," her father said sadly. "A lot of trouble."

"Where are 'these places'?" Liz asked, and noticed Alison glance at her mum.

Kenneth lowered the newspaper and eyed Liz.

"I'm not starting. Just wondering what you meant. What constitutes 'these places'?"

His eyes returned to the paper and a page of the *Daily Telegraph* was turned.

Judith tried to intercede—"It'll be great for your profile, keep your name out there"—but Liz persevered.

"Ethnicity? Poverty? Race? It's a genuine question."

The *Telegraph* came down again and Kenneth lowered his reading glasses to the tip of his nose, enabling him to peer with a tired kind of menace over them.

"I'm not trying to annoy you," Liz persisted. "Does it depend on distance from Ballyglass? What constitutes the foreign? It's an interesting philosophical question—what comprises the Other?"

Kenneth lowered his jaw slightly, and pushed his tongue to one side of his mouth. This was the face of sufferance, of a man who is set upon by life but stoically endures it.

"Just forget about it."

"I didn't mean to annoy you—"

"I'm not annoyed. I'll just keep quiet over here. In my little corner."

A car horn went. No one had noticed Spencer swing his A4 round the back of the house.

(ii) Anthony Carson, 72

Anthony spent the afternoon moving a wardrobe, or watching one being moved, as his nephew joked in the van on the way back. He knew it was a kindness for Jamesy to ask him along. Get a lonely man out of the house for a bit of a jaunt, let him feel useful. He didn't feel patronized by it—he was grateful. It's what family was meant to do. Afterwards, Jamesy came in to check the TV aerial for him while Anthony got them a bottle of stout each. These big, boxy sets were out, according to Jamesy, you had to get a sleek, flat one. They bantered for a while but then the inevitable moment came and Jamesy took his leave. People had their own lives to live, of course. Anthony fed the cats and put on a record and opened another bottle of Murphy's. Mary had given him all these Bach concertos on vinyl for their twenty-fifth wedding anniversary, and he sat at the table and drank and listened to the complicated celestial music. He lifted the deck of cards and dealt a hand of patience. After three failures, a game came out, and he stopped the record player and placed the fifth concerto back in its sleeve. He examined his shirt in the mirror for stains and decided to change it before heading up the lane to the Day's End.

There was no seat at the bar, but Paddy went out to the back to find a spare stool and they squashed him in at the end by Jonty McLellan, who was well on his way.

"How's young Anthony getting on out in Thailand, is it?"

"Ach, very good indeed. He loves it. He has a wee boy now with a native."

"Oh very good. I'd say now there's a few of them mixed children out there."

"There would be."

"Fish farm going well?"

"I believe so."

There was a pause.

"Now what exactly would the fish in a fish farm be eating?"

"They feed them."

"Oh they do."

"They do."

"But now would they be eating each other's feces and so on?" McLellan asked happily.

"I don't believe so, no."

"Would they not be? So pellets, is it?"

"I'd say so."

"Like fish meal?"

"That would be my understanding."

"You been out there?"

"I have not."

"Get yourself a wee squeeze, what? A wee honey."

"Ah well now, actually we were booked to go the year Mary died, but then, you know, Mary died."

"Now it's a shame."

"It is."

"You haven't had to seek your troubles."

"We all have crosses to bear."

In silence they looked down at their drinks and considered their crosses, then looked back up at the band going full throttle.

"Not bad, this lot."

"Not bad at all."

"You like the rock and roll?"

"I do."

"Me, now, I like two kinds of music myself. Country—"

"That's an old one."

"And Western."

"Look at these ould yahoos."

"An affront to come in like that and bang the door."

"Who do they think they are anyhow?"

"Sure, they have the Halloween masks on. Now why in the name of God—"

CHAPTER 9

The shaker bottle fitted too well into the cup holder of the Audi. On the way to his viewing, before heading back to his parents' house to see Liz, Spencer stopped at the light and tried to pull it out, but the bottle was stuck fast. The lid flopped back and spilled Vanilla Pro Performance AMP Amplified Mass protein shake—augmented with a handful of Quaker Oats, a dollop of extra-crunchy peanut butter, a few blueberries, and one banana—across his khaki Dockers. He wiped it off as best he could as the light changed, and almost immediately someone behind began beeping his horn. It was Ballyglass, for fuck's sake. Where was the fire? He considered pulling the hand brake and getting out and having a go at whatever gipe was in the black car behind. He snapped the rearview mirror up to stop himself eyeballing the driver, and eased the car away from the green.

At the next light by Molesworth, the same black motor had pulled up alongside him. It was only Hutchy, the idiot, in his 5 Series. Spencer waved and Hutch flipped him the bird, the cheeky fuck. They rolled their windows down.

"You still on for golf on Sunday?" Hutch shouted.

"I'll be there."

"Bring your fifty-pences."

"I won't be needing them."

"Aw I think you will. I've got my new driver. It's *ti-TANE-ee-um*."

Hutchy warbled the last word like the pop song, then winked and sunk the boot. The BMW purred off ahead. Spencer watched it crest Oldtown

Hill and disappear, feeling the usual mix of guilt and grief and wild cheeriness that Ian Hutchinson triggered in him.

Atop the Oldtown Hill, Spencer looked automatically downwards to see the field still sitting there, still empty. It sloped down from the car park behind the TV shop and the offices of the *Mid-Ulster Mail*. It was a large field, a hundred meters across and double that in length. When Spencer was growing up they'd played football in it after school—the agency was only across the road from the TV shop—and it was the only large empty piece of land in the center of Ballyglass. And it was what had broken Lynx Property, the company set up by Spencer and Ian Hutchinson.

They were best friends. Spencer passed most of his childhood in the Hutchinsons's tidy detached five-bed in the Oaks—long since downsized in favor of a bungalow in Forthglen. The front room had a collection of porcelain ballet dancers in a corner display unit, and a pungent smell of potpourri, back when potpourri was a thing. Mrs. Hutch—Miriam—floated in and out of his infancy and adolescence with tea towels and traybakes, dispensing glasses of orange squash and optimistic multipurpose aphorisms, as all the while Ian rolled his eyes and told her they were hungry or thirsty or busy or bored. She loved Ian like he was a little prince, and it turned the cruel and funny boy into a witty narcissist. Anyone could see that Hutch had been too adored. Even Spencer, who'd been pretty adored himself, could see it. It was only natural for these two much-doted-on boys to go into business. Spencer—because he'd been working at his parents' agency since he was sixteen—had access to the properties; Ian had the endless chutzpah.

It was 2006 and the mood in the town, in the country, was wildly optimistic. A shop selling only mobile phone cases opened. A shop selling designer children's clothes opened. There was an ice cream "shoppe." There was a deli selling "organic produce." The citizens of Ballyglass watched these developments with disbelief, amusement, anger, and finally despair. When the economy collapsed, the main feeling was one of vindication; it had always seemed ridiculous, fantastical, and so it had been proved. The town had been poor for all of its five hundred years, and by

God it would be poor again. People had got "above themselves," had been "carried away," were all out gadding about living "beyond their means." The inevitable reversion to a hardscrabble existence was accepted like a natural order returning, like water finding its own level. MacGill's Delicatessen shut and was replaced by a Poundland. MobileCovers4U was boarded up and destroyed one night by fire. The town's unwritten constitution—which was something like, "If it seems too good to be true, you're not in Ballyglass"—was restored.

But for those early years the mood was unstoppable as an avalanche. It was madness *not* to get involved. Townhouses were being built on the sites of the old factories and people would surely be found to buy them.

Ian and Spencer were both nineteen when they bought their first house together with a loan—a two-up two-down out on the bypass; thirty-eight grand—and they rented it to Mrs. Montgomery, who wanted to be closer to her daughter. But they soon wanted to go bigger, better, higher. They set up Lynx Property—named after the scout patrol Ian had been sixer of and Spencer seconder—and by the time they turned twenty-one, they had five houses on the books.

Time to develop. They heard from Simon Conway in the Railway Bar that the TV shop crowd might be willing to entertain offers for the field. They could buy it and go into partnership with Dennis Mahon to build thirty townhouses there. They bought it from Wilson Espie for eight hundred thousand pounds, not one pound of which they had. Spencer didn't tell Kenneth until after they'd signed the deal on September 12, 2008; Lehman Brothers collapsed three days later. The interest payments on the loan amounted to thirty-seven thousand a month. They had to build immediately and make a lot of money. Dennis Mahon the builder announced he already had twenty-three houses he couldn't sell in Omagh and fourteen in Magherafelt, and there was no way he was starting more.

Going bankrupt was the kind of humiliation that makes you feel physically smaller, weaker. For three years after he turned twenty-two, Spencer had no bank account and was paid an allowance by his father again, as if he were twelve.

When he got to the house in question, a girl sat on the outside steps, head down in prayer to her smartphone; another peered in through the glass panel of the front door. He pulled up right outside and waved. Curt was the nod that came back from the steps. They could be very snappy, the foreigners.

Ballyglass had got mostly Lithuanians and Portuguese. Nearly all the immigrants worked on assembly lines: cutting, boning, packing. There was the bacon factory, the cheese factory, the cement works. There was Moy Park, the big poultry plant over in Dungannon. He once sold two Korean chicken sexers a nice two-bed flat in Newmills. Then there were your Polish, your Romanians, Hungarians, Indonesians, a scattering of Africans. You saw these very black girls pushing prams up and down the main street. Brave new world. The new Café Ali on the corner of the Old-town and Burn Road was filled with dwarfish, swarthy men—they were your Portuguese—hunched over tables or standing out front smoking. Never any women. Used to be you could walk the length of the town with-out seeing a soul you didn't know by name, or know to see, but those days were long gone. There was, anyway, less fighting now between the RCs and the Prods; all the trouble at the weekends was between the migrants and the locals. So that was one thing they'd done for the community. And wasn't it for the best, in the end? Adding a bit of color to the old two-tone, to the faded orange and the washed-out green? And if it was a shock to hear people speaking some funny tongue in the petrol station, well, it was only a shock once. And they were generally pretty good tenants. Quiet, punctual with rent. You might find there was an extra body or three sleep-ing there, but no, overall, not bad. Not too bad at all.

"Spencer, nice to meet you."

The one at the door tripped down the steps to shake his hand.

"Katarina."

Nose ring beneath the heavy-framed glasses, three ear cuffs on one ear, her lengthy black hair tied back and dyed inexpertly with purple streaks. She wore a black hoodie and was skinny up top with a very large lower half. Her elfin friend gave him a tepid smile as she tucked her phone into a little pocket on the strap of her backpack.

"Now this place has just come on—let me get this open—but it's not going to be on long."

Katarina liked the kitchen but disliked the hill you had to walk up to get to the house. Greta liked the hill because she loved this view from the kitchen of the fields and mountains—the Sperrins, Spencer clarified. Katarina liked the view but disliked the way the garden opened at the side onto the car park. It wouldn't be difficult to put a gate up there, Spencer reassured them, gesturing with one hand to demonstrate how a gate might swing open and closed.

"Would the landlord make that?" Katarina asked.

"I'm sure that could be sorted out," Spencer said, and added brightly, "So where are you girls from?"

They looked at each other. Girls had been perhaps the wrong word.

"I am Czech," Katrina said.

"Great football team, Czech Republic."

Spencer gave her a grin and got nothing back. Greta finished taking a picture of the kitchen units with her iPhone and slid it into the back pocket of her saggy jeans. She was not unattractive. Too skinny, but she had the face. Eyes like blue ice. Viking cheekbones.

She gave a sigh of spiritual annihilation and announced flatly, "I come from Latvia originally."

"Latvia."

He was drawing a blank on that.

"Lovely," he added. "Ballyglass must be a big change."

Upstairs, Katarina fiddled with the cord of the window blind in the big front bedroom, and said that she liked this room. One of her rings was a silver skull with purple eyes. Greta said she liked it too, retrieving her iPhone.

"You'll have to draw straws." Spencer smiled, and then, thinking this might be a little lexically complicated, added, "Or you could throw a coin, you know, flip it." He noticed the little darting glance Greta threw at

Katarina. They were a couple. He threw open the door of the hot press. Takes all sorts.

After he waved the prospective tenants off, he lifted the post and piled the letters to a dead woman on the kitchen counter. The house had been cleared of most of Mrs. Shannon's effects, though the stripped beds and a fairly inoffensive oatmeal sofa in the lounge had been left. The son was a radiologist in Glasgow, and he'd rung up to put the house on with them. He'd let Kenneth set the rent at 450 a month and told them anything left in the house should be donated to Cancer Research. Mrs. Shannon had been in a hospice in Belfast for months, but even so, it was quick in the end. And they had the house on the market before her body was cremated.

But you couldn't second-guess other people's grief. You never knew. You couldn't know. There was a hardening of circumstance. Spencer thought about his mother telling him to sit down one Sunday afternoon and drink his tea and then saying, "I have this swelling in my stomach." And he'd been sick at heart, oh how he'd cried like a baby. But after a few weeks or so he'd begun to sleep again, could think of it without a hard knot forming in his own stomach. It was awful it was awful it was awful, but he was used to it. You could get used to anything. Wasn't that the lesson?

They didn't sit around discussing it, not anymore. It had been three years since Judith's "debulking," the initial chemo, an infection that made her left leg swell up as hard and thick as a tree trunk. He'd driven with his dad every day to the Royal—and every day argued over whether to take the Boucher Road or the Westlink—and every day parked up on the top level of the rooftop car park, where she could see them from her window.

Spencer stopped at the sunburst mirror in the hallway and adjusted his hair.

He sat back down on the sofa and removed the tie that Kenneth in his wisdom still felt all estate agents should wear. His shoulders sagged in his boxy pin-striped suit. Impossible not to feel slightly wired after a showing. Game face. Real face. His left arm ached from a series of drop-set preacher curls he'd done in the gym last night. He tensed and let his fingers trace the swollen bunched cords of his bicep through the jacket and felt the reassurance of his own body, his capabilities. There was the familiar knock at the door. He let her in.

"Hey."

"Hey."

"Where'd you park?" Spencer asked.

"On the main street, down by Conway's."

"Are you OK?"

"I'm OK."

"When do you have to be back in the office?"

"Before the hour. Your dad's at Ray Mullens's funeral, but I told Judith I'd be back at work by two."

"You work too hard for my family."

"And Liz is coming home."

"I'm off to see her after this."

"This?"

"You know what I mean."

He slipped the camel coat off her shoulders and she let him.

"Were they keen?"

"The lesbians?"

"They were lesbians?"

"I think they'll probably take it. You're looking fine today, Mrs. Hutchinson."

"Don't call me that."

As Spencer sat on the edge of the mattress, buttoning his shirt, he watched Trisha fasten her bra at the front and twist it round. The pale tundra of her back, the outposts of three moles by her left shoulder. She was tall, taller than Spencer, but neither willowy nor voluptuous. She had a strong athletic physique that over the years and after one child had softened now to what to Spencer seemed all shades of glorious.

"Stop watching me."

"Why?"

"You've seen it all before."

"That doesn't mean anything."

She stopped and slipped her blouse on. It had a high collar and she squinted in the mirror now to find the catches. The varnish of her self-possession cracked occasionally, as now, and the sly silliness that lived beneath came out. She said, "You're a bad egg, Spencer Donnelly."

"Me?"

"Well, me too."

"How's it been between you?"

"OK, you know. Sure, you see him more than I do! I think he's probably sleeping with someone new; he gets texts at all hours. I don't ask. He was up in Castlerock again at the weekend."

"He get you anything for your birthday?"

"Did you?"

"I wanted to. You told me not to."

"He got me an iPad."

"Well, that's *nice*."

"I think he thought it would keep me company. He spent about forty minutes hooking it up to my computer and downloading all the music on it."

"He'll use it for porn."

"Don't say that."

"I saw him this morning. He beeped me at the lights and then flipped me the bird."

"Let's not talk about him."

Trish paused, and Spencer saw the conversation was about to take a familiar, tedious turn.

"Do you think we'd be doing this if it wasn't for him?"

"Don't. Let's not go over this."

Spencer cupped her buttocks, newly captured in her skirt, and tried to pull her back onto him.

"I mean, you get to sleep with your best friend's wife, and I get revenge on my husband with his best friend."

"You make it sound a little ruthless."

"Isn't it?"

Spencer spun her round and took pleasure in how easy it was to move her.

"Well, that's all true but you didn't add in the bit about me loving you. You know that."

"I don't know anything."

She looked genuinely distressed now; the flushed, mild giddiness of having fucked was giving way, inevitably, to guilt. She bit down on her lovely lip.

"We can stop," Spencer said, knowing that they couldn't.

Spencer tied his second shoe in a double bow and stood up sharply. Trisha was applying lipstick in front of the mirror.

"We could always tell."

Trisha winced.

"We've been through this."

"Didn't he say you're free to do as you choose? Just as he does?"

"Yeah, but not with you, Spence."

(iii) Angela Downey, 26

It wasn't that she didn't like London, but in the end you missed where you were from. That was just a fact. And when there was a child involved, you wanted them to have the same sort of upbringing you had. No big mystery, even if people treated her like she'd come from Mars, or like she'd failed somehow by returning. Especially if you came back like she had—a single mum with a brown child. "A wee half-caste girl," as her Aunt Yvonne put it. What a beautiful child, they all said to her, and she heard the unspoken qualification. Perhaps that was unfair. Sophia *was* beautiful, like a tiny Nefertiti, Angela thought, though who would she say that to? The father had never been around. He was French-Nigerian, Claude, and a personal trainer in the gym she'd joined when she moved into a basement flat in Brixton. He was nice, but he already had three kids and when she told him she was pregnant, he warned her that he had all the children that he needed. She'd assumed, stupidly perhaps, that he'd change. And he did—he stopped coming round. Her mum had been great about it, and what her dad thought she didn't know, because he would never have told her anyway, but they loved Sophia. You'd have known the wee lassie wasn't "fully Derry," but she might have been taken for Italian, her mum said once, meaning to be kind.

And you should have seen her father with Sophia. He doted on her. Jesus Christ, he loved her. You'd think there wasn't any other kid in the world when he got down on his knees in the conservatory and started building the Lego with her. She never remembered him taking her to the park—but with Sophia he was always walking her down to the swings, or taking her to play Pooh Sticks off the bridge at Callaghan Cross. And to-night they were keeping her without a word of complaint, happy to do it. So she could go out on this . . . outing. It wasn't a date. No, you couldn't call it a date. Eugene worked as a salesman in McCulloch's garage, and she was the receptionist. They'd spent four months smiling at each other before he even stopped to chat. When she looked up his employment file and saw he was thirty-two and never married, she thought, *What's wrong with him?* But the answer, based at least on three evenings out, was: *Nothing.* Or nothing much. He made bad puns. But he stood six foot one and was skinny with a little button nose, and when he'd kissed her last week he'd laughed afterwards with such sheer dizzy joyfulness that she had found herself laughing too. He hadn't met Sophia but he knew all about her, and said that he loved kids. He had three nieces of his own, and claimed never to forget their birthdays. His Uncle Derek was playing in a *céilí* band out in the sticks and they were going to have a drink and a wee dance. What harm could come of that?

She said a vodka and lemonade and Eugene turned back to her and asked if Sprite was OK and she said of course and then there was a noise so loud she fell into his back, and the other drinkers pushed against her. They all crushed up against the bar and she wouldn't ever see her daughter again, and Sophia would never see her. A bullet moved with exquisite speed from the metal barrel of a gun into her skull and out the other side again, erupting.

CHAPTER 10

Spencer jumped out of his car, as the women who loved him watched from the kitchen window, and bounded into the Donnelly house. Liz embraced him.

"Good God, it's like hugging a tree."

He grinned, delighted, and pulled up the sleeve of his polo shirt to flex his bicep.

"Seventeen inches."

Liz poked it exploratively.

"You ever read books?"

"Actually I do. Well, I listen to them in the Audi. Just finished a great biography of Carlos Lambada, the Mexican drug lord. *Kingpin of the Badlands*."

Kenneth—who thought of himself as the family correction to this kind of feminine Spencer-fawning—shouted from the depths of his red chair, "You sort out Brian Hughes?"

"I don't think he's going to go for it."

"Why not?"

"Another house over in Cullydown, one of the wee terraces up on the Dromore estate. He thinks it's a better buy."

"Nelly White's?"

"Not sure. I didn't push him on it."

"Why?"

"Didn't think to."

The red chair sighed; no one in the universe possessed an ounce of sense. Spencer grinned at Liz.

"My whole family in the one room!" Judith said, and her eyes took on an instant sheen of maternal insanity.

"Well who's this?" Spencer stooped and picked up Atlantic, who licked his left ear, and then his right. "Aren't you a dote?"

"Spensy, Spensy."

Spencer looked down and Michael was tugging on his jeans.

"And you're a dote too."

"Liz, Spencer, can you two carry out the trestle tables from the garage? The marquee people are going to be here in the morning."

"How are things then?"

"Oh, you know, shitty."

"On the shitty scale?"

"Pretty fucking shitty. Lift your end a bit higher."

"Watch the coal bucket. And that lamp."

"I came home to find my boyfriend in bed with someone else."

"Fuck. Go left."

"He was in bed with another man."

"Oh *fuck*. My left."

"Not ideal. On the plus side, I'm trying to look at it from a Donnelly perspective, like I'm losing a tenant who never paid rent."

"That *is* a plus."

"I like your haircut."

"Do you? Dad calls it the Ian Brady."

"Is he a footballer?"

"The Moors Murderer."

"It looks good. You seeing anyone?"

"Not really."

"No Myra Hindley?"

"Funny," Spencer said, meaning the opposite.

There had been girls—always described to Liz when they were on their way out—but never anyone who stuck. This one was "too clingy." That one was "too bossy." Used to the intrigues of sisterhood—the competitive self-denigration, the tart protectiveness—Liz always found her brother comfortingly open and uncomplicated, transparent as clean glass. Still, for all his straightforwardness, her little brother was curiously guarded about his love life.

Now he stopped walking and leaned the table against the low brick wall dividing the fruit trees from the lawn. To avoid answering her questions properly, he nodded back at the hulking shape of their father standing at the window, observing his children momentarily not doing what he had asked them to do.

"You notice he can't find the right words all the time? He says video for radio and document for argument, and I'm off to bad for off to bed. You can't mention it or he gets wound up about it. You have to pretend it didn't happen. He said care bear for burger the other day."

"He did not."

"No ketchup on my care bear."

They lifted the table back up and began moving again.

"What do you make of Stephen?"

Spencer shrugged. "He seems up for it."

"Up for it?"

"For Alison, for taking on two wee ones."

"But do you like him?"

"Well enough. He's quiet. Maybe a bit of a breathe-in-breathe-out. You seen the tats on his arms?"

Liz nodded at this. She thought about the driving license but wondered at her own motivations for wanting to tell Spencer about it. It made her feel like Alison, pouring poison in your ear just to make conversation. She held her tongue and Spencer lifted the table back up, nodded at her to do the same, and summarized the situation.

"Alison certainly knows how to pick 'em."

CHAPTER 11

Only one day to go now. It was important to remember it was her second marriage. You didn't want to do everything the same. You didn't want to make a similar kind of fuss. Her dress was cream, a fishtail with minimal detail on the shoulders. No train. Judith had been very against another white wedding, and she was probably right. Her hair would be piled up on her head with a small diamond tiara to hold it in place. She'd seen a thing in *Northern Woman* in the hairdressers about releasing doves at weddings, and they had ordered two for tomorrow morning—but only two. No overdoing it. Spencer was meeting a fella from Coleraine half an hour before the service to get them. Tomorrow there'll be doves, she thought, a dress and a tiara, but for now she stood in her old leggings and her Everlast tracksuit top holding hands with Stephen in this draughty church.

She'd asked Trisha, who worked in the office, and whom she'd known for donkey's years—if never particularly deeply—to be her maid of honor, and she'd turned up in a pair of tight jeans and a sleeveless top that gaped at the back showing her bra, God love her. She had a six-year-old, but you would never have known it. It was just a question of taste, really, and Trisha, nice as she was, had none. Thank God she'd chosen Trisha's dress for tomorrow for her. She looked nice in lavender, as long as she didn't overdo it on the eye shadow. If there was time, the beautician could do Trisha's face in the morning—after she'd done Alison's, and concealed this bruise beneath her eye.

Stephen did really well. He mumbled a couple of times, but Reverend Gifford was so patient. Afterwards she and Stephen walked hand in hand in silence through the car park at the side of the church and then he pulled her to him and they hugged for a long time. A crowd of wee lads was playing a football match on the far side of the wall, and they could hear the game dispersing as the boys headed in for the evening, exchanging their serious farewells—Aye, see youse now. Take it easy. Keep 'er lit, fellas. Overhead the rooks were circling loudly, also getting ready to settle for the night. He was leaning against the bonnet of his Focus and she was standing between his legs, leaning into him. She closed her eyes and it felt like she and Stephen were the still center of a noisy turning world.

"Do you think he'll remember to mention the bit about us meeting here in the same church we're getting married in?" asked Alison as they watched Reverend Gifford lock the vestry door, back in his civvies though still with the collar.

Stephen lifted his head and waved to him.

"Because it's almost like fate, isn't it?" pressed Alison, awaiting his confirmation.

"Like, what goes around comes around, you mean," murmured Stephen stupidly, nestling his head back into her neck.

"No, no," said Alison, trying not to get cross. "That's something else altogether."

Stephen liked to say he started as her handyman and ended up her husband, but for Alison it was this bit about the church that mattered, because it seemed to sanction her good instincts, which is all Alison ever wanted: external confirmation of whatever she felt inside. But yes, he had painted her lounge. It was just after she moved in to her new place, when housewarming cards filled the kitchen windowsill. They weren't really housewarming cards, of course; they were Congratulations on Your Long-Awaited Independence cards, Condolences on the Demise of Your Shitty Marriage cards, Sorry to Hear You Were Mentally Ill When You Got Yourself Hitched to That Drunk Cop cards . . . People in the street who hadn't given her the time of day were now smiling and stopping to chat and laying a hand on her arm and reassuring her that if there was anything they could do, anything at all . . . She'd run into Carol Hutchinson, Trisha's mother-in-law, in M&S by the biscuit tins, and she had recommended someone called Stephen McLean, who'd just painted their living room and papered one of the bedrooms, and had really done a fantastic job, a super job. Very clean, very quick, really very reasonably priced. He goes to Ballyglass Presbyterian. You must have seen him there. Sits by himself at the back in a gray suit. Bald.

That Sunday she sought him out after the service. He stood on the steps, and she watched him shake hands with Maurice Sheldon, one of the elders, and then help him down the stairs. He moved purposefully, carefully, as if he were carrying something breakable within him. Reverend Gifford appeared beside him, and Stephen listened intently as the minister talked in his ear. Alison found she was staring at him and his eyes met hers—he smiled. But it meant nothing. Everyone smiled at each other at church. That was the whole point.

"Stephen, is it?"

"That's right."

"I've a wee job that Carol Hutchinson thought you might be interested in."

He had a little patch of stubble on top of his bald head, but at least he shaved it. And the eyes, under the level brows, were so brown.

"Oh yes. A painting job?"

"Aye, well, painting and maybe fixing up a few things."

He pulled a slim diary from his inside pocket, unexpectedly professional, and extracted a thin pencil from its spine.

"Let's see. I'm putting in conservatories during the week, but what about Wednesday evening I come over and you can show me what needs doing? Then I can give you a quote."

He took off his shoes at the door, without being asked. All smiles and comments on the fine weather, the solidity of the house, the lovely cornicing in the hallway and no questions about the absence of a man living there. His rollers and sheets and brushes were nicely ordered in a plastic crate and he removed his black leather shoes again—school shoes, really—and left them paired at the front door. He locked himself in the toilet and came out dressed in gray tracksuit bottoms and a plaid work shirt, both heavily spattered with paint. When Alison had taken Isobel and the baby to Tesco's, they'd returned to hear him whistling proficiently in the bathroom upstairs. She'd never found bald men attractive, but by the time she offered him a cup of tea at 6:00 p.m. she'd noticed how gentle and patient he was with Isobel, who'd stood and watched and talked at him for a good hour and then trod emulsion all over the bathroom tiles. He cleaned it off with white spirits and told her she was lucky to live in such a nice house. There was something attractive about a mind that moved in a straight line.

The second night she came into the kitchen, where he stood at the sink, sleeves rolled up, washing his brushes. As she set the children's empty plates on the side, she saw on his left forearm the British lion reared back on its hind legs, though unsteadily, as if it might be tipping over, and under it, in Gothic script, was "No Surrender." On the other arm the bloody hand was red and bright, and below it a dagger with "Made in Ulster" written along the blade. But he looked so mild, so bald, so normal. Well, didn't they all. Weren't they all just normal-looking idiots. The ruiners. The mentals. Still, she was surprised. Though it wasn't unusual, it wasn't out of the ordinary. The way things had been, the way things had gone, you never knew what challenges, what problems, what circumstances led . . . And then there was the question of class. Not everyone had had the same start out the gates. You had to remember that. But she didn't want Isobel asking about the tattoos. It'd be like her to notice them. It held her off: It reminded her that she knew next to nothing about him. She stayed up in the nursery with Michael, and when Stephen shouted, "I'm off then, cheerio," she shouted down, "See you now, cheerio," and only when she heard his car pull away did she go downstairs and put the chain on the door. It was not hard to keep away from him for the two weeks of evenings and Saturdays he worked on the house.

On the last night, with the last wall painted, the last socket fitted, the paving laid and the lawn cut, she offered him a cup of tea and he accepted, and she felt unexpectedly glad, and he sat down at the kitchen table. He sat straight in his seat, a little stiffly, and there was a kind of tender nervousness in his demeanor. She found herself wanting to know more about him, felt that there was something here that she could not define but wanted to see. He was partly in shade. Now that she knew he was finished, that he wasn't returning, she felt free to be friendly.

She was talking about teaching, and about a favorite teacher of her own, Mrs. McElhone, who'd become a missionary in the Gambia and had been recently kidnapped, tied up, and finally shot in the leg in her own home in . . . in whatever the town in the Gambia it was, she couldn't remember. And as she was talking she found something strange occurring. All the time the children made her feel like her single role in life was as a mother, and she found her life moving happily and unhappily along that road. But Stephen, his back to the sun coming in low through the kitchen window, nodding and asking questions, spoke to some other potential in her, of being an adult, of being a woman, equivalent and opposite to this man sitting at her table. How could you be lonely with two kids? It wasn't loneliness exactly. It was emptiness, a whole part of her life was so empty.

It was with some surprise that she realized that she liked having him around the house.

"She's in Belgium now, in a hospital, recovering, but she devoted forty years to that country and now . . ."

Stephen shook his head.

"Shocking."

"I mean why would someone do that?"

He shook his head again and then said, "Money, I suppose."

"It's evil."

"You ever been to Africa?" Stephen asked.

"No, I've been to Egypt once."

"That's in Africa."

"Of course it is. Well yes, then, I have. Against my knowledge!"

She laughed a little hoarsely and Stephen smiled again, took a dainty sip of tea.

"Actually, Bill, the kids' dad, is out there somewhere, God knows where, in Afghanistan."

There was no response from Stephen, no little glimmer of a private pain. He simply nodded, widened his eyes sympathetically.

"The forces?"

"Private security."

"Good money, I'd bet."

"We're not together."

"Sorry to hear that . . ."

His eyes met hers and there was a wee flicker of irony in them. Not sorry at all. Alison felt the kitchen drop slightly like an elevator. Lovely, kind eyes he had with those long lashes that made him almost handsome.

The first time they went out it was to the Dragon Bowl, and she found herself delighted by the fact that he made a single bottle of Heineken last the entire evening.

When they pulled into the space outside the house, he'd stared for a while through the windshield. Anxious of the silence, she put her hand on the door handle to get out, but he said, quietly, "I have to tell you something."

"You're not married, are you?"

"No, nothing like that."

"Well, what is it? You're scaring me now—"

"Look, I've done things in the past, things I'm ashamed of. Things I shouldn't have done."

Alison said nothing. If she didn't move, if she kept staring out the side window, maybe this would stop. Finally she said, "We've all done things—"

"Not like that. I don't mean some wee thing. I mean I was involved. I've done things no one should ever do."

He stopped. Alison was motionless. All the hope, all the pleasure, all the desire turned slack and rancid. Couldn't he have waited a month, a year—forever?

"What—what did you do?"

He was silent.

"Tell me."

"The worst things you can do."

Her mouth felt very dry suddenly. She swallowed and said, "What's in the past . . . ," but stopped.

Stephen spoke quickly, "I paid for them things, I paid for them and I regret them. I do. I regret them. But I thought you should know from the start."

She realized he was crying. She couldn't bear it when men cried.

She turned to him and said, "Don't get upset. . . . Stephen!"

She barked his name at him, as if he were one of her pupils, and he looked at her surprised. He laid a hand on hers and said, "I need to tell you . . ."

"You don't. You don't need to tell me. I don't want to know. I don't want anything to do with this."

She realized she was making a decision. He was nice and all, he was great really, but no. She didn't need this. Whatever it was, she didn't need it, and Isobel didn't need it, and Michael didn't.

She couldn't remember getting out of the car or into the house. She lay in bed and heard her phone buzz with one, two, three texts but didn't pick it up to read them.

She tried his name in Google, and found an ophthalmologist in Arkansas, a schoolboy footballer in Glasgow, a professional magician in Lancashire. She added "Northern Ireland," and found a quality control officer in Oakdale Meats in Dungannon. She added "murder" and hit return. Nothing. "Bomb." Nothing. "Terrorist." Nothing. Whatever it was he'd done, she told herself, it couldn't be that serious.

Over the following weeks the texts kept coming. Dinner again? Just lunch. What about a drink? She said no and said no and then said not now, not yet. She was too nice, as she explained to Trisha as they sat and drank their Cup-a-Soups. She didn't tell Trisha about the shadows in his past. She said that it was too soon after Bill, that she had a baby, that she wasn't ready to see anyone, that she was flattered, of course, but it was madness, wasn't it? Though he was such a sweet guy. Trisha told her to go for it. "He's one of the good ones," Trisha said, standing up and washing her mug out in the sink, "and the good ones don't come along too often."

When she did finally answer a call of his, he sounded so pleased that the next thing she knew she'd agreed to meet him for lunch.

They kissed all the time.

They sat in his Focus outside her house, the car switched off, after an evening out and kissed until her lips hurt, and his hand would still be on the outside of her blouse.

Well, that was like starting a fire inside her.

She wanted to drive him so wild he couldn't control himself.

She found herself looking at the phone waiting for him to text or call.

If he came in for a coffee after they'd been out, they'd stand in her hallway, kissing goodbye for ten minutes.

She felt like she was seventeen again scobing Grant McCartney by the bins outside Eastwood's pool hall.

After three months they had still not made love—not for religious reasons really, though Alison did allow herself some smugness at the virtue of the action—but because Stephen hadn't ever taken it to that stage. Plus, there was always Isobel and Michael. Isobel came down a few times when they were on the sofa, and only the fact that she'd the gait of a baby elephant meant they heard her on the stairs and separated in time.

One Saturday Judith and Ken kept the kids and Stephen took her to the Tall Trees Garden Centre and then back home, where he swiftly planted everything up, fixing trellises to the back wall with nails and garden wire, rolling the plants out carefully from their plastic pots. Afterwards they stood in the kitchen washing their hands together—and standing beside him, sharing the tap's single twisting ribbon of water, she felt very close to him, closer than she'd felt to anyone for years. She thought how the tattoos on his forearms were really quite faded. As he dried his hands on the towel he observed, "We'll need to water them in," and she'd said, "Well, you do that and then meet me upstairs." He said, "You're on."

They lived in a terrible country. What sort of chance . . . What start in life . . . She heard him down beneath the window, unwinding the hose. People aren't monsters. What good can come from dwelling on it? You only had to look at him. A good man. A take-you-to-the-garden-center type of man. She took off her tracksuit bottoms and pants and T-shirt, and put on her black silk nightgown. She got into bed and then got back out again and put on her dressing gown and sat on the edge of the mattress. Then she got back into bed with the gown still on. She picked up the *Tyrone Courier* and turned the pages, not seeing it. She heard the hose stop. Could you be good and do bad things? The country made everyone mad. She felt overwhelmed and heard his tread on the stairs and the next thing she was kissing him and he was warm and naked and they were under the covers.

He was careful, even a little timid. Also tender, shy, and incredibly quick, as she knew somehow he would be. They lay in the bed and self-consciously, like lovers in a movie, shared one of his Mayfair cigarettes—her first in five years. He dropped the dying fag in a glass with an inch of water left in it, and turned to her. They both slid down the bed together and faced each other on the pillow, their noses an inch apart.

"Where'd you get those eyes?" she said.

"I dunno. My da. He looked like Charlie Chaplin."

But that hadn't been quite what she meant. She didn't know what she meant exactly. Only eyes like those weren't given out at birth. So much brown, so much despair. She felt out of her depth suddenly. It was almost five o'clock and her mum would be dropping the kids back soon.

"We should get up."

"He used to tell people he *was* Charlie Chaplin. He was a desperate one for fibbing."

"You take after him there too?"

"I do not."

"We should get up."

"Aye." He pushed his forehead against hers, and his hand fitted onto her face. "Or maybe not."

She slid backwards off the bed and stepped into the shower without looking at him. When she came out he was fully dressed again, even wearing his shoes, and sitting in the corner on the chair reading her *Grazia* magazine.

"You look like you're waiting for the dentist," she said, wrapping her hair in a blue towel.

And the next time she turned round he was on his knees, in her bedroom, asking her to marry him.

(iv) Janine McFadden, 32

Janine had that new pain in her stomach. It was everything stretching, everything making room, but definitely her body was older and more worn than it had been with Bobby.

She would cancel the evening with her mum and dad, only they'd be disappointed. And she had said she'd drive: This time she was determined that David would have a beer with her dad. There had been that bother over the silly toy rifle her dad had given to Bobby—to, as he said, "his own grandson"—and which David had insisted they secretly put in the bin. Hadn't he a right to decide if his son should be encouraged to pretend to shoot people? Especially nowadays? What with everything. I mean Jesus, what was your father thinking . . .

But then Bobby told his granddad that Daddy had taken his shooter away, and it was all a bit awkward. And now Bobby was obsessed with guns—which David blamed on her father. He'd take a branch from the apple trees, or a tennis racket, and shout bang bang bang and hide behind the oil tank. And anyway Vanessa from next door was booked to watch him, and she always got so shirty if they canceled. And it might well be her last time to go out before the bump emerged.

When they arrived at the house Mum was still upstairs and her dad started coughing as he answered the front door. He beckoned them in and hacked and hacked, and hurried off to the bathroom. When she went in after him she saw him spit a lump of brown phlegm flecked with blood on the toilet bowl.

"Did you make an appointment yet?"

"I said I will, and I will."

"You're worrying me. Can't you go and get it checked?"

Martin looked at his daughter with a hooded, angry stare: "I said I *will*."

Mum's footsteps on the stairs.

"Well, make sure you do."

The pub was busy and there in the corner was her friend Niamh with her boyfriend. She'd kept them seats. Dad went to get the drinks, and she sent David to help him. Her mother was wearing the new perfume by Armani that she'd got her for their fortieth anniversary last month. She took her mother's hand as they crossed the dance floor. The band was starting up and there was a wee note of jollity in both of them suddenly, unforced and easy and lovely. Niamh raised that eyebrow at her again as she tried to fit herself around the table. It was so loud, the music. The singer of the Cotton Mountain Boys was good, a big raw voice, all feeling. *For six long years I've been in trouble.* Janine wondered if the baby could feel the music. Maybe this would be the first song the baby would hear. Some idiot was shouting "Trick or treat" behind her. Then she felt her mother's arms around her, gripping so tightly, just full of love.

CHAPTER 12

Since Stephen rarely talked about himself, it made it easy to live always in the present. He'd arrived on Alison's doorstep without a past. Once, on the sofa, watching a program about endangered white rhinos, a diminishing box of Maltesers between them, he said, "That's like my family. Getting themselves extinct." But the fact he had no kin to speak of made wedding planning easier. Everything seemed smoother than the last time, especially her relations with Reverend Gifford—she could still feel the humiliation of Bill being drunk throughout their meeting concerning "spiritual preparations for marriage."

This time he led Stephen and her down the book-lined hallway to his little cluttered study, and they followed, meek as lambs. A row of tight white curls round his baldness like a hedge circling a hillock. He motioned to the sofa, though several commentaries on the New Testament were stacked on it. His ancient computer was on and a page filled with words open on the screen. Beside it on the desk a chipped side plate with a half-eaten buttered slice of barmbrack sat by an empty mug. There were papers everywhere. Alison lifted the books from the sofa and set them in a pile on the carpet.

"Just putting the final touches to the sermon."

"Do you have to write a new one each week?" Alison asked, because it seemed like she should.

"Well, I don't *have to*, but I find it focuses the mind."

The sofa was too soft and she and Stephen squashed against each other, separated. It was odd to see the Reverend in his home and his ordinary, rather shabby clothes. He had a wee piece of barmbrack on his beard and Alison must have been staring at it because he reached up now and found it, then looked at it for a second as if unsure whether or not to eat it. He dropped it on the plate.

For the next ten minutes Gifford reminded them of their marital duties and responsibilities, the ancient nature of the commitment. He talked about the nuclear family, and Adam and Eve, and the fundamentals of human need, companionship and support, the legitimacy of sexual urges. Alison examined the large swirling galaxies in the carpet and coughed.

"Well, as you know, Reverend, this isn't my first time at the rodeo, as it were."

"Of course, yes, Bill." The glasses came off. "How is he getting on?"

"Ah, we've no contact. He's in Afghanistan, far as I know."

"He had a problem with the drink," Stephen offered, and Alison threw him a quick reproachful glance.

"And you have the two? From the first marriage?"

"Mickey and Isobel."

He turned to Stephen.

"And are you committed to raising them as your own?"

"I love the children very much."

"And they get on with you, do they?"

"Well, they're children, you know. So some days they're a handful, let's say."

"Of course—"

"He's great with them," Alison said.

"And we should discuss—the past. I'm assuming you've talked about it?"

"You mean Stephen's past?"

"Yes."

"We've discussed it," Alison said. *Kind of*, she thought.

"We have," Stephen confirmed.

"And you have made your peace with it?"

"We're putting it behind us." Alison took Stephen's hand in hers. He squeezed her fingers to reassure her and said in a steady voice, "I'm living a Christian life now."

"I know you are. I know you are, Stephen."

Gifford put his glasses back on. They gave him an owlish aspect. He cocked his head to one side and sighed and Alison realized she passionately disliked him, always had. He made a slight humming sound and touched his fingertips together and said, "Have you forgiven Stephen?"

"It's not up to me to forgive him, is it," Alison said. "It's up to God."

Gifford smiled, as one might smile at a small relentless child, and said, "And those who suffered at his hands."

They sat in the car and before he'd even started the engine, Alison said, "I don't even want to know. I don't even want to know the details. What happened. Or where. Or why. It's in the past. Let's leave it there."

CHAPTER 13

"You wearing that?" asked Kenneth.

Liz looked down at the navy shift dress she'd put on. She'd tied a navy and white scarf round her neck and parted her hair neatly to the side. She had, in other words, made an effort, a conspicuous effort, to dress for a wedding.

"I was going to. Is it not all right?"

Liz never could find her proper voice to talk to her father; it went up an octave.

"It's fine."

"What's wrong with it?"

"It's *fine*."

Kenneth filled the water tank of the new Nespresso machine, and then turned the rack of the coffee capsules, looking for his Chococino. Much of the enjoyment he got from using the machine was due to the fact he could complain, each time, that it wasn't quite hot enough.

"Well, obviously something's wrong with it or you wouldn't have brought it up."

If Judith had been in the room, Liz would have let it go. She would have been able to meet her mother's eye and exchange a look of sympathy and exasperation. But Judith was at Alison's, helping her and Isobel and Trisha get ready. They had to be at the church at 11:00 a.m. and it wasn't even 10:00 yet. Plenty of time for an argument.

"I think it's pretty clear I'm not wearing pajamas. What else would I have on? An intermediate outfit?"

"Jesus Christ! I just asked you were you wearing that. Is that a crime?"

Her father closed the cutlery drawer with double the force needed.

"But why? To undermine my confidence? To make me feel bad about myself? I thought I looked nice. But now I don't think that."

Her father, steering his way out of the kitchen, stopped and turned. The expression on his face was one of curious hurt.

"You *do* look nice. I didn't mean anything by it. I'm sorry."

In Liz's memory, her father had never—ever—apologized for anything, and in shock, she followed him through to the living room, watching as he set his cup on a coaster and lowered himself into his seat.

"Are you OK?" she said.

"I don't want to argue," he answered in a very small voice.

"Me neither. I'm sorry too. Everyone's stressed. . . . I was thinking this morning about the rituals of marriage. Something old and something new, something borrowed, something blue." She sat on the arm of the sofa, babbling, trying to prolong this intimate moment. "It's about continuity, and novelty, your old life and family and your new one—and the borrowed must be about the necessity of community, about relying on the network—but what's the blue one about?"

Her father picked up the remote control.

"Rhymes with new, I suppose."

The church door opened and thirty-four heads swiveled as Ruth Johnston—the alcoholic organist—took the cue to plunge ahead a little frantically with Mendelssohn's dreary march. With her head bowed slightly, Alison entered, looking up from under thickened lashes. Down the aisle she advanced like a large pale pupa being dragged by another insect, this one dark and a little stiff-legged in his morning suit, the tails of which hung behind like folded wings.

Kenneth's face maintained a grave, momentous expression, although he winked almost continually at various people, excepting Liz. What was the deal with her father? When he was ten he'd won a scholarship to a boys boarding school in Dublin, and been sent away from the butcher's shop in Ramelton, Donegal. He was the youngest of seven, and had always been spoilt, but that all-male environment had broken something in him; he had no way to reach the emotional content of his life. He couldn't quite enjoy the company of women. He needed to mock whatever undertaking he was engaged in. He needed a jokey competitive level of conversation—the way boys talk in a locker room or dormitory. He couldn't tell you how he felt—only wanted to assure you that he felt the way any normal man would feel, and why would you think otherwise?

Alison stared forward, concentrating on keeping her head still, her hair elevated, and on not showing too overtly the pleasure that she felt. When she reached the second pew she turned to her family and widened her eyes at them as if to say, *Can you believe this?*

Liz could believe it. The bad, boxy cut of Stephen's hired jacket, how pale he looked. She watched wee Neil, the best man, beaming at Alison, his round face freshly scrubbed and the color of cooked gammon. He also belonged to the prosaic, believable world. The church was cavernous and cool, but even so Stephen wiped sweat away from his forehead. The Rev. Gifford stood on the step and waited for Alison to arrive, gently nodding his head to show he approved of all he surveyed.

Kenneth handed her over to Stephen. Though Liz knew the transference of the woman from one registered keeper to another—like a car— suggested that the female would live with the husband's group, in this instance the husband appeared to have no group, or at least no local group. His side of the church was filled up with friends of the Donnellys. She tried to think of it in academic terms; she hunted for the word—"uxorilocal," was it?—when the newly wed couple shacked up near the wife's group. It was textbook endogamy; she was marrying within the tribe. Stephen's group, if there was such a group, was part of the larger tribe of Protestantism—one of the two moieties, say, that lived in the area.

During the vows, the Rev. Gifford read out Stephen's name as Andrew McLean, and added, "known as Stephen," and Liz felt she was the only one who found this odd. Known as Stephen?

Though as it was, if she could pick a name different to her father's, she would. Who'd be a Donnelly? Who'd be Kenny Donnelly's little girl, the elder one, the dark and prickly one, the one with brains to burn but still unmarried, and wasn't it sad?

Alison swallowed hard and concentrated and bit her lip and wiped the tears away, but the contagion spread, and Judith and Liz began snuffling and crying. She wanted her sister to be happy, and if marrying this skinny unprepossessing bald man who wore a signet ring and said "Scuse I" when he burped and whose eyes looked wet and dead was what made her happy, then she should go for it. He was kind to her, and Bill had never been kind. Judith passed a Kleenex for her along the row.

Up in the pulpit Reverend Gifford beamed at the happy couple and praised the dress, praised little Isobel the flower girl and the lovely flowers, praised the "clement" weather—and then began to sermonize as if leading the congregation into battle. A marriage had to be "protected," it "needed securing," one must "keep others out of it to guarantee that it stays strong." One needed "to hold it close and defend it," needed to be "watchful," "vigilant," "wary." The mood was somber as they stood to sing "All Things Bright and Beautiful."

Hadn't Lear in "The Owl and the Pussycat" got the analogy down pat? Dear Pig, are you willing to sell for one shilling the ring at the end of your nose, your nose? Marriage was, as Lévi-Strauss remarked, an economic institution, not an erotic one. Except that watching the ring slide—not entirely smoothly—onto Alison's finger, it occurred to Liz that the symbology was as much about penetration as possession, that they were always intertwined.

At least they'd taken out "obey," even here, in Ballyglass. It was time for her reading. Ecclesiastes. A time for this, a time for that, a time to read, a time to stop reading, a time to sit back in her seat and feel the burn of other people's attention only lift when the next hymn began.

Be thou my vision oh lord of my heart
nought be all else to me save that thou art
Be thou my saviour

When they went out to sign the register, the Ballyglass Primary School choir trooped in, arranged themselves, and began a Westlife medley. Liz was very close to crying again. It was to do with the passage of time, the relentless forwardness of the serious enterprise of living. Liz was middle-aged. Was thirty-four middle-aged? Her parents were definitively old. The church, the wooden struts and beams above, the tapestried cushions for kneeling—stayed the same. But she aged, her parents aged, her brother and Alison aged. Everything around them would outlast them. This hymnal in her hand would be here long after she was dust. What would she outlast? Atlantic, possibly.

After the choir filed back out into the vestry, there was a surprised silence when the congregation found they'd been left to their own devices. Silently, diligently, Spencer plowed through the levels of *Candy Crush* on his iPhone.

Next to her, in his pin-striped suit, her Uncle Sidney smelled of carbolic soap. It was binary; if he didn't smell of pigs he smelt of soap. He was scratching amicably with his fingernail at a dried stain on his tie. Even now, at seventy-two, Sidney looked more than capable of hoicking a calf up onto his back or plugging a sheep under either arm or flinging a bale up into the hayloft. The Sperrins's elements had tempered his face, polishing and coarsening the skin. Thick tentacular hairs emerged from his nostrils and his ear canals, probing the atmosphere. There was a gentle wryness to him caused by negotiating with the earth on a daily basis. Now his eyes closed and his huge hands moved to his lap, the fingertips touched—a structure representing this church they sat in. And here are the people, the lost tribe of Ulster Protestants. Along the whitewashed walls were affixed brass and marble plaques for the war dead—the Great War, the Second World War, policemen and soldiers murdered in the Troubles—all the men who had been turned to names, to sounds. Not even first names—initials, surnames. One of the plaques had space left at the bottom, in anticipation of more dead. Everywhere imagery of sacrifice and offering, memorials and altars—but even while disguised as just the opposite, a sanctuary from materialism, the church functioned as a marketplace of cold transactions. For it was here that all the contracts were proposed, signed, enacted. Right from birth the Ulster Protestant was steeped in metaphors of hardship and reward, of temporal disadvantage and eternal compensation. Portrait of the Christian as a stakeholder, as a shrewd and patient small investor.

This was the same pew she'd sat in for the first fourteen years of her life, until her parents agreed that if she got confirmed she wouldn't have to come to church again. And so it had gone. She'd last been in here for Bill and Alison's wedding. Or no, it must have been Isobel's christening. The church was unchanged; the lectern had the same gold eagle with its wings spread in the act of taking flight, though never actually flying.

Her mother stood up and she heard her give a little moan of effort. She looked at her and understood. She touched her hand and said, "Are you sick again?"

She could see Judith considering a lie but then she nodded and squeezed her arm.

The many-headed snake of the congregation shuffled down the aisle— well wishing, swapping niceties—out into bright sunlight. Confetti was not allowed in the church grounds but rice was fine. Maybe the birds dealt with the tidy-up of rice. They waited for the bride and groom to exit. The road was twenty feet away and passersby had stopped to have a nosey. Liz stood beside a tall, soberly besuited man and a tiny woman in a brown tweed twinset with pearls, both in their seventies. He was watching the proceedings through his thick glasses with a lugubrious air. His wife unsnapped the clasp of her handbag and fished out two toffees. When she saw Liz watching her unwrapping them, she offered her one.

"I won't, you know. They get stuck in my teeth. But thanks."

"And mine," the man said forlornly.

"It was a lovely service," offered Liz. "Bride or groom?"

"We're Andrew's aunt and uncle," the man answered.

"Stephen's," the woman corrected him.

"Stephen's."

"Ach, right, I didn't realize he'd got relatives here."

"Just us two, I think," the lady said, looking around.

"And we can't stay."

"You won't come out to the house? Just for a cup of tea?"

"We've got to get back to Belfast, love."

"It's sad about his family."

"Well, they don't really see him, after everything. They moved to England, you know."

"I didn't know."

"Oh yes, they're in Shrewsbury. He's a carpet fitter."

"Who is?"

"The brother, James."

"He's not dead?"

"He wasn't when I spoke to him last week," the man observed equably and unwrapped his toffee.

And just then Alison and Stephen appeared in the Gothic arch, laughing and ducking the handfuls of long-grain and saffron as the photographer Bob Buchanan directed them this way and that. They all had their phones out, and there was another man, whom Liz didn't know, snapping away with a big professional camera. Wee Neil stuffed a handful of rice down the back of Stephen's shirt and got a boxed ear for his trouble. Kenneth stood on the first step of the church, swollen with success, glad-handing, laughing. Judith moved among the crowd, shaking hands and thanking people. A cardboard box covered with gold foil sat on a folding picnic table on the church lawn, and Alison and Stephen pulled the red ribbon off it together, and one white turtledove came flying out and alighted on the topmost strut of a telegraph pole. He wore a jaunty purple bow tie around his neck. As for the other, there was no sign so Stephen gave the box a little shake until it emerged and hopped up onto the rim, ruffled and guilty looking. It jerked its head round at the circling onlookers then unsteadily took off, only to land on the top of the open church door, where it proceeded to defecate copiously, leaving a stringy white streak down the burnished oak.

(v) Moira Sheehy, 52

The door to the lounge bar banged and she saw them, the two men, coming in wearing masks. She knew right away. One waved a pistol round his head and the other, the one with the vampire mask, was pointing one of those big automatic rifles at everyone. There was the crackling sound. Moira put her arms around her daughter's back— her lovely daughter, her only daughter—and the same bullet went through them both.

CHAPTER 14

Liz found that if she offered to take the gifts from the arriving horde in order to "set them somewhere safe" (one of the desks in the study), she could curtail every little interrogation (*Not married? No children?*) with a semblance of basic courtesy. She surveyed the landscape of wrapped shapes. Ulster—a gift-based culture. You received, you returned, you passed it on. The statelet ran on quid pro quo, on tit for tat—and the rules applied as much as to toasters given at weddings as sectarian slaughter. These spoils were functional reciprocation for the dozens and dozens of bamboo salad servers and Cartier stationery sets and Waterford decanters and Belleek fruit bowls that Judith and Kenneth had bestowed over the years. Where was Alison going to put all this shit? The sight of so much pointless excess made Liz almost giddy. All these gifts evidenced the kula ring—the exchange system—that ruled Ulster life as much as it ruled any Melanesian people. There were rules for guest and rules for host, and they were nonnegotiable. Liz thought sometimes of writing something on the tribal aspects of life in Northern Ireland—how it resembled, like all cultures infected by violence, an older, atavistic way of life. (For wasn't the typical state permanent war? Weren't all the cities of antiquity walled?) A society that worked on the process of peace was a relatively new invention, and not just in Ulster.

But sooner or later she had to emerge from the room of gifts into the party itself. A maiden aunt—a spinster aunt!—had certain duties to ful-fill: Liz fetched Isobel a glass of Shloer and wiped Michael's nose, then used the few survivors of a bag of Jelly Babies to lead them down the lawn.

The three of them sat on folding chairs in the little shed-cum-sunroom at the very far corner of the garden and surveyed the mania unfolding. Judith came fluttering across the grass, leaning forward oddly to stop her heels sinking into earth. Her face appeared serene, but the eyes told a different story. She put her head around the door.

"Liz, we could use you in the house."

"I was just looking after these ones. I think Michael needs a change, but I wasn't sure where the nappies were."

Judith tightened the drawstring of her mouth, swooped on Michael, and bore him away.

"Granny's cross with you," Isobel offered thoughtfully when the door swung closed.

She was taking refuge in the kitchen, downing a glass of wine, when Spencer came in, followed by Trisha Hutchinson from the office, who looked a little disarrayed and carried a trifle in a large glass bowl. She still wore her lilac maid-of-honor dress. The cream of the trifle was studded with circles of maraschino cherries.

"I'm sorry this is so late. I'd left it in the back of Ian's car but sure I forgot all about it. I thought it might be useful for your mum, you know, with having you all home."

There was so much food, the fridge was so full, there were going to be leftovers for weeks, but better that than arrive, as they said in Ballyglass, with your two arms the one length. Liz found a space for it on the windowsill of the utility room.

"How long have you been in the office, Trish? Must be ten years."

"Almost twelve," Trisha blushed. "I know. It's hard to believe."

"They were lucky to find you," Liz said, and meant it. Trish was famously—within the family—"good" with Kenneth. It was an uncommon and discrete quality, like being sickle celled or double jointed.

"Ah now, I don't know what we'd do without Trisha," Spencer chimed in, grinning.

———————

Upon their arrival, Alison and Stephen began a victory lap around the garden that lasted until Wee Neil clambered up on the garden bench and clapped his hands twice and shouted, "Ladies, gentlemen, and Stephen, the buffet is served—or as they say round here, 'Yer tay's waiting on ye.'"

Entering the wedding marquee, Liz ran into Cousin David. Bug-eyed, snub-nosed, prematurely portly, now married to an improbably cute adult woman called Cynthia, he remained frozen in Liz's memory as the twelve-year-old who explained at great length that he'd heard a voice talking to him as he was falling asleep, and believed it was the call to dedicate his life to the Lord. Soon after he'd stood up at the Lighthouse and accepted Jesus Christ into his heart as his "personal savior." Jesus wasn't, Liz always thought, *that* personal a savior. It wasn't like he was a personal trainer or a personal assistant. He'd save anyone, literally anyone who asked. Liz was not asking, though, and so David looked at her now, as he always did, with pity. Not married still? No children? David patted the heads of a couple of his own nearby children—he had five—and began speaking, as usual, of what was going on with him. Which was more of what he'd always been doing. Spreading God's word to nations less fortunate and less white than Northern Ireland, where so much good had sprung from Christianity. Liz nodded and tried to smile as he finished "updating" her, all the time gripping her hand as if she was his very favorite sinner.

"And we just met your wee dog!" he enthused.

"She's such a cutie!" Cynthia added. It was her turn to touch Liz and she took both of Liz's hands in hers and gave them a squeeze. "Is she your little baby?"

"Oh not really. She's my dog."

Liz took a dainty sip of wine, as if she were drinking it under duress.

"Oh, but sure you love her like a child!"

When you saw such relentless positivity up close, Liz assumed it had to

be hiding something so unutterably sad, so dark, so tragic that she herself
wished never to know it. Spencer was hovering behind David. It was one
of her brother's dearest wishes to wind David up so that he cussed or lost
his Christian rag. He leaned in and whispered in his cousin's ear, "D'you
see they've discovered a gene which makes people more likely to believe in
God, kind of a genetic weakness, like?

David wheeled round.

"I see you haven't got any smaller."

Liz spoke, "Actually, David, I wanted to ask you: Do you know anything about *new* religions? Specifically about Papua New Guinea?"

David's beatific grin faltered.

"What's a *new* religion? Like a sect?"

"I'm not sure—I'm off to investigate one at half seven tomorrow morning," she added, with an involuntary smile, and the realization that she
was probably drunk, and very definitely happy to be imminently free.

"I know there's a lot of very good missionary work done in New
Guinea. Our home church network raises a lot of money to send people
and supplies out there. It's a place that needs—"

"Here, and David," Spencer interrupted, "d'ye see on the news they've
done these studies now that show religious children are much meaner than
normal ones?"

David gave an authentic laugh.

"It's true. They want more severe punishments, and won't share, and
stuff like that," Spencer continued.

"You've been saving these up for me."

Spencer smiled and Liz thought he blushed a little.

"I just thought you'd be interested. I was listening to the news and I
thought, now, David'll want to know . . ."

David took his arm and started to steer him towards the marquee.

"You know where I get my news? It's a big book that's been passed
down to us—"

"The dictionary?"

"Close—"

"The encyclopedia?"

"Almost."

"Oh I know what one you mean," Spencer said. "*The Guinness Book of Records.*"

"On behalf of my wife and I—"

A roar went up. Stephen grinned and let it die down.

"On behalf of my wife and I, I'd like to thank you all for coming today. I'm a lucky man. I know that. I'd like to thank Ken and Judith, who've been only kind and welcoming towards me, and also for putting on such a great day here, at their lovely house.

"I don't have any fancy speech prepared. I find myself a bit tongue-tied when it comes to Alison. As you can see, I've had a bit of luck here—meeting her and marrying her. Isn't she beautiful? And Michael and Isobel, they're little smashers. I hope that I'll be able to deserve their love. She's the best thing that ever happened to me, Alison. And I'd like to thank her for agreeing to be my wife."

There was a collective ooh from the female half of the audience, and Alison reached over and squeezed Stephen's hand. She felt famous somehow, even more so than the first time because the story this time was so . . . uplifting. Alison's had a hard time—she deserves some happiness. Alison's been through the mill—but look at her now. It was almost like the stories on the front of the rags you bought at the supermarket checkout.

CHAPTER 15

The house was dead, locked in heavy, hungover slumber. She dressed hurriedly and gave Atlantic—still curled under the duvet—a valedictory tickle on the chin. Her taxi was already in the driveway and they drove in silence to the airport, ambushed by patches of low-lying mist and sudden clarity. Her head kept falling forward and waking her back up. She was through security and buying a bottle of water when she saw the newspaper. On the front page of the *Sunday Life*—the whole front page of the *Sunday Life*—Alison and Stephen on the doorstep of Ballyglass church, coming out from their wedding.

Murderous McLean's Doves of Peace: Trick or Treat Killer
Living Life to the Full . . . Unlike His Victims

> Ruthless gunman Andrew McLean got married yesterday in a lavish wedding ceremony, celebrating the big day by donning a top hat and tails and releasing white turtledoves—despite the blood of five people on his hands. . . .

There was a description of the shootings, and details of the wedding, of the family, of the estate agency business, of the fact that Alison had two children from a previous marriage. . . . Comments from the local SDLP MLA for East Londonderry, who said she was "shocked" to hear of the marriage, and added that McLean could move on but his victims and their families would never have that luxury. A side column was headed: OUTRAGE OF PARENTS

Whose Children Sang at Killer's Wedding. "I wouldn't let my child perform at the wedding of a pedophile, why would I let my child be at the wedding of a cold-blooded killer?"

There were photos of the Day's End pub after the massacre. Some of the bodies were covered with sheets. Stray limbs emerged. A bracelet on a dead wrist. Shoes on lifeless feet. Dark blotches on the dance floor were blood. She found she was sitting down on a bench. They were saying it was the last call for her flight to Heathrow.

Queuing for the gate she phoned home and Judith answered, slightly breathless.

"We heard. Your dad's away now to buy it."

"Did you know?"

"What?"

"Did you know he was wrapped up in that? Five people! Five people he killed!"

"Of course we didn't. I can't believe Alison had any—I mean, how could she have . . . If she'd known . . ."

Her mother trailed off, helpless.

"The plane's boarding."

There was the sound of her mother crying. Spencer came on the line. "You OK?"

"Yeah, I mean, what a fucking disaster."

"It's unreal."

"Unreal."

Stephen was still asleep. His face all squashed against the hotel pillow. Her head was ringing. She slipped into the bathroom and found the Anadin. She washed them down with water from the tap and then, while she sat on the toilet, turned her phone on. It buzzed, and buzzed again. She opened the message from Liz:

You need to ring M&D.

More messages appeared. Texts from Spencer. Her mum. Liz again. Neil Taylor, the best man. A girl from work. Trisha Hutchinson. She opened one from Spencer:

All those people?

She felt the room, the town, the world turning away from her. She looked at herself in the mirror and found she looked guilty, terrified. There were three tiny flecks of toothpaste on the mirror and she scratched them off with her fake wedding nails. In the bedroom she pushed Stephen in the back to wake him from whatever dream they'd been living.

PART 2:

IN THE WAY THAT FIRE WANDERS

CHAPTER 16

Belfast. London. Hong Kong. Cairns. Port Moresby. Wae. Fifty-two hours. And they still had the flight to Wapini and then on to Slinga in front of them. It was a long time to spend traveling cheek by jowl with your crew—no matter how much you liked them. And Liz did like the cameraman Paolo: He seemed to her atypical for an Italian. He kept his cool always, did not fuss about the poor culinary pickings in the increasingly small airports, and when she was tired of talking he understood and fell silent himself. Margo, her producer, was more annoying—more fussy and more liable to complain—but she was a known quantity. Paolo had been the wild card. Now, as they all lay exhausted with their bags alongside the airstrip in Wae, their legs stretched out companionably in front of them, she felt grateful for Paolo and their friendly chemistry: It bode well.

"How you doing, P?"

Paolo made a little—impossibly Italian!—pout and let a puff of air out of his lips: "Oh, I am doing." Across the tarmac the slubby Australian approached them again: They were to shift on out to the tarmac now. The plane—an eighteen-seater twin-prop Cessna—was ready and up the little stairs they went.

On board, a high-Afroed man in a beige colonial suit sat in the front row clutching a brown leather briefcase to his chest, and stood up to greet them when they got on. His curt bow was formal, his smile deeply intended. It seemed someone once had told him a firm handshake was the mark of authenticity and he'd taken the advice to heart. Liz's fingers hurt. Without lowering the briefcase from his chest, this Mr. Kent Raula, vice-prefect of

Odango Province, insisted they were most welcome to New Ulster, that they had chosen a fine time to visit. He assured them the country was really nowhere near as violent as people claimed.

They sat behind a native family in old acrylic, patterned jumpers with string bags full of cans on their laps. Creamed corn. Peaches. After Liz and Margo and Paolo settled in their seats, the same face on different people kept turning round to look at them: deep-set friendly eyes, prominent cheekbones, a very dark complexion. Father, son, daughter, another son. Only the mother, light-skinned, moonfaced, ignored them. She was reading a Bible bound with yellow flock wallpaper, running a fingertip under the words. Across the aisle from Liz a white girl sat, a tall strong-looking teenager dressed in an old-fashioned school uniform—white blouse, plaid kilt—utterly inappropriate for the weather. Her face was heart shaped and hopeful behind pink-framed nerd-specs. She read a thick hardback novel. On the far side of the girl sat a small man in an old blue baseball cap. His eyes were closed and his head tilted back. There was something martyred in his sleeping expression; he could have been a little Christ carved out of ebony. On his T-shirt was a faded portrait of Britney Spears.

"That's some nail varnish."

The girl smiled, rearranging freckles. She held her hand up, fingers fanned out.

"Sonic Boom Blue."

She pulled the bottle of nail varnish from a pink furry pencil case and offered it to Liz.

"They won't let us wear it at school. So, you know. . . ."

"Where're you at school?"

"I board in Port Moresby. Mission kid. My parents work for the New Truth. Sarah."

"Liz. What's the New Truth?"

"Oh, a Christian mission. I thought everyone knew it round here. We've been out here in PNG for over forty years, but my dad opened the Slinga station himself, eight years ago. Before that we were in the Philippines for two years."

"Wow."

The girl nodded bravely.

"I only get out here for holidays. Like, I've three months now, and I'll look after my little sister and two brothers."

"You must miss them."

"In September Esther—she's ten now—is coming back with me to school. They won't know what's hit them. My mom teaches her now, and she just lets her run around outside, smashing things with a pole."

"Sounds like you'll have a long summer."

The disheveled Australian appeared in the doorway of the plane and looked the passengers over.

"You." He pointed at Paolo. "Can you sit in the corner there? Someone give him a poke."

Paolo opened up the drawstring hood he'd closed tightly round his face, looked out, moved two seats across, and promptly pulled the drawstring closed again.

"I'm going to teach the local kids how to play softball. They're all into soccer, but I bought a bat and a ball from Kennings, that's my school."

"That's a good idea."

The girl beamed.

"It's about rules, you know. They don't even know what rules are really."

She looked across at the man beside her; his eyes were still closed. She lowered her voice.

"They really have nothing. They're so far behind, it can be hard to get them to accept Jesus into their hearts."

Liz concentrated on sweeping the little brush over her left thumbnail, leaving it a few shades brighter than the sky outside the window. She held it up to the girl, who nodded approval.

"Doesn't it make it easier—for the mission—if they have nothing?"

"What do you mean?"

The Australian—now sitting in the pilot's seat—shouted over his shoulder, "Fasten those seatbelts. This baby's got the gliding angle of a brick!"

"Just that . . . you know, if people lack all sorts of basic things, food, health care, schools . . ." Liz trailed off. Something bright and defensive had risen in the girl's face.

"We help them live Christian lives."

The plane shuddered into life and it was astonishingly loud—like sitting in the bag of a hoover. Conversation was impossible. Liz smiled at Sarah, who smiled tightly back and opened her novel again. Part of Liz felt vaguely abashed: Why was she trying to convert a schoolgirl to her way of thinking? What was wrong with her? Why did she always have to be right? She gripped the arms of the seat as they rattled down the runway and miraculously ascended. The great shimmering bay rose into view— little white pleats appeared and unpleated on the dark metallic surface. The plane banked and turned inland and climbed. The city spilling down the hillside was fast replaced by jungle. Deep-piled, invariable, bright green. Peak and vale, peak and vale, though here and there the verdancy gave way to a sluggish muddy river uncoiling in great oxbows along a valley floor. Gardens, stubbly cultivated patches, could be seen on the lower reaches of the mountains out to their right.

The man with Britney Spears on his T-shirt came to life and said something to Sarah, who began to pick at her nail varnish unhappily. She took out a bottle of nail varnish remover and cotton pads from the pink pencil case and began undoing all that she had so far achieved. Liz read— pretended to read—the shooting script off her laptop. She was having an attack of nerves about the entire undertaking. The smell of nail varnish remover wasn't helping. The farther she traveled from home, the more unqualified and ridiculous she became. At the back of her mind came the thought of her sister's shame, her family's shame, the shame of her brother-in-law . . . At Heathrow's Gate 23D, after vowing not to mention what had just happened with Stephen and the newspaper, she blurted the whole sorry tale out to her producer. When she started to cry, Margo'd held her hand and said, "I wish someone would explain Northern Ireland to me," and Liz replied, "Me too." Paolo returned with three coffees to find them both drying their eyes. At Hong Kong's futuristic techno airport she googled his crime and saved the pages. Now she flicked between her script and these notes on terror—reading the autopsies, reading the criminal case recounted in some decision on the tariff, whatever that meant. It meant Stephen walked into a bar in 1993, along with his fellow Ulster Freedom Fighter Lenny McAteer, and shot dead five people. There was a boy of nineteen, Patrick Creighton, the barman; a married middle-aged woman, Moira Sheehy; Moira Sheehy's daughter, Janine McFadden; an old man called Anthony Carson—the list went on. The barman was struck by three bullets. One entered the front of his abdomen and passed to the left, lacerating the liver, the stomach, the spleen, and the left kidney before exiting through the left flank. Another bullet entered the right side of the back and passed upwards, lacerating the right lung before exiting through the front of the right shoulder. The combined effect of these injuries caused his rapid death. A further bullet passed through the left arm, fracturing the bone. However, this injury was less severe and so would not have accelerated death to any material extent. . . .

Wapini appeared in the distance. Out of the green came a long silver torsion of waterfall, the black slice of rock face it tumbled down. An extensive jumble of red-tiled or green-corrugated structures had gathered and multiplied where the water fell. A huge whitewashed pile with a Gothic turret—it must be the hotel—perched on a rise and a few jeeps and vans were parked about the earthen lanes like bright counters in a complicated board game. There the river escaped the town, and there a single dirt road wound down the mountainside, and there a pale grass runway was cut like a scar into the saddle below, the one horizontal among the slopes. The plane hurtled towards it and landed and bumped back up and landed again. When they finally stopped, Sarah, pinching a little stack of cotton pads stained with blue, said, "Are you filming the birds of paradise?"

"We're actually doing a thing . . . It's for a special season on religion for the BBC—*The State of Grace*—we're making a program about new religions. You know, what gives rise to them, that kind of thing. The show's called *The Latest of the Gods*. At least at the moment it's called that. These things have a habit of changing."

"Are you going to . . ." She leaned towards Liz and whispered, "You're not going to film Belef, are you?"

"That's right." Liz smiled. Sarah did not smile. She threw a glance beside her at the man, whose eyes were closed again, and whispered, "You should keep your voice down."

They had three hours before the Australian, Hastings, flew them on to Slinga, and they lunched in the hotel, the Wapini Arms, where Stan Merriman, the writer of the original newspaper article about Belef's cult, had arranged to meet them. In the center of the dining room a large wicker structure hosted a silent, balding, melancholy parakeet called Josephine. The lunch arrived in metal trays with warm cans of Coke, and they sat at a long canteen table eying each other.

"Now this," Stan explained cheerfully, lifting his fork, "is manioc, and this . . . is sweet potato . . . and this is rice."

"I know what rice is, Stan," said Margo. She looked up from her laptop and saw his face and said, in a gentler tone, "So, you do fieldwork with kangaroos?"

"Tree kangaroos. Actually they're not related. Tree kangaroos are closer to large rodents, nocturnal, very cute, and I've been fitting radio collars to them to study—"

"And it's your sister who works in Sydney . . ."

"She's an editor at the *Morning Herald*."

"But you're English."

"From Reading. Well, from a little village outside Reading called Checkendon. I've been here a couple of years. Gemma emigrated with her husband to Australia in 2011."

There was a long pause.

"And how's your pidgin?" Margo asked.

"Pretty good. Not perfect."

"And where is Belef now?"

"You know I'm not totally sure."

Margo stopped typing. Stan had his hands palms down on the table. His hair was decisively parted in the middle with styling gel and he'd put on a clean pink T-shirt for his first meeting with the BBC team. Liz could see he only wanted for things to go well, but was finding, if he was really to be honest with himself, that this was not happening.

"Stan, we're time-limited here. We did discuss this on e-mail. We need all our ducks in a row."

His smile kept coming. It was remorseless. Liz felt she had to look away.

"No, no, sure, of course. It's just—it's quite hard to keep track of people in New Ulster. It's not like they have phones. And sometimes she goes off to the forest to talk to the dead."

"To the dead?" Margo began tapping in her MacBook again, not looking up.

"To speak to her dead relatives, get advice, that kind of thing . . . And sometimes she stays in her ancestral village. It's several valleys over. But I'm sure she'll be at Slinga now. There's been a lot of activity to do with the Story."

"And how many followers would you say she now has?"

"I mean, it's hard to say. What constitutes a follower?"

Stan tilted his hands upwards in query. Margo sighed. She'd pushed her laptop a few inches away from her and now she pulled it closer again, but didn't type anything in.

Her voice had a metallic tint to it: "Someone who follows her?"

This got a small laugh from Paolo. Stan sat back slightly in his chair. She was probably just tired. If he felt awkward, well, the situation was awkward, but it would end soon. He just had to wait it out. He folded his arms and smiled harder.

"You said in the *Herald* piece that she'd hundreds of disciples."

"Yes, sometimes when she speaks, there're hundreds there, easily. They come from all round. But you know, it's secret, a lot of it. Even in Wapini, you can get in trouble talking about her. The missionaries are very powerful here. So the locals want to stay in with the New Truth, but many of them are working her magic too."

"And porters? Where are we on that?" Margo asked.

At the other end of the dining room, Malcolm—the hotelier—leaned across the polished wooden bar on his elbows, watching them, his gut hammocking beneath him and not entirely contained in the white polyester of his short-sleeved shirt. For some minutes he had been very involved in picking a fleck of something out of his teeth with a key, one of dozens he kept on a retractable clip attached to his cargo shorts. Now he roused himself and called over, "I've done that. There'll be five at Slinga airstrip and they'll cook and carry your stuff and"—he gave a brief piercing whistle—"we've got a bodyguard for you to take from here."

"OK, terrific. Thank you for organizing all of that."

Liz knew the implication from Margo was that Stan meanwhile had failed to sort out anything at all. It was growing apparent, though, that Stan was not alive to implications. Like a puppy now he looked happily from face to face, in no doubt someone had the ball. Malcolm's waiter appeared in the doorway.

"Go get Posingen."

"Working her *magic*?"

It was the presenter lady, Liz, who had spoken. She had been mostly quiet so far, writing things down occasionally in a big red notebook and throwing Stan encouraging glances.

"That's what they call it. Or working her law. Doing her ceremonies. A lot of it is the old traditions, pagan dances and so on."

The waiter returned to the dining room, trailed by a tall, impassive, and very dark-skinned man in military fatigues, an AK-47 slung over one of his impressive shoulders.

"This is Posingen. He'll make sure you're safe."

Liz looked over at Margo; she was nodding as if to reassure herself that everything was completely and totally and absolutely fine.

There was no Wi-Fi. Malcolm directed Liz to a superannuated Dell in the lobby. She assumed the unforgiving wooden chair and examined the patch of blistered damp on the flock wallpaper as she waited for the heavy machinery to boot up. It groaned, hummed, gave a low whistle, hummed in a slightly lower key, made a series of breathless clicks before the screen seemed to enlarge slightly as it turned from black to gray, and then to a screenshot of Malcolm standing in front of his hotel, looking a couple of stones lighter and a couple of decades younger. Internet Explorer. Among the junk mail and phishing scams was an e-mail from Spence. He never bothered with a salutation:

> The in-law's an outlaw! Can you credit this cunt? I thought he seemed a bit *mild* . . . Think Alison knew? I texted her but silence. And she's not taking calls. I knew there was something weird about him. And I don't mean to be a dick about it, but do you think it's all right that he's with the kids all the time? Is he legally a psychopath? What about Bill? And how are Mum and Dad going to face the golf club quiz—

Liz signed out and shut the computer down.

Margo and Paolo sat at the bar of the hotel, bottles of Big Island beer in their hands, their laptops and battery packs and mobiles arranged around the room, attached to various adaptors, replenishing themselves. Hastings the pilot was playing pool with Stan; a local girl of about seventeen stood silently near them. She stared at Liz with a perfectly empty face, as if Liz were a picture on a TV screen and not a real person in the room with her.

"Hey, BBC," Hastings called across. "Want to join us?"

The girl was called Vali and introduced as Hastings's "friend." Stan and Liz against Hastings and her. The balls were racked. Liz broke and unaccountably one of the reds went in. Hastings gave an appreciative nod and chalked his cue. She tried for the blue and missed.

"Bugger," she said, and Hastings laughed. "Bugger," he repeated. "You Brits got the best slang."

"Did you ever come across Belef?" she asked.

The pilot gave a terse nod, and waited for Stan to take his shot before he answered. "I did. And I hear she's getting a bit of a tailwind behind her."

"You know we're here to make a film about the Story."

"She'll like that. That girl with you on the plane?"

"Sarah."

"Yeah. Belef was her nanny. Worked for the family."

"Really?"

Hastings leaned over Vali as she bent to take her shot.

"You want to get right down."

He pushed the back of her head down towards her cue, not gently, and his stubby fingers disappeared into the tight black curls. Stan looked away. Vali's face remained unwritten, clear of expression; she was used to this. Hastings must be at least fifty. He lifted his hand off and she kept her head lowered and took the shot.

"Way too soft." He gestured to show where the ball should have gone. "I saw it happen with the Catholics, I saw it happen with the Lutherans, I saw it happen with the Independence crowd. But this one, the Story—it's got wheels I think. Depends how the administration plays it."

"Saw what happen?"

Stan potted a red, then moved quickly round and potted the black. He was surprisingly adept.

"They come in promising everything, so long as the locals do what they say. Stop doing this. Start doing that. They promise things'll change, that they'll get their reward, and the natives do what they tell them, but what do you know—nothing comes. Then what?"

Stan potted another red, sending it in off a cushion.

"That was a fluke. Or this guy's a fucking hustler. Look, they all want what the priest has, what the minister has, what the big man has. Not God or independence or whatever. A generator, a fridge, a radio."

The girl, Vali, spoke for the first time. "For music."

"Right, for music. And you know, Belef has had enough of waiting. More power to her!"

Stan missed and Hastings efficiently potted a red, a green, the last red.

"Why not? Why shouldn't she? You know how it started? The leaf?"

Liz shook her head.

"I'll let her tell you then. But I will tell you something. I was flying back round the Suvla Pass and I saw that someone's made a start on clearing a sort of landing strip on the slopes. You might want to ask her about that."

Hastings missed the black but left her snookered on the green.

"A landing strip?" Liz asked.

"Means they think the cargo's on its way."

Liz played a shot—the cue ball struck all four cushions and managed to miss the green, and all the other balls, before spinning to its rest.

Vali said, "Painim six natings."

Hastings laughed. "That's what they say for getting fuck all. It's from snooker. You missed six pockets. You got six nothings."

Emboldened by Hastings's laughter, Vali moved close to Liz and touched her blue thumbnail where she held the snooker cue.

"This color is fun," she murmured.

"Oh thanks."

"I can make some?"

"Oh, I don't have it, I'm afraid. The girl on the plane . . ."

Vali nodded: She didn't believe her but she wasn't surprised.

The hotelier Malcolm drove them back to the airport himself. Margo in the front seat, Stan, Liz, and Paolo crushed in the back. Their gear followed behind, strapped onto a small flatbed truck. Wapini might have known grandeur but not for some time. Faded pastel clapboard houses with verandahs in poor repair, a few red and squat brick buildings, one of which read **WAPINI POLICE STATION** in yellow tile across its forehead. Its blinds were pulled—perhaps forever or perhaps against the sun. The whole town appeared to have given in to the heat and light, gone inside to lie on its bed. And behind the settlement, waiting in the rising distance, the dark jungle with its waves of green, its encroaching tendrils and creepers.

"There's the vice-prefect with the iron handshake," Margo said.

"Raula, you met him?"

He sat outside the bank on a bench, smoking a cigarette. On the other side of the entrance a queue of maybe thirty people had formed.

"They're waiting for the money he just brought in to be distributed. . . . You see that fig tree where those old boys are sat? That's the tree they used to hang prisoners from. The last kiap, the district officer, he lived over there in the yellow house, and would hang a man for stealing a loaf of bread, before breakfast. Wouldn't cost him a second thought. Raula'd love to do that. He's a genuine piece of shit. Excuse my French."

Deeper and deeper inland the plane flew, towards the blank heart of the island, over the endless mountainous jungle so vivid and monotonous. Sarah and her friend in the Britney Spears T-shirt had reappeared, but were now sat—as per Hastings's barked instructions—in the back, and their seats taken by two sturdy foresters whose brute chainsaws were stowed in the belly of the plane. The Cessna banked and pure blue filled the windows. They were descending again and fast. The little plane made contact with the earth and rattled and whined and whinnied quickly to a stop. Outside Liz's window a little posy of children waved to them from where the long grass started. All their mouths moved in unison; they were singing. They got off and stood, a little lost, by the plane as it continued to tick and whirred into silence. A much more sticky heat, and the foliage around the edge of the runway so dense and sinuous it looked like it would wrap itself around your limbs if you stood still too long, entangling and entrapping you. Liz watched one of the foresters hand over a few parcels wrapped in newspaper to a waiting villager.

"Tobacco," Stan said at her shoulder. "They're crazy about it."

Liz waved Sarah and her minder Usai off. Sarah had promised her it was an easy hike, thirty minutes tops, and she wanted to wait for them, but Usai—who kept looking at the BBC crew with open hostility—insisted they get going. Now Liz needed a wee and there was no clear procedure. Margo was happily berating and directing four of the five promised porters Mal had arranged: small wiry bow-legged men who loaded bags onto each other. Paolo was smoking his vaporizer and letting Stan point various things out to him on the horizon. Liz crept off into the edge of the forest and squatted down among the ferns with one hand on a tree trunk to keep her balance, the relief of emptying her bladder tempered by the fear of wetting the jeans gathered round her ankles. Someone giggled close by, and she waddled round to see three of the children watching her from behind a clump of ferns.

"Shoo, shoo."

They did not. One, the boy, made an unexpectedly vicious hissing sound.

"Yes, that's what urine sounds like," Liz replied. "Well done."

They followed her back across the runway, and stood about twenty feet away, watching, until Paolo got out his smaller camera and began filming them. They came closer then and the boy began to mug into the lens and the girls danced, the larger one twirling the smaller around as she screamed with delight. Then the youngest put her hand out and said, "Some dollar please."

She sat on a log—they were waiting for the missing porter—and took her folder out of her bag and started to leaf through it in preparation for meeting . . . who exactly? A prophet? A god? An ex-nanny? An independence leader? There wasn't much to go on. Apart from a few newspaper articles, she wasn't mentioned in any of the literature, though there were certainly precedents. Liz had pored over the essays Margo had the researchers photocopy from the British Library. They were from journals called things like *Oceania* and *Human Organization* and *Anthropology Matters*. Liz had highlighted paragraph after paragraph—she was at heart still the conscientious scholar, the head girl—and as she flicked through them now her eye picked out words she'd underlined: rebellion, revival, time, language, civilizing, reclamation, the Other. Three times in red biro she'd underlined "the Other." "Phenomenology" she'd drawn a box around in green, but she had no idea what phenomenology meant. She used to know what it meant. How had she forgotten? It was suddenly incredible important to know what phenomenology meant.

"Have you bars on your phone?"

Paolo shook his head. Margo had none either.

She set her folder across her very white knees. The sixth page of her notes, the last page, consisted in its entirety of:

> *Fusing the* MAGIC *of contacting the* DEAD *with the power and knowledge of* WHITES.

Her phone gave a little buzz and she hurriedly tugged it out of her shorts but found it was only a low battery warning.

They began the walk, and in their little single-file caravan she followed Stan. He had done a PhD in zoology at Bristol, and had been here for almost eighteen months, attaching radio collars to tree kangaroos and playing a lot of football with the children. She kept him chatting because it was important to her, she realized, to normalize the situation. The porters' chanting and the sudden rustlings—birds, probably, though the foliage was so thick it was impossible to make them out—all of it unnerved her, and she knew that if she didn't distract herself then the strangeness of the scenario would make her retreat inward, and that couldn't happen. She was a TV presenter, thus upbeat and capable and calm, in possession of exceptionally normal cognitive function. Also, almost immediately, her new hiking boots had started to rub on her left heel.

"And then when the Japanese invaded, thousands fled from the coast. Most hid in the forest and were hunted down. The rest tried to get inland and cross the island to the southern shoreline."

"But that's hundreds of miles."

"One hundred and twenty. It gets slightly marshy here."

"How did they survive?"

"They didn't. There were something like seven who made it. That they know about. And all of them had native—Look!"

Stan stopped in front of her.

"A skink with his dinner," he whispered.

A dark brown lizard—about six inches in length—sauntered down a broad buttressed root carrying a cricket or a cricketlike insect in its mouth, much like a dog might carry a newspaper. The tiny dinosaur stopped and swiveled its hard triangular skull round to look at them, at their impertinence, then jerked its head down and bashed the insect on the root once, twice.

"He's softening it, to eat it."

Liz moved around the side of Stan, to see it better, and slipped her camera out of the side of her rucksack. Then something was in her hair and on her face and she shrieked, brushing frantically at it.

"It's just a web," Stan said.

"Is there a spider?"

"I can't see one. I think this is an orb-weaver's web, probably a golden—"

"I don't care! Get it off me."

She did a little twirl, as if showing him her outfit, and he repeated, "I can't see one. I think you're fine. I was just going to say—"

"Liz? You all right?" Margo called from up ahead.

"I'm fine."

A long strand of spider silk wafted from her hand and she rubbed it against her thigh.

"The webs of these spiders are so strong they can trap a small bird, and you'll find local people even use them to make bags or fishing nets. It's absolutely—"

The look Liz gave Stan halted him midsentence. The remnants of the vast web swayed from a branch and the trunk of a palm tree. Two porters in front of Stan had stopped and were staring back with amused curiosity.

After fifteen minutes of trekking in a zigzag through forest that thinned as they ascended, they now emerged in a clearing inhabited only by grass and low, desiccated shrubs and one enormous, roughly cuboid rock, the size of a small car. It stood by the edge of the clearing, where the flatness began to fall away so steeply one could, if one were braver than Liz, reach out and touch the sharp needles of the conifers, whose roots were five storeys below.

All of them stood for a moment in silence. A warm breeze came up from the valley. Landscape unfolded as far as vision allowed. To the north were immense mountains, sheer cliffs, thin chimneys of black rock, plunging slopes, gullies, valleys thickly carpeted in all varieties of green. Three long white ribbons of waterfall fell from a far cliff, cutting through stillness, athletically twisting and twisting but remaining the same. Above it all the blue sky stretched tall, the unchecked sun shone, and a few tufts of cloud drifted.

"This is approaching perfect," Paolo said, with a certain grudging respect.

Liz looked at his broad back and had a brief desire to touch his shoulder.

"It's beautiful," Liz said, which seemed inadequate. She tried again. "Breathtaking."

"I always think if you get high enough above the cloud forest," Stan said, "it looks just like a crate of broccoli."

Paolo filmed Liz pretending to arrive at the rock and take off the rucksack that one of the porters had carried so far. They did the shot three times and already her shoulders felt the impress of the rucksack's straps. It was obscenely heavy. She could hardly have walked the length of herself had she actually to carry it. She felt a low, familiar pulse of guilt about the falsity of the situation, and asked Margo, in a whisper, "Are we paying these guys properly?"

Margo gave her a patient look and replied, "We're paying the standard fee."

"Ours or theirs?"

Margo was short, strikingly dark, heavy thighed, and her lips forever pursed in appraising situations. She hadn't seen her since they'd made *The Use of Myth* program, but everything came back. The trick was to keep her on a very casual level of intimacy, at a friendly arm's length. If you wandered off the main road with her, you faced the real risk of being lost for some time in the outskirts of her complicated backstory. There was Javier, a Cuban ex-husband, and Bella, the teenage anorexic daughter who lived with Margo's mother and stepfather, because Margo herself was Bella's "trigger." There was a litany of professional grudges and gender slights and the humiliating difficulties of middle-aged dating. Liz knew they were coming, these conversations, but they must be held off as long as possible. Conversely, though, you had to keep her sweet. If Margo felt snubbed, the fallout was chilly, immediate, lengthy. You wanted to keep her star within your orbit, but not so close as to get burned up, not so distant as to lose all light and heat.

"Liz, stand here . . . No, forget that. That's not going to work."

The rock was black—basalt?—and scraped with white geometric shapes and patterns. On the center of the side facing north, towards Wapini and Ibaki and the coast, a rudimentary tableau had been etched in outline: a huge snake crawling up from the ground in a winding pattern.

Its head split open into two fanged jaws and fleeing from it were all manner of creatures: a rat, a fish of some kind, a pig, a spider, a long-legged bird, and several tiny white stick men. The dell was like a giant altar awaiting sacrifice. Liz felt exposed. She looked at the tree line round the ring of the clearing. Were they being watched? Margo paced back and forth with her clipboard, deciding on shots, general views, cutaways. Liz read her Piece To Camera and tried to memorize the first paragraph. Take it slow. Make it natural. Something had bitten her on her neck and it was starting to itch.

Stan appeared behind her.

"That's new."

"The carving?"

"The snake. And that's new too. The little figures fleeing before it."

"Over here, Liz. When you're ready."

"This astonishing landscape behind me"—Liz swiveled, made the sweeping gesture—"is the island of New Ulster. For centuries this harsh mountainous terrain, not to mention the legends of the local tribes' ferocity, kept Europeans away. But over the last fifty years the missionaries have started coming. In that time many of the natives converted to Christianity, turning away from the gods and rituals that had been their way of life for millennia. But here, in a high valley in the very heart of New Ulster, one woman has begun a revolution."—Dramatic pause—"She's started a brand new religion, perhaps the newest religion in the world, and I've traveled here to meet her."

Thirteen times. The first time she said "trocal libes" instead of "local tribes." The second she forgot what came after "Christianity." The fourth time one of the porters coughed. Halfway through the sixth take a fly landed on her chin. The sweat on her back was making her shirt clammy, and Margo's encouraging smile had morphed to a grimace. Liz's mind began to turn on itself; helplessly she started smirking at the absurdity of the situation, the way she was wafting her arms about for accentuation, the enthusiastic manner of her speech, the odd collection of human animals ranged around and watching her. The ninth take was good until the same guy who'd previously coughed gave a sneeze, just as she was finishing. With a wave of her hand Margo exiled him from the clearing. The eleventh try she nailed but her voice dropped off at the end. Finally:

"That was great."

"I'm so sorry about—"

"It takes as long as it takes."

Margo gave the same dismissive wave. It was a mistake to apologize.

"Let me watch it back. Paolo, good with you?"

The cameraman raised his head from the lens and presented his crooked, reassuring grin, holding Liz's eye for a moment too long.

"Great with me."

"Are we almost there?" Margo asked Stan.

"Ten more minutes tops," he said, though his eyes looked less certain.

They followed the path that led from the glade through the trees. There was an eeriness to this place; the forest seemed alive. The branches stretched out to embrace her. After a while the forest began to thin again and the path opened up and straightened and a small boy stood up ahead of them, staring. Liz was third back—behind Stan and Margo—and one by one they all stopped, with the usual, slightly comic domino effect. The boy was some way off, watching them as a statue might, giving nothing away. There was some kind of whiteness in his hair, white feathers maybe or white blossoms. He wore a tattered pair of red shorts and nothing else and after a few seconds turned and bolted sudden and easy as a hare, as if his body were all lightness.

"Hello there!" Margo called out after him. "Hello!" But he was gone.

A few minutes later they came out of the forest gloom to arrive in a village. Wooden huts dotted either side of a grassy clearing. In the space between, two groups sat in lines facing each other. The men wore faded T-shirts, a few baseball caps, shorts—and some had sticks or clubs across their knees. The women all wore meri skirts, long, patterned dresses. In the firebreak between them a woman in the same kind of patterned dress walked up and down, gesticulating and talking loudly. She also wore, improbably, a white sailor's cap pushed back on her head. She was shouting, repeating the same phrase enough times for Liz to make a basic phonetic copy in her notebook:

"Em I strongpela sia. Yumi tupelo I ken sindaun long en."

Some of the listeners were mumbling and whispering, but most sat rapt. Now she turned to their little group—sheepishly they'd filed in and stood along one edge of the clearing—and she seemed to Liz to look directly at her. The woman made a shape in the air with her brawny arms and announced in her low raspy voice, "It is a strong *strong* chair. You hear? Good news! We can all of us sit on it."

CHAPTER 17

Some force from the dreamworld pushed sharply and repeatedly on Stephen's lower back until he rolled across, towards her, and forced his eyes open. They hadn't lowered the blind properly. A wedge of bright light snuck in from the bottom of the window, picking out the scene. His hangover greeted him first. The tangle of his morning suit, the twist of his white shirt on the chair. Her head was not on its pillow. She was sitting up, her rounded, colorless shoulders facing away. She stared at the screen of her phone. He reached up and over and tucked his index finger under one of the straps of her burgundy silk nightie, tried to slide it down but she pulled away.

"What is it?"

She angled the pixels of the phone at his face.

"What is it?"

"Can you sit up?"

Her voice had a frayed, dangerous edge. He raised himself on one elbow as she pushed the smartphone into his hand.

"It's from Liz."

He read, and then flicked through the next few texts, and handed the phone back. One part of him peeled away from another. His heart thumped, full of blood.

"Aw fuck," he said, and lay back on the bed, breathless. There, it had happened.

"What have we done?" Alison said, still not turning to face him.

"You haven't done anything. The story in the . . . Did you read it?"

"Not yet."

He sat up beside her, and swung his legs off the bed, spindly and hirsute beside her plump, pale thighs.

A siren was going off somewhere at the other end of town, and Stephen had the absurd but very real notion that they were coming for him.

"It's not letting me in." She looked down at the half obscured *Sunday Life* Web site. "You need a subscription."

"You know, we could just put our clothes on and go to the airport and pretend it never happened."

Even as he spoke he knew how ludicrous this sounded. Alison looked at him, a level unloving gaze.

"And that will stop everyone we know reading all about it, will it?"

Stephen grimaced.

"What do you want to do?"

She felt very cold suddenly and stood up, snatched the hotel dressing gown from the back of the bathroom door and put it on. Once she was wrapped up, defended, she sat back down on the bed and turned to him.

"You have to tell me what you did." Loosely she was hugging herself, braced for the response, and her round blue eyes brimmed. "You have to tell me everything."

"You know. Killed people."

"Yourself?"

"Yes."

"With a bomb?"

She watched him lower his head to his hands.

"With a gun."

"How many?"

Now a whisper: "Five."

"In one go?"

Now only a nod. Alison too buried her face in spread fingers. Stephen put his own hand out towards her—he watched it move across this strange new distance between them. When he touched her shoulder she flinched and he drew back.

"You OK?" he whispered.

After a few seconds she looked up and asked in a dry, compact voice, "Where was it?"

"In Eden, Londonderry."

"That pub they shot up?"

"Yes."

"Jesus Christ! I remember it!"

"Yes."

"*Who* did you kill?"

"Whoever was there. Four Catholics, a Protestant."

An early-release prisoner, a beneficiary of the Good Friday Agreement: two years for killing five people. Mostly it lived at the side of his vision, that great darkness he'd brought into so many lives, and into his own. It existed, a vast island, just beyond the horizon, its presence confirmed by the way the light above it deformed and colored. Nine years in Ballyglass. Nine years building it all up brick by brick till the wolf of the past comes along and blows it over, one puff. He had planned this morning: breakfast in bed, lengthy baths. Check in at 10:30 for the 12:55 to Faliraki. They needed to get sun cream in Boots, but they'd have plenty of time. Plenty of time to order a couple of flutes of champagne in the Voyager bar, snapping pics to stick on Facebook. They would be giddy with love.

Now he gripped his knees and wondered if he was going to vomit. It was that huge falling feeling he had when the police came to the house on Erskine Place and banged on the door, shouting, "McLean, McLean, open the fuck up." Part of the sensation he'd felt was relief. He realized he'd been half waiting for them to turn up. Don't we want to be known? Don't we want it all out there?

The blind was hanging down wonkily. At the top its blades were horizontal, evenly spaced, and then as it got lower one of its strings had got caught up and the lower half was lopsided. She looked at the desk, the fire exit notice on the back of the door, the landline phone, her wedding shoes—white slingbacks lying on their side under the chair. Every object was suddenly giving off tiny vibrations. She turned back to Stephen.

"I've no idea who you are."

When he'd imagined it—and he had, many times—the moment of admission and unburdening brought such a deluge of relief that he and his dear wife were brought closer; it cemented their love. Not immediately, obviously. He wasn't a fool, he knew it would be difficult. But she had seemed so accepting of his past, so fine with it. Even—could he say it?—thrilled that he had been involved. Her eyes glittered when she obliquely referred to it. His dark secret. His terrible past. But now in the wake of its explicit revelation his wife sat at the desk and stared at a point about three feet above his head. He tried to meet her gaze, but she refused and stood up and walked to the window. She twisted the blind open without fixing the bottom of it, then twisted it shut again.

The door had closed on the old life. The man who cut the church's lawn and stood for six hours at the door of Tesco's collecting for Cancer Research. The man who had come through. That man was discarded. He felt himself slipping irrevocably back into the old Stephen in the eyes of others, Mad McLean, despicable son of a bitch. And in his own eyes. Bastard with a semi-automatic and a black heart. Everyone knew what he was. It was not the past to them. It was once again the eternal truth of him.

Alison looked directly at him, a new thought forming.

"What *age* were those people you killed?"

"I—I don't know."

She just kept on staring.

"The youngest was nineteen. The oldest was seventy-something."

Over and over she said, "I can't believe this is happening" with slightly varying cadence as she pulled her jeans and a hooded gray top on over her nightie. She pulled on her honeymoon sandals and lifted the card-key and went out, pulling the door behind her. Almost ran to the lift, and waiting for it felt the silent tears slide down her face. As soon as the doors closed on her, a raw sob came out of her mouth, shocking in its loudness. She looked at herself in the mirror and wiped her blotchy face with the sleeve of her hoodie. By the time she arrived at the ground floor, she'd tied her hair back and sorted herself out with a few deep breaths. She strode out briskly to face the morning, to cross the road and walk to the Spar on the corner.

Stephen lay in the bed with his head under the pillow, a flock of thoughts continually roosting and alighting inside him. In the interrogations the police kept showing him photos; of the inside of the bar, of the horror, of the autopsies, of the bodies. "How does that make you feel, son? Take a good long look." There were casualties in war, but wasn't he also one of them? Wasn't his whole family? He thought of his mother looking at him through the tempered glass, her features hardening, setting. She died after he'd been inside eighteen months, poor woman. What he had done had solidified her face into a mask of sorrow, of shame. Now he would do the same to his wife. The door opened. She was back, he sat up. She set the paper on the bed, unfolded.

She looked fat in the photograph. There was no denying it. She knew it was irrelevant. But she looked fat in it, on the cover of a newspaper.

He looked at it in silence. Undressing the wound. His eyes fell on a random paragraph.

> I knew Angela Downey and Eugene Boyne, who were out on a date on that fateful night, and I've always wondered if they would have married. But there will never be any ceremony for them, no doves of peace or top hat and tails. Instead McLean left a wee girl to grow up without her mother.

He looked up and she was standing there crying. She allowed him to hug her and after a few minutes, she sat down in the chair at the desk and looked at him, imploring him to make it not true, not real. He sat back on the edge of the bed and wrapped the coverlet over his shoulders. He felt the insufficiency of the actual facts. There was nothing adequate, nothing useful.

"I mean you have to remember," he began, "where we were, what had happened. They were killing us for being Protestant, just for existing. We had to strike back. We had to. We had to let them know that if they were going to kill us in shops and bars and going about our business, we were going to do the same. It was war."

"I'm so stupid. I imagined . . ." She spoke very quietly. "I thought—you'd helped people."

"What do you mean?"

"I don't know." She looked at his Adam's apple, then his shoulder, moving her eyes off him, away, away. "Like you had a friend who'd done something and he came to you for help and you hid him or hid his gun or something. I just thought you'd have done something that was a mistake. That you were being too good to someone."

"I wasn't myself."

She turned to him suddenly. "Who were you?"

"Someone else. It was twenty years ago."

She sat down in the chair by the desk. He wanted to take his wife's soft, sturdy body in his arms and tell her everything would be all right, but how could he?

An invisible shutter had been lowered into place between them. He couldn't get round it to her. Her forceful and settled way of seeing everything had always been refreshing to him. Alison, in a judgmental mood, enthralled him. She gave the impression that she hated everyone except him, that only he was all right, that only he was bearable. But now he felt himself pushed from the circle of her light.

He let himself look at her. She'd a few stone on him, but there was just more of her, he always said, to love. And he loved the excess of her body, the soft wide waist, the large low breasts. Her hair had been done new for the wedding. There was an openness to the face that Stephen had always liked; you thought she had no side, no edge, at least until she started talking. It wasn't that she loved life, but she had a way of *expecting* it, anticipating certain patterns, that moved Stephen. She possessed no capacity for surprise or wonder or ambiguity of any kind. The universe was clockwork and windup and behaved as she anticipated. Actions and reactions—she expected Isobel to be overtired after swimming on a Thursday; she expected

Michael to fall asleep in his car seat on the way back from nursery. She had her grasp on things and it worked, it held. She understood that there were no rules, fine, but certain principles could be discerned, and followed onto death, beyond if we were lucky. The little regulations with which she ran their lives constituted a kind of handrail round the abyss. But now he had upended all those laws and statutes. She was a good person, a *good* person— not like some saint or whatever—just an average, normal, good person. And she conferred a kind of average, normal personhood upon him. He had felt compelled to be the person she expected, to conform to her idea of him. But now. He stood up and walked past her into the bathroom. The extractor fan labored into life and he realized the other noise that had started up with it was her sobbing. He slid the bolt on the door across and flicked the tap on to drown the sound out.

CHAPTER 18

Belef gestured for them to follow her. She had a slight limp, was not tall, but there was a physical power about her. Broad shoulders, thick forearms, unsmiling in the long flower-patterned meri dress and plastic flip-flops and ratty cardigan—plus, the yachting cap, its gold braid and stiff brim and nonsense insignia. Nothing more had been spoken, and Liz felt they'd all been bound with a spell into silence. Even Margo made no attempt to tell her who they were or what they wanted; she simply followed like the rest. Liz looked back behind her. She couldn't figure out which way they'd come into the village now; a mountain stood behind them, covered with moss forest, and they must have come round it somehow. Or—and the thought took hold for a second—they must have come through it, through the mountain. They must have come through it like the children led by the Pied Piper, and this was the world that lay beyond their world. She walked alongside Margo and found herself taking the producer's hand in hers. Margo accepted it without a word and gave it a little reassuring squeeze.

The village was a scatter of buildings along a sloping grassy highway. Most were small huts, fronted by enclosed gardens. The roofs were thatched and the walls timbered. The windows were square holes in the wall, shutters propped open above them. And here was Belef, the prophet, the fraud. Was this what she expected? Did she resemble a deity, this stout middle-aged Melanesian woman in a sailor's hat?

"I've met God," Margo whispered to Liz. "I've met God and she's black."

Liz wished very much she would shut the fuck up. Belef marched at the head of their little retinue, straight-backed and with her hands held behind her as if inspecting the village, a suggestion that intensified when she began to weave back and forth across the grass highway between the huts, stopping to crouch down and look closely at the scraggy patches of land enclosed in front of them by means of stakes and twisted vine, muttering to herself, or bending her head back and adjusting her cap to better see the roofs. It was apparent that this was a performance for them—and that they in turn were being paraded around the village, to demonstrate Belef's importance. Liz realized suddenly who Belef was reminding her of: the Duke of Edinburgh, with her hands tucked behind her back, examining proceedings, occasionally stopping and passing a remark. Quite a crowd of children—a dozen or so—had gathered in their wake or ran alongside them, though none were the boy with white in his hair who'd met them on the path.

The girls hung back and giggled, covering their mouths, whereas the boys ventured right up and shouted, "Hello! Hello, mister!" Liz tried to smile. She found them intimidating, the way they'd challenge each other to come close enough to touch her and then tear away shrieking.

Belef stopped outside a hut where a young plump woman with no front teeth was sitting, holding a piglet like a baby. Belef said something to her. It sounded like "Bless the day" or "Blessed day."

"Oh look," Liz exclaimed in a whisper. "She's breastfeeding the pig. I read about that."

"Get it on film," Margo hissed at Paolo, but the cameraman was already zooming in on it, framing the piglet working his little pig jaw, pulling out on the woman smiling broadly at Belef, throwing a slightly uncertain glance directly at the lens.

They walked past a hand-painted New Truth Mission sign that stated: CLEANLINESS IS NEXT TO GODLINESS: WASH YOUR HANDS. They walked past another: LOVE ONE ANOTHER AS I HAVE LOVED YOU: BEATING WOMEN IS WRONG. Another, in a jaunty yellow, with a border of hearts and flowers, stated: THE WAGES OF SIN ARE DEATH BUT THE GIFT OF GOD IS ETERNAL LIFE.

In the distance were a cluster of larger structures, made of the same thatch and wood and wattle—the Spirit house, the haus tambaran, the men's house, perhaps the village rest house—but also, set up on a rise, a small compound of three white buildings. Glass glinted off real windows and galvanized roofs. A little shining city on a hill. The mission.

Belef had stopped at a house; like all the others, it had a roof thatched with sago palms and woven matting for walls, though the garden was overgrown and untidy—except for one corner cleared of all greenery, where for several feet the soil was inlaid with rocks and stones and pieces of bone or shell in concentric circles and geometric lines. Paolo swept the camera lens slowly over everything.

She gestured for them to sit on the logs by the entrance. She herself sat down on the highest log, smiling slightly tensely, and faced them. She tilted the yachting cap backwards on her head so a wave of thick tight curls rode up, and her metaphysical confidence returned. She was a god! With a face perfectly round, eyes hard and bright as onyx.

Liz crouched in front of her—Paolo stood filming a few feet away—and delivered her rehearsed line: "Nem bilong mi Elizabeth. Mi kam lukim yu."

Belef nodded.

"Welcome to here," Belef said carefully in return, and gestured to suggest the entire solar system was happy to host them. The voice was low-pitched, accustomed to being heard, and came out of a mouth of piecemeal teeth stained red by betel nut.

"We're from the BBC," Margo said, and handed over her clipboard, containing, presumably, a release form. Belef made no motion to take it.

"I am Belef."

"Well, at least we've got that right," Margo said, forcing a chuckle.

"Belef, as we discussed, we're here to make a program about the Story," Stan started.

"We're here," Margo took over again, "to talk to you about your organization"—this seemed a neutral word—"and if you're happy to let us, we'd like to film you, follow you around for a couple of days and talk. Visit some of the important sites."

Belef gave no indication she understood a word, but instead stared directly at Liz and smiled broadly and said, "I knew you would come."

Liz looked at Margo. Was Belef claiming to have had a premonition of their visit?

"You mean you got Stan's messages?" Margo said.

"I knew you would come," she repeated. "Elisssa-bet, elisa-bet . . . we will have tea."

Malour, the porter with the Blue Jays baseball cap and bandiest legs, the carriers' foreman and spokesman, took his men off to prepare the dinner and the village rest house. Paolo set up the camera on his tripod outside Belef's house. Posingen—the bodyguard—kept his usual distance, sprawled under a tree in the distance, his AK-47 across his lap. Margo kept repeating that they really should get *something* on film today. Belef sat on the log bench, her elbows on her knees, her long purple skirt hanging down between her legs. She chewed betel nut and spat and stared at the four white people with friendly defiance.

Liz worried that Margo was going to remember the present for Belef. In Heathrow's Terminal 2, outside the Pret a Manger, they'd stood and debated what gift might be suitable, and in a final panic ended up buying a teddy bear dressed as a Beefeater, some Harrods tea bags in a Big Ben tin, and a striped dressing gown—on sale—from the Paul Smith store. Sitting looking at her house and her life, and the endless rainforest stretching every direction, each of these gifts—now sitting by Liz's feet in a green plastic bag, waiting to be handed over—seemed equally implausible. She glanced down at her list of questions.

"I'm going to ask you about the organization you've started, and then we'll talk a bit more about you. Go into depth about your childhood, defining moments, that kind of thing. Sound OK?"

Liz beamed and Belef gave back a brief tense grimace. Now she sat up, now she rearranged her hands, now she held onto her knees, now she set her hands in her lap.

"Can you describe how it started? The movement? Just talk through—"

"Is that angle working?" Margo interjected. "Would it not be better to get her from here, with the light coming in—"

"Hold on." Liz held her hand up to Belef to tell her not to answer yet. Belef's response was to hold her own hand up to Liz's and push gently against it. Her hand felt very rough and dry.

"Do we need to get Stan to translate the questions?" Margo asked no one in particular.

"Liz, can you start talking?"

"Hi Belef, it's an honor to meet you."

Belef's nod confirmed that the honor was indeed Liz's.

"Can you tell us about the leaf? The leaf that started it all?"

"Ask a more general question: What started the Story?"

"Can you tell us about what started the Story? The beginning?"

Belef paused and looked from face to face, then raised her hand and touched her shoulder.

"Leaf," she said, and then, with the proper solemnity, "it landed here."

Margo set the boom down.

"Can we get one of the porters to take this? They could manage that surely. I have a twinge in my shoulder."

Stan took the boom himself. The team sat in suspended silence, with Belef fidgeting until Stan had the sound bag round his neck. Margo continued to wear the headphones, and now she waved them on.

"Belef, can you tell me what started all of this?"

"I am inside my house and I am thinking about this leaf when it landed." She touched her shoulder again. "On me. It was Sunday, after time of church. And I am lying down on the mat now. Inside my house."

Liz nodded, and Belef rose to the encouragement, clapping her hands lightly and smiling.

"You must all believe in this something. Where do you believe this came from? The door was all closed up. I was asleep when it came onto my body. This something is just like when people write and send it. The letter. But it had come from Papa and to me."

"Papa?"

Belef looked surprised.

"The Big Boss. You say God."

"And I hold the leaf like this"—Belef had her hands raised in prayer before her—"and Leftie brings the paper and he draws in it: balbal leaf. He draws all the marks found on it. And all of the village must copy all the writing of this something something, and must follow it. And this would be the Story. For the house was totally closed shut, so how could this something come inside? It was sent by my daughter."

Liz turned to Margo. "Who's Leftie? Is this going to work? Shouldn't we get the story straight first and then film it?"

"Keep going," Margo overruled her.

"Have you got the leaf? Could we see it?"

Belef stood up and walked stiffly into her house, undergoing a trial of some importance. She reemerged bearing a large label-less can, such as might have held chopped tomatoes or peaches in syrup. Across the top of the can was a piece of gauze, kept in place by an elastic band and she carefully removed it, storing the band on her wrist, before drawing out the leaf. It didn't even look particularly old. Though dry, it was still green.

"This came and slept on me, and now I hold it."

Belef sighed like she was remembering love and for a moment nobody spoke.

Finally Margo said, "You know, her English is really pretty good."

"Why did Papa send you the leaf?"

Belef sighed again, this time for sadness, and fixed Liz with a look that said she should not have to explain. "To tell me my daughter is angry and wants me to fix it. Come."

She stepped around the side of the house and pointed at the space in Belef's garden where the grass had been pulled out and the shells made swirling patterns and little wooden crosses were arranged.

"This is where Kasingen sleeps."

"Is this where she's buried? Kasingen?"

"This is where she sleeps." Belef said again simply, and leaned down and touched the tip of a cross with a finger.

"It's a very beautiful grave."

"Yes."

"Did you make the crosses?"

"They are not crosses."

Liz bent closer. What she'd thought were crucifixes were aeroplanes: some rough approximations, but others elegantly carved with cockpits and pilot's heads, twin propellors, tail fins—but each landing badly, planted nose first in the soil.

Abruptly Belef got up and went into the house. They listened to a hurried conversation inside and Belef reappeared with a walking stick, the head carved like a snake's head.

"I will bring you to my spirit children's place."

She walked briskly, even with her limp, and the path came alongside a wide stretch of a slow river pocked with stepping-stones and larger rocks. Farther back a small waterfall dropped a few feet into a pool, where several russet leaves spun aimlessly as if they'd been spinning there forever. Trees dipped their fringes in the water. Everything was ease and sunlight and enclosure. A bluely iridescent dragonfly careened above the shallows to a stop, hovered, motored loudly off.

Margo had become all business, and that made things easier, clearer between them all. She replaced her tortoise-shell sunglasses with her tortoise-shell reading glasses; the black clipboard she held across her chest and referred to as if she herself were also following instructions. Now the sky was visible again; against the uniform blue a few white clouds tumbled in slow motion out of themselves. Paolo set up his tripod. Margo held them off with one raised palm, and then, when he started filming, Liz followed Belef onto a large rock down at the water's edge.

"This"—Belef gestured with her snake walking stick—"is the Tractor Rock. When the land is all flat my children will farm it with this."

The rock did look vaguely like a tractor, at least from this side. Margo gestured at Liz to sit on it, and Liz pretended not to see her. She was concentrating on ignoring her sore heel and not rubbing the spider bite on her neck. Stan had been put to use again with the boom mic, and was doing his best to please Margo by staying as still as possible. Belef took a farther step out into the river onto a stepping-stone, a smooth spherical rock.

"And this is their football."

"Your children's?"

"Yes. My spirit children."

"How many do you have?"

"Three boys and a girl."

Belef stepped back onto Tractor Rock and sat heavily down. She inserted the tip of her walking stick into a crevice in the rock and worked it like a gearstick. Liz sat down beside her, sidesaddle. From the bank Margo gave the thumbs-up and Paolo kept rolling.

"Where are we going?" Liz asked but Belef ignored her. She had been struck by some new thought and she pulled her stick from the crevice, dipped the end of it in the water, opening a new grain in the river's surface, a flurrying. Liz patted the rock like it was a docile beast and felt the heat of a whole day's sun in the black basalt. Belef whispered urgently, "Elisabet, I know you are in grief but you are here for purposes."

It seemed to Liz like the rock beneath her shifted. How could she know? What did she mean?

"What? I am?"

"My children bring me secrets. They tell me you are powerful and sad. So sad. You will learn the why you have come here." Before Liz could respond further—she felt wounded suddenly, suddenly breathless—Belef had raised her head to the riverbank, to the camera lens and Margo, and shouted, "This is my promised land! This waterfall is Jordan. All this is *our* worlds."

A few minutes later, when the camera was off, Paolo offered Liz his water bottle and asked, "What was she saying to you out there?"

Liz shook her head, meaning it didn't matter, and said, "Have I a bite?"

She pulled her hair back and showed Paolo her neck. It felt like a gesture of vulnerability, like how Atlantic might expose her belly for a tickle, and Paolo touched the skin.

"There?"

"Yeah."

"It's a little red. Itching?"

His fingertip lingered on her neck. She felt the contact shiver through her. It was just an offhand, natural thing, she told herself.

"What was she saying to you out there—"

"You guys notice there's no birds here?" said Stan, kneeling a few feet away, touching a patch of bare earth with his biro. No doubt some insect, bravely confused, now trekked up the shaft. No one responded. "I've always noticed you don't get birds where there're waterfalls. I think it's the sound. It means they can't hear predators approaching."

Liz said, "Oh yeah," but Margo—head in her clipboard—and Paolo continued to ignore him. Ignoring Stan, she realized, was going to be a useful bonding exercise for the team. Margo dropped her clipboard on her daypack and clapped her hands.

"Right, terrific. Let's do a couple of pickup shots—Belef, if you could walk with Liz down the path . . . Where is she?"

"She must have gone to the toilet," Stan offered.

"We'll fill the rest in on commentary. Liz, just say for now this is the Tractor Rock where devotees come and pray, that right behind you is the waterfall they call Jordan. Maybe mention a lot of the iconography is based on Christianity, but reflects the local landscape. Or something. Are they baptized here? Stan? Do we know if they're baptized here?"

After the shot was done, Liz decided to confront the inevitable and slipped off her left boot to take a look at what was happening in there. Nothing good was the answer. The red welt had already bloomed into a loose pasty globule. She dipped her heel in the cool water. Margo had blister plasters—"Of course I have blister plasters, I have everything"— and these blister plasters were, Margo explained, revolutionary. "If it weren't for these I wouldn't be able to wear heels on dates with awful men." Liz stuck the false skin to her own and put her boot back on, without rising to Margo's conversational bait about awful men. She watched Margo walk a few meters into the forest, shouting "Belef," occasioning a screechy, flappy evacuation in the canopy above. Margo stepped quickly backwards and fell over a root, landing on her bottom. She sat there looking suddenly small and defeated. Liz helped her up, and granted that this place was a fucking deathtrap.

"What the hell were you doing, Stan? You're meant to be watching her. And where's the bodyguard? Isn't he meant to come with us everywhere?"

"You told him not to come," Liz said softly.

"Was I meant to know we were going to be abandoned in the middle of the jungle?" Margo sniffed.

"I think I know where she might have gone," Stan said a little sadly, and stepped off into the thicket of greenness. Paolo sat on the ground, puffing his vaporizer, then set about unpacking his lenses and cleaning them.

They sat—the three of them—and waited. Liz kept her head down, studying the next PTC. Margo made various grunts and sighs of discontent.

"And now we've lost Stan," she said.

"Do we know how to get back?"

"There was basically a path, wasn't there?"

A scuffle in the undergrowth and they all turned to look at—nothing. Stan was right. There was no birdsong here, just the steady singing of the river passing through. A feeling began to close in on them and it was not pleasant. Liz stood up.

"Should I call for him?"

"Why would he just walk off like that?"

"Maybe because you were rude to him?" Paolo offered, not looking up.

"Stan, Stan!" Liz shouted.

They waited and waited. They did a few pickup shots. Liz peering into the hole of a tree. Liz coming down a path, spangled with sunlight. A lemon-colored butterfly the size of a paperback flapped into the clearing and alighted on the Tractor Rock. Slowly it parted and shut and parted its wings, semaphoring something. Paolo filmed its secret message, then it left. Only motion and event could hold the sense off that they were lost in a forest. They checked the footage again. Liz kept asking questions about it—did that work? did this come over?—trying to prod a compliment from Margo that was not forthcoming.

"It's been thirty minutes," Paolo said. "Should we try to head for the village?"

"I think we should wait here," Liz said, and Margo nodded.

They sat for a few minutes in silence. Around them insect life continued, sun played on the surface of the water, the leaves above breathed.

"I just meant he should keep an eye on her," Margo said. "It wasn't the worst thing anyone's ever said."

Neither of them responded. The more Liz looked at the cloud forest the more it appeared to be a single sentient creature. They were in its fur, on its skin, enveloped in its grasp. The lianas and creepers began to seem tentacular, prehensile. She got the impression that the jungle could snap shut around them. There were forever little movements happening on the edge of her vision, of her comprehension. She took a few steps down to the riverbank, by the Tractor Rock, and lay back on the grass and looked up through her sunglasses. Their yellowy tint made everything nostalgic, televisual, cheerful. Far overhead a plane dragged its dissolving plume through the blue.

"Shall we do the checklist piece? About religion?"

"I haven't sorted that out yet," Liz said.

"It's going to be cut with shots commenting on the list, though, so piecemeal is—did you hear that?"

"Anyone want a banana?" Paolo said. "Stan found them, growing on a tree."

"Are they definitely bananas?"

"They look like bananas."

"Shush!" Margo said again, sharply.

"What?"

"Listen."

A beating sound. Far away something wooden being hit by something wooden. Distant shouts. Chanting. It seemed to grow louder as they listened. Perhaps the wind changed. Were the shouts in anger? Silence again.

She looked across at Margo. Before the producer noticed her watching, Liz saw the fear in her face, then she turned to Liz and gave a little professional unpersuasive smile.

The shouting started again. Margo gave a little "Huh" and stood up, began to walk towards the forest.

"Hello?" she called. "Stan?"

Paolo got to his feet.

"Hey, you shouldn't go too," he said, and stood in front of her: Margo suddenly hugged him. Paolo raised his face to Liz. He was making an expression that said, *Help me*.

Just then Belef stepped into the clearing, beaming at them, bearing a parcel made from a large wrapped leaf, tied up with a fiber of some kind. Stan appeared behind her, blinking at them apologetically. Margo immediately released Paolo and launched into a speech.

"Belef, hi, good to see you again. Listen, this isn't going to work if you head off and leave us behind. We're trying very hard to keep to a schedule and it relies—"

"I had to go to Sydney."

"Excuse me?"

"Did you see the plane?"

"We didn't see any plane."

"I saw a plane," said Liz.

"That was my plane," nodded Belef.

"Your plane?"

"I had to go to Sydney for business."

"OK."

"I saw Kasingen and she sent back this for you."

Belef unwrapped the leaf parcel and presented Liz with some sticky-looking yellow sap.

"Thank you. What is it?"

With both hands, Liz took the leaf from her. Behind Belef, Margo motioned to Paolo to film the proceedings.

"This is cream from Sydney. For the bite."

"My bite?"

"On your neck."

"Oh."

Liz's hand rode up to the swelling on the nape on her neck.

"It is the tears of a tree in Sydney. It is for just this."

Belef pinched some of the sap from the leaf and dabbed it on Liz's neck in a tender gesture. Liz felt infantilized, and had a sudden urge to hug this woman in front of her. She was so sturdy, so stable, so sure of everything.

"Michael Ross was flying the plane. I wanted to stay here but he pulled me and he was strong."

"OK." Liz nodded.

"And this will help you." Belef had a length of red string in her hand—it matched her own bracelet—and she tied it round Liz's wrist without asking whether she could, then she turned her broad back and was off across the clearing.

"Where did you find her?"

"Actually she found me, by the telephone tree."

"Did you hear the shouting?"

"There was shouting?"

It was enough for the day—they had arranged to trail Belef for the whole of tomorrow. They climbed a hillside, crossing scrubby kunai grass. Belef trekked some way in front with Stan. A freshening breeze came down over the mountain. The sun was out. Anything was possible. Margo asked Liz, "Did you really see a plane go by?"

"Yeah, and she must have too."

"Did that stuff help your bite?"

"Not really. Just made it sticky."

Just then, coming over the crest of the hill, was the boy with white blossoms or feathers in his hair, leading a huge pig all badged with sores on a piece of vine. When he saw them he stopped, and then turned and led the animal calmly the other way.

"Hey, hello! Hello!"

"Leave him. He doesn't want to come near us."

On its delicate feet, the pig started to trot away from them, its massive buttocks slipping past each other and the boy broke into a jog to keep up. He didn't look back.

"What's wrong with us?" asked Margo.

"Oh," Stan replied. "The white skin, I expect. Probably thinks we're ghosts."

CHAPTER 19

"We all have secrets."

"I suppose it's a question of magnitude, Alison."

Ken sat at one end of the kitchen table, Judith stood by the sink. Alison sat awkwardly on the arm of the sofa. She'd kept her coat on. They were heading to the airport, and at first she'd been glad she stopped in. Both of her parents had given her long meaningful hugs at the doorstep, though the meanings of these hugs were only now becoming clear.

"I didn't know all of it. I mean I knew that he'd—been involved. But I didn't know—"

"It's about as bad as it could get," her father said. "And this man is meant to be a stepfather to my grandchildren, a husband to my daughter—a murderer." Her father tipped his head back, and asked the ceiling, "Is he coming in?"

"I didn't think you'd want to see him."

Ken looked at Judith.

"I suppose we don't, really. But."

"I think he's ashamed. I'm ashamed too. I don't know—"

She coughed out two startled sobs and sat down suddenly.

"*You* don't need to be ashamed," her mother said.

Alison twisted her wedding ring round on her finger and looked at her.

Judith went to hug her again. She felt insubstantial to Alison, unexpectedly hollow and light.

She saw her father had a teaspoon that he kept twisting in his fingers, like he was reeling something in.

"And what about the school? Did you see the headmaster's comments?"

"I did."

"He's incoming president of Rotary this year . . . It's just—how could you not tell us? How could Stephen—or Andrew or whoever the hell he is—not tell you? I can hardly credit it." Kenneth sat back, set the spoon on the raffia placemat. He liked the line so much he repeated it, "I can hardly credit it."

"How could I talk to you? I didn't know exactly what—I didn't know."

Judith could see the change coming. In an argument when Alison felt cornered it was never long before she'd turn to the attack.

"I think you should stop making excuses," her father said. "You know damn well you should have told us, or he should have told us, and for you to get yourself mixed up in—"

"It's not like you're easy to talk to. It's not like Spencer or Liz or I can bring our problems to you—"

"Oh don't make this about other people, Alison."

"Do you think Spencer can come to you and tell you—"

"Spencer and I talk all the time, every day—"

"You have no idea who Spencer is, no idea—"

"What are you talking about?"

Alison stood up.

"It doesn't matter."

"No, tell us, what *are* you talking about?"

"I don't know. Don't you wonder why Spencer has never had a girl-friend? I mean, like, never. Why he's in the gym every day? Have you seen his hair? All the attention he pays to his clothes?"

Kenneth blinked and looked at Judith.

"I'm sorry, are you saying Spencer is—"

"Well, I don't know!" shrieked Alison, her volume rising relative to the unstable ground she knew herself to be on. "Maybe! But don't you think it's odd? You say you know us. But sure you never ask us anything or if you do you don't bother listening to the answers. I have to sit and listen to you talk me through each game of golf hole by hole, shot by shot, but if I try to talk to you about anything—anything at all—you just switch off. And it's the same with Spencer and Liz. You should ask them. Ask them for once in your life."

Her father made a huge exhalation and shook his head slowly; he closed his eyes. Unfair, untrue, and he would not continue to look on a universe where such lies were bandied about. There was a large gentle core to Kenneth, the hedgehog's tender underbelly, and it was only his children who could reach it. When someone attacked his sense of himself, undermining the received history of the family, belying the sacred texts of his clan, something of a religious wounding occurred, and Judith thought for a second that he might cry. Instead he picked the spoon back up, returned to twisting it in his fingers.

Judith glared at her daughter. It wasn't conscious on Alison's part. Of her three children it was for some reason Alison—the middle one, the teacher, the mother, the committed Christian—who practiced most fervently and effortlessly the policy of slash-and-burn.

Judith said, softly, "You need to get going if you're going to make your flight."

Alison nodded.

"Good that you're getting away for a bit. Are you going to ask about your children?"

"Where are they?"

"In the lounge. They're watching *Mary Poppins*."

Alison gave her mother a hug.

Kenneth put his head in his hands.

"There are twelve thousand people living in this town and you choose him. I tell you it's going to be terrible for business."

"Oh shut up, Kenneth," Judith snapped. The kettle had boiled and she went to attend it.

As Alison went through to the lounge to see the kids, Judith said, very quietly, to Kenneth, "I suppose everyone deserves a second chance."

"Oh really? And if he was IRA? If he was the one who shot Davy Smith? Or blew up Geoffrey Irwin? They were *murdered*," he added emphatically, as if she'd contradicted him.

Judith said nothing. There was a bit of hardened porridge from Isobel's breakfast on the tabletop, and she picked at it with her nail.

"It's so hard to believe," she said softly. "Little Stephen. Seems so harmless. When he came here and piled the logs for us that first day, I just thought now here's one is shy and kind. Opposite of Bill."

She was looking in the big cupboard for the Tupperware with shortbread in it.

"I never trusted him," Kenneth said, with the same sour finality Judith had heard so many times when a rent check failed to arrive or a buyer pulled out.

She knew Kenneth thought belief in the goodness of people—of life!—to be essentially a mug's game. And it had always been her role, in the marriage, to "look on the bright side."

"It's so hard to believe," she said again now, with a different intonation, and let herself for once hold her stomach where it hurt and sat down.

CHAPTER 20

The rest house was about half the size of the other village huts and raised on foot-high stilts. The floor was halved logs, the walls wattle, the interior divided into two small gloomy rooms. When she entered there was a silent moment when Liz tried to realign her expectation with the reality. She had imagined something like a guesthouse—a room with dormitory beds, white sheets: plain, functional, clean. This was a hut, a tiny filthy one at that. Also, dark. A little door, only a few feet high and a couple of feet across, allowed access to the second inner chamber—the "panic room," as Margo dubbed it. The ladies, she announced, would sleep in there, since it was enclosed, with all the gear, and Paolo would sleep across the entrance. There was a front door they could tie shut with wire from the inside, and in case anyone tried to get in, he'd be there to fight them off.

"Fight them off?" Paolo asked. "What with?"

"Your charm," Liz offered, smiling.

"A stick," said Margo, not.

"I don't think anyone's going to try to get near you two. Maybe near my camera. And where's Stan going to sleep?"

"He'll bunk with you."

Even though it was still light outside, they needed lantern torches inside the rest house. They left one hanging in the back room, and one in the front section. Liz donned the head torch Margo had brought for her, and they rolled out their mats and sleeping bags in a determined silence, then stored the gear, locking the rucksacks together with a chain.

In front of the hut a delegation was arriving.

"You guys must be the BBC. Sarah told me. I'm Josh Werner. Come up and eat with us. We have more than enough."

His hand was outstretched. Beside him stood Sarah, the girl from the plane, smiling, a little shyly, at Liz. Three more children appeared from behind her, descending in height to a scrappy little toddler in a washed-out Texas Rangers T-shirt and a low-hanging terry-cloth nappy. He held a thin yam pointed at them like a gun and said, "Prepare to die."

"You know, I like to make this joke," announced Josh from the top of the table, in his utterly humorless way, "I say we're basically like *Star Trek*, the New Truth Mission. We boldly go where no one's gone before! I came out here by myself for six months and just lived among them. Got to know the culture. Learned how to make their food and build their houses and talk to them in their own tongue."

"You earned their trust," Liz said, adding in her head, *in order to betray it.*

"Exactly. I'd go off hunting with them for days. Got pretty good with a bow and arrow. Can take a tree kangaroo down at thirty yards. I mean I'd done a bit of hog hunting back home, but this was the real deal. You don't eat if you don't hunt, you know. We took everything very slowly. The initial steps in discipling were pretty tentative, you know, pretty—"

"In *disciplining*?" Paolo asked, and it was impossible to know if it was a genuine question.

"In di*scip*ling—though the Lord knows there are times they need some disciplining. But we had to teach them to read and write in their own lan-guage. So me and another guy, David Lawrence—he's dead now, God rest his soul—we spent a year just teaching them basic literacy, and then those we taught would pass it on. But you want them to be able to read the Bible themselves. You need to see the truth with your own eyes"—he pointed at his—"and not just take our word for it."

A Frisbee appeared in midair for a moment below the verandah of the Werners' house and they saw Stan's hands reach up and pluck it. He'd disappeared with the kids as soon as the dinner was finished.

"You're the piggy," Liz heard him shout. "You're the piggy in the middle."

"The thing is," explained Josh, "you have to start at the very begin-ning. My first choice was what to even *call* God. I mean what word do we even use for him in Bible lessons in Koriam or tok ples, the pidgin. The first choice is just to use the word God, and I know that in some missions they've done that. But the word God has no meaning for the Koriam. And we thought of using the name of one of the most powerful spirits in the Koriam culture, but none of these spirits had attributes that were even remotely similar to the creator of the whole universe." Josh raised a finger and twirled it, including the evening, the mountains, the children. "In fact many had negative characteristics that should not be associated with God. And then I thought of this word they have—Collinka—it's a verb that means to make something out of nothing, to create. It's an archaic word, they hardly use it. Pata Al-Collinka—it's the term I came up with to mean the Father of Creation. That's what they call God now in their language."

The man who had managed to name God smiled broadly at Liz. The Father of Creation had placed some green fleck from the stir-fry between his two front teeth.

Paolo was avoiding the conversation by playing with the dog Nipper, tug-ging a rope chew away from him and then waving it in his face again. The mongrel had a lengthy, chunky body, short strong legs, and an unquench-able desire for the rope. His soil-brown coat was patched with white and his little wispy beard made him appear the wisest of all dogs, a dog phi-losopher.

"I was losing the battle with the bottle. Had lost it, really." Josh's laughter like the rattle of coins in a tin. "I mean I was *far* from God, about as far from God as you can get."

There was something needy in the way he hunched forward and talked to them now, eager to convince them of the depths of his depravity.

"It wasn't immediate. Lord knows it took time. But through God's will, when I was twenty-six I gave up the demon drink, and joined the Fleeting Pentecostal Church of Our Lord God and Savior Jesus Christ. I began to understand that God had called me—to leave behind my old ways, to leave behind Kansas, to serve him . . .".

His wife, Jess, reappeared with a wooden tray of cups and a teapot, and Josh eyed her with a dimly guilty air.

"I was telling them how I came to God—"

"From Kansas," Liz said, and got a guarded laugh from Jess.

Liz was thinking about landscapes. The flatlands of Kansas. It was no surprise that the deserts of the Middle East had given birth to the three big monotheisms. A landscape's character directed the minds of those born in it, their imagination, their interactions with the seen and unseen. Out there in the Kansan prairies—or the wilderness of sand where Jesus fasted forty days and nights—it was just you and God under the sky, staring down the huge horizon. It was unilinear. It was strict. It was personal. The jungle spoke a different tongue. It talked of fertility, the immanence of objects, the many spirits lurking in the trees and ferns and rocks and rivers. There was constant activity, displacement. It reminded one of mortality, the endless simmer of rot and renewal. And where was her own Ireland in the system? A tidal zone. A recurrence of folds. Early mist rising up like all the ghosts in the hollows of the fields.

"Oh, we make what we can get," said Jess, in response to polite murmurs from Liz about the stir-fry. "Kaukau with everything. Had you had kaukau before? It's basically sweet potato. Maybe not so flavorsome."

Jess's nose was a pale dorsal fin, a perfect quadrant. A nose like that led its owner through the world, parted it before them. It entailed a certain affirmation to truths on the side of life and made Jess difficult not to like. Her blond hair was tied back loosely in a ponytail and she had the capable aura of someone used to physical work. All of her was freckled and taut and full with a cheery American tension.

"We had it for lunch," Margo said shortly.

"You make your peace with it," Josh added. His eyes narrowed. He was staring at Liz's arm, at the red string tied round it. "I see you've already met Belef."

Jess said, "They have lots of onions and cucumbers, this time of year, and the plane comes once a fortnight, if the weather's fine. I meant to say, Josh, the water pump's still not working properly. Could you even hear yourselves talk out here? Inside it sounds like the house is about to take off—"

Liz understood Jess was trying to keep her husband in a good mood, trying to divert the river of his anger. Darkness was beginning to fold in over the valley. Moses—a short, broad-shouldered eight-year-old with tangled brown curls—stood on the grassy slope, waiting for the Frisbee to come to him. Behind him, at the edge of the rainforest, the trees seemed to step backwards into the darkness, and it all made Liz almost unbearably sleepy.

Sarah banged the screen door, carrying out a wooden platter of cookies.

"Here she is," Josh said.

Sarah replied, not looking at him, "You know the oven still doesn't work either. I had to stand in front of it for forty minutes to make these. It turned itself off like every three seconds."

"I'll have a look at it tomorrow. And the water pump."

"And the showerhead. It's still cracked," Sarah added.

"So can you tell us a bit about the Story, about Belef's movement?" Margo asked, pushing her plate away from her as if she were in a restaurant.

A look was exchanged between the spouses. Jess bent down and swept the plastic tablecloth with only her hand, swiftly herding crumbs into the other cupped against the table's side. Josh sighed.

"Movement is a very *grand* word to give to it. Look, we were sad to lose her from the church. She was part of the church family."

"And *our* family," Sarah added.

"And she was very close to us, the six of us. I think God is still in her, somewhere," Jess said, "and we pray for her to return to His ways. She's just a little lost right now."

"More than a little," Josh corrected.

Margo asked, "And what actually happened to the daughter?"

Josh spaced his hands as if for cat's cradle.

"It was a tragic accident—"

"I will eat you up!"

Stan's voice shouting from just beyond the verandah.

"Gobble gobble gobble!"

He was ambling around like an ogre, growling and howling and lunging at the kids as Esther and Moses tried to throw the disc around him, and Noah banged an empty plastic bottle off his own head.

"I can see the difficulties she's placed you in," Margo said softly. "It must be very"—no other word came—"difficult." She added, in an even softer voice, "And *can* you tell us what happened? How did she come to start her religion?"

That hard, metallic laugh again from Josh.

"I'd hardly call it a religion. Maybe a cult. Look, with Belef, like with so many women, she takes it all personally. If a leaf falls on her when she sleeps it has to be about her. You see—"

"I suppose Margo only means it in the way all religions begin as cults. Even Jesus started somewhere," Liz offered reasonably. "Yeshua of Nazareth as a protest movement against the Roman occupation and all that." Josh was staring at her with light amusement in his face but she continued. "It's just that some village religions achieve a kind of full spectrum dominance and then we begin to accord them—"

"You know"—Josh's turn to interrupt. He spoke calmly but irritation flickered in his eyes—"things here in New Ulster, in all of PNG, they were very dark for centuries. Cannibalism. Constant tribal warfare. Widow-killing. Even when we first arrived, there was so much violence. They were sick of their lives. They wanted the light of God to enter them. I remember Usai telling me that they were starving for the truth. That was the phrase he used in pisin—starving for the truth."

"Usai is one of our church's elders. I don't know what we'd do without him," Jess added. "Will you have tea? I'm afraid the milk's only the powdered stuff."

"You met him on the plane," Sarah said, offering a cookie to Liz. Liz had the impression that Sarah wanted to get her away from here and talk openly. There was a censored aspect to her presence. She seemed years younger, smaller, plainer than the girl she'd met the day before.

"He sat beside you? Britney Spears T-shirt?"

"Normally Sarah would have flown on an MAF flight, but there was none coming this week so we sent Usai to go get her and take her with Hastings. And then she met you. Imagine the BBC coming all the way out here—"

"Do you have Internet?" Margo asked.

"Sometimes," Jess answered brightly. It would be hard to rile this woman, Liz thought. She had the hard patience of a pioneer. This woman was the kind of mother Liz knew she could never be, if she ever did, if it ever happened, if she ever met . . . Capable, calm, many handed.

"You see that stump by the crest of the hill? Where the post sticks out of the ground? I stand there with my Samsung held in the air for hours at a time. You can sometimes send e-mail, but so slowly. It must depend on where the satellites are, but I haven't figured it out. And there's no point in thinking about downloading or uploading anything. And forget Facebook or Twitter. People send me photographs sometimes and I want to scream. The villagers think I'm mad standing out there, my arm in the air."

"Waving at planes," Sarah said.

"What about electricity?" Margo asked.

"We have solar panels on the back here, facing north, and when the weather's good like today, they're more than enough. Do you want to charge your phones and computers? You're more than welcome—"

Josh sat back up and interrupted, unable to help himself. "We're more than happy to give you every help we can, but I would ask one thing of you."

"Of course," Margo said, and Liz could hear in the intonation that her producer was seriously enraged by the qualification. Margo's sense of entitlement—she said "We're from the BBC" as if she were saying we're from NASA or NATO or the FBI—thrilled Liz, but it was not balanced in her with the institution's slightly embarrassed sense of public service. Margo believed in Margo, and in the BBC as an extension of Margo, and she believed in that combined divine right to direct the way of all things entirely.

"I'd ask that you talk to one of our converts. You should speak to Usai, since you've already met him. Would you say Usai—Jess, Sarah—would Usai be a good one to talk to?"

Something in his tone revealed this question was not a question, and she realized that this had been prearranged—maybe not between Sarah and her parents, and maybe not even between Jess and Josh—but the Reverend had certainly been planning it.

"Usai would be good to speak to," Jess dutifully responded.

"Usai is the reason we're here at all, in some sense, you see. And of course he's Belef's son."

"Her son?" Liz asked.

"Yes, but a Christian, a pillar of our church. He's from Kirlassa, one of the villages nearby, from the Oguru tribe, and they'd heard that the gospel had come to Kutang, that the Kutang had received the word of God. Kutang's a day's hike from here, where the New Truth began to missionize in 1984. Usai went to live there, learned a bit of the language and realized he was in the dark, and all of the Oguru were being left in the dark, so he asked the mission there to send people, and *we* came to Slinga. All of his village, all of Kirlassa, moved here. And his mother and sister. That was thirteen years ago."

"Amazing," Margo said, sounding distinctly non-amazed.

When they left, Sarah left with them. She had to shut the chicken coop up and she touched Liz's arm as they said goodbye at the foot of the hill and whispered, "You know . . ." She waited until Paolo and Stan and Margo had walked a few steps farther on. "My father's trying to get Belef arrested. I heard him talking on the CB radio. He says it's illegal that she has her daughter's body buried next to her house—that it's unsanitary. He's told her already, but he's serious about it. You should tell her that he's serious."

They parted and Liz hurried to catch up with the rest of them, the tiny, ranging, tangled beams of their flashlights.

On the walk back, Stan said he'd heard there'd been an accident, that Belef's daughter had been killed, but that the villagers would not speak of it freely, and he had never asked Belef outright. She blamed the missionaries for it, though: He knew that. They talked of Josh, of his image of himself as Captain Kirk, and made loud jokes against the darkness around them. By the time they reached the hut, giddiness had overtaken all four of them. Back in their section of the rest house, as the women got ready for bed, Margo whispered, "And what was the story about the diapers? Dishtowels and duct tape? Why would you even need a nappy? The kid's running around outside."

Liz laughed, and there was a desperate flavor to it. If they stopped joking for a second they might start crying. Laughter and more laughter because the world around them had shrunk to a small dank hut and the cone of light cast by a hanging torch. The walls of the rest house, like the walls of all the constructions in the village except Josh and Jess's compound, were made of pitpit, a thin reedlike bamboo that was beaten out and woven. They were not walls in the sense of barriers; the insects came and went as they pleased, and when the wind rose above a whisper it whistled through the gaps. Liz donned her Thinsulate gloves and a wooly hat, tightened the drawstring of her sleeping bag around her face, which she'd doused with insecticide. It was amazing how loud the jungle became when they stopped speaking and lay down in the darkness. It was an entire ecosystem of sound: every species of noise, near scratches and distant shrieks, tenor bellows and shrill whistles. She found her hands were clenched into fists and relaxed them, and attended to the weight of her entire body pressing heavily into the sleeping mat, into the planks, into the earth—and in a few minutes was asleep.

When the rain started in the middle of the night, it woke her. It would have woken the dead. There was urgency about it; it meant to tell them something, to impart their transgression, their trespass. They had no right.

"Margo?"

Her voice rang small and tremulous. She said it again, louder.

"I'm awake," came the response.

"It's raining pretty heavily."

Margo didn't respond.

"I feel like the whole hut is about to slide down the hill."

They lay there and listened. A tapping sound began and Liz realized water was dripping from the roof onto the foot of her sleeping bag. She freed her arms and found her torch and turned it on, stood up unsteadily and hooked it to the ridge post.

"I'm going to have to move your—"

Margo screamed.

"What is it? What is it?"

Her sleeping bag thrashed around and unzipped and Margo was out standing in her tracksuit bottoms and fleece beside Liz, then holding onto her, then standing atop the rucksacks.

"Eyes! Below the boards!"

"What?"

"A pair of eyes below the floor, looking up! I just saw them."

"Human eyes?"

Paolo's face appeared at the little entrance to their room.

"Someone's under the hut!" Margo screeched.

They shone their torches down between all the gaps but saw nothing now but mud and darkness.

Margo insisted that Paolo sleep in with them. Stan had slept through the whole thing and they left him now in the outer part of the hut. Paolo settled in by the entrance, and Liz lay between her cameraman and producer. Paolo stretched out on his back, and she faced away from him. She tried to forget that he was lying beside her and shut her eyes. But she could feel Margo's breath fluttering across her nose. She pulled a T-shirt out of her bag and covered her face with it. She found herself pushing her bottom backwards an inch or so against Paolo, and he turned and pressed against her and she pressed back. They lay there spooning and neither of them moved for several minutes and she didn't know if he was awake or not. She tried not to hold her breath or think to herself what it meant. It was nice, for a moment, to try to live without meaning one thing or another.

CHAPTER 21

The lobby of the Mitsis Alila Exclusive Resort & Spa in Rhodes was a cool sanctuary of soft wicker seats and white marble. A girl in white offered them flutes of pineapple juice in which small pink flowers floated. All the staff wore white, as if they were manning a sanatorium, or were members of the cult of luxury, gliding behind the marble desks and between the marble columns and around the tinkling marble fountain diligent and capable and silent as angels. She and Stephen had barely spoken for the previous three hours, but to enter this grand, quiet space soothed them both. Like Heaven's waiting room. Now, as they stood at the check-in desk, Stephen took hold of her hand and she let him.

They were on the seventh floor with a sea view. A large, clean, anonymous hotel in a hot country is an Ulsterman's idea of paradise, provided it's not too hot, and provided the all-inclusive deal they've booked includes alcohol. Alison opened the door to the balcony and the heat came at her like she'd opened a furnace. There was the steady iteration of the waves, hissing intake and backwash, and she stepped out to see a narrow strip of yellow beach dotted with the hotel's white umbrellas, the cloudless sky, the sun dazzling on the toiling sea. How happy she would have been.

"Stephen, come out here and look at this view."

"I'm coming."

"Isn't it lovely?"

"It is."

They ordered up steak and chips for two, a bottle of local Shiraz, and watched a movie about fishermen caught in a horrific storm. Alison had gone through the movies they could choose and tried to pick something in which no one was shot, a surprisingly difficult task. Stephen made Alison turn off her phone. It sat there on the desk, though, and she kept glancing over at it till finally he lifted it and placed it in the drawer. It was a portal to sadness. The sheets were clean and white and cool, but when Stephen reached across the bed to hug her, she pulled away. "Not yet," she said. And: "I feel too far from you."

The next morning the beach was busy, but they had loungers and umbrellas reserved for hotel guests. When they came up to get changed for lunch, Alison, who had been quiet but calm, went into the toilet and came out looking distressed.

"You want to tell me?"

"No."

"Are people saying stuff to you?"

"On Facebook. And I made the mistake of reading the comments under the *Sunday Life* piece."

"I thought you couldn't get it online."

"I subscribed."

"Alison. Why don't you just go off-line for a while?"

"But maybe we need to go through it. To see how people are going to react." She lifted her phone, and read, in a flat, emotionless voice, "I was at school with her. She was always desperate. Didn't realize she'd go this far, though."

"Don't, Alison."

"I can see why she married a mass murderer. He was the only one who'd have her."

"Leave it alone."

"I know it's off point but did anyone order a meringue? . . . It's like the twenty-first century never made it to Mid-Ulster. . . . He should have been shot years ago. It's scum like that—"

"Stop it," Stephen shouted and grabbed her phone from her.

———————

On the second day they lay under the umbrellas and drank beer by the smaller pool, where there were no children, while Alison tried to signal to passing parents, with her smile, that she did have kids and liked them, but was glad to be rid of them just now. After the buffet lunch they slept all afternoon in their room with the curtains drawn. Alison woke first and sat on the balcony in her new purple sarong and straw hat and watched the beach below. Rows of white umbrellas obscured most of the occupants, but here and there you could see a hand reaching for sun cream or the pink exposure of some brave soul who wanted the full force of the rays. Several children ran in and out of the shallows shrieking. A saggy old man in board shorts and a young woman in a leopard-print bikini walked hand in hand along the shore. Far out, beyond all the cheery activity, the flat expanse of the blue sea shivered and roiled.

Stephen came out in his boxers and sat across the plastic table from her. Since it had all come out, he'd adopted a dozy expression and a kind of ambling gait, as if he'd early-onset Alzheimer's and a vaguely sprained ankle. It was all, Alison felt, too self-conscious to be real, and in any event it seemed to suggest that *he* was in pain, that *he* was struggling, which she thought was a bit rich in the circumstances. She looked back down at her guidebook.

"Anything interesting?"

"Oh this and that."

"Like what?"

"Waves of invaders. Crusades. Sieges."

"The usual."

"There were two thousand Jews on the island that the Nazis deported and killed."

"Terrible."

"One of that band Pink Floyd used to have a house here."

"Oh yeah?"

She nodded and stood up, handing him the book.

"I'm going to have a shower."

"Want me to join you?"

Alison looked back at him with such a withering glance that Stephen blushed. He heard her lock the bathroom door.

In the evening they chose the Zorba restaurant—the hotel had five—and ended up drinking two bottles of red wine over dinner. They'd both ordered moussaka, and Alison had finished with the cheese course and Stephen had chocolate tart. A band had started inside, and was embarking on a shaky cover of Lady Gaga's "Alejandro."

"This is the life," Stephen said.

"It is," Alison quietly confirmed.

"Are you going to be miserable all holiday?"

She looked up at him, shocked.

"I'm devastated." He said nothing so she repeated it. "Devastated."

"I know."

"You shouldn't talk to me like that. You might have had time to get used to—"

Another couple was being led through the doors outside to the terrace, towards the empty table next to them.

"Anyway, we'll talk about it later."

The couple nodded hello and they nodded back. Once they'd sat down, the woman said quietly to her husband, "Well, this is better."

Northern Irish. Alison looked over and said, "You fleeing the band?"

The man laughed. His striped shirt was very similar to Stephen's. He was midthirties perhaps, the woman a little younger.

"Right enough, they set up just by our table."

The woman nodded. "I couldn't believe it. I thought they were going to wait till we left, but they just started playing. I couldn't hear myself think. At least we'd finished the food."

"It's much nicer out here anyway."

"Is there someone in swimming?"

"We thought so too, but I think it's a buoy bobbing about."

There was a silence and finally the woman said, "The hotel's lovely, isn't it?"

"You want to hear these?"

Stephen sat in the bath and Alison stood in the doorway, iPad in her hand.

"What?"

"Messages."

"Do I?"

"Not all bad. Some very sympathetic."

Stephen said nothing.

"There's one from Judith saying they had three phone calls last night and the person hung up without speaking."

"Jesus."

"I got one through the Donnellys' e-mail from someone called Ivan Clements from the *Belfast Telegraph*."

"Delete it."

"OK, but there's one headed 'University of Ulster Oral History Project.' Can I read it to you?"

Stephen nodded.

> *"Dear Alison,*
>
> *My name is David Boyd and I'm a researcher at the CAIN Centre for the Study of Conflict at the Coleraine campus of the University of Ulster. We have put together a large archive of oral testimony to do with the Troubles, and I wondered whether it would be possible to interview your husband Andrew Stephen McLean. Our archive includes interviews with hundreds of people involved in and affected by the Troubles.*

Please rest assured that the interview is for a sealed
archive and would not be opened or released until after
the participant's death—

"There's a whole load of documents attached from something called CAIN, C. A. I. N., and it's—"

"Delete it."

"Well, hold on."

"Delete it."

"Shouldn't you think about it?"

"Alison." He sat up. The water in the tub sloshed back and skited up on the tiles.

"It's just that people think of you . . . You should be able to tell them your story . . . What happened to you—"

"What happened to me isn't relevant. It's what I did."

"It was a different time . . . Don't you remember you said—"

Stephen snorted.

"If people knew the situation. You were almost a child—"

"I don't want to talk about it."

"Maybe it shouldn't be up to you."

Stephen looked at her. "Who else would it be up to? You mean you?" He blinked at her.

"No, of course not. I mean . . ." She lowered the toilet lid and sat on it. "There's no point arguing. I only meant maybe you owe it to everyone, to the country, to tell the truth of the situation. To tell the whole story, warts and all."

Stephen sighed.

"In the classroom, you know, I'd sit my kids down and make them tell me exactly what happened. Then make them apologize to each other."

"In your class?"

"Yes."

"With six-year-olds."

"Eight- and nine-year-olds."

"Alison, I—I killed people. It's not like I stole their lunch money."

"Maybe you need to put your side of it."

"My side?"

If he said he regretted the deaths, if he let remorse in, then wasn't he admitting that the whole foundation was rotten? That his whole life had been a waste? That he had killed all those people for no reason? No, you couldn't do that. You made your bed and you lay in it. You could be forgiven only by God. It wasn't like a switch was flicked: lights on. There was forever slippage, confusion, uncertainty. Of course he regretted it. His life, his whole life . . . But how could you draw a line between what he regretted for himself and what he regretted for others?

"Well, you did what you did but you had reasons, didn't you? They might have been terrible reasons, they might have been inadequate, they might have been wrong, but there were reasons. Shouldn't you give them? Shouldn't you try and explain? You're not a psychopath."

"I said no!"

It occurred to Alison now that she wanted Stephen to suffer. She was suffering and it was his fault. It was outrageous that he was here, alive and well, and all those people he had killed were not. It also felt important that he have a story, a linked chain of events that explained—thus excused—why he'd done what he'd done. The terrible things. She found she was looking at his hands intently.

"What about when the Shinners tell their story—their glorious freedom fighting."

This was an argument Stephen could never resist. Whataboutery. Northern Ireland's favorite form of rhetoric. She closed the three folds of the iPad cover gently.

"He says the project's talking to lots of"—she baulked at "terrorists," which wasn't the word the e-mail had used either—"of people who were involved. The protagonists. You'd be one of a whole load."

"I couldn't be using anyone's real name."

"Isn't it all out now?"

"Mostly. But. You know."

"What?"

"There's others, like, that were involved, you know."

He looked up at her with his usual squint amplified into something approaching discomfort.

"Like who?"

"For one, the guy who gave the say-so."

He turned on the hot tap.

"What happened to him?"

"Nothing."

"Nothing at all?"

"You don't betray your commander."

Alison nodded as if she understood. She felt she was being asked to share in some elaborate fantasy and couldn't, even if she'd wanted to. She said, "I'll tell him you'll think about it."

What is a honeymoon for? Alison knew that they were meant to make memories they could live off for the rest of their lives, salt away the incidental moments they could return to and talk about. She booked massages, she booked a boat trip out to see some birds.

It wasn't that she was always thinking about it.

But she was never not thinking about it.

Every glance between them now was freighted with this new, shared, terrible knowledge. Complicity.

They drank hard at night and during the day lay by the beach or the pool. In the afternoon Alison went wandering by herself for an hour or two. She visited the Lindos acropolis, the sailors' houses—wandered the cobbled lanes and seafronts. Each shop selling beach mats, brightly colored beach towels, inflatable animals to ride in the pool, bats and balls for the beach. She picked up trinkets—painted Marianic icons, ships in bottles, blown glass elephants and seals and lions—and set them all back down.

On the day of their boat trip round the jagged headland, they waded in from the beach up to their knees to get to the boat and then two of the skinny little Greeks had to haul Alison up over the side. They picked up six more passengers from another hotel's pier and started out. White birds took turns to fold themselves up and plunge into the sea. Little blocky white cottages sat high up on the parched yellow mountains. Stelios, the captain—or at least the one steering—called out distances and dates and facts, but it was impossible to hear him above the noise of the engine. They finally reached a bare rock in the sea where hundreds of cormorants hunched together and gabbled and squawked and shat. They were wretched, charred, evil-looking things. The boat circumnavigated the island and headed back, and Alison wasn't sad to leave the shivering, ragged birds behind. The repetitive throb of the outboard, the lift and drop of the boat were hypnotic, and with the sun on the face, with the sea spray, the smell of petrol and salt, she felt herself relax, and inserted her arm into Stephen's, and they sat there like an old couple, arms linked, watching the lacy wake behind them disperse, the surface resume its pitted façade.

When they went back to shower and change for dinner, she found the man Boyd from the University of Ulster had replied with a list of possible dates. Stephen, sitting on the balcony, eating a packet of foreign crisps whose flavor he could not discern, suggested—casually—the day after their flight home. Suddenly there was no drama about it: It was like he was setting up a meeting for a wee painting job. Which maybe he was. The newspaper article, the messages, the unending knowledge of being hated, of being really hated again by the large anonymous public, had worked on him. It felt unfair. She understood he wanted to tell someone why the thing had happened, how he was not that person, how he was a changed man. He wanted to offer the view his own mind had provided to his soul. *Don't worry*, the mind said. *You did your best with a bad hand.*

Alison felt she had come round to the opposite opinion; she'd worked out that in the privacy of a room, in the silence of a mind, you didn't have to confront or reflect, you could just pretend that everything was fine. For whole hours at a time they appeared to be normal people, and anything that brought it back to her—the violent cover of a paperback book by the pool, or the family at the next table talking about "terrorists," even if they meant ISIS—had to be ignored, out-talked, refused completely. The thought of Stephen speaking about it in detail—to anyone, anywhere— suddenly repelled her. It was precisely the details she couldn't handle.

On Thursday they found the beach loungers the attendant had allotted them were beside the Northern Irish couple. He was sitting up under their parasol wearing a Hawaiian shirt and playing something on his iPhone. She was lying in a sensible black one-piece in the sun, reading *Glamour*. Alison noted with approval the stretch marks like tidemarks all over her thighs.

As the attendant laid out their towels, the man looked up from his phone at Stephen and said, "You're a good man."

"You what now?"

"I was just saying you're a good man"—he pointed at the Liverpool football shirt Stephen had on—"to be wearing that, especially after how they played last night."

"Ah, you know, through thick and thin."

"Mostly thin."

"We're biding our time."

All day they lay a few feet from the other couple. There had been no further friendliness from either side, and after a while it became too late. If anyone had spoken it would have given the lie to the agreed pretense that they were not listening to each other's brief conversations about sun cream or the attendant's unwillingness to take a beer order or the Greek word for towel.

At lunchtime they found themselves in the queue for the buffet behind them. Alison'd gleaned that he was called Paul, but he hadn't mentioned her name yet, had referred to her as darling. Alison and the darling smiled at each other.

"You guys here for two weeks then?"

"We are."

"We've just got the week."

"You on the Sunday flight back to Belfast?"

"We are."

"We're all on the same flight then."

"Ach lovely."

"You in Belfast?"

"Antrim, actually. Paul works in the hospital there and I teach."

"*I* teach. Well, I did teach. I work in the family business now. Estate agency."

They talked and talked but somehow the automatized sorting processes—the reflexive threshing, sieving, straining—were not working. Paul and Stephen drank six beers between them, and Alison and Claire—her name was Claire—shared a bottle of locally grown Chardonnay. For approximately fifty minutes the women discussed their children, the rewards and trials of parenthood, the importance of sun cream and other products that provide defense against the foreign climes. Meanwhile the men talked about Louis van Gaal, his mistakes, his aims, his rubbery muppet face. And still Alison had no idea whether they were Catholic or Protestant, Cathestant or Protholic. She felt the refusal of context as frustration and then as a kind of mild delight. It was like meeting someone from England, but they didn't have that brittle cold veneer the English had, where you were always worried about being overfamiliar or too blunt.

"And where's the school exactly?"

They had eaten together in the middle of a table meant for eight.

"Do you know Antrim?"

"Not well."

"It's down in the Markets—it's a nice wee school. Integrated, you know, so—"

"And does that work all right?"

"Ach really very well—we're about half and half. I mean there's teasing issues. And not all shades of the community would be behind it, you know."

"Shall we head back down to the beach for a drink?"

"Let me put this on my bill."

"Sure, we'll stick it on ours."

"It's all paid for anyway."

Paul said to the waiter, "Can you put it on room 405?"

"Certainly sir," said the diminutive teenager in the snowy Nehru jacket. "What's the name?"

"Devlin," said Paul.

———————————

Back in their room an hour later Alison said, "They were very nice."

There was a pause and Stephen said, "Surprised?"

"I didn't know, to be honest."

"Mixed, do you think?"

"Which way?"

"Well, he's Devlin."

"She teaches in the integrated."

"Yes."

"But they were nice."

"I'm just saying."

"No, I know."

CHAPTER 22

Liz stood on the little hillock Jess had recommended with her arm in the air, clutching her iPhone.

"Getting anything?" Margo called.

Tendrils of wood smoke rose from the huts on the hillside and flavored the cold morning air. They had traveled back a million years. Or forward. Time had gone strange. There was no sign of movement from the Werners' little compound. The mist below them in the valley was already clearing. A few of the porters sat round a campfire smoking and chewing betel nut and drinking tea. Paolo walked towards her, his camera hoisted on his shoulder. He might have stepped off a black run in St. Moritz—silver wraparound shades and a neon yellow anorak. Liz smoothed her hair down, while trying not to look like she was doing it. For her on-camera outfit, she'd bought five plain black, but not unstylish, blouses in Bally-glass, along with three pairs of identical beige cargo pants—the edit could rearrange the scenes in any order and it would still work—but now she thought she should have worn something less . . . austere.

"Can you walk down there, towards the trees, and then turn around and come back? Don't look at the camera."

"OK."

Walking, strangely, was one of the hardest things about presenting. At soon as you knew someone was watching you walk, it became almost impossible to do it. Where does this arm go? Why is my back so hunched? Am I walking too slow, too fast? Her limbs swung like they were very loosely attached.

She settled on a brisk, determined stride and then remembered to slow up and look around her, marveling at everything. The problem with TV was you had to *perform* experience rather than actually have it.

What she felt now was fraudulent, more than a little ludicrous.

She touched her neck and found the spider's bite, the marble under her skin, had almost disappeared.

"Guys?" Margo was shouting across to them. "Can you get ready to go? We're picking Belef up on the way."

Paolo filmed Liz walking up to the hut. She felt she was bobbing her head to some inaudible rhythm. Stan was already there, sitting on the log beside Belef, and Margo motioned to him to move out of the shot, but he didn't see her or anyway didn't comply. He held a hand-drawn map out in front of him and was asking Belef to point out various places on it. Reconciling her 3-D world to the 2-D map somehow amused her; she smiled and smiled at the piece of paper. As the crew approached, her face took on a rigidity and she said, "Do you make work with the New Truth?"

"We're from the BBC."

"What is the Beeby Say?"

Margo's face managed to express both rage and pity.

"The BBC. The British Broadcasting Corporation. From Great Britain."

"David Beckham?"

"He's also from Great Britain."

"You work for the New Truth?"

"No, no, not at all."

"You know Mister Josh?"

"We just met him. But we're here to learn about you. We've come all the way from London—"

"And Ireland—"

"To learn about you and your movement."

"The Story?"

"Yes, the Story. Sorry."

There was a pause and she looked at the map again, pointed to something on it. Just then a low insectile whine started above them, and they looked up to see a white twin prop plane coming from the north, heading for the village. It banked steeply against the blue, readying itself to land.

"You should get this," Margo said, but Paolo was already filming it.

"What is the plane for?" Stan said.

"For the mission," Belef answered, and dismissed with a wave of her hand. "All their stuff, all their good stuff."

"I'd never get up to the landing strip in time to film it coming in."

"No, well, let's leave it."

"Here." Belef struck the map with a finger. "We must go here and make a telephone call. I need to speak to my children."

"To Kasingen," Liz began.

Belef nodded impatiently. "I have one daughter and three sons. Come, we will talk to them."

Belef stood and took the two steps across the grass to meet Liz and grabbed hold of her wrists firmly. Her hands were rough, chapped, and her mouth looked shocking, vampiric, blood red from betel nut. She stared into Liz's eyes.

"You and me, Lizbet, we died. Long time ago. But we did not know it—"

"We died?"

"We go on with walk and talk, but our spirits are gone from us. At Kirlassa I have visits of the tambaran who comes to me at night from the five stones. And last week my three boys came to me when I sleep. I was like this."

Belef let go of Liz's wrists, closed her eyes sleepily and pushed her head onto Liz's shoulder. Liz stumbled backwards slightly. She could see the camera from the corner of her eye and tried to stay completely calm. Part of her wanted to laugh and part of her wanted to turn on her heel and go home. She raised her hand and patted Belef on the arm. Belef pulled her head back and slowly opened her eyes; there was a dazed half smile in them. *Your mind is very far from mine*, Liz thought.

"Kasingen, she comes every night and brings a flashlight so I can see them all well, all my boys and girl, and she told me Lizbet is your friend but she is dead, and you also are dead."

Belef looked into Liz's eyes again, insisting. Liz found herself nodding.

"Michael Ross told me: 'The spirit of Lizbet entered your body and Lizbet's body now has your spirit.' So you must tell her this, and tell her the message also."

The hands again, gripping. Liz let herself be held. She stayed very still, though inside her heart thrashed and she found she was swallowing hard. Belef's face was very near hers. The woman spoke matter-of-factly and Liz managed to match her tone. "And what is the message?"

"Johnson told me this. Soon the whiteskins and all Chinese will leave New Ulster. They will go and not come back." Belef widened her eyes; moats of white surrounded the deep brown irises. "The goods that the white spirits have stopped will be given among you. They say tell Lizbet this for she is our friend."

Liz nodded and tried to gently pull her wrists free, but Belef held fast. A tall thin woman appeared in the doorway of Belef's hut, carrying a broom—twigs tied to a branch—to which she bore some resemblance. Her face was impassive, though her eyes imbibed the scene, pausing briefly at the fabulous eye of the camera. She wore a yellow cotton shift with small red flowers and butterflies embroidered along the hem, around the neck, and along the frayed sleeves that stopped halfway down her stringy upper arms. Among all the strangeness the dress looked familiar; Liz realized it was exactly the same one her sister had worn for her confirmation. It was in the photograph on Ken and Judith's mantelpiece: them all standing outside Ballyglass Presbyterian's stone arch doorway, the adolescent Alison in the middle, a kind of Elvis quiff that Judith would tong back for her in the mornings, her arms folded, a smile being coaxed out under sufferance . . . From Monsoon or Whistles or somewhere.

Liz freed herself from Belef's grip to gesture at the woman and say, "My sister has the same dress. That yellow dress."

Belef glanced behind and said: "That is your sister. And I am also."

The woman disappeared again into the shadows, and they heard the *swish-swish* of the brush start up.

"Let us make moves. We have much to get done."

Belef gave a shrill whistle, and from behind the hut a skinny wide-shouldered man appeared wearing only a grass skirt—his torso reminded Liz of a kite, all struts and concave stretched membrane. And there was something steerable about him, his eyes eager for instruction as he stood shifting from foot to foot, waiting to catch a breeze and veer off.

"This is Leftie."

"Leftie?"

"He carries my tools."

She pointed to the string bag over his shoulder. In it were stones, twigs, some rough yellow papers covered with indistinguishable marks.

"You like mango?"

"Sure."

"Leftie, bring 'em mango. Good and soft."

A figure was making his way down the wide grass fairway. He wore sunglasses and beige slacks and a khaki short-sleeved shirt. Raula was lighter-skinned than most of the New Ulster inhabitants; he looked to have Indian blood. In his right hand he carried the briefcase, allowing it the tiniest of swings as he tramped down the slope. When he moved his arm the dark crescent of a sweat patch peeped out and was covered again. Behind him strolled two policemen in blue shirts and shorts.

"That's the deputy administrator," Margo said.

Belef looked up at the approaching delegation and gave a little half smile.

"Leftie is *my* deputy."

They watched the delegation approach. When Raula was within a few meters of the hut, Belef got up and stood in the doorway with her back facing out. She spoke languidly to the woman inside, "Smel nogut i kamap," at which the woman laughed loudly. Raula stopped at the edge of Belef's garden and gave a little rigid bow.

"Good morning."

Leftie appeared with a bark plate of mango and offered it round, ignoring the delegation. The two policemen stood a few meters away, one with his arms angrily folded, staring at Belef's hut while the other fidgeted with his moustache and threw an occasional shy glance in their direction.

Both had pistols on their belts. Finally, Belef turned round. She'd put on a pair of black glasses—glasses that had no lenses in them.

"Mr. Raula, it is so nice to see you."

Liz wasn't sure why she was so surprised that a person who professed a daily interaction with ghosts and who lived in a hut and who assumed that different spirits inhabited each rock and tree would be capable of high-grade sarcasm—but she was surprised. She liked Belef even more.

"The Development Committee tells me you are causing much trouble."

A little pearl of spittle appeared on Raula's lower lip as he talked. Out of the corner of her eye Liz could see that Paolo had started filming. She wiped mango juice from her chin.

Belef chuckled meanly at Raula and said, "How could that be? I sit right in this place and watch the sun go up and it come back down."

"You are preventing the quotas being filled."

Belef sat down on the other log. She removed her glasses and closed them.

"I don't see that."

"The village gives two days for work on the coconut fields, one day for development, one day in the gardens, and two days in church work, Belef. I understand your followers have neglected their duties."

Raula looked at the camera.

"Please do not."

Belef stood up and put her pretend glasses back on.

"I see it all clearly. You want us to do the work for you."

"It is not the work for me. Please." He turned to Paolo. "Please do not." He wagged a finger at the camera.

"Aren't you the government?"

"I work *for* the government, but, Belef, this is no good for the village. No good."

"I stop no one, I tell no one nothing. And who am I? I am no one. You have said it yourself to me."

This angered the administrator. He looked back at the two policemen, before turning to Belef again. "It is illegal to disrupt the development plans. I have asked you, please do turn the camera off."

Paolo set the camera on a log, but Liz could see the recording light stayed lit.

"But I do nothing wrong."

"Nothing?" Raula stepped forward into the garden. "Is this a grave, Belef? Is this where Kasingen is buried? Isn't it illegal to bury bodies anywhere but the graveyard?"

Belef stood up. Raula was standing on top of the grave. He began to kick over the little crosses and shells. Belef's eyes, for the first time, showed fear. Liz wondered if Raula was here because of them, to perform this power play for the cameras.

"Are you keeping her close because you expect her to bring you money—to bring you law? You are malas, Belef. Malas. Bodies in the graveyard. There are rules for death. Rules!"

"I keep all them rules."

"You are a nothing troublemaker. Your husband was bad as. And I hear the stories of your followers breaking Christian law. I could have you taken to Wapini and put into the jail. I could have your house burned down and all your followers put into the jail. Napasio! Napasio!"

The tall woman appeared in the doorway of the house. She held her broom still and stared at Raula with open contempt.

"Do you want to go to jail? I can send you into jail too. I can send all of youse. You need to put your house in order, Belef." He lowered his voice. "Start going to church again. Stop all this nonsense."

Liz watched as Belef—her new sister—hawked and spat a red stain on the grass.

"One of the most important aspects of any religion," Liz whispered, "is how it deals with its dead." She peered behind her and the camera moved with her, seeing what she saw: A few meters distant, between two of the huge buttresses that supported the massive trunk of a date palm, Belef stood like a third buttress, pressing her forehead against the tree.

"Belef is in the process of what she calls 'talking on the telephone'—in this case through a hole in the side of the tree. And it's through these telephones—these portals in the natural world—that she contacts those who have passed on."

A long pause as Paolo came panning round the side of her face as she watched Belef.

"Did you get her lips moving? Can you move down there and do one more tracking shot where you get her lips?"

Margo wore a headscarf close over her skull, decorated with nautical motifs; it gave her a piratical if vaguely cancerous look. The orange laces on her hiking boots bounced as she stamped from decision to decision, cheered today by progress, by getting "shots in the can."

"Lizzie, let's do that long speech now. Just come in when you're ready."

Liz placed one hand a little awkwardly on the tree trunk and looked meaningfully at the lens.

"Again and again we find particular objects repeating in Belef's iconography—certain things that are good to *think* with. Some objects fulfill metaphysical needs with their physicality, so you get trees"—Liz knocked her knuckles on the tree trunk—"which exist both above and below ground. You get pools of water, running water, mountains, unusual natural phenomena—the shape of some rocks, the habits of certain animals. These are ways of doubling the world. There's no distinction, really, in Belef's worldview between the natural and the supernatural."

"Terrific—but can you go from 'These are ways of doubling'? I think you rushed that last sentence."

There was a pleasure, Liz was finding, to trailing along in Margo's wake, being told to face this way, to look up, to say that. Margo ducked and shielded the viewfinder to watch the take. It had to be done again. And then again. Part of the reason she sped through some words and fluffed others was that every PTC was simultaneously a piece to Paolo. They were a little shy with each other. Nothing had been mentioned about the night before. After they finished filming she crouched down beside him—he was cleaning a battery pack with a soft cloth—and asked, "Everything all right?" and he barely looked up.

"Have you seen the bubble wrap for my SLR lenses?"

"Isn't there a case?"

"The case fell out of a helicopter in Cuzco last month."

"Right. I haven't seen it. You sleep all right?"

"It was in this bag."

"I haven't seen it."

He stopped then and looked at her directly. "I slept well."

He smiled. It was an unexpected smile; it bestowed a kind of blessing. She wanted to see it again.

As they tramped back to the village from the telephone tree, Belef and Liz walked abreast for a while. Even Liz felt tall and angular next to her. Belef was one of those women who consisted of a series of circles: round face, round eyes, round cheeks, plump bosom. She carried a thick walking stick, which she didn't need. Her stride was purposeful, low slung, and it took no effort for her to avoid roots, rocks, marshy patches—everything Liz stumbled on or tripped over or squelched in.

"Can I ask what you talked about on the telephone today?"

Belef gave her a sly look.

"Mothers in the earth. Mothers in the earth who need to be straightened."

"What do you mean?"

Stan turned to look at Liz and Belef, and then dropped back to join them.

"There were many dongen underground and they all were talking at me."

"The ghosts of widows who were killed," Stan added.

"They killed widows?"

"They broke their necks."

"When?"

"Up till thirty, forty years ago."

Belef swung her snakehead stick to lop the heavy curling head off a fern.

"They said to me, 'Pikinini, I want to know why we of the underground were killed by all of youse. We of the underground were killed for what reason?'"

"Why *were* they killed?" Liz found her voice was quiet. "Was it a question of resources—"

"They said to me, 'Why was it that all the men worked at killing us?

You must talk about its meaning, what was the reason?' And I said I knew about this law, but I do not know about these times. I will ask the men and the men will give their answer to youse."

Belef swung her stick again, cutting a swathe through a patch of grass.

"I am the new God now and we do not kill them. I told my mother that. She was crying. 'Why they kill me? Why? What the reason?'"

In the evening, Liz and Margo sat outside their rest house, eating manioc from enamel tin bowls, and Margo made an attempt to gather the experiences of the day into a neat and simple explanatory package, tied with a bow. It reminded Liz somehow of her own sister. "It's plainly grief," Margo said. "It makes people mad."

"Do you think she's mad?" Liz asked.

"You don't?"

"She seems very sane. She just seems pissed off. It's a resistance movement, really. And she's negotiating how to deal with the dead, how to listen to them, how to keep them close."

"Hmm," Margo said, standing up. "I think you're taking it all a bit seriously." She threw the rest of the white slop in her bowl into the trees.

CHAPTER 23

"That's a heavy-looking sky."

"Do you want to stop at McElhinneys?"

"Have we time?"

"I mean afterwards."

"On the way back up?"

Ken didn't reply. The implication was too obvious: Wasn't that what "afterwards" meant? Where else would they be going but back up to Ballyglass from Mullingar? He shifted gear down to second with undisguised impatience, and pulled up behind a van going through the tollgate. Judith looked out the window at the low green fields, the tall metallic sky. A rainbow arced faintly out to the west and she kept it to herself.

"You got the two euros?"

"I just gave them to you."

"Did you speak to Alison?"

"She texted this morning."

"And?"

"She's OK."

"Did she ask about the kids?"

"Of course. I told her Trisha was happy to take them for the day."

"I don't know how she can stand it."

Judith said nothing.

Ken continued, "Don't you ever think . . . Don't you ever think that if a man like that knew what destruction he had brought—I mean really brought to people, how he'd ruined them—"

"Yes."

"What?"

"I'm agreeing with you."

"I haven't finished."

"Sorry."

"If he knew what he'd really done, he wouldn't be able to live."

It was a wee estate on the outskirts of Mullingar. The semi-detached was pebbledashed and Ken pushed the doorbell. Hugh Treacy was tall, bald, overweight, and possessed of less than the regulation number of upper teeth. A benign ogre in a navy velour tracksuit, he talked and talked as he ushered them into his small hot living room, where turf crackled in the grate and the blinds were shut.

"The cross was my grandmother's and before that I don't know. I don't think it's particularly old, though. Will you have tea?"

"Not for me, thank you. We stopped outside Louth and had a coffee."

"Oh very good."

Judith's heart had a kind of twisted energy in it now. She set her bag down on the little side table; it was covered with a lacy tablecloth, galactic swirls of crochet. It was yellow and Judith couldn't decide if it was age or dirt or meant to be yellow. She noticed that every surface in the room was covered with drapes, materials, fringes.

"My wife had a brain tumor and she prayed on it," said Hugh Treacy, without preamble.

"And how is she now?" asked Ken.

"Ach, she's dead. She died, unfortunately."

Judith looked at Ken, who was staring hard at the fire. She could see his determination to keep his temper; it was in the set of his mouth, the clasp of his hands.

"Sit yourselves down. I'm just going to get it."

Hugh disappeared, and a cushion came alive in the depths of the sofa, stretched itself, and walked along the sofa arm.

"Hello, puss puss," said Kenneth and scratched the cat's neck.

Judith perched on the edge of a rickety wooden seat by the little drop-leafed dining table. A pack of cards—branded with Benson & Hedges—sat by a folded up *Irish News* with a half-completed quick crossword. A little vista of the lonely days of Hugh Treacy unfolded itself before her.

"I see you met Buster. Aw he's a terror."

Hugh stood in the doorway, cradling the cross, his smooth brown eyes shining. It was maybe eighteen inches tall, and he set it on the coffee table in front of them. Old carved dark bogwood, naked, no Jesus. It had a circular copper base. He pulled a prayer card from a bookshelf stuffed with John Grisham and Patricia Cornwell novels.

"Ken?"

"Yes."

"No, don't stand up. Now I want Judith—if you could place both your hands on the cross here."

Hugh held his white puffy hands out and Judith leaned forward and rested her own hands on the cross's bar. Ken saw the nervousness in the pools of his wife's eyes, and it made him straighten his back and square his shoulders and give her a little supportive smile. Her own shoulders were hunched forward in sorrow and apology. Hugh moved around them, arranging. He set the prayer card beside the cross.

"And if you read this prayer out three times while Judith holds the cross. I'm going to leave you to it now."

Hugh held the door to the kitchen open for Buster, who gave one bored clean yawn and paraded out first, steered by his tail.

They sat facing each other now across the coffee table. Their eyes made contact—for the millionth time in the forty-four years they'd shared—and Judith raised her eyebrows. Like all long marriages, theirs had been sustained by many forms of surrender and deceit and kindness, but in all those forty-four years they had never prayed together. Ken again tried to reassure her by widening and brightening his glance back at her.

"Shall I start?"

"Yes."

"I should turn my phone off."

"Yes."

He did that and then picked up the card and read out the prayer.

"Lord, we ask that you look upon the sick with eyes of mercy. May your healing hand be set upon us. May your life-giving powers flow into every cell of our bodies and into the depths of our souls, cleansing, purifying, and restoring us to wholeness and strength for service in your kingdom. Though we cannot see a way, Lord, we are sure that you can. Amen."

Hugh must have been listening at the door. As soon as Ken had finished reading the prayer the third time—his voice getting stronger each time—he pushed the door open, and smiled at them.

"All done?"

"All done."

"Now you're more than welcome to come back any time you like."

"Ah, well, it's a long enough drive."

"You're Ballyglass, aren't you?"

"We are."

"Do you know O'Neill's Butchers? Declan would be a cousin of my mother."

"Oh very good."

Kenneth stood and put his sports jacket back on. Judith was already by the door.

She said, "Can we pay you for your time?"

"Ah, well, I can't take any money for myself, obviously. But if you want to leave me fifty euros, say, I'll give it to a charity."

Ken slid his wallet out of his jacket and plucked a note from it. He laid it carefully on the table by the pack of cards.

It was a relief to get back out to the pale light of afternoon, the cold air. Judith felt curiously weightless, almost floated to the car.

"Thanks for coming down with me. I'm sure it was all a waste of time."

"Not a problem."

"Wave to him. He's stood at the doorway."

Both of them waved.

"The house was so hot and dark," noted Ken.

"I feel I should try everything," said his wife very quietly, hardly aiming to be heard. "Might as well."

"Which charity do you think the money'll go to? The Hugh Treacy Memorial Fund?"

"Shall we stop at McElhinneys?"

"Do you want to?"

"I think about it sometimes. About when it began to grow and I never noticed."

She felt the warmth of the prayer, of the blessing, fade out as he started the car.

He held his hand to the key a long time and looked stoically out of the windscreen. "Just one of those things."

"Do you think it was there the summer Isobel was born?"

Ken didn't reply.

"I know you don't want to talk about it."

Ken stayed silent. He pulled out of the estate and onto the N14. The steering wheel passed under his hands smoothly, the car swallowed the tarmac.

"I don't see what the point is," he said eventually.

"*I* want to talk about it," Judith said quickly. "That's the point. Don't I get to talk about it if I want to?"

"Of course," Ken said softly.

"It's inside me, not you."

She had the sudden sense that in all their years together she had failed utterly to get a single point across. If they dovetailed together, if they fitted, it was only because she had deformed and shaped herself out of all recognition. Where was that glossy, hopeful little girl with the navy book bag and the hairclip with red butterflies on it?

CHAPTER 24

"**T**his is the second most holy place of the Story. Do you see the rocks over there?"

Five rocks poked up out of the water.

"I see them. Are they engines?"

Belef gave Liz a saddened look and said, "The first is the Gold stone. This is where all the money come from on the last day. The next one, the sharp one, is the Power stone and help us make the new law. On the last day it make the country level and easy to work, easy to plant. These other three stones are the Story of the old times. The pointed one is the tries of our first parents to make the white man's life. It failed us. The flat one means the tries of our last parents, but it also failed. And this stone—the last, the largest—it means us, the Story. And it will not fail."

"And where did you learn this?"

"The Big Boss told me in my sleep."

"And what happens here?"

"You will see."

"What will we see?"

"What happens here."

Margo nodded to tell Liz to keep on.

"Can you tell us about how the Story explains the world? How did the world come to be?"

"The pool holds the spirits of the ancestors, and when we chant here and dance the ancestors hear us. The frogs cry back, the birds make answer, the fish jumps from the water."

"But who made this place?"

Belef nodded, preparing to explain. She held out one calloused hand, palm up.

"This is Dodo, the creator. He sent his son Manup"—the other hand came up—"to Sydney and Manup built the city for the white kanaka. He wanted to come here, to New Ulster, but the whites tricked him. He died in Sydney and became the ghost who entered Mary, and was reborn as Jesus. But the Jews didn't want to share the cargo. They captured Jesus to stop him getting to New Ulster and killed him." She put two fingers to her throat and pressed. "They killed the Black Jesus who was coming to save us."

She spoke factually, without much emotion, but her eyes burned bright and clear. Liz felt the gaze pushing against her person. She shifted on the rock and asked, "And do you believe in a Second Coming?"

"We believe He will come again—Amulmul has told us—and when the new Jesus comes he will give us what is ours."

Margo gave her the thumbs-up and Liz let the look linger between them.

"And cut. Great. Belef, if you come off the rock. Liz, can you talk about what that means—let's move you round to face this way—"

Belef slipped off into the forest. She was not beholden to formal entrances and exits, staying for as long as something was interesting to her, leaving when she had something else to do, and apparently never feeling the need to alert others in either case. For a moment Liz felt an intense envy. She turned and spoke to camera.

"It's becoming clear to me that the Story is a syncretic structure . . ."

"Lizzie, can we hold off with words like that? BBC Two, not BBC Four. Simply as you can."

"It's becoming clear that the Story is a mix of Christianity and the traditional myths Christianity displaced. Manup and Dodo are part of a creation narrative common on the island, but Belef has also brought modern elements into the mix, such as the imagery of technology, which seems to the indigenous mind miraculous—these machines like aeroplanes and tractors."

As Liz spoke she became aware of a low rumbling, a chanting that varied in intensity and pitch. Margo held her hand up to stop her speaking. Paolo swiveled the camera on its tripod to point it across the river, towards the source of the sound. Among the trees figures began to appear. They wore native clothes, grass skirts, loincloths. There were maybe fifty men and women, all naked from the waist up. Some held hands, some carried babies or trailed children behind them. They moved slowly, and sang in pidgin or Mouk, then repeated a line in a rough, strangely accented English. There was a happy emptiness in their eyes.

> *Wait and see the sky crowded with airplanes,*
> *Wait and see the sea crowded with ships,*
> *We will sit down like whites at the tables,*
> *Amulmul will make us all rich.*

At the water's far edge they halted, looking across occasionally at the camera crew but not otherwise acknowledging their presence, not making any sign to them. Leftie was there, his bilum strapped across his forehead, and then Belef appeared, somehow on the other side of the river, changed into a man's filthy white shirt, and she had put her yachting cap on. She was the only one not in native dress. The people's song changed when she appeared:

> *Black Papa will come to save us.*
> *Black Papa will come for he loves us.*

Belef stepped into the water, her face serene, abstracted to a higher plane—though she still managed to throw a few glances at the camera. In she walked until she was up to her waist, and beckoned to Leftie, who took the shoulders of a flat-chested teenage girl wearing only a grass skirt and pushed her forward. Fearfully she stepped into the river, looked back at someone on the bank, and waded on. As she got to Belef she stumbled slightly and Belef caught her. They stood hugging in the water for a few seconds and then Belef ducked her backwards in a full immersion, like a ballroom dancer might dip his partner. She held her there for a moment and then the girl erupted, dripping, still holding her nose, her eyes opened wide. She gave a little shriek of happiness. Belef pulled a red string from under her cap and tied it round the girl's wrist while the watchers behind on the riverbank cheered and banged sticks on the trees, and there was a scramble to be the next baptized. They pawed at Leftie and he ordered them in, one by one. After ten or so—old, young, male, female—had been transformed by the water, Belef raised her hand and the chatter stopped.

"All our lives," she shouted, "we give 'em to the Story."

She took off her cap and held it to her chest and closed her eyes.

"We ask you Papa to open the road, to forgive our stupid fathers for their sins against you and to send us the good cargo. O Papa, we have been waiting this long time. We did what you wanted and we watched the white skins take all that you wanted to give to *us*. We will not forgive them their trespasses, Papa. We ask you to send Amulmul the snake to chase the rubbishmen away. We ask you to send us our things from Sydney and Heaven and Brisbane, to send us fridgerators and the motorcars, guns and bigscreens and radios. We ask in the name of Black Jesus, who will come to save us. Amen in Black Jesus. Amen in Black Jesus. Amen in Amulmul."

The crowd answered, "Amen in Black Jesus, Amen in Amulmul."

It was just after lunch, but Liz had an urge to climb into her sleeping bag. She wriggled down into the bag inside the mosquito net in the back room of the rest house. She wanted to insulate herself as much as possible. A bag in a net in a box on the side of a mountain of trees. She imagined some hand reaching down from the sky and lifting the lid of the hut and finding her, exposed, squirming like a maggot. She turned over on her back and looked through the gauze at the outline of the rafters, the thatch roof. Manioc with rice, rice with manioc, taro with rice, manioc with taro, assorted non-identifiable greens—she should have brought some pasta and a jar of pesto. She lay on her back for a while and thought of Belef's face. It seemed to be coming at her if she closed her eyes, looming out of the mind's dark. She lifted one side of the net and looked out. A bulbous thumb-sized reddish spider negotiated its crazily long legs—like guy-ropes tied to its body's hot air balloon—across the plastic sheeting on the floor, towards her. One leg after another was freed and waved around and refastened. She dropped the net and used one of Margo's sandals to weight it in place. The wall separating their quarters from Paolo and Stan's was like a world map, though not of this world. Continents of white-bubbled mold. Everything in this place grew on the back of something else—eating it, rotting it, strangling it. Everything was on the turn. Everything stank. A tropical stench, things feeding on other things. Missionaries preying on natives. This morning a dog gnawing on the carcass of another dog behind the hut.

How did Belef know she was "in grief"? What did she mean they had both died some years ago but did not know it? Belef defied the surface of things. She resisted the men of the world. Her unwillingness to submit to Werner or Raula or Usai or whoever . . . She was an answer to a question Liz was unaware of asking, but still Belef offered her some clarification, some reply, some understanding of the world system as it really was beneath the sheen of its accepted and inequitable surface. There was a wildness in her, some terrible knowledge, a certainty, a base refusal—Liz found herself smiling up at the hanging knot of the mosquito net. All they wanted was to bring Belef into line. But she would not go. She would not.

Liz got her notepad out and tried to write up the day's filming. She had a halfhearted idea of trying to get a book out of the trip. But she felt insufficiently rational to make proper sentences. She thought of the baptism, and tried to write out her feelings when she'd watched it. What she had sensed at the edge of her consciousness was that she too wanted to be held in the cold rushing waters and to rise again, cleansed, reborn, grinning with salvation. In her notebook she wrote, *We saw*—she crossed the verb out. *We witnessed the mass hysteria of religion in action. Query: Immune system responses? Q: Attaining in-group status? Q: Water as process of rebir—*

Voices outside, raised, at some distance.

In front of Belef's house a crowd had gathered. Two men hunkered on the ground—she recognized them as disciples from the river. They looked like brothers, though many of the men here looked like brothers. Between them, being loosely held by them, sat the boy with white in his hair. It wasn't feathers or flowers, in fact, but little bits of white root, rhizomes, or pulp perhaps, which he had woven into his thick Afro. Big-eyed and fearful, he clutched his bilum in front of him and in it were little packets of stitched leafs. He talked very quickly and in a high-pitched voice, but Liz couldn't catch anything.

Paolo, using the smaller camera, was filming. It was a courtroom scene playing out. Belef sat up on her log, judge on her bench. Margo stood a few feet by Stan, out of shot, wearing huge insectile sunglasses. Liz whispered to them, "What's going on?"

"I can't make out all of it," Stan said, "but the boy's called Namor, and Leftie brought him to Belef. That's his pig."

He pointed to a huge pig—the one they'd seen him leading through the village—tethered now to one of the posts marking out the garden of the nearest hut. It lay on its stomach, massive head on the ground, and watched the proceedings from its tiny eyes with considerable interest.

"Why?"

"A lot of them have pigs. They spend their days wandering and come back at night, to be fed. They don't usually take them round, although—"

"No, I mean why is he here? What's happened?"

"I think he's been selling relics, the skin of Amulmul."

Belef threw a glance at them to stop them talking and leaned back on her log, legs apart, one hand on either thigh, her flowery skirt dipping in the middle. The court was now in session.

She motioned to Napasio, who scurried into the hut and reappeared with a few small green betel nuts and a little gourd of lime. Belef tore at the husk of betel nut with her teeth and started chewing, then after a while daintily scooped out a trace of the white powder with a little wooden spatula, wrapped it in a leaf, and popped the package in her mouth. All the time she regarded the boy, not kindly nor with any particular malevolence. She spat between her feet, chewed some more, spat again.

"Namor," she said finally, "raise up."

The boy stood and was walked forward, towards her, by his guards. He was tiny, nine or ten, and so thin his little thighs were the width of Belef's upper arms.

"What have you in bilum?" Belef demanded, and Namor made no move to respond, so she asked again, in pidgin or Mouk, and the boy came forward and opened the bag for her. The English was for their benefit. Belef drew out a small leaf parcel, and then another and another, setting them in the lap of her skirt.

She looked at Liz.

"This boy, he found the skin of Amulmul. The skin Amulmul leaves behind."

Liz asked, "The snake god?"

Belef nodded severely.

"He is many things. He is half snake, half human, and the father of us all, father of Jesus and Manup and Moses and Dodo, of Moro and Titikolo. The world came out of the great snake Amulmul like an egg. Or he made this"—she made a motion of vomiting—"and the world came."

She grinned around the circle at her disciples. Her eyes were wide and Liz felt an apprehension in her presence that she hadn't felt before. There was a sharp edge to her showmanship.

"Ah, and here are kina. Kina and toea."

She tore open one of the leaf parcels and let the little copper coins fall into her hand. The boy with white hair looked at her without expression now.

"Namor tried to steal from the Story, and he must be punished."

A woman holding a baby stepped forward—young, maybe twenty-five, but clearly Namor's mother. She said something desperate sounding in Koriam, then spoke in halting English. "Belef, please. Namor is such young'un. He not know—"

"We love our children, Mosling. All us love our children. But the gods we must love more."

She raised a hand to prevent further interruptions and opened another of the small packages in her lap. She drew out a transparent scrap of something, and rubbed it between her fingers. She smelt it. She touched it with her tongue. Then she held it against her ear, narrowed her eyes in an expression of intense listening, and finally she nodded.

"Truly, this is his skin. Amulmul has returned to us, to open the road for cargo."

While Belef held the tiny clear fragment to the light, the onlookers murmured and sighed and a few of them clapped.

"See. Leftie, bring it to 'em."

Delicately Leftie took the relic, pinching it in a large rubbery leaf. He walked among the crowd, the faithful, his eyes darting from the object to the faces of the flock. When he got to them, Margo said, "May I?" and Leftie had not time to object before she'd lifted it and pursed her lips and handed it to Liz. The relic was a tiny piece of bubble wrap—a tiny piece of Paolo's missing sheet, with the bubble popped. Liz set it back on the leaf and looked at Margo, who was refusing to meet her eye. The relic was returned to Belef, resealed in its leaf. Napasio went into the hut and came out with an empty tin can. The rest of the little leaf packets, each presumably containing a scrap of bubble wrap, were ceremoniously transferred from Namor's bilum into the can.

"And where you find it?" Belef asked, "Yu gatim we?"

"Tractor Rock," the small voice said.

"The snake needs to rub itself against a stone to loose up the old skin. We have all seen this."

A few of the onlookers nodded at the truth of this.

"And you did not want the Story to have it? Amulmul returns, and behind him leaves this to tell us. And you take it and you hide it? You try to stop the Story? You have made my stomach hot. You have made all our stomachs hot."

Namor said nothing.

"And more again you sell the skin for kina for your pockets." She shook her head sadly, and addressed the circle. "Namor tried to keep the return of Amulmul for himself. He tried to turn profit on it."

She looked back at the boy and shook her head.

"You forget that Amulmul means riches for everyone. It means the road is open, but you sell his skin for these coins that have no use, that make rubbish. What work have we for coins? We will receive the treasure Amulmul has in store for us. The rivers will get wide and deep and the land flatten out and ships will come up them and they will be loaded with cargo. The sky overhead will be full of planes coming to give us cargo."

She made a sucking sound through her teeth.

"You all know me. You know that I have been up to certain places. I have spoken on the telephone to Amulmul, father of you and father of me and father of all the birds and pigs and creepy-crawlies. Our old ones chased Amulmul away and he went to the whites, and gave them the cargo. But he wants to come back. He wants to come back to us. But the whites will not let him."

She clapped her hands once, hard. An electric thrill passed through Liz, through the crowd.

"And we are still punished for the longlong stupidness and bikhet and pighead of our fathers. And Namor shows Amulmul more of this longlong work. And now Namor must be punished."

The boy's head was downcast. His body went limp, and the two men at his side had to hold him up.

Belef brought a finger to her cheek and held it there, then pointed it at the boy.

"Five strokes and lime in the cuts."

Napasio nodded and went inside the hut, reappearing with a lithe switch the length of the boy. His yellow T-shirt was yanked up by one of his guards and his little brown back looked so smooth. He made a little puppet dance of resistance but went nowhere. Liz started to move forward, to explain, to stop it, and Margo took hold of her arm. She gave it a hard pinch, and added a warning look.

"Shouldn't we—"

"No," Margo hissed, "we should not."

Leftie stepped forward and took the sapling. He looked at Belef, who nodded her sad assent. Efficiently the strokes were administered. When the first lash connected, the boy's body jerked forward and he gave a little yelp. From then on he made no movement or noise. Paolo stealthily moved round the circle to film him from the front and he zoomed in for a close-up on his face for the last two strokes. Could they even show this? Leftie paused for Paolo to get back in position.

"He's bleeding quite badly."

"He'll be fine," Margo whispered.

The boy stood shaking and giving out little bleats of sadness. There was a stony satisfaction in some of the onlookers' faces, but others were twisted in upset. Belef nodded at Leftie, who, grimly unsmiling, retrieved a clump of white lime powder from the gourd on the ground and smeared it on the boy's back. Released, the boy fell on his knees and began coughing out angry tearless sobs. Napasio took the baby now, so Namor's mother, Mosling, could go to the boy and fall on her knees and embrace him. Belef strode towards them—Liz thought she was about to pull them apart and remonstrate with the woman—but she crouched and hugged both of them, and all three of them were in a huddle crying together. Belef looked up, her face lit with grief and righteousness, and shouted at Liz, "But it is *good news*! Amulmul has returned. The Story has beginning."

Sarah sat outside the rest house on the log bench, an unopened book balanced on skinny brown knees. Her blond hair was tied back and she wore black sunglasses. She might have been a Valley girl on the bleachers at the local high school—but the valley she was staring down into was the Wahgi, a vast earth wound of a hundred miles of rumpled green jungle and mosquito swamps haunted by hunter-gatherers who'd never seen a white man, who lived now as they had lived for millennia.

"That's a fat book," Liz said in greeting.

"Oh, hi." She held it up. "Same one. *Great Expectations*. I don't know that I'll ever finish it."

"You like it?"

"I do. I mean he does go on."

"He does."

She stood up, and took a step towards Liz then stopped and folded her arms, holding the book across her chest.

"So Mum thought you might want to, like, think about moving into our storeroom."

Liz laughed.

"Your mother's a wise woman."

"It was so wet last night."

"It was wet, it was cold, it was sort of frightening. Are you sure it would be all right? I'm not great with bugs, I've realized. Or rain."

A real glass window with a metal grille. Real plaster on the walls. Malour, their head porter, and his little toothless buddy in the orange woolly hat carried their bags up to the compound and Liz and Margo sat on camp beds in the storeroom, absurdly delighted to be beneath a bare electric bulb and this corrugated iron roof.

In the Mission's washhouse, even though the water pressure was feeble and the little drizzle just warm enough to stand in, it became almost impossible to get out of the shower. After days of sweat and dirt, the water took on epic properties; she felt it as ritual, as rebirth. She lifted her face up to it, let it thrum against her forehead, against her eyelids and cheeks, stream down her nose and gather in the little hollows of her collar bones . . . Finally she ratcheted it off and saw that on the pipe behind the showerhead a little frog sat watching her contentedly with completely black eyes.

She was writing up her notes, trying to describe some of what had happened: *Belef's movement clearly embodies a wish of the people of the Slinga district—of New Ulster, I suppose—to be liberated from forms of control. We might cite the late-stage colonialism of the New Truth, the imposed nationalism of the country of Papua New Guinea on eight hundred or so different language groups, the insidious pressures that capitalism takes, even here. But we also see in Belef's Story, the people's desires being co-opted and integrated into NEW forms of social control— disciplinary practices like the whipping of Namor, his public shaming, the enacted rituals of forgiveness, etc. . . . . It is only by strict adherence to*

*these new edicts that she claims the cargo will come. But how long can
you enforce belief based on some future event occurring? How long can
Belef promise and not deliver?* Here Liz drew a little asterisk, then, at the
bottom of the page, its twin, and wrote: *Of course, Christians have been
waiting for two thousand years for their own cargo! The trick is to keep
them on edge—on red alert—"one cannot know the hour." The event is
always just around the corner, always just about—*

Writing quickly in a notebook is like whispering furiously into someone's ear; anyone else in the room assumes you're talking about them, and
Margo sat up suddenly and said, "Look, I know *completely* where you're
coming from on this, but all I was trying to say was we have to remain
neutral. It had nothing to do with us. We're observers. What Belef does is
up to her. I mean it's fly on the wall, and that tradition of reportage is
not—you know—it's not inherently a bad tradition."

"It was *our* bubble wrap."

"He could have found that anywhere."

Liz didn't bother replying. She lodged her ballpoint in her notebook
and set it on the lino, then lay back on the bed and looked up into a sur-
vivalist's fantasy. Above her towered orderly shelves of packets, jars,
boxes, and tins: pasta, flour, sugar, coffee, and all manner of vegetables
and fruits in syrup. Kenneth would have surveyed the room and given an
approving nod, and his eldest daughter had inherited his ability to feel
soothed—or at least marginally less agitated—by the presence of an epic
amount of nonperishable foodstuffs.

She said, "If there's an earthquake I'll be taken out by tinned corn."

Margo lay back down, deciding to be placated.

"I have kidney beans. Who likes kidney beans?"

"I suppose it's whatever they get sent."

"I'm sure they make a shopping list out and it gets delivered."

"You don't think it's donations?"

"It's not like there's a food drive for missionaries. Or maybe there is."

There was an indecisive knock at the door and Sarah's head appeared.
"Everything OK?"

Liz propped herself up on her elbows.

"Thanks so much for this."

"Will you guys come over for dinner?"

"You know, we should probably eat with poor Paolo and Stan. They're stuck in the hut."

"They could come too."

Paolo refused, having discovered that the bodyguard Posingen possessed a large bag of marijuana and was happy to share it. Besides, he and Stan had plans to go with Malour into the forest later to look for an albino cuscus that a porter had seen the previous night. So only Liz and Margo sat holding hands with the Family Werner while Josh, at the head of the table, lengthily articulated grace. It seemed overly intimate and unnatural to Liz to hold hands with these people, but there was also a kind of ancient power here. As soon as she'd touched Esther's and Noah's hot little hands she felt the voltage of it—to make a circle, a human ring, warding off whatever forces gathered outside it. She watched Noah, the little three-year-old, open his eyes, his head still meekly dipped, and wait for his father to finish talking.

Margo had her eyes tightly closed, an open helpless look on her face that Liz hadn't seen before; a great affection for her producer blossomed in her. Josh spoke the usual routine of gratitude and petition. He thanked, he asked, he hoped that Belef might come to know the error of her ways and return to the fold. Thanking and asking, thanking and asking. Waiting. Hoping. Prayer was much like sending in your shopping list, Liz thought, but getting back random donations, whatever God had knocking around in the back of his cupboard. You wanted corn, you got kidney beans. Amen. Liz shut her eyes.

Amen in Amulmul.

"So how did the British Broadcasting Corporation get on today?"

There was an edge in Josh's question but Margo was unfazed.

"I've got to say I think it's going to work very well. Belef has a lot of charisma. I mean I know you've had your differences, but she comes across very well on camera. She has a naturalness, and a real power, and the whole setup, the scenery, the little children . . . it's going to be beautiful."

"It's certainly a stunning part of the world you live in," Liz added, neutrally she hoped.

"And the stories she has about everything. She'd have been brilliant in brand management," Margo said and laughed, alone. "Or in advertising," she persisted.

Everything in Josh's face tightened, like someone had pulled the skin from behind.

"Will you come to church in the morning, do you think?"

Margo speared a piece of fried pork and held it in midair.

"Would you like us to?"

"I think it might be good in the interest of balance. For your program. To show what Christianity has actually achieved here. What we're dealing with, what we're trying by God's grace to do."

"Of course we'll come," Liz said, and Sarah smiled her small closed-mouth smile.

The talk turned to the politics of New Ulster, the corruption, the AIDS epidemic, the drug problems, the "rascal gangs" who ran the towns. The government was useless and crooked, lining their pockets with international funds meant to kick-start fair-trade coffee industries or organic coconut plantations or whatnot. There was still large-scale intertribal war. The poverty was astonishing. Women were treated as chattels. Children were beaten and abused. Men sat around all day chewing betel nut or getting high. The country needed stricter governance, leaders of stature, a vastly improved infrastructure . . . and the answer to all of these problems, it turned out, was God. It seemed to Liz that Josh was living out the longings of a mystic who'd pitched up in the desert two thousand years or so ago. He'd staked his life—and his wife's, his children's lives, the little time he'd got on this good green earth—on something he could neither see nor hear. He had a hunch, a feeling in his gut, and on that he'd bet the farm. As Liz watched him talk, his liquid eyes shining, she found herself almost admiring him. Again and again he rubbed his chin in wonderment and looked from Liz to Margo for some validation of his choices.

As Liz scraped a little desperately around the bowl for the final vestiges of pink strawberry mousse, he said, "And I hear there was some hooping and hollering this afternoon."

"How'd you mean?" Margo asked, knowing perfectly well how he meant.

"I hear Belef attacked a young child."

There was a silence.

"Jojo got whipped," said Jess, with a certain curt brutality that seemed to give a flash of something dark beneath the All-American mom exterior. Only now had she sat down, and started to eat her dinner of cold pork and rice and floppy boiled greens.

"There was an incident, yes. It was certainly unpleasant," Margo said, shifting gear into a formal seriousness. She was always impressive in this mode.

"Jojo?" Liz said, "I thought he was called Namor."

"He was called Jojo before she baptized him into her cult. She changes their names. It's—well, it's a way of throwing her weight around, I suppose," Jess said, now meek again, eyes wide at the very idea of a woman throwing her weight around.

"Can I leave the table?" asked Esther, the ten-year-old, possessor of one magic dimple and an irritatingly scratchy voice.

"That kind of viciousness, that kind of wickedness . . . The problem is she has a little knowledge, but not a lot, not enough." Josh wagged his spoon. "Proverbs 29:18 says, 'Where there is no vision, the people perish.' A newer translation might say something like, 'Where there is no revelation, the people cast off restraint.' The Spanish version of the Bible—I did a year in Venezuela—says, '*Donde no hay visión, el pueblo se desenfrena*—Where there is no instruction about God, the people don't have any *brakes*.' Belef has no brakes. I see it. I know it."

Josh motioned a car speeding along the tabletop gathering speed.

"She saw a book of ours, one of Sarah's. It was a guide to the national museum in Sydney. We'd gone there as a family for a faith refresher course, and the kids had spent a day at the museum with one of the junior pastors."

"Can we play badminton?" Esther asked.

Jess nodded.

"It was a lovely way to renew our beliefs. We saw the opera house, and we had the most wonderful boat trip out into the bay—"

"Tell them, Sarah. Tell them what she did." But his daughter was not quick enough. "She was sitting in Sarah's room looking at this book one afternoon when she was meant to be doing the washing—and she got enraged by it."

"It was the pictures of the exhibits," Sarah said. She looked down at the table. The *thwock* of a shuttlecock from outside.

"They'd put their idols in glass cases," Jess added. "You know, in the museum. The graven images. All the funny little wooden figures."

"Totems, they're called," Liz said.

"Well, whatever they're called, she saw the photographs of that and she got mad, like *really* mad," Sarah said. She was very slowly peeling a red apple with a dinner knife: the apple was a compromise, in lieu of the strawberry mousse she'd refused.

Josh elaborated, "I came back from a vestry meeting and she was standing in front of the house shouting. She was cursing, saying all of them had been told by us that these gods of theirs, these statues and carvings and idols they kept in the haus tambaran were worthless—but now here they were being kept in a special house in Sydney. In a glass house. In a glass cage. Because they were so powerful. Did we ever find that book, by the way? Things just disappear here. Anything you leave outside overnight just goes. Anyway, she was giving quite a speech. There was a crowd gathered round. It was undermining. Undermining to the mission. And the anger. Like a switch had been flicked. There was no question. I knew immediately of course we'd have to let her go."

"It's time for your bed, little man," Jess said then, scooping Noah out of his high seat, ingeniously fashioned from an ordinary chair, a fruit crate, a cushion, and a luggage strap.

"Her view was: 'We've been tricked!'" Sarah offered. She set the half-naked apple on the table; it was plain she wouldn't eat it. "That the white people had stolen their gods and kept them for themselves. That they'd lied and if those gods were not worth anything, why did they lock them up? Why did people come to see them?"

Josh laughed his tinny laugh: *Har har har.* He said, "I mean, how do you *begin* to explain something like that?"

CHAPTER 25

Flight BA187 descended from the blue through the immaculate clouds. The plane entered an underworld of muted grays and greens. Rain throbbed across the round-cornered window.

"We'll be glad of our jumpers."

"Yeah."

Alison's anxiety came out in little well-worn patterns of speech. All morning, as soon as her mind saw a phrase bobbing in the distance it had leapt on it like a life ring. For his part Stephen said less and less. She noticed his bottle of diazepam had been left out that morning and had asked if she could take one. It hadn't done anything except make her fall asleep on the minibus to the airport. When she woke the anxiety was just the same as before, as if she were connected to a higher current than normal. Reality was coming up to meet them at three hundred miles an hour. As the plane bumped onto the runway, Alison took Stephen's hand in hers and squeezed it tight.

She thought of the kids. She knew what children said and did to each other up close; she'd seen it again and again, and little Isobel already found the slightest unkindness intolerable. A girl in her class called Jenny had once given a marble to all the other girls but her and told them they were now the Marble Club, and Isobel was not a member. She cried for an hour on her lap. She would have to toughen up. At least she'd have the summer and maybe by the autumn it would have died down a bit. But what about when they grew up and read about it? How could she explain?

In Ballyglass they'd called at the house but there was no one there, and finally her mum answered her mobile. They were in a café, they'd head back. Alison sat oddly frozen on the edge of a sofa arm with her phone in her hand for a long ten minutes, and then stood to attention when she heard the key in the lock. She observed Judith greeting Stephen in the hall with a quick kiss, not meeting his eye, and thought: Can we do twenty years of *this*? But Mickey's wailing at being both woken up and parted from his grandmother was enough distraction for them all to pretend that normality—at least for the moment—had been resumed.

Stephen reached out for Isobel and Judith noticed that her granddaughter responded by hugging her mother's legs and positioning herself behind Alison, where she stood now, peeping out. Alison's arms were bare and brown and goosebumped.

"You've got good color. How was it?"

"We'd a nice time. Hotel was good. Food was good."

"I'm just going up to make some calls, Judith," said Stephen.

"You go ahead."

"Your hair's nice," Alison said and Judith touched the side of the arrangement of highlights, and gave the slightest narrowing of her eyes.

"I haven't had it redone."

Alison beckoned her into the kitchen and said in barely a whisper, "I feel on edge the whole time. He's hardly spoken about it."

"Do you want him to?"

"I don't know."

Alison turned on the television on the counter for the children and took two packets of crisps from the tall cupboard.

"What can I do?"

"Nothing. I'm worried about him. About his job. And the kids. And you and Dad. What have people been saying?"

"It's been OK. A lot of people said to Kenneth they felt for him."

"Who?"

"In the golf club. Protestants *and* Catholics."

Alison was aware that a formal distance had arisen between her and her mother. They stood on opposite sides of a border, in different countries. Her parents were the unhappy victims of history, ambushed by circumstance—but to choose Stephen, as Alison had, meant complicity.

She could hear the intermittent rumble of Stephen talking through the ceiling.

"He's ringing Jason Newell, his boss at Glencore, to see if he still has a job."

"They can't fire him over something he did in his past."

"Depends on whether he told them. And depends on whether it stops him doing his job. Like if the other guys don't want to be on site—"

They heard Stephen coming down the stairs and Alison stopped.

In the afternoon Stephen disappeared to do a "message." Half an hour later the kids spotted him in the driveway with a huge box visible in the boot. They stood on the sofa to follow his progress through the front window, lugging the huge thing towards them, surely towards them. He got a rapturous greeting in the hallway.

Isobel tried to pry the cardboard walls of the box apart with her hands.

"And look, Mickey look, there's a slide. And ooh there's a swing. Can I help? Can we help you? Are there monkey bars on it? Can you make it? Can you make it now?"

"I'm going to do that. Can you give me a minute to get the toolbox?"

"I'm going to swing," Isobel said, holding imaginary ropes on either side of her shoulders and tilting her head up and down.

Her brother looked up at her, wide-eyed, and said dramatically, "Her going to swinnnngggg."

"Just stand back there, Isobel, stand back, and pull Mickey back too."

Stephen already cut his thumb on the inside of one of the tubes and he hadn't even unpacked all the pieces. The metal tubes looked too thin, and the ropes for the swing were cheap nylon.

"When will it be done?" Isobel said.

"Oh honey, it'll be a while yet. I haven't even found the instructions. Can I take a baby wipe?

"Wipey wipey," Mickey said, and offered the packet.

"I just need to go and put a Band-Aid on this."

The cut was deeper than he'd thought, and every time he applied any pressure to his thumb it bled. By the time he'd got the bare skeleton, the four-legged mainframe, constructed, every piece of bright blue tubing bore several bloody thumbprints.

"Is it ready yet?" Isobel whined. She sat on the back doorstep, pulling petals from a daisy.

"Can you please stop asking me that, honey? Why don't you go inside and watch the end of *The Jungle Book*."

"I want to swing."

"Swinggggg," Mickey echoed, looking up from a piece of cardboard he was stabbing with a screwdriver.

"You shouldn't have that," Stephen said, and lifted the screwdriver from him, precipitating a wailing that was not stopped by the presentation of an adjustable spanner, a spirit level, or the bubble wrap the screws came in. Finally Stephen handed him back the screwdriver.

"All right, all right, knock yourself out."

At the first spot, as soon as he'd gone down about four inches, he hit stone. The builder of these houses, who'd bulldozed the UDR center to make way for them, must have just dumped a load of the rubble in their back gardens.

"Stand back. You two! Stand back."

Stephen swung the spade over his head and brought it down with a crack. His hands shook painfully with the reverberation. Isobel gave a nasty little chortle and Mickey clapped with glee. He'd have to dig around it, lever it out, whatever it was. He was hot now, and he stopped and took his flannel shirt off. His T-shirt was already wet with sweat.

"Stephen, can you put this up?" Isobel whined.

"What do you mean?"

"Can you put the swing on?"

"You can't use it until the legs have been buried."

"I won't."

The frame stood at the other end of the garden, by the back door. Isobel was holding out the swing to him. Couldn't she call him Daddy? He'd asked Alison about it on the honeymoon; he wanted it to happen, and she said she'd tell the kids when they got back that he was their new daddy. It sounded so cheeky when she called him Stephen, like she was making fun of him.

He heard the back door next door being unlocked and then the neighbor Eric's footsteps going down his gravel path.

"Can you put the swing on, with the ropes?"

"What's the magic word?"

"Pleeeezzzeee," the kids chorused.

The footsteps stopped halfway down the path. He glimpsed Eric's head through the topmost open trellis of the slatboard fence. It wheeled round and went back up the gravel path.

They'd spoken several times across the fence, him and Eric, when he'd been cutting the lawn, and that time when he was planting up the garden, putting in the clematis and honeysuckle. As he knelt to unravel the red nylon ropes he heard Eric's back door softly open and softly close. Well, fair enough. And also fuck him.

"Now you aren't to swing on this, do you understand?"

"We won't."

"Let me get something to stand on."

He carried out a kitchen chair. It was two simple G-clamps to hold the loops of nylon and he screwed them into place. Even the threads of the nuts were poorly cut. His thumb opened again and as he tried to get the wipe from his pocket he left a smear of blood on his tracksuit bottoms.

He started digging a second hole and found that the spade—its lug nestled against his trainer—struck stone almost immediately. The rubble started after only a couple of inches. It was ridiculous. The builder'd simply *sprinkled* topsoil over the hard fill—the cheap fucker. After a few minutes of strenuous digging, the hole had expanded on the horizontal plane but not the vertical one.

When he looked up he saw Isobel swinging and Mickey hanging onto one leg of the swing set; it was shaking as if it might tip. She reached the top of her swing, and both back legs of the A-frame lifted a few inches off the ground. He screamed at her, "Stop that, Isobel, it's not ready, you were told—"

Her white, terrified face turned to him. He ran up the garden and yanked her off the swing. She was holding fast to the ropes and somehow in the struggle he managed to give her rope burns on the inside of both arms, and on her stomach—on her soft white skin.

He kept saying, "It's for your own good. It's for your own good," as he wrestled her little body into submission.

Between sobs she spluttered, "You hurt me, you hurt me."

He carried her towards the back door and saw Alison, standing at the sink looking out at him. In her white dressing gown, hair wrapped in a towel, she was staring with her mouth open in anger, and not, it turned out, at Isobel.

The child ran from his arms and buried herself in her mother's dressing gown.

"Stephen, take it easy with her. She's only four."

"I was trying to stop her tipping the whole swing set."

Mickey appeared in the back door, also bawling, but he had managed to pick up the screwdriver en route.

Isobel turned towards him, the wee face all red and twisted up, and screamed, "You're not my daddy. I know what you are."

Alison fell asleep in Isobel's bed that evening, having tickled her back until her own eyes had closed. After an hour, when she hadn't come back downstairs, Stephen crept in and woke her by shaking her shoulder. Wordlessly she got up and followed him back downstairs. He sat on the sofa and waited for her to join him, as she had always done, but instead she sat in the blue armchair and hugged a cushion to herself.

"We could move," he said.

"Where? To Scotland?"

"Why not? Or England."

"My family."

"I'm your family."

A look passed over Alison's face that she did not successfully disguise. It was a tiny grimace of disgust and Stephen saw it.

"I'll think about it," she said.

She never expected marriage to be easy; Bill had taught her that. A second marriage meant substituting old ceremonies and traditions with different ones, meant trading in the old gods for new, but Alison couldn't help it; she didn't believe in it any longer. She'd lost her faith and found the new gods to be false gods. What desire she had ever had for him now dissolved entirely; she knew what his hands—his small pale hands—were capable of.

And beneath the disgust was a deeper shame. She understood that she could claim when she had married him she didn't know, she didn't know. But it wasn't true, not quite. Underneath the continual earsplitting alarm of disgust was a tiny ticking drip of shame, her own shame, the shame of not wanting to know, of choosing not to know. She had been happy to have her eyes half closed. And she knew that her whole life she'd always been like this, chosen the downhill path, the passenger seat, the prevailing wind—and the humiliation of that knowledge made her revolted with herself as much as with him. As she passed the mirror in the hall she looked down at the carpet.

CHAPTER 26

When they went outside, the sky was so wide and tall and filled with so many stars that Liz gave a little helpless sigh. The far mountains were in silhouette. Below them, the empty valley dropped away forever. Bats whirred through the dusk, darting and veering off like they were on strings yanked from above. The vast cacophony of night was tuning up.

"Is that the chicken run down there?"

"Yeah, we keep Buff Orpingtons, a few redshanks."

"My Uncle Sidney breeds Buff Orpingtons."

"Oh no way," Sarah said, and then sighed. "You know my dad feels she betrayed us, Belef. I mean maybe she did but I think she just went mad when her daughter died. She'd worked for us for years. With us. My mum taught her English and really she and Kaykay—that's her daughter—were like part of the family, you know."

The coop and the run were enclosed with wire. A few trees stood by themselves on the slopes before the forest began and they looked lost, wounded, abandoned by the vast retreating army of the tree line. The moon had not yet risen and the Milky Way was visible, its dark spine fringed untidily with light. They walked silently downhill.

"What happened to her, the daughter?"

"It was awful. She was leaving church one Sunday after evening service and a branch fell on her and killed her."

"Oh God."

"It smashed her skull in. We were all there, outside the church. Just before Christmas."

"But why does she blame your dad?"

"He'd just given a sermon about the Wind of God. It's what they call the Holy Spirit. The Wind of God. There was no way to translate it. And then—outside—it wasn't even that windy, but the branch was dead and it snapped off. Dad carried the body back into the church. It was a real mess."

The coop was already closed up and silent. The chickens had been locked away for the night and Liz wondered why she and Sarah were here. The far edge of the forest appeared to breathe in the semi-darkness, moving in, out, as the eye struggled to define it. In there, in the all-day permanent gloaming, beasts crawled on their stomachs, crept on all fours, stalked and pounced, rutted and died and rotted. The tree line marked the edge of civilization as much as any city wall.

"And Belef thinks it's God's fault?"

"She says it was punishment for breaking with the old ways. Kaykay was singing 'Jesus Bids Us Shine with a Pure Clear Light'—it's the only hymn they seem able to learn—when the branch fell and killed her. Belef says it was Amulmul. Amulmul wanted to show her who was the real Wind of God."

"Is that why the husband left? Because of the death?"

Sarah fiddled with a piece of wire on the coop door and they started back up to the house.

"Oh no, he'd been gone years before. He just disappeared. One day he'd gone out to get honey from a tree, but no one knew exactly where the tree was. I mean he knew, but he wouldn't tell anyone in case they stole the honey, and he'd done it before. He'd come back before with a huge honeycomb wrapped in leaves, apparently, but this time he just never came back. Dad arrived in the village a few weeks later and Belef was hysterical. She was screaming at him. She thought he was her husband come back. The dead turn white, they think. Or they used to think. And so it was a weird start to the relationship, you know. They used to joke about it. But it was always pretty intense between them. She always loved my dad, I think. But then, well, you heard, things started going wrong."

Outside the storeroom Liz stopped, intending to say goodnight.

"I was going to show you my collage."

"Shall we do that tomorrow?"

"But you're going to be filming. It'll only take a minute."

Liz followed her into the house and down to Sarah's room. Sarah shut the door behind them. It felt curiously illicit. There was light from the porch where Jess and Josh were, but they had gone straight past them.

"Here, sit here."

Liz sat at the little school desk and examined the "collage."

"My cousin Erin in Indiana sends her old magazines to me at school."

Sarah had cut and stuck hundreds of images onto an enormous sheet of cardboard salvaged from one of their food deliveries.

"Have you a theme?"

There were animals, celebrities, furniture. A deck chair. A kitten. Some pop stars, actors, mouthpieces.

"Not really. It's just things that strike me. I don't think I'm going to have enough to cover the board."

"They did this in Victorian times."

Except the women in those collages were not so . . . naked. Nor pouting like that. Nor were they so skinny. It was lovely, almost innocent, and also pointless and terrible. There was a sense of someone held at some remove from all life, in the prison of her days. All the men were in suits or T-shirts and jeans, but the women—it was hard to find one in a proper outfit. Liz felt a tenderness towards Sarah. Motherly. She tapped her fingers on the pile of magazines—fashion, lifestyle, "interiors"—and thought how awful it was to be young now, even here, at the end of the earth. It pressed in, the wider world and its stupidity and pornification, lust and greed and envy and hatred. Sometimes she forgot how hard it was to be female, and then she was reminded. There was no way to protect a girl from the world—it was like trying to hold off a tidal wave of shit with Sellotape and string. But she was clever, Sarah. She would be all right. Would she? She was so skinny, so on edge, so eager and nervous and unhappy.

"You know a lot of the stuff in these magazines is nonsense, right?"

"Of course. I was just . . . I was just making *something* from it. For something to do. The other side's more interesting."

Sarah turned the board over and Liz started to laugh. This side was like Hieronymus Bosch.

"You haven't showed this to your parents, have you?"

"Of course not." Sarah grinned.

"Have Esther and Moses seen these?"

"They're not even *allowed* in here."

On the board, Kim Kardashian's head was split in two and a Formula One car was driving into her mouth. Several arms came out of a dollar bill, holding the mounted head of a deer, a Molotov cocktail, a can of Budweiser, a tricorne hat. A long row of heads—John Travolta, Scarlett Johansson, several models—appeared to be on a skewer turning over a fire made from yellow and red furnishings cut into the shape of flames. A pair of legs—Beyoncé's?—missing a torso but attached to the top half of a spaceship stood in a forest, the trees made from skyscrapers topped with lettuce leaves.

"This is great."

"Cool, isn't it?"

"This is super cool."

"And I did Donald Trump." She pointed. "Just there."

Trump's head was on the body of a flamingo, and somehow the juxtaposition made sense of the glassy fear in his eyes, as if he were scared he might topple off his single spindly pink leg.

"And look."

Sarah handed over a photograph she pulled from the inside of a book—a diary perhaps—by her bed. It showed Sarah, Esther, and Moses with Belef and a little black girl, grinning cheekily, overflowing with mischief, sitting on the front steps leading up to their verandah.

"That's Kaykay?"

"Uh-huh."

"She's the same age as you."

"Two months apart."

"Were you friends?"

"Yes," she said simply.

Belef looked so young in the photograph. She wore a yellow head wrap, and the bright smiling face that looked out from the picture was almost unrecognizable. Since then pain had come and done what pain does to a face. Liz passed the photo back and Sarah slipped it into her book, then sat back on her narrow bed.

"So . . . *do* you like Stan?"

"Stan? He's too old for you."

"I don't mean that! I just wondered if *you* liked him."

"I like him fine."

"What about Paolo? Do you think he's cute?"

"I think he thinks he's cute. What about boys? Do you have a boyfriend in PM?"

"Not as such."

"What does that mean?"

"There's a boys' school across the road, but . . . Doesn't Stan seem so good with kids?"

"I think he's at home with them. That's not quite the same thing. Anyway, I don't want to talk about boys."

Sarah gave her a meaningful look, and said, "Me neither."

She got up off the bed and took the two steps to the desk and stood in front of Liz, then awkwardly bent and tried to put her arms around her. She brought her head down and tried to kiss her. Liz rerouted the movement into a hug and said, "Oh honey."

"Forget it." Sarah pulled away strongly and was back on her bed. She turned her face away towards the wall.

"No, it's . . . Oh Sarah, I'm like twice your age."

"Forget it. Let's forget it. Could you go?"

Liz sat down on the bed beside her.

"Don't be bonkers. Nothing happened. We're cool, OK? We're cool."

Sarah turned towards her. Her neck and face were blotchy, puce with embarrassment.

"I'm not even like that."

"Of course not. Whatever. I remember being fifteen. Look, we're cool."

"OK."

"Honestly. *Everything* is fine."

But everything was not fine. Liz stayed for another five minutes, trying to kick-start fake conversation. She waffled and waffled and all through it she found herself thinking, *What would it be like to kiss this fifteen-year-old girl? She was pretty. A delicate neck.* And then she would think, *Liz, what are you doing in here? Get out. Get out.*

She told Sarah that she could make her own way back to the storeroom. She had her Margo-issued torch. In the corridor, she saw a light on under a door she'd not been behind and heard a chair scrape, Josh's voice, a crackle of static and Josh's voice again.

"That's what I said. Physically attacked. I understand he was whipped, the poor child."

More buzzing static. There was a click as Josh plugged something in and the static stopped.

"I haven't seen him. I told you they're filming here. It's getting out of hand . . . Daniel, I ask you to get the police down here, and you send Raula. She's running rings round him. You need to get the body reburied in our graveyard. . . . Ten years work, ten years of my life! She cannot stay in Slinga. I can't allow it."

There was a long pause. Liz began to tiptoe down the corridor. Josh spoke again and his voice was softer, sadder.

"No, I know. But it's not a situation I *can* bear. The church needs support. I'm asking you for help here."

The chair scraped again as Liz reached the back door. Sarah came out of her room and saw her, but only raised a hand in silent farewell. Liz waved back and undid the latch and slipped out into the night.

"We were *all* longlong, we were *all* in darkness, *all* of us knew nothing, and then God gave his ten laws *on* to his people. And the *second* of these laws was—You shall *love* your neighbor as yourself. Wantok bilong mi em I husat? *Who* is my neighbor?"

You couldn't call Josh a natural preacher, but he had watched enough sermons to pick up the basic tricks. He grinned and cajoled and glowered. He raised and lowered his voice, although his stresses did not always fall on the appropriate word.

"You shall love the person *near* you as you love yourself. This is the second law, and we must obey *all* of these ten laws to gain eternal life, so that we might live forever."

Josh walked across the little raised dais of the church and back again. There were two men with guitars, who had, a minute before, been playing "Make Me a Channel of Your Peace." They stood on either side of him watching, impassively. Josh pointed at one of the guitarists and said, "Watna knows that."

Watna dutifully grinned back.

It was a small building of wooden planking and a corrugated roof. In lieu of the expected rows of wooden pews, there were red plastic stacking chairs. The congregation consisted of twenty or so people, about a third of the church's capacity. The women wore meri skirts and blouses, the men short-sleeved shirts and shorts. The earthen floor was covered in raffia matting. For ten minutes before the service started, Moses ceremoniously bashed "the bell," a rusted wheel arch hung on a chain from a nearby mango tree, in a one-two-three rhythm. Inside, the air of expectation and tension was resolved into genuine joy when the singing began.

Josh started the service with a list of reminders: They were not to chew betel nut in church, since the red spit got on the prayer books. If the children cried they were to be taken outside. They were to remember to give their hymn books back by the door at the end. Paolo dutifully filmed from various angles. He'd wired Josh up before the service started—running the wire under his shirt and into the transmitter at the back of his trousers—which had involved much off-key joking from the missionary: "Now careful, Paolo, we're not even engaged. Buy a guy a drink first." Paolo smiled and nodded and laughed, and finished clipping on the mic, before glancing over at Liz with a look that conveyed the single word "prick."

"So we can *split* it into three parts. Who am I to love? My neighbor.

What am I to do? I am to *love* him. How am I to do it? I am to love *him* as much as I love my *self*."

It occurred to Liz that the second commandment made no sense. Such a formula required certain preconditions that were not, commonly, in place. Most people loathed themselves.

Usai leaned his head back against the church's white clapboard, his Britney Spears T-shirt stretched across his lean frame. The sun shone very brightly on the whitewash but they'd tried under the coconut palms and it was just too dark, Paolo said, to pick out Usai's features. Usai watched them from under his baseball cap, nervousness playing on his face. When Margo gestured that he should remove the cap, he lifted it off and exposed sharp cheekbones and wary, intelligent eyes, Belef's eyes.

Josh stood forty feet away, talking to Watna and his tiny wife; on her hip she held a squirmy baby whose baptism—whose consecration—was being finalized, unknown to him, at that moment above his head. Usai, who during the service had helped with Communion, proudly in charge of the platter of wafers, did not need much prompting. In a rush he said, "Mister Josh brought us to the light of the church of Jesus Christ."

Liz nodded like a real TV presenter—reassuring, fascinated—and asked, "Could you describe how that came about?"

Usai looked blank and Stan, holding the boom like a standard-bearer, added rather theatrically, "How you come to work this law? The law of Christ?"

Usai nodded gratefully.

"They come because of me. In Kutang they have God, but in Kirlassa we are in the dark. It was because I spoke and rang Papa that the New Truth come . . . You all hear the talk. I was a nothingman in my tribe. My father had gone and I had no pigs. But I am Christian, I am someone. We were in darkness." He held his hands out, palms down. "And now we live in light." He turned the palms over. "Before, we knew nothing, we were longlong and now we know it good. We work it like this. We go to church"—he leaned back and with one hand delicately pushed the side of the building—"on Wednesday, Saturday, and Sunday."

"And how do you get the people to come?"

"We believe in going on top to Papa . . . We all watch out good. Each man will boss his skin and keep it clean by what he does. But say a man fouls in the bush and loses his church for two or three weeks, then I will put a man's name in the church book and tell it to Mister Josh. Mister Josh will point to this man in the church who was pigheaded or he will come to see the man and talk to him, and tell him that he will send it to the Big Man—"

"God?"

"Yes—the Big Boss God will know that the man has not worked the law good, and he will be punished. He will get no reward, he will not live forever, he will burn in the fires of hell underground."

Usai smiled, pleased with his explanation.

"What about Belef? Your mother?"

Usai paused and looked at his hands. He glanced over at Mister Josh, who held Watna's baby over one shoulder and was explaining something to the parents.

"I am crying for her." He gave a little shrug. "I tell her, 'You cannot live with this anymore. You cannot follow this thinking. It is the lies of ancestors, and they are all now underground burning in the fires.' Mister Josh showed us pictures of them all burning in hell. I said to her, 'You must forget about this old way of thinking and come inside the Bible school. You must finish with the old thinking for all time.' I am crying for her. I tell her, 'You will be in hell. You will be burning in hell for all time.'"

"She's your mother—"

Margo looked at Liz with her special steely-producer glare. Liz shook her head unlike a real TV presenter—dismayed, a little disgusted.

Usai grimaced. He paused and then decided to say it.

"Belef doesn't like that I am an elder, that I am an important person in the church. She thinks of me as little Usai. She is not with God, my papa. She uses muso. But it does nothing to me."

"Muso?"

Stan said, "Magic."

Usai pulled apart the steeple he had formed with his fingers and gestured towards himself.

"For me, I am not afraid. I can drink from a stream where a woman has washed or eat mushrooms from where the women walk along the path. Sorcery is not strong enough. Nothing can touch. The Lord is with me and bids me shine. I drank poison once and it was not strong enough."

"Why would you drink poison?"

"To show the power of Jesus! I drank bleach! Watna ate the poison put out for the rats in the church. It is impossible to hurt those who believe in Christ Almighty."

Usai closed his eyes and opened them slowly; he had a courtesan's long lashes. The steeple was re-erected.

"I am sorry about your sister."

"Of course."

"Your mother thinks she died because Amulmul was angry and wanted to punish her for leaving the ways of the old gods. She says Amulmul wanted to show he was the true Wind of God."

Usai looked from Liz to Margo, but he saw that the producer wasn't going to interfere. He scratched his eyebrow, shrugged again and said, "The Wind of God killed Kaykay because she didn't believe enough. The true God is a jealous god. Belef causes much trouble in Slinga. But we should talk about the one true church of Jesus. He bids us shine. He will bring rewards."

"What do you mean 'rewards'?"

"The rewards of Christian life. And when we heard about the Mission coming, about Mister Josh arriving, we were so happy."

"Why?"

"We knew that God was coming."

"But I understood that God didn't even exist, as a concept."

Usai looked at Stan.

"Did you know Papa, before?"

"We didn't know Papa, but we knew we wanted a new life."

"Did you think the planes that would come to the airstrip were bringing stuff for you? Did the villagers all think they were going to be rewarded?"

"The reward is the Kingdom of Heaven."

"And where is Heaven? Near Sydney?"

Usai looked at Liz with a flicker of confusion.

"It's in the sky."

"Just behind the clouds?"

Usai leaned back a little in his chair and said nothing.

"And how do you get there? To Heaven? By aeroplane?"

"No." He gave her a long, cold look. "You have to die."

CHAPTER 27

After a lunch of rice and manioc outside the rest house, Margo went for a nap in Paolo's mosquito net, a feat involving much detailed negotiation about when exactly she would remove her boots. Paolo—though he always looked like he'd spent several days evading capture—was as fastidious about his belongings as he was about the cameras. It was his habit to represent them like their lawyer: My sleeping bag will not like muck upon it. My rucksack does not want your feet on it.

Paolo and Stan were playing cards and smoking with the bodyguard Posingen. Liz decided to walk down to the square. Paolo and Stan called over to her to come and join them, but she waved them off and went on. Leftie was weeding Belef's garden on his hands and knees. Stan had said that her main garden was an hour's walk away, that the land here was poor and had been farmed out years ago.

"Hello."

Leftie looked up.

"Do you speak English?"

"Little, little."

"Where's Belef?"

Leftie pointed round the side of the mountain.

Outside the school, a few boys played with a tree kangaroo they'd tied by one leg to a stump. It was brown with reddish patches, its nose an obscene pink. Part koala, part wallaby, part baby bear, it squealed and showed its teeth as they poked it with sticks, and she was thinking how she could persuade them to let it go when she became aware of a presence at her side. She looked down to see Namor, the boy with white in his hair, looking at what she was looking at.

"Hello."

The little hand inserted itself into her hand, and he pulled her along, up the path.

"Oh OK, where we off to? How's your back? Your back, it's better?"

He said nothing.

They entered the forest by a path she hadn't been on before, an opening down at the edge of the square, and the trees in here were closely spaced. It was dark and felt cool and his hand was dry and tight on hers. After a few minutes, satisfied she was definitely coming, he let her go suddenly, and jogged a few steps ahead, turning every so often to smile at her.

It made sense that Belef would find telephones to the dead in trees; they were taller than us, they touched the emptiness of sky, and went deep into the earth. They reached down to the dark past and stretched up to the open future. She pushed a palm against a narrow trunk as she walked past and there was a sudden rustling above and a shuffling of the light scattered on the forest floor. She couldn't see the boy.

"Hello?" She walked a few tentative steps into the collage of green stems and cords and vines climbing, draping, veiling. "Namor. Namor." She tried "Jojo." She looked at her watch. 13:37. Realistically they could only have walked for ten, maybe fifteen minutes into the forest. And he'd only been gone a few seconds. He'd probably stepped off the path to go to the toilet. She should just wait here. A gloomy spot, dense thickets on both sides of the path. She backtracked a few meters to a little clearing where a tree'd partially fallen—the forest was too tightly packed to achieve horizontality—and stood propped and rotting against its neighbors, swaddled in moss and ivy. Several saplings strained upwards in the new light its death occasioned.

She waited. 13:48. She decided to head back, but after a while the path split and she wasn't sure. They'd been walking at a slight downwards gradient, basically, so she took the higher option; it wound round several thick-trunked acacias and petered out in an unfamiliar patch of dusty-looking ferns. She retraced her steps to the fork and tried the other route.

This path split several times and she hazarded guesses. She was staying mostly level, and appeared to be rounding the side of the mountain. But she hadn't come from a bigger path onto a smaller one. Or had she? And she didn't remember seeing this rock with feathery yellow moss on one side of it. But then if she had been coming from that direction . . . The trees were too dense again to see much now; it was like being indoors, like being in fog, the world up close and within arm's reach. Slightly breathless, she stopped and called again and listened. Was that the river? Or a breeze rounding in the canopy?

She turned and tried the alternative from where the path last split, but after only a few minutes, the path wound back on itself and she was returned to the rock with yellow moss. Now she could find nowhere that looked familiar. She walked on and on, unsure if she was heading towards Slinga or not; the path curled and sloped up for a bit and then down and she thought she recognized this silvery tree trunk with peeling bark but wasn't sure. 13:56. She shouted Namor again, as loud as she could, and there was a movement in the bracken. She turned expecting to see him but there was nothing.

The fear she'd been accumulating needed, all at once, to be tallied, and she sat down at the foot of a tree. The trees themselves constituted presence, so many presences. They made a company of beings round her. Discreet company they were too—silent, incidentally protective from the sun, whispering among themselves. They were not hostile, nor were they on her side. They were bystanders, witnesses, they would not intervene.

It was impossible that no one would come along from Slinga. If she just sat here, very still. Several hundred inhabitants. Hadn't Stan said? Or a thousand, was it? Her backpack: three pens, a banana already soft at one end, a bottle of water with an inch or so left in it. Her notepad. Her phone. She checked in the small inside pocket. A fifty-pence piece. Some paper clips. She turned the phone on and checked that there was still no reception. She took a selfie against the tree trunk, looking at the camera blankly. Immediately she took another, trying to appear suitably lost and scared and alone, trying to respond outwardly, adequately, to the situation. Her hair looked greasy. She tied it back properly and tried again. She looked appropriately worried now, and her cheekbones looked good. She deleted the two previous. She wished she had a real camera with her; this would have played well within the episode, this incident—"an unguarded moment," Margo would have called it.

She leafed through her notebook, finally writing on a fresh page in large looping cursive, "I got lost in the forest." She added, "It's not the sort of forest you want to get lost in."

She stopped and leaned back against the tree trunk. A great vitality ticked round her, invisible. Each corner filled with insect traffic or a feathered consciousness flicking from bough to branch to ground. But all remained just out of apprehension. Ah here was a small, dull, brown bird on a branch. Hop hop and away. She looked down at her boots and grew aware of a large, black, glossy beetle moving across the space between her feet, hauling the shield of itself along. It climbed the hillock of her right hiking boot and descended and continued its journey.

She counted—five slow breaths taken all the way down into her chest and back out. She watched a single ant traverse the acreage of a broad heart-shaped leaf two feet from her nose. She stood up and held onto the tree trunk and pressed her head against it.

She thought of Belef on her telephone tree and found herself thinking of her parents' phone number. She murmured it out loud and heard herself say, "Mum?" The forest breathed around her, an immensity of listening, of attention. She found herself whispering to her mother that she loved her, that she didn't want her to die. She saw her mother sitting on the edge of her mattress, high on morphine and steroids, her eyes half closed, her fingers fumbling at the buttons of her nightgown.

She raised her head from the tree trunk and the thought occurred to her that she could just walk into the forest. Just keep walking forward and forward and forward until she fell down. She had the old urge she felt at the edge of a cliff or with a bottle of pills in her hand. There was a deep desire within her to join the teeming machine around her, to go back to the timeless and inanimate . . . She took a few steps into the jungle, into the thickness of shadow. Two more of those small brown nondescript birds sat silently on a branch a few feet above her head and looked at her.

One flicked itself upwards, and a second later the second followed. It occurred to her with the clarity of a slap that she didn't want to be alone in the world anymore. She wanted a partner. If she had a partner—or even children; but slow down Liz, slow down—would she take this step into the forest? Or this one? She stopped. She was tired of being on her own. She didn't want to have to stop herself from walking into oblivion. Where was her partner? Why was she always alone? She felt a rush of hatred. At herself, at the jungle. She was scared and she was sick of this. She hated this place. She hated the desperation of everything, the poverty and filth. She hated the way the day dropped away to night like a shutter slammed down. She hated the way even the trees reached out to grab whatever they could. Everything was naked and real and awful. She hated Belef and Leftie and Napasio. She hated all of these people, with their inability to give a straight answer, with their filthy clothes and ignorance, with their idiotic faith in magic and the dead. She hated the fact they made her distrust the things she knew were true. She hated the Werners. She hated their tragic faith. It was so frightening, so dangerous, so boundless, so extreme. She hated this island and its insects and its mud and its labyrinthine paths where there was no escape, where there was no hope, only more leafs and more bugs and more ways to disappear.

There was a sound, a glugging sound, like how a bath concludes its drainage with a deep *glug-glug-glug*. Then an incredibly low frequency purr. She heard it but felt it also—it vibrated inside her. The richest deepest bass she'd ever heard. Next a clicking noise and a dry bark, then about ten feet away a cassowary strutting into sight. Its bright blue head down, then up, picking a way through the undergrowth. Obscene red wattles swung from its neck and on its head jutted a large black crest like a dinosaur might have.

Huge, taller than Liz. According to Stan they could kill with one kick, its middle claw a dagger, its leg effectively a piston.

It turned its head and stared.

A long, narrow beak curved unpleasantly out from a face with a garish quality of drag about it—inexpert makeup, lavish lashes. The bird gave her a haughty once-over and Liz stayed perfectly still. It registered nothing of interest and ducked its head back down, shaking the black, frilly ball of its body. Another few clicks, a baritone purr, and it strutted off-stage. Still she stayed completely still.

Was it gone? Back to its life of insects and leaf litter and rotting fruit? She looked hard into the patchwork of greenery and shadow and it was not there.

She clapped her hands, thinking that might drive it deeper into the undergrowth, away from her. The echoes snickered briefly. She clapped again and the echo came back a second later, slower somehow. She clapped, twice, and two echoes came back, even slower. She made three claps and *four* echoes came back. She heard what sounded like a laugh. Over to her left Namor sat in the crook of a tree about ten feet from the ground, clapping in response and laughing, the little shit. She ran towards him but he shrieked and jumped down and skipped off.

Liz shouted, "Now hold on. Just wait one minute please. Where the hell—"

She stopped shouting. He moved fast and it took all her concentration not to lose him again. She glimpsed the white of his hair between the trees and he darted off barefoot. He would turn back at corners to watch for her and wait for her approach, but when a few meters were left between them he slipped off again, his body unimpeded as a fawn's. She felt old and heavy and tired. He sat now on a decaying tree fallen across the path and she reached him and pointed ahead, in the direction he was leading her, and said, "Slinga? Slinga? We are going to Slinga, yes?"

He laughed and skipped off but she wasn't playing anymore. She sat down where he'd sat—a clutch of seedlings sprouted from the trunk and she brushed their heads with her hand. He looked back and slowed, then stood at a distance, watching her with curiosity. His stare seemed to bear down on her, to plead with her, but no, she would not move.

She opened her bag and took out the notepad and began to write in block capitals: "NAMOR IS AN ASSHOLE."

She tore the page out and held it up to him. He looked and looked and came closer to see it properly. As he neared she put it down on her lap and began to fold it into a paper plane. He watched and watched and she finally lifted it up, adjusted its wing tips, and launched it down the path ahead of them. He ran after it and snatched it up. He came back and handed it to her. She pulled the fifty-pence piece from the pocket of her jeans and showed it to him. He held his hand out for it and she pretended to give it to him, but changed her mind at the last minute. He laughed and she did it again, then flicked it in the air and he caught it.

They walked together. She said, "Slinga?"

And he answered, "Belef, Belef."

They came to a shallow river dotted with stepping-stones and crossed it easily. A long winding path upwards led them to a roughly worked gate. It would have been easy to walk around it, but Namor whistled and a short man Liz hadn't seen before appeared from behind a tree. He held a stick like a gun, across his chest, and looked them up and down, eyeing Liz with barely hidden fear. Namor said what sounded like, "Spin-Jo-Spin-Jaw." The man nodded and with maximum ceremony opened the gate.

On they walked for a few minutes in silence and then the forest ended. They stood in a clearing.

CHAPTER 28

A rough formation of men—forty, fifty—marched at the far end. They carried sticks like the man at the gate, propped against their shoulders like guns. A few wore parodies of military uniforms, matching khaki cargo shorts, and long tennis socks, but most were dressed unalike. Swim shorts, flipflops, some were in jeans. But every one was bare-chested, and across their torsos, from hip to shoulder, each wore a red woven sash. They stopped and stood in five loose rows. Something about their self-conscious pomposity reminded her of the Orangemen back home. A man facing them shouted, "Attention." They all shuffled slightly taller. Liz fingered the string on her wrist. The sergeant major, she realized, was Leftie. How had he gotten here? Hadn't she just walked away from him in Slinga? She waved at him and looked around the encampment.

The "runway" was neither level nor large. The trees had been chopped down, but many stumps remained, though there'd been an effort to burn a few of them out. The surface was churned soil, though here and there little patches of green stubble had started to show through. You could see where they'd tried to stamp the ground flat, the prints of bare feet and flipflops. Leftie shouted, "Fall out!" and the men began to disperse. Most moved off to the shade of the tree line. Two lifted an iron railing and inserted it under a root, then bounced and jiggled it, trying to lever the root loose.

None of them joined the women and girls picking stones and rocks from the soil, carrying them in wicker baskets to the edge of the forest to be emptied. Some reddish, scrawny chickens scratched and pecked around the churned-up soil and beyond them several older women sat singing at a fire—squeezing liquid through muslin sheets twisted into balls, and collecting it in plastic buckets. The song they sang was in Koriam but the tune was "Jesus bids us shine with a pure, clear light." A solitary hound, black with dirt, lay on his side at the edge of their circle, and Liz watched his ribs appear and disappear as he breathed.

A squat hut sat by the side of the runway and a bamboo aerial had been lashed to its side, reaching twenty feet into the air. Namor touched her arm and pointed at another hut, larger, at the head of the runway, partly ensconced in the trees.

"Belef," he said.

The structure was the usual wooden beams and pitpit topped with a thick circumflex of branches, but higher and wider than the huts in Slinga, stately by comparison. The door of the hut was closed, and above it, at the top of the pointed gable, a carved wooden aeroplane had been tied in place. It was a church. Liz took her phone out to take a photograph and found her phone was dead. Not that the battery was dead, but that the phone was dead. She had charged it the previous night and when she was lost in the forest, taking the selfies, it had still been fully charged, but now there was nothing. She pressed the black mirror of the screen and sent a little ripple of color over the surface.

Inside the hut people talked in Koriam. One voice—quavery, intense, querulous—pleaded and stopped. The other—placid, mournful, tolerant—began to respond.

"Belef? It's Liz."

The church grew silent.

"Belef? Are you in there? I thought I was going back to Slinga, but Namor brought me here."

"Please enter," said a third voice, Belef's, low and even, and Liz pushed the stiff door aside with a scrape and edged her way in. It was dark inside and Liz put her hand out in front of herself. The room took shape. Long and empty, ribs and struts exposed, the boards on the floor covered with woven sacking, and at the far end sat Belef, alone. Cross-legged. A darker pyramid of cloth and limbs against the matting of the wall. Pungent incense burned somewhere, a sweet sickliness.

"Oh I thought you were with some people."

"My children were here but they had to go."

Belef made no movement.

"Were you arguing?"

"All my boys were here. Michael Ross and Johnson and Bullet. They didn't want their sister to come in, so they locked her up underground. They tied her to a tree and I was telling them to let her go. To let her come up to me."

Madness comes abruptly. Liz felt a curious admixture of embarrassment and thrill, and it occurred to her that Belef was extremely high functioning for a schizophrenic. If that was what she was. Did she believe what she said? Was she possessed? Was she a fraud? Both? Authentic power— and Belef had that—could be founded on anything, although nothing, no inheritance, no beauty, could guarantee it.

Liz turned her head away, the better to disguise her response, because she had none. She placed her hand against the wall for balance and started untying the lace of her left boot. Her blister was bothering her and her limbs were like stone. She sat down.

"I thank Amulmul that Namor found you."

"I saw some boys playing with a tree kangaroo . . ." began Liz, but this was from the prosaic world and Belef did not live there.

Silence. A dog barked distantly outside. All of a sudden Belef slapped the floor of the church with her palm.

"We have much law to work. Michael Ross said, 'Mother, what you must do is make this, and he gave me a pikcha of a flagpole.'"

"A picture?"

"Yes, a pikcha, a pikcha. The flagpole is found underground and we are to make it up here to open the road. We do the correct working of the pikcha, and around it is marching, singing, and we raise the flag."

Liz nodded.

"Did you see the army of Amulmul, Liz? My army?"

"Listen, you must send word to Margo and Paolo to tell them where I am."

She tried to sound angry. She *was* angry, and yet Belef's aura, her personal force, drove every other emotion out of the hut. Something was centered in Belef, some energy was held in her. She added, almost as an afterthought, "And *where* am I? Where is this?"

"Kirlassa. My village. Before the mission came, there were many families here. They grew scared of the darkness and moved to Slinga. They were all afraid of Hell, this new place they heard of. And all the villagers who went got shoes given 'em. All the others were getting on and they were not."

"Where did your children go, just now? I heard their voices."

"Back underground they go. Bullet didn't want to leave."

There were shadows in the church. It was possible there were people in the shadows. Was it? False floors and trapdoors. It felt like they were not alone. Belef stood up slowly and walked down the length of the hut. Each step she took Liz felt through the boards. It certified the woman's dominance, her physical, ramifying presence in the universe, and when she sat down beside her and leaned back so that they were sitting side by side, Liz had to steel herself not to pull away. Something in her cowered. She felt she lacked agency, had entered a room—had entered a country—that she did not belong in, and did not understand, and whatever table she had thought she was sitting down to dine at, had been unveiled as an altar.

Why did she feel so tired? Belef reached across and took Liz's hand in her leathery fingers. She spoke in no more than a whisper.

"I dreamed and knew one day that when the sick-moon came up on me, I would work it good. I took a mat and put it under my bed so the blood that fell from me made a pool on the mat. And for all those days the pool grew there. And when the sick-moon finished I took the mat and tied it tightly. I buried it in my garden. The first white child to come was Michael Ross, and he was tall and good and he helps my garden make food. He pushed up the taro. Then Johnson came and he is strong and warm. He makes the loads lighter and the nights less cold. The last to come was Bullet. He is quick and fearless and laughs all the time. He carries me great distances and tells me not to be afraid."

"They're white?"

"Of course."

"Is your daughter white?"

"Not yet. Her eyes are red when she comes back. Her stomach is hot."

"Kaykay?"

"That was what the mission children called her. Her name was Kasingen. She lies in the ground by my house. The dead must be kept close to talk to."

Belef tightened Liz's hand in hers.

"I'm so sorry that she died."

"Five months ago, December, he killed her."

"Someone killed her?"

"It is because of Mista Josh that she is dead. But she wants to cut all of our necks."

Belef stretched and yawned and stood up. She went out and Liz, after a moment, trailed her like a little child staying close to its mother. Outside, Belef stood with her feet planted far apart and placed her hands to form a cone round her mouth to call across the runway to Namor. The laboriousness of the gesture was inauthentic, and Liz knew she'd seen a *waitskin* do it. Josh himself had done it when he called to his kids when they were playing below the balcony.

Namor's eyes were sullen as he received his instructions from Belef—Liz could pick out the word "BBC." He ran to the tree line, and Liz saw his pig was tied up there. He patted it and whispered something into its ear and then broke off into his effortless run towards the path.

Belef led Liz around the camp, pointing out this or that, and was only ready to move on after Liz gave the appropriate nod or smile. The structure by the runway, as far as she could tell, was meant to be an air traffic controller's hut, and the controller flashed his gums in a helpless smile when they entered. He wore a woman's red cloche hat and fingered his long gray matted beard. His toothlessness meant his mouth leaned inward, giving him a vaguely tortoiselike gormlessness—but the eyes twinkled sharply. He jumped up to await instructions, and nodded intently at Belef's explanations to Liz, though it seemed he couldn't understand them.

The large square block of wood on the floor was a radio. Its dials were made from strips of fabric and twisted bark. Rounded river stones and translucent fragments of shell served as buttons and switches. Beside it, on the floor, lay a pair of coconut halves, held together by several inches of string. Belef saw Liz notice them, and she pointed at them. The man pushed the red cloche hat off his head and let it fall on the floor. Gingerly he lifted the coconut halves and fitted them over his ears; he looked terrified, as if someone might speak his name out of them.

"Buggle," Belef said, as they left the hut. "He is Buggle."

Perhaps if Margo or Paolo had been there it would have been a cause for some joke or smirk. It was true, of course, that no plane would be greeted and guided in by this wooden block adorned with mother-of-pearl shards for buttons—but that didn't seem of much importance somehow. Not all actions result in success. Most don't. Another definition of the real is that which can be reproduced, and Liz found there was something persuasive in the gravity of the enterprise. The man in the red hat had not *appeared* embarrassed or humiliated or empty or sad. He was doing his job with as much purpose and dignity as it deserved—no more, no less, like all jobs. He was waiting, and who wasn't?

Belef led them to the campfire and Liz found a spot at the edge and tried to be inconspicuous. She got her notebook out and jotted down, "What constitutes action and what ceremony?" She wrote, "Semblance of the real?" She wrote, "As far as the world allows, you choose reality."

People kept arriving. Ten, fifteen, thirty. Belef walked among them, shaking hands, a serious dignitary, exchanging concerns, nodding with warmth. Leftie came over and squatted down beside her.

"Welcome to Kirlassa."

"I just saw you in Slinga and now you're here. This is your army?"

The man smiled.

"You think I am my twin. No, he is him."

"Ah. Let me guess. You're Rightie?"

"Alan. My name is Alan."

"What are you—marching for?"

Alan wrinkled up his face and laughed.

"Everything!"

She sat with a large rock at her back, making rambling notes, and felt herself also to be a rock that the others flowed around. They never stopped, the women—fetching water, firewood, shelling beans. One woman pounded sago so loudly that Liz thought the beating was a drum announcing the beginning of festivities. Napasio brought her black tea in a tin cup and she gulped it down.

> *The Story—in fact any story—acts as an excursion to the hyper real. The dailiness we inhabit is replaced by a copy of the world, one where we find closure. Belef fictionalizes the world after the fact to justify where she finds herself, where her people find themselves. Life is moving from space to space, from person to person, from moment to moment; it is a story, a litany of anecdotes and mythologies. Belef uses them, she lets them all in. It's a plural vision.*

She wrote "ADD TO FINAL SUM-UP BUT SIMPLIFY" in the margin and made four small five-pointed stars beside it. She paused. The tip of the ballpoint hovered over the page of the ocean, and dived.

> *We are time traveling into the future at the blistering rate of sixty minutes an hour!*
> *Amazing fact!*
> *All the illusions we maintain are a form of ritual. Without them, what would we have? A man called Buggle sitting in a hut twisting an unconnected dial on a solid slab of wood seems as good a way as any to address the situation.*

CHAPTER 29

Napasio had just brought Liz a slushy pile of steaming white manioc on a peeled sheet of fresh bark when a large group of men arrived, maybe twenty, and at the rear of the procession walked Leftie and Margo and Paolo. Behind them came Posingen carrying the shock of his real gun, as well as one of the camera bags and the tripod and Margo's pink daypack.

Namor pointed at Liz but they'd already seen her, were now cutting across the runway, Margo with her hands out. "We were worried about you." Liz scrambled to her feet and hurried over to Paolo and threw her arms round him. He grunted something and took a step backwards but then returned the embrace. His arms around her felt as hard as timber. When she let go, Margo kissed her on the cheek and patted her on the back and said, "You really should have said you were going for a walk. Are you OK? You don't look OK."

"Namor led me here. I'd no idea it was—anyway, I'm sorry."

Margo needed more contrition.

"We were *incredibly* concerned."

Paolo nodded, not appearing worried in the least.

"I told Belef to send Namor to tell you. I didn't realize he was going to bring you back."

"We insisted. Imagine the headlines. 'TV Presenter Lost in Jungle.'"

"Isn't that already a show?" Paolo said.

Margo tutted and gave her a long demonstrative hug—though what was being demonstrated wasn't quite affection.

"Well, did you get anything good at least?"

"I got the grand tour."

Posingen stood a few feet away, his forehead creased with disapproval.

"This is not a place to go walkabout alone," he said, pointing the nose of his rifle at the ground. "Women here are not treated like they are in London, England."

"They're not treated all that well in London, England."

"Here they get raped. All the time raped."

"Lovely," said Margo, as she unlooped the pink rucksack from Posingen's shoulders.

Paolo steered her by the elbow across to the fire. He, too, wanted to impart something.

"I was actually worried."

"Were you?"

"Semi-concerned."

"Oh?"

He sighed dramatically.

"I've grown to like your face."

"What about now?"

She crossed her eyes and gurned.

"Especially now."

She smiled but he turned and looked across the clearing. Was he embarrassed? By the tree line Namor was rubbing his pig's broad head with his knuckles. The pig gave a two-note grunt of satisfaction and turned back into the boy, wanting more.

"On the way here"—Paolo pointed at Namor—"that one tugged on my T-shirt and said, 'Hey Beeby Say, more paper? More paper?' and he made like this"—Paolo clicked his tongue—"popping little bubbles of bubble wrap. Cheeky fuck."

"You think he took it from your bag?"

"Those were his eyes under the floor."

"The little shit."

"I told Margo I was going to give him some more just so Belef could whip him again."

They watched Namor take the pig's cheeks in both his hands, almost lovingly, and then slap it on the face. It squealed and went chuntering off into the forest.

Margo pulled the Paul Smith bag from her pink rucksack and handed it to Belef: she took it, peered in it, and set it by her feet.

"Say 'Liklik samting tasol,'" Stan prompted Margo, and she tried it.

And Belef said, "It's very fine."

She picked it back up and tore away the blue tissue paper.

She looked at the multicolored, striped dressing gown and held it up this way and that and pushed her face into it and decided to put it on there and then.

Napasio and the other women came across to see what was happening, and one by one they came forward to feel the hem of the garment. A young girl smelled it. Belef let them, then drew apart and gave a little twirl to many encouraging sighs.

"Joseph and his Technicolor dreamcoat," Liz said.

"Can you ask her if she'll take it off now? I don't think we should film her in it," whispered Margo. "Looks a bit . . . artificial."

"You're not getting that off her now," said Liz, as Belef tied the dressing gown cord in a bow around her waist.

They were setting up to film Leftie when Stan arrived. He shook Liz's hand and looked away towards the fire pit. One of the women cooking waved at him and he waved back.

"Have you been here before?

"Never, but I've heard of it. Kirlassa. This is all sacred space to Belef's clan. I understand they had quite a haus tambaran here. You should film in there, Paolo, if it's still standing. It would give you guys a really good idea of the culture here. Benches where the men just slept all day while their wives worked. The garamut drums and the secret pipes they played in the roof—they'd tell the women and children it was the spirits coming back."

Paolo gave a small Italian shrug and reattached his eye to the camera.

"How was *your* afternoon?" Liz asked briskly and Stan took his glasses off and wiped them on his T-shirt in his customarily apologetic manner.

"I went to the tractor pool with the Werner kids actually, to look for you."

"I'm sorry about that."

"Shall we film?" Margo asked.

"Oh it was fine. They had a swim and I found this banded weevil. Fascinating. It was pale blue with black stripes, but a kind of lighter iridescent blue I hadn't seen before—"

"Liz," Margo said firmly, indicating Leftie, who sat on the log bench, waiting.

"Sorry, yes. Have you seen his twin, Alan? He's over there."

Leftie's eyes, deep-set and black and sad, flicked to either side, as if they couldn't quite bear to land on her.

"Before," he began, "we did not live good. We stayed in the men's house and ate the animals we hunted and told the women and the children all the meat was eaten by the spirits. We fought with other tribes and beat the women."

All the time he spoke his hands twisted round and round, a pair of snakes trying to get the better of each other.

"What did you fight over, with the other tribes?"

Leftie stilled his hands and gave a rueful smile, but still he didn't make eye contact.

"Everything. When I was a boy, everything. When the rains did not come. When the food was short. We fought the Lusi for two years over baibai nuts. We fought with Nainal over a woman. Twenty-three men got killed. We used bows and arrows. We would wait for them and—"

He stopped, aware that he had grown enthusiastic. The hand-twisting resumed.

"They were very bad times."

"And what happened with the mission?"

"When Mista Josh came he wanted to know everything. We storied him on Titikolo and Amulmul and Black Moses. He visited and wrote the stories down in books. And we were pleased because there are many hills in New Ulster and they had come to ours."

"He was learning about your history."

"It happened like this. He took all the stories and told us, 'You must all now follow me, and I will work this.'"

"What did he mean?"

"All these other stories that youse are working, these are not real, these are not true, they are Satan tricking you all. These are the lies and the longlong tricks of your ancestors, the law of darkness."

"And did you know who Satan was?"

Leftie shrugged.

"He said Satan is the baddest of all spirits, the most bikhet. He is not masalai. Satan is more strong than that. And he will come to get you. Satan will pull you down to the belowground and keep you there and burn you every day. Mister Josh stood up in this church and made fire of all these papers, of the stories of Amulmul. He burned them in front of everyone." Leftie waggled his fingers in the air, imitating the fire. "And he said, 'You cannot live with this anymore. You cannot live in darkness. All of your ancestors died in sin because they did not know the real God. They are all in hell burning and crying forever. This is a fact. They are calling out to you. And that is how he turned our thinking."

"And what about Belef? How did you come to follow her?"

Leftie shrugged again.

"They are keeping secrets from us."

"What do you mean?"

"Belef saw the truth. They say we are rubbish, that we are nothing-men, but they put our gods in a big house in Sydney in glass cages. They steal our gods and give nothing back. They live in a house with plenty food and plenty water and give us nothing. We follow them and our children die. It's same same."

Margo nodded.

"That's great. That's more than enough."

Belef led them around, resplendent in her Paul Smith dressing gown. Paolo walked behind, filming everything, scanning the cleared earth, the women cooking, the church, the controller's hut. Stan and Margo followed. Margo held her trusty clipboard across her chest like a breastplate against the world. Liz and Posingen were the beast's straggly tail. As they set off, Posingen produced a stick of sugarcane from his pocket and broke it in half, offering it to her. Like chewing a twig, but delicious.

"I'm fine," she said when he produced another one.

"No, no," he said. "Look."

"What is it?"

"From the leg of the cassowary."

It was a small bone flute, seven or eight holes roughly carved into it.

Posingen placed it in his mouth and played, unmistakably, the opening notes of "Danny Boy."

"That's an Irish song."

"I know," he said, and smiled. His handsome face looked goofy.

"The 'Londonderry Air.' How do you know it?" Liz asked.

"My school in Wapini was St. Ignatius mission school, run by Irish nuns. An Irish priest. Father McNally."

"How was it?"

Posingen gave his massive shoulders a small shiver, and allowed himself a wry smile.

"I learned to read some and write some. And some songs. But the nuns were very angry. They were cross patches. They did not want to be there."

"How angry?" Liz asked.

Posingen held out his forearm—a crisscross pattern of welts stretched from the wrist to the elbow.

———————

Stan stopped Belef by an okari tree at the edge of the runway. A bulbous blister the size of a football erupted from the trunk at head height, a few bright heart-shaped leaves sprouting from it, in contrast to the okari's darker foliage. The carbuncle looked like a frog's vocal sac, smooth and swollen. Stan pointed.

"What do you call this in Koriam?"

"Bomba."

"Bomba," he repeated. "We call it an ant plant in English."

"Bomba," Belef declared again and tapped it with her stick. In response ants swarmed from it down the trunk and Liz saw the underside was honeycombed with galleries, ant real estate. Belef hit the plant again and another wave of émigrés erupted. "It takes from the tree, the bomba, and gives nothing back."

Kirlassa had succumbed to forest, been swallowed by it, and they walked through the ruination. Nature had paraphrased each hut into a mockery, a prototype of hut. The idea of a wall might appear, but rotted, mossy, subsided at an angle, and now a platform for a roost of saplings, underpinning for a bank of dank ferns. A center post stood sentry oddly by itself, robed in white-flowering clematis. The ardency of the greenery cast a spell of silence over the group as they walked among the dereliction.

Hundreds of years might have passed—these ruins could be Mayan, Aztec, Khmer—but it was only a decade. Nothing really. Cities dealt exclusively in human time: working hours, last minute, the final call. But out here one encountered other kinds: insect time, bird time, grass time, fern time, the time it took a river to erode a hole in a rock so it looked like a seat of a tractor, the time it took a cloud to pass across the blue roof of a clearing . . .

"What are they doing?" Liz asked, pointing. One woman sat near a little stepped stream that came down through the trees and then disappeared into the ground. Her lowered head was very still, as if in prayer. She was staring at the hole where the water disappeared.

"Ah this is Mupil, a holy place. The river is called Power. Come."

As the procession came towards her, the woman stopped her earth vigil and looked up. One of her eyes followed them and the other did not. Belef pointed at the hole in the limestone where the water disappeared. The falling water made a low-pitched, repetitive rushing sound, and Belef cupped one hand to her ear—another inauthentic gesture, Liz thought. Belef was also a "presenter."

"Do you hear the noise?" she said. "It is our generator. This place belongs to Michael Ross and Johnson and Bullet."

"What is she looking *for?*" Liz asked.

"Pikchas of the cargo."

There was a brief exchange in Koriam between Belef and the woman, and Belef knelt.

"These ones—"

A column of ants—little ebony centaurs—passed over the edge of the limestone. With their raised front legs, they carried tiny white specks.

"Are they eggs, the little white things?"

"These ones make a pikcha of what is coming. They carry rice to show us rice is coming. And this one—"

A beetle—testaceous, thuggish, low-slung—plodded across another part of the rock.

"This one is a truck going in, and look . . ."

Another ant walked towards it, and then round it.

"There is a car, avoiding it. It is a mark, it is a sign, and now we must get up the songs."

"That was pretty good, but let's try it again."

"Give me a minute."

There was just Margo and Paolo and Liz left by the stream now. Liz leaned back on her hunkers. Her thighs ached but the shot looked good and she had to hold the pose. She repeated the same spontaneous gestures at the limestone rock, the little river.

"This is a culture that strives to re-present reality through metaphor. From Anglo-Saxon to Native American cultures, traditional magic focuses on *miming* the object you want to capture or create. Charms, spells, poetry—they're incanatory; they call forth what they desire. And wanting something badly enough makes you see it everywhere. Religions involve mapping our desires onto objects. Christians see the body of Christ in bread or his blood in wine. And as we've seen with this stream, whose rushing and falling, to followers of the Story, sounds like the generators they hear at the white men's houses, and these insects they liken to cars and trucks, everything is proof, everything is evidence that they are right, and that some God—their God—is sending them signs to tell them so."

Belef sat on a tree stump carved into a seat. She was shaking in time with the drumming; her eyes were closed. The dancers faced her and took small rhythmic steps back and forth, chanting, "Amulmul, Amulmul." Some had adorned themselves with small headdresses of foliage or entwined leaves, but they wore their usual mix of Western and native clothes.

Belef raised both hands and the crowd responded as if on invisible strings, letting themselves be jerked upwards and upwards. Her eyes were closed. She conducted the mass around her. Suddenly one of the men began hooting, high pitched and eerie.

At the call, the people parted and a conga line, a snake of six figures appeared, shuffling from foot to foot, hands on the hips of the one in front. The leader—Alan—had the face of a snake drawn in white on his bare chest. The rest had painted bones onto their bodies, as if the skeleton showed through. They were animalized—some wore headdresses of cuscus or tree kangaroo, others sported the fantastical plumes of paradise birds.

Stones, shells, bottle caps adorned their ears, their necks, their fingers. One had a nest of broken twigs in his hair, and one wore a cape made of matted reeds, held with a clasp fashioned from a pig tusk. They wore anklets and wristlets of dried grass. They carried spears and chanted, "Mon-eee Mon-eee Mon-eee," as they circled the central fire. They were go-betweens, Liz thought—offering a lesson about life and death. The rainbows of feathers, the mother-of-pearl, the adornments spoke to vitality, but the skeleton beneath had been made visible, and it said, *What you are, we once were. What we are, you will be.*

The men separated to rush an invisible enemy, hooting and brandishing their spears.

Liz asked Belef, as she sat on her makeshift throne, "What is this?"

"The dead will repay us with cargo. We show how much we do for them. We give everything away so they will help us."

She gave a loud sniff and spat some scarlet betel juice on the grass.

Liz stood a few feet in front of the skeleton men—they wheeled behind her with their arms out, like kids pretending to be planes. The chanting was so loud she had to shout into her mic. "This dancing is to *please* the dead. Belef and her followers don't want the dead to be banished, or be invisible, or to be sectioned off in a graveyard. The whole point of tonight's ceremony is to indebt the dead, to make the dead owe them something, to oblige them to deliver the cargo, to send the living their reward. The Story wants to make a future by entering into ethical relations with the past."

Napasio led Namor's huge pig to the clearing. Several men descended on it and the squealing started. When they drew back it lay on its side with its legs trussed, a block of wood tied in its mouth. So much living poundage of pork and salt and fat. It strained and jerked and threw its head back to moan. Namor watched from the edge of the group, chewing a fingernail. Leftie knelt beside it, whispered to it, and with a quick twitch of a blade slit the pig's throat. Blood came in blackish spurts, a curtain of it falling from the pink gape of flesh, darkening the grass. Even with the wood wedged in its mouth the pig didn't stop squealing. Paolo went in close on its eyes; they were clouding over. Namor moved beside it and stroked its broad shuddering flank. When it stopped moving and was silent, he disappeared at a run into the forest.

"I was instructed by Michael Ross. We work it like this so the tumbuna are close and the tumbuna want to come up now and they have sorrow for us. They are moved, we give worry to them."

She adjusted her cap and walked back across the front of the fire, pausing to point at the pig already being roasted on a spit over the flames.

"We kill the pigs and we abandon our gardens and we march and go hungry and we stay awake. They will help us for this. When they see how much we do, they will give us the cargo they have. The living need cargo more than the dead. Who would deny it?

She turned and looked around at her listeners. A few nodded agreement. Some were talking among themselves and she raised her voice.

"It is like this: The men kill the women. The men kill the dongen. My own mother screams from underground. And the women want to send the cargo to us, but the men say no, they cannot have it. The men stop it. The mission men want to keep it all to themselves. I have some knowledge to pass on. Michael Ross told me this last night."

Belef waited until the entire group was silent. Only the fire sizzled and cracked as fat from the pig dripped on it. She spoke softly again, imparting a secret.

"I have told you before that Jesus is a prophet of Amulmul and wanted to help us. He wanted to come back to us, but the white men stopped him. I have new knowledge. The truth is this: Jesus is a woman. They have lied to us about it! She has no penis! In all the pictures, what is there? Just"—she rubbed her thumb and fingers together—"a little hair. They know the female is powerful—they try to stop it. They are fooling youse. Before they told us we were free we had a queen. I saw this queen again on the secret medal Lizbet gave Namor this afternoon—"

Belef pulled a coin from the pocket of the meri skirt and held it up. It was the fifty-pence piece Liz had given Namor. She waved it towards Liz.

"I know this pikcha. She is Queen, Queen Elissabet. You wear her name. You work for her. And the woman is the most powerful, but men have placed themselves between us and the queen; if they were not there we would be fine. And the white men know it, for they do not hit their wives or cross them. The whites put a silasila around the cargo. They stopped us with a fence. They buried it underground. They burnt it. They made it disappear. But we will find it. Elissabet will lead us to it."

Maybe a dozen fires were lit across the runway now, and they sat in a circle around the fire nearest the church. Margo had brought spare clothing for Liz, and she put on her North Face jacket and a woolly hat. Belef stepped from person to person and held a battered tin bowl of warm cloudy liquid up to their mouths. She said, "Take, drink, do this in remembrance of me."

Stan whispered, "It's basically kava, which they have in Fiji. Do you know it? They boil the roots of the kava plant and strain the water through muslin. They call it isa here."

"Is it alcoholic?" Liz whispered back.

"Mildly hallucinogenic. It just sends me to sleep, though."

"You know, I don't think I'm going to have any—but Liz, you *should* try it. So you can talk about it."

Margo put her hand up to reject the bowl, but Belef just stood there, waiting.

"*Fine.* I'll just let it touch my lips."

"It tastes like shit," Liz confirmed.

"I like it," Paolo said. "Like drinking earth."

Finally, the meat was ready. Long dark strips of pig, carved off with wooden blades, were served on banana leafs. Liz watched Stan and Paolo tuck in. She waved the plate away. Belef called Namor and finally he sloped reluctantly across and sat at her feet, chewing his pet. The isa began to work, warmth spreading through her body. Her ears grew very hot. When she turned her head it took a second for her vision to catch up. Eyesight was slowing down just as her brain began speeding up. It was dusk, and the orange tinge was giving way to gray. The first few stars were coming out. The edges of the trees waved like hands, imparting something but she didn't know what.

Belef's followers—maybe a hundred in all—lounged around campfires. Belef, and her surrogates Leftie and Alan, visited each circle in turn and served up the isa, leaving a bowl and a full plastic canister behind for them to keep drinking and serving themselves.

People lay on their backs and sides, chatted softly, stared into space, fell asleep. Margo was sitting very still and humming to herself. Stan curled up in a ball and put his head on his rucksack. Paolo sat beside Liz and kept saying that it didn't seem to be affecting him, that it wasn't working, that he couldn't feel anything.

Liz lay back on the grass and looked at the sky. She had the distinct impression she was not looking upwards but was in fact hanging above everything, looking down into space. She felt as if she might fall off the surface towards the starry floor beneath her. She took hold of Paolo's hand and gripped it like it was the single filament connecting her to earth. She was aware of existing within the frame, within the cage of her body.

She lay for a while and watched the sky turn. The crescent moon appeared from behind a silhouetted peak and began drifting upwards through the deep arrangement of stars. She sat up. The fires, the people, the trees, the grass—it came with the force of revelation that she herself existed as a wave of energy, and that this wave of energy flowing through her flowed just the same through all these other things. The fires, the people, the trees, the grass. They were all secretly the same thing. They were all one. She was overwhelmed with a sense of the world's clandestine harmony, and looked at Paolo, and could see by the way he was now grinning stupidly at her that he felt it too.

CHAPTER 30

Ian Hutchinson was kept busy by betrayal. Lies were hard work—you had to keep up with them. For example, the night before he'd stayed up at their holiday house in Castlerock, not with his family but with Charlotte, the eighteen-year-old receptionist he was sleeping with, whom he then had to drop off at her hair salon in Portrush before heading back to Ballyglass. He'd already called the office and left a message that he was seeing clients on the road all morning, and timed it all so he got back just after Trish and the kids had left for school. The kettle was still warm; two soggy bowls of cereal sat on the kitchen table.

Now he lay on his marital bed masturbating; beside him, propped on a pillow, the iPad showed a shop assistant with improbable cleavage getting fucked standing up in a changing room. It occurred to him that the sheer obvious discomfort of her position appeared to be what turned him on. He was efficient, brief, and just wrapping a tissue around the raw head to catch the semen when a small box appeared in the corner of the screen. A sent message from Trisha to Spencer.

Ian Hutchinson dropped the tissue in the toilet.

He was neither outraged nor angry. Instead, the knowledge entered as a sadness. The tone of his wife's message was soft, a softness he recognized as belonging once to him. Even with all the work he himself did with lying, he still felt tender towards Trish, or at least had not moved his old tenderness entirely to anyone else. He just fucked other people, and for a moment now the text had the strange inverse effect of making him feel guilty about that. It took a good ten minutes before he could sufficiently transfer all the guilt, lock and stock, onto her. Lying is work but righteous fury is so easy, can be slipped on like a coat.

He takes his time. He showers and dresses and drives to Donnellys Estate Agents. He parks outside the office and waves through the glass at Trisha sitting behind the desk. She waves emptily back. When he doesn't come in immediately, she gets up and walks out to the car and raises one hand to ask what he wants.

He is very clear about what he wants. He beckons her down to the car window and reaches through and grabs her by the throat.

CHAPTER 31

I t was dark.

The dancing had begun again.

The kunda drums pounded out a beat and feet stamped the ground in time, and Liz lay on her back in the grass and felt it rising through the earth.

"You have to just give in to it," Paolo shouted as Liz tried to sit up.

"Are you going to be sick again?" Stan asked.

"I wasn't sick."

"Not you. Margo."

"Where is she?"

"I'm here. I'm right here. Has anyone noticed how the trees are rippling, like flames?"

Margo was lying on her side behind Stan, next to a puddle of vomit.

"Those *are* flames," Stan said.

"Is something on fire?"

"The fire is on fire."

"I am so high."

"Me too."

Stan stumbled to his feet and began to dance. His jerkiness reminded Liz of the cassowary. And she wondered for what seemed a long time if he *was* the cassowary or if the cassowary was his spirit animal and what hers was and why. Now she was in the circle dancing and so was Margo and so was Paolo and there were many grinning faces dancing at them and round them and there was this pounding beat that just went on and on and on. She was smiled at more than she'd ever been smiled at.

She tried to emulate the way the dancers shifted from foot to foot, but in the end she just stood there and bobbed in the traditional Northern Irish manner like a cork or an aunt at a wedding. There were drums and chanting and a thin reedlike warbling. Maybe it was someone singing, maybe it was pipes or something. She looked around and around but couldn't see anyone playing anything. The music came out of the earth itself.

Suddenly the smiles stopped and the dancers got to work with intricate routines—dipping, turning, swaying, barking. She staggered over to the side and sat down by Margo.

She raised her hand to her face and watched as it aged in front of her. She knew, from reading about it, that this happened to everyone, it was Hallucinogenic Experience 101, but this did not make it any less extraordinary. The hand wrinkled and aged and finally the skin dissolved, the bones, the cartilage fell away. There was only space, trembling space, where her hand had been.

The dancers formed concentric circles. Suddenly the outer circle crouched, and then the next one and the next one and so on—until only the innermost circle, the decorated dancers, the skeleton men, were left upright. They turned and faced outwards and moaned and pretended to fall down dead. Belef stood there, the center of all circles, the sanctum sanctorum.

She shook and shivered. She wailed, she stomped. Around her the crouching people chanted, "Amulmul, Amulmul."

She raised a hand and pointed it at Liz and shouted, "I see Queen Elissabet. She has the message from Kasingen, from my daughter, from the dongen, from all the dead women. What are we to do? Speak to us."

Liz found herself lifted and pushed forward. Margo tried to grab hold of her arm, but there were too many hands on her. She floated on a sea of hands. The circles opened for her and closed behind her. Belef's eyes were ecstatic, hard, and empty.

"Kaykay! What are we to do?"

"I'm Liz," shouted Liz.

"Kaykay talks in you. What must we do?"

"No—I'm Liz. Just keep having, just keep on—"

Belef gripped the sides of Liz's head and pulled her face into hers. Bodies were all around them. Belef shouted, "You gave your Elisabet coin to Namor. You gave your money away. And we must do the same."

"No, there was no—"

"We must give our money to the dead. So they see we have nothing and send us cargo."

"I didn't mean anything by—"

"We must follow you. We must open the road like this."

The music stopped. The bodies peeled away and Belef released her.

Liz stumbled backwards, but dozens of strange hands kept her in the circle. She felt panic rise within her. All along she had thought Belef was the gate, the key, the strangeness, the location of the magic, and Belef had thought it was her. She was the alien visitor, the unlikely revelation, named for the most powerful woman in the world, a real queen, a vehicle for the dead daughters, for the dead mothers. Liz tried again to break out of the circle and found herself pushed back in.

"I have nothing to do with this," she shouted. "I don't know anything about this."

Somehow a chain of followers formed and began to throw their bank notes and kina into a circle at Belef's feet. When there was a pile of notes there—crumpled autumn leaves—Belef motioned to Leftie and he retrieved a burning branch from the fire.

"Queen Elisabet says you must do this! Kaykay says you must do this! You must burn the money."

Liz looked around for Margo or Paolo or Stan, but there were only the faces of Belef's followers—of Napasio, of Namor's mother, of Leftie and Buggle and Alan.

"No," Liz said. "No, I can't, I can't do this."

She tried to hand the branch back to Leftie, but he stepped away.

"You must open the road, Lissabeth. Kaykay chose you. Kaykay sent you."

Liz felt her own judgment begin to crumble to circumstance, to some-one else's power and personal force. Belef was nodding at her, willing her on, and it made a very real sense suddenly to walk to the little scatter of crumpled orange and green notes.

They watched her intently. She took the burning torch Leftie offered her and dropped it on top of the money. The paper began to crinkle up and then the whole lot flared into life. The followers roared and the kunda drums began again. Liz found her way back to where her group had been and slumped to the ground. Margo sat with her head between her knees. The rest were nowhere to be seen.

Then Liz heard shouts of anger, they were coming from the direction of the church, and two of Alan's army appeared a few feet from her, car-rying some large resistant object. The thing twisted and yelped and Belef looked on with vague interest as it was dumped in front of her. The thing got to its feet: Usai, one sleeve of his Britney Spears T-shirt ripped along the shoulder seam.

"You spying on us? You working for the New Truth?"

Usai looked at his feet.

"Mother, you must—"

Alan stepped forward and efficiently punched him in the stomach. He doubled up and went down on his knees.

"We found him behind the church, with matches and paper. Going to fire it up," Alan said.

Usai looked at Belef.

"Mother, that isn't true. I came to tell you, you need to come back to Christ. Come back to the real church. They will put you in jail."

"This man betrayed all of us. Kasingen and me and the Story. It is time Usai is stopped."

"We have to do something." Liz wiped the hair away from Mar-go's face.

"Leave me alone."

"Snap out of it."

"They've found Usai in the trees and they're hurting him."

"I need to lie here and never move again."

Margo rolled onto her side and curled up in a ball, hiding her face in her hands.

"Margo!"

"What!"

"They're going to hurt him."

"*I* hurt."

Liz stood up. Her vision was still unsteady. Everything flowed. She couldn't see Paolo or Stan. She stepped towards the circle. The ground moved up to meet her feet.

"Belef, please, let him go. He's your son."

The woman grinned diabolically.

"No. He betrayed us."

"Please let him go."

"Lizbet, you are soft like water. We should tie him to the flagpole. We should raise him as our flag and slit his throat."

"Please. He's terrified."

Usai's face was bleeding. He knelt in the firelight.

"He wants to burn the church and stop the cargo."

Usai stared at the ground. Belef raised her hand.

"He must be punished by Amulmul."

"You have to let him go. He is your son. He is Kasingen's brother."

Belef waited. She made her thinking face, squinted. Scratched her chin.

Liz hesitated, then shouted, "Kasingen says she wants you to let him go. Kasingen says you have to."

Belef grinned, a huge grin bloody with betel nut. Liz had the impression suddenly that Belef had been waiting for this.

"All right, all right, you have come to open the road and we will learn from you." She turned to Usai. "Go," she said softly. "Run away, little one."

Usai got up and walked through the followers, pushed and jeered at but granted passage. His silhouette was swallowed by the forest.

She lay between Margo and Stan now in front of the fire. She was still high, and the sensation came and went, came and went. Had she killed someone, saved someone? Neither. She had not added her weight to the wrong side of the scale. Perhaps that was the best any person like her—not brave, not a God, not a leader—could ask for. She felt she had been thrown out of the universe and hauled back in. Staring into the flames, surrounded by bodies, by the slowly rising and falling sounds of breathing. Galactic time, nighttime, deep time, the time of stars, time of the moon. She must have fallen asleep.

CHAPTER 32

Alison ushered David Boyd into the living room. He wore a sports coat and a pair of green corduroys, and he carried a brown briefcase. With the thick glasses and the wiry red hair and the tall-thin build, he was exactly what she'd always thought a professor would look like. In his late forties, or thereabouts. He wouldn't meet her eye and she thought of a boy who was like that in school. They'd called it shyness then; now they'd say he was on the spectrum. She helped him along: "Come in the car, did you? Will you have a cup of tea?" She left him and went into the kitchen to split and butter a few scones while she waited for the kettle to boil. Stephen stood by the fridge, and she could see by his face he was having second thoughts. She gave him a quick hug and asked him was he OK. He turned and hugged her back.

"You'll go out, won't you?" he replied. "I don't want you in the house."

She nodded and called through to the academic.

"You from Coleraine, David?"

"From Derry. Londonderry."

"Oh yes?"

"Yes."

She arranged the tea things on a tray and handed them to Stephen. "I'm just going to pop out and leave you to it. I'll be back in a couple of hours. D'you reckon that'll be enough time?"

"I'd expect so," Stephen said. His voice faltered and he said it again. She knew it was stupid but didn't she feel a little proud? Here was this man from the university to talk to her Stephen. To let Stephen explain.

———————

Thanks for agreeing to meet. I'm sure this can't be terribly easy for you.

The interviewer, this fella Boyd, kept rearranging himself on the sofa, and his discomfort put Stephen more firmly back into himself. It was not easy to talk about that night—partly because it had been hardened into certain details by the police and the courts and by his own telling and re-telling of it, and those details, while not exactly false, didn't give a wholly true or representative impression. The evening was not to be caught in words or conveyed in them. The hurry and the panic, the slip of the moon appearing and disappearing over the hedges as they roared along the back roads towards the bar. All the wild excitement. How cold the steel felt as he lifted out the semi-automatic from the Adidas holdall. The solidity. The grip of it. The dry mouth. The fear of it. The long walk to the door. And then the punters in the bar ignoring them as they entered and a few of them laughing at the masks. And then the fresh rage coming down—once the first shot went off. Once the first one was fired. Once the thing began, it all turned so unreal so fast. It was getting the first one off. Then: easy. A crumpling. The brief song of each shot. Casting madness into the crowd. *Pop-pop-pop* and how they dropped and crumpled. How they went. How they disappeared like that. *Click*. Whole beings discontinued. How his ears had rung. He couldn't hardly hear the boys in the car afterwards at all. They'd been whipped up to a frenzy, whooping and laughing. Only when the two police cars hurtled past them, sirens going, heading to the Day's End—the place of the dead, the place they drove away from, the mess that they had made—did the chatter stop for a second, did Stephen think what has been done, what have we done, what have I done.

No bother.

He felt himself clam up, his throat close down. He coughed and swallowed.

Can you just talk us through your involvement with the UFF? Your childhood, et cetera?

My childhood, et cetera?

Stephen tried a wry smile, but David was working at the Dictaphone.

He watched David lean forward slowly and set it—red light flashing—on the coffee table.

You happy enough for me to use this?

Oh aye. It's not going to be played anywhere, is it?

Just in the archives. But it won't be available, obviously, until you're dead.

Cheerful.

We're all passing into history.

David gave a small smile at last and handed a stapled contract and a biro across to Stephen.

I'm the undersigned?

You are.

He squiggled his name on it—one of his names—and handed it back.

You done many of these?

David smiled again. It appeared he was beginning to get the hang of this cheeriness business.

I'm not at liberty to disclose that.

Fair enough. Stephen touched his nose as if they were in on a secret.

They'd been back two days and Alison's only trip out in public was dropping Isobel at her nursery that morning. The staff treated Alison normally—all smiles—but they knew, they must know. After she'd driven back home, she sat in the car and rang Judith, and cried a bit on the phone and asked her to pick Isobel up after nursery, just for today. "It'll get better," her mum said. But why would it? Nothing could change.

Now she pushed the buggy purposefully past the Ancient Order of Hibernians's Hall, the Ballyglass Furniture Centre, O'Neill's Butchers. It was half eleven on a Wednesday, the town was sleepy. Three smirking, mitching schoolboys in Ballyglass High blazers went past and she felt a sharp pang of nostalgia for the uniform, the rough polyester of the blazer, the narrow slippery tie. A black Honda Civic went past and beeped its horn. Was it at her? She didn't know. But it shook her, the long sounding of the horn, and she began to lose her nerve. She could easily go and sit in the kitchen without disturbing Stephen. Sure, she'd promised not to listen to the interview but she should listen. She should hear it. Wasn't it important that she know?

She unlocked the back door quietly, left a sleeping Michael in the utility room, draping a towel out of the drier over the front of the buggy, and sat down quietly at the kitchen table, by the radiator, still wearing her coat. She held her purse. If he came in she could show him that she'd just come back for it, that she was on her way back out again.

The door to the living room was closed, but she could hear everything easily.

I mean, a Protestant background but nothing so unusual. My dad was in the forces for a while.

The army?

UDR reservist.

And you were from Derry? From Londonderry?

Prods from the Cityside. My granny lived on the Foyle Road and a few days after Bloody Sunday there was a knock at her door and four men in balaclavas came in and trashed the place. She was given a day to get out. Sixty-six years old and they forced her on the floor and one of them stood on her back. We lived in the Fountain area until I was ten, I think, and then we moved out to the countryside, out to a wee farm of about three acres near Limavady. It used to be my uncle's and he left it to my mother.

What happened to your granny?

Lost everything. Moved in with her sister in Coleraine. The IRA kicked twenty thousand Prods out of the Cityside of Londonderry in that month or two after Bloody Sunday. They lost everything. My granny got two hundred pounds from the government for her house—which was all paid off and worth four thousand. When she went back to get her stuff two days later, the Official IRA were there moving another family in. When she asked the man for her belongings she was told it was all dumped. All gone.

Was your father involved?

Well, you have to remember where we were. The Fountain area's surrounded by republican enclaves. I wasn't born yet but my dad would have been . . . lightly involved, let's say—like all the men. He wasn't in any organization. He wasn't in the UDA or anything, but he would have been defending the area. Everyone was.

What happened to him?

He joined the UDR as a reservist. He wasn't particular as to the Union or anything. He joined for the money. You got well paid and it let him run the farm. He'd do some lorry driving too for a while there. Haulage for a crowd over in Eglinton. Anyway, the Provos got him when I was thirteen. They were waiting out behind the barn when he went to feed the pigs on a Sunday night, and they shot him twenty-six times. We all heard the shooting and tried to run out, but my ma blocked the back door of the house. Sure, there was almost nothing left of him.

There was a long pause.

He was a good guy. He always thought the Catholics had a just argument. He'd say, You can't treat anyone like a lesser citizen and expect them to put up with it. You're sowing dragon's teeth. A religious man. I'd come into the bedroom at night and see him on his hands and knees at the end of the bed. I asked him once what he was doing. I was only a wee lad. And he said, What do you think I'm doing? I said, I think you're talking to God. And he laughed and said, I'm negotiating. Is that working properly? The light's flashing on it.

I put new batteries in it . . . Let me check.

Click. Click. Stephen's voice, smaller, tinnier, came out—*the light's flashing on it.*

What was your family life like?

What do you mean?

Were you a happy family?

Couldn't say that exactly. Not unhappy neither. There was five of us in a three-bed terraced in the Fountain. Me and my brother Roy shared a room. Bunk beds. My sister Susan, she was a bit older, she had her own room. But my mum and da fought like billy-o. Not often. But when they went at it, they really went at it, if you know what I mean.

Did you join the UFF because of, because of what had happened to your dad?

Well, you know, I'm sure that was part of it. But when we lived in the city, in the Fountain and on the Waterside, well it was part of the local culture. I mean you knew who the local bigwigs were, who the men were you didn't want to cross, and you admired them in a way. They had power. They were the ones who could sort stuff out, if you know what I mean. And I wanted to be a part of that. And you have to remember what was going on then. I was looking around and we were being killed left, right, and center, you know? It was tribal. There was no pushback. It was all one way. I was just convinced that it was time for me to do my part.

And what age were you then?

Eighteen, nineteen. It was 1990, 1991, that kind of time.

And how did you get involved? What steps did you take?

I was back in the Waterside by then, staying with a friend. Looking for work. Not very successfully—or thoroughly, I might add. I began selling magazines to raise a bit of cash for the LPA.

Which was?

The Loyalist Prisoners Association. We'd set up a stall on the Twelfth and the Last Saturday and all that. Loyal Men and True—that was one of them. The Defenders, that was another. We'd sell badges, magnets, scarves. Aye, and we had tapes and CDs of Paisley giving it what for to the Papes, and pipe bands, and bands singing loyalist songs. That sort of stuff. Would you like a heater in that tea?

Alison stood up to hide in the toilet. Her chair gave a tiny scrape, but David answered.

No, no, I'm good, thanks. But if you want to make yourself a cup?

Aw no, I just had my breakfast. Too much tea gives me the shakes.

And then what happened?

Well, I waited for a year or so. I was in no hurry to rush it, you know. But I was sure in my heart of hearts that I wanted to do it, you know, to go further. And then a man asked me did I want to join. Obviously I won't be telling you any names.

You understand this is sealed.

Well, that's as may be but you never know what'll happen now, do you? I don't know you from Adam. And I'd just as soon not mention any names. Some of these guys are possibly still in the game, and some are respected members of the community, as it were. So let's just say a man asked me did I want to join.

And you said?

I said I did. Because I did.

Alison found her stomach was cramping up. The voice was Stephen's but it didn't sound like Stephen. He was very sure of himself. She looked at the fridge, the magnet saying ONLY BORING WOMEN HAVE TIDY HOUSES, at Judith's recipe for lasagna, at the primary-colored magnetic letters Isobel had used to spell out MICKEE, MVMMY, ISOB3L, LOVE.

This was the UFF, you understand. And this fella asked me was I sure, had I given it thought. He said that there were things that I would be asked to do. But it was a question of belief. I had faith in the Union, in the fundamental right we had to be British. And I accepted we were at war. In war people had to do difficult things.

What else did he say?

You know, detailed the things. Handling explosives, hiding guns, moving shipments, all that stuff. Just what you'd expect.

David nodded. He capped his pen and uncapped it.

And you said?

I said yes, I accepted that.

Was there a ceremony? A swearing-in or anything?

Nothing like that. Myself and another man just had to go to a wee house—I won't be saying where it was—and meet some people. And that was that. Some shaking hands and then I was told, Well now, you're in, you're a member of the Ulster Freedom Fighters.

And then?

Well, nothing, not immediately. After a few weeks there was a phone call and I had to drive a few lads to a house to give someone a beating then take them home again. I waited in the car. Then I had to pick up a bag and deliver it. Small things, you know. And there was a weekend in weapons training, on a farm in Carryduff.

Do you know the name of the people you killed?

What do you mean?

I just wondered if you knew the names?

That's not really the . . . I mean . . . What's that got to do with it?

I was just curious. You were saying—

There was the Shankill bombing. You remember. They killed nine Protestants in the fish shop. And Adams carried the bomber's coffin—Begley, it was, who'd got himself killed. I mean when I heard about the bombing I was shocked, you know, but then afterwards there was this rage. They were just killing Protestants. It was genocide. It couldn't have been more nakedly sectarian. I wanted revenge. You know, at that time. Everyone wanted revenge.

Right.

And a few days after the bombing we were summoned to our CO's place and—

The Mexican?

Ah, the Mexican. You know about that?

That's what the judge called him.

You've done your homework. No comment. I can't be saying anything about that.

Stephen thought of him: Patton Andrews. He answered the door and they followed him into the living room. Little porcelain figures of Disney characters on a side table. Photographs of children in blue school uniforms. Two girls and a boy. Andrews was a tall bald guy in glasses but with dark eyes so deep set and penetrating they suggested a certain natural force. He was used to being listened to. He congratulated Stephen and Lenny. He told them he was proud of them. Andrews would move to a much bigger house in Ballycastle, buy a villa down in the Algarve, drive a BMW. And never spend an hour inside.

Just strange, now, so long afterwards, that they never got the guy who ordered it, you know. You served two years, and the guy who told you to do it, who sent you in, got off scot-free.

There was a long silence.

Well, it's like this. When you sign up, you know what you're getting into.

What were you told?

Just that there was to be an operation. We were going to see action, you know. Something would happen. You were taken to a location and told what weapons you'd be using. But we didn't know where. We'd be told the target on the day. I mean, we knew already this wasn't going to be an IRA member or a Shinner. This was eye for an eye, tooth for a tooth. We were going to hurt the Nationalists for protecting the IRA.

You mean Catholics?

We were going to be indiscriminate like they were indiscriminate.

When did you find out about the Day's End?

We were told to go to a certain place and we stayed the night there. On the morning of the shooting we were picked up and split into twos. And that was so if there was an informer among us they wouldn't have a chance to contact the army or the police. And then we were told the target would be that pub in Eden.

The Day's End.

Aye.

And what was the plan?

Simple enough, like. We were to head in and spray the bar from top to toe with gunfire and kill as many people as possible.

Alison found her breath was coming very quick and shallow now. Her lungs were refusing to cooperate. Three blue tits kept alighting on and leaving the feeder by the kitchen window. Flashes of blue and black and yellow, little flurries of peck and displacement. They seemed to have a freedom she longed for, right now: the power to leave.

As many as possible?

Yeah. We made a recce, myself and Lenny McAteer. I mean that's public knowledge. We stopped off at the bar about seven p.m. to see the layout, and there were only a few people there. We headed into the wrong bit at first. The lounge bar. There was only a young fella getting set up. So we went out and went back into the front bar. Ordered some food—

What did you eat?

What did I eat? Stephen laughed, but the laugh was only to cover a terrible fluttering inside.

I mean, I don't know. Fish and chips I think. We just generally looked around, you know. After we got our food we upped and left. Didn't eat it, you know. Too nervous, too excited. And we realized we'd have to go into the lounge bar later, really. The front bar layout was too difficult. We could get cut off and blocked in too easy. We went back to the safe house, just sat round and waited. By the time we actually left it was about nine o'clock and by then we were running a bit late. Because we had to go to where the weapons and boiler suits were.

Where were they?

At another house, not far from the bar, actually.

How were you feeling when you were doing all this?

Well, it's funny. When we got to the pub I was in a kind of trance. Mind more or less empty. You're going into war, you know. Like over the trenches. I mean over the top of the trenches. The body takes over.

Not quite war.

David Boyd had not looked up for a while. Stephen noticed now that the researcher's left leg was jiggling up and down. Too much caffeine.

How do you mean?

Well, you weren't going to fight anyone.

Boyd's face was pale and Stephen saw dark circles under his eyes he hadn't noticed before.

Yeah, but see your body's wired. It's flooded with adrenalin!

Sure.

Things seemed like a dream kind of thing. Like you weren't really there. Everything made no sense and a very real sense. Do you see what I mean?

Not really.

Maybe it sounds mad, but that's the best way I could tell it—we were all hyped up and crazy. Laughing and on edge, butterflies. When the driver—

Mark Agnew—

You know it all already. Yeah, when Mark pulled into the car park we'd gone silent. We had to get down to business. John and Lenny and I pulled our masks on and got out and went in.

Alison knew it was a mistake now, this not leaving. How could it ever be the same again? It was like floating down a river, the Niagara River, and something was coming. The river was speeding up, there was a rushing sound, a hissing in the distance. She sat there rigidly, hands holding the purse on her lap, powerless.

Not running or anything. Calm as you like. And I remember one of the customers in there, an ould fella, telling us to wise up and put the guns away or something. Like he thought they were toys. And Lenny just shot him in the face with his pistol. That was it. We were away. I walked into the middle of the dance floor and just whirled around and around, letting the semi off. But you know everything was quiet. Things were going in slow motion. I mean, I knew there was gunfire happening but I couldn't hear it.

Stephen couldn't get it into words. Even if he was the instrument. Even if he was the one doing it, moving from thought to action, abstract to concrete, intention to execution, intention to *execution*—he couldn't quite believe that it was really *real*, not then or now. The people screaming, falling, crying. The Guinness mirror behind the bar exploded, and the disbelief broke into an understanding of this new clarity he was forcing on the world. His finger ached upon the trigger. His whole body roared.

Could you see what you were doing? Could you see the people in the bar?

I mean I could see it. It was like a video game, you know. Unreal. The people were just crumpling up. There was a lot of blood but it didn't seem real, you know. It didn't seem like I was doing it. They were just falling over and this blood was coming from them. But it wasn't anything to do with me.

Although it was, of course.

It seemed to last for ages but of course it couldn't have. A minute, two minutes tops.

In the kitchen Alison was falling out of one life and into another.

Were you picking victims out? Were you aiming at people?

I just had my finger on the trigger and was trying to keep control of the gun. The kickback on an AK-47 is pretty stiff. I managed to get two magazines out.

You managed to?

Yeah.

Stephen leaned forward and set his elbows on his knees, knitted his hands. The slight smirk on his face rearranged itself to sternness.

It's like this. It shouldn't have happened. But it was necessary, you know. It was necessary to show the IRA that they couldn't just kill innocent Protestants. I wish *none* of the atrocities had happened.

Necessary?

I'd say so, yes.

Do you know the names of the people you killed?

Sorry?

I'm just wondering again if you knew the names of the dead.

I . . .

I'm sorry—

No, it's all right. I don't dwell on that stuff.

And what about the families?

How do you mean?

Well, do you think *they* dwell on that?

David sat back a little in the chair and stared at Stephen then looked away.

I suppose they do, yes. It's terrible to lose anyone.

Why do you say it like that?

Like what? Stephen asked.

It's terrible to lose *anyone*. It's terrible to lose someone, someone specifically. It wasn't just a random event.

Well, no, of course—

It wasn't an avalanche.

Sorry?

It wasn't an accident. Or a natural disaster. It wasn't a tsunami.

David's voice had gotten louder.

I just mean—Stephen's tone was slow and soft, but Alison knew he was close to losing his temper—losing anyone is terrible.

David stared hard at his notepad and with the point of the Biro traced along one of the lines.

I'm not sure where this is going—

You know what I don't get, said David, digging into that line, working it over and over. You see them sometimes on the TV, don't you? People who've lost someone who was close to them? A daughter or husband or whatever, and they say stuff like they don't feel any bitterness towards the killer. They forgive them, they hope they have made peace with it, all that.

Are you from the University of Ulster? Stephen asked, his voice furled and tight.

I thought when I saw you I'd feel sorry for you even. Feel like it made something better.

Are you a—a relative of someone?

Oh, everyone's a relative of someone, Stephen. Don't you know that? We live in a small world here. A small corner of a very small island.

Oh God—

After a long pause, Alison heard one of the armchairs being pushed back along the laminated floor. Stephen had stood up. Now she heard the other one move.

Wait.

What?

You say, 'Oh God.' You should be keeping that word out of your mouth. But 'sorry' wouldn't help me either. What use is that? What force does it have in the world? What does it do? I don't know how people do it. Your man who lost his daughter at Enniskillen. He was full of mercy. Full of forgiveness. I don't feel like that, not at all. I'm full to the brim with bitterness and hate.

I didn't know . . . You should leave. My wife will be home soon—

Don't talk to me about your wife.

What's your name?

Don't you worry about it. You don't keep those names around. You don't want to dwell on that.

There was one called Creighton. There was one called Downey—

McFadden. Janine. And her mother. Moira Sheehy. Janine was having a baby. And she had a wee boy, Bobby, five years old then. Moira and Ja-nine. Two ordinary people. Ordinary people have rights like everybody else. But they don't get them. They don't fucking get them.

I don't think we should go on with this. This isn't what I thought it was going to be.

Sit down, Andrew.

I'm Stephen now.

Alison set her purse on the table. What was happening?

I understand you've found God now.

Who are you?

Just talk to me as we were talking. It was going well.

She heard the coffee table being pushed away.

My wife will be back in a minute with the kids.

Alison moved to the living room door and pushed it open; both men started at the movement. David sat on the sofa and Stephen sat in the armchair by the fire.

I'm back already.

Stephen stood up. He tried to push her back out through the door.

Alison, take the children and get out of here.

She ignored him and sat down on the arm of the sofa. David's eyes looked uninhabited; he stared at Alison like someone sleepwalking. He nodded at her.

David McFadden.

Your name's David McFadden?

The man nodded again. He began weeping and through a tremulous sigh murmured: Sure, you took my whole world from me.

The thing Alison knew she wouldn't forget was the man, David, speaking of the child, the little boy:

> *I wasn't much good at consoling him, really. I had my own grief. I wasn't much use to him. But that was the way it was. I was so shocked I couldn't cry. I had no feelings. I couldn't love*

and I couldn't hate. I was like a zombie. Imagine you've no
feelings about you. It wrecks you.

They were almost at the front door at that point, and he was crying again, and Alison started sobbing properly, big shuddering spasms. Then she was hugging McFadden. And all the time Stephen sat on the lowest stair in the hallway, waiting, motionless, staring straight ahead into the future.

McFadden was gone. Alison came in and went straight upstairs past Stephen. She knew she should embrace her husband, but she had no feelings left.

CHAPTER 33

They woke at first light, all the fires burnt out. Liz's head was on Paolo's thigh, her hand gripping his knee. There was dew on her hair, on her eyelashes. She shivered, she coughed, but her head felt remarkably fine. When she climbed to her feet, Paolo stood too and put his arms out, and she let herself be hugged for a long time by him. A few feet away, Margo lay in the shelter of a log, wrapped in some sacking from the floor of the church. Liz saw her watching them embrace with something close to amusement.

Stan led them all back to the village and the stunned, trembly silence gave way—as the sun rose higher—to the swapping of stories. Paolo said he'd filmed all night, and at one point saw a three-headed demon rise from the fire. Then his camera and the tripod and his battery packs turned into robots—robots with distinct ages and genders and personalities—and started insulting him. When he tried to tell them to stop they just laughed their weird metallic laughs.

Margo unlocked the storeroom and they lay down on their cot beds and made grunts of appreciation. A banging woke them.

"Hello?" Margo said.

"Hi, it's the Werners. Could you open up?"

"We're just taking a nap." Margo's voice was sharp.

"It's important that we talk now."

"OK."

Josh and Jess stood outside holding hands. Sarah stood a few feet away, holding Nipper in her arms.

"Where's Liz? This concerns both of you, I'm afraid," Josh said.

"Is everything all right?"

Liz appeared in the doorway.

"We had a visit from Usai this morning and we're just, we're just really shocked at what's been going on."

"What do you mean?"

Margo zipped up her fleece.

"We heard about the carnage last night. Liz burnt their money. I mean do you know how hard they work to make anything here? The salaries are like nothing. Whatever they have is—"

"They were doing it themselves. We just watched. Liz might have held the torch for them, but they asked—"

"They think she's going to open the road to cargo for them, that she's a representative of Queen Elizabeth, that she's the one they've been waiting for. There's a whole load of confused ideas out there and you've exploited them to make an idiotic TV show—"

"Now hold on a minute."

Margo reached in and lifted her glasses from the shelf. She put them on with one hand, assuming her prosecutorial air, and held the other hand up to silence Josh.

"We saved Usai from a beating, and maybe more than that. I don't know who sent him to spy on the Story, but if we're talking about blame here, I think you need to go and take a look in the mirror."

"You don't know what you're talking about."

Liz spoke. "We didn't mean to cause any harm."

"Well, you did. You'll need to move your stuff out now. You can go back to the guesthouse. You've made a mockery of our trust and kindness. Those ceremonies you took part in are heathen witchcraft. We've done a lot of work to eradicate the immoral dancing and licentiousness and the taking of drugs in this town—"

"You've done a lot of work to eradicate *many* of the local traditions," Margo countered.

"OK, that's it." Josh moved towards Margo and his wife pulled him back. "Pack up. Ship out. Your time's up here. I won't be taken for a fool. Lord knows I tried with you people." Josh put his hand out. "Keys."

Margo handed them over.

"We'll need ten minutes. Thanks for your hospitality."

From behind her mother, Sarah looked at Liz with anger, not embarrassment.

Liz and Margo gathered up their stuff in silence—though when they were rolling up their sleeping bags they made eye contact and each pulled a face of mock horror to stave off the real pain. No one liked being shouted at. They needed to get out of here and down the hill to Paolo and Stan.

They were explaining to Paolo what had happened when the plane whined into earshot. It looked like Cannick Hastings's little red and white Cessna.

The delegation trooped past them as they sat outside the rest house eating manioc and rice. Raula, the deputy administrator, walked past, in conversation with Josh. Behind them walked another administrator in a beige suit, and three stern policemen in navy shorts and sky-blue shirts; two carried semi-automatic rifles on straps across their chests, and all three had long knives in black leather sheaths hanging from their belts, along with truncheons. The one without a gun carried a spade against his shoulder.

About thirty feet behind came Cannick Hastings. He stopped beside the rest house, out of breath, and slid his mirrored sunglasses up onto his head.

"They mean business."

"What's going on?" Margo asked.

"Werner's worked Raula up. He got the chief of the New Truth in Texas to put a call in to Raula's boss, and the mission has threatened to cut grants to all schools and development funds if the administration doesn't put a stop to Belef and the Story."

Belef sat in her usual throne, on the log outside the door, and Raula stood before her, waving a letter in her face. Belef wore her Paul Smith multicolored dressing gown and her yachting cap and her glasses without glass.

"Witness. Witness the paper, Belef. Signed by the police chief *and* the head administrator. The body must be moved today or we can take you into jail."

Belef didn't respond. Finally she reached up and scratched her ear, then resumed her middle-distance stare. She called to Napasio.

"Me liklik samting."

Raula turned to the policemen. One of them stepped forward and poked the muzzle of the gun at Belef's arm. She merely turned her gaze towards him and he retreated.

Napasio came out from the house and handed her some betel nut and lime from the gourd. She whispered something to Belef, but Belef didn't respond. She moved in slow motion or like she was underwater; even the way she chewed was dreamy and measured and removed.

Raula came forward again.

"Belef, we can knock this down, make your house level, and we can lock you up in jail in Wapini. Is that what you want?"

"Do what you think is right."

"What I think is right is what the administrator has ordered. And what the chief of police has countersigned. Under twenty-nine C of the 1996 Health and Hygiene Provisions, any corpse is to be buried in an officially designated space set aside for such a purpose, and your garden is not such a space."

Belef said nothing but looked up at him and smiled. Raula turned to Josh Werner, who stood between the police, his baseball cap low on his head.

"Belef," he said, "you have to do what Raula says."

"What *you* say," Belef responded.

"Dig up the body," Raula said with a note of finality. The decision was made.

Belef got to her feet. Calmly, she said, "Do not touch her."

Werner stepped forward, brandishing a Bible in his hands.

"Belef, you were told—we told you that you couldn't bury Kaykay in your garden. It's not an example that we can let stand. And all this

MODERN GODS 293

nonsense about cargo, burning money, talking to the dead. I mean what did you think would happen? You can't go against God like this."

Belef looked at Josh and said, "When the law breaks open and Kaykay comes back she will find you."

"We were only ever trying to help you, Belef. But you can't challenge the Lord. He has only so much patience."

"Dig it up," Raula repeated.

"My children will stop you. My sons."

The policemen started forward, but Belef stood up and the men halted. She walked around to the patch where Kaykay was buried, where the little carved aeroplanes marked out the plot, and held up her hands.

"Get out of my garden. I will do it. I will do it. Let me go in for a minute."

Raula nodded at the policemen.

Belef turned and entered into her house and there was silence. No one met each other's eyes. Napasio came out and began muttering at Raula. She had her broom in her hands and pointed the twig end at him.

"You are a rubbishman, malas. A bikhet. You think you bigman but you nothing."

Inside the house Belef was talking in Koriam. A man's voice answered, then another's.

"Who is in there?" Raula shouted. "Come out, come out."

"It's her children," Liz said. Raula looked across at her and noticed that Paolo was filming.

"Stop that, stop that camera."

Paolo took a step back but didn't lower the camera.

Raula turned to the policemen.

"Get them to come out. Bring them out."

"They're not real. The children."

The short policeman pushed his gun onto his back and shoved Napasio out of the way. He entered the house and there was a minute or so of silence. Belef came out with the same blank expression as before. The policeman walked behind her, the nose of his semi-automatic pressed in her back.

"Oh, Belef, I'm so sorry. May the Lord keep you and bless you."

Liz turned. It was Jess, who'd appeared with Sarah and Usai. Quite a crowd was forming behind the policemen. Leftie was there, and Namor, and the boys who'd been playing at the river. Her neighbors had come out to see what was happening.

The policeman with the spade came forward, but Belef held her hands up and he halted, looking back at Raula. The deputy administrator pulled out a folded sheet of blue tarpaulin from his briefcase and threw it into the garden.

The policeman who'd come out of the hut behind Belef continued to press the nose of his gun into her back. She looked around at the assembled crowd of thirty, forty people, and said, "I will do it. I will dig up the body of my child. As they put the gun on me. Under the eye of the waitskins."

She sank to her knees by the grave and began to pull out the wooden aeroplanes. She laid them in a pile by the side of the hut. Margo spoke to Raula, "Surely there's no need for this. It's not like she's a danger—"

"She is. She *is* a danger," Raula said. "And stop that filming. This is not for BBC."

Paolo lowered the camera from his shoulder and then walked round behind Raula and the policemen and lifted it back up.

Belef collected the shells and pebbles off the grave and set them into piles. Napasio knelt down and began to help her.

Jess was crying now. She was hugging Sarah and soon Sarah was crying too. Josh stood apart from them, holding his Bible, watching intently.

Belef and Napasio began to dig with their hands, like dogs. Leftie appeared from around the side of the hut and got down on his knees too. He carried a digging stick and began churning the earth with it.

Usai stepped forward, and placed one hand on his mother's shoulder. She stopped scrabbling in the soil and looked up at him. He helped her up and they stood with their hands held for a long while. Belef said, "My son" and they hugged. He led Belef to her log seat and she sat down and looked at her hands, covered in soil. Usai took her place at the grave, scraping away the dirt. Belef took off her cap and set it on the grass at her feet. Her face was sweating and she would not look towards the administrator or the police, but she stared at Liz with a look of pure puzzlement, as if Liz had brought this whole situation about, as if Liz was the one to fix it now.

The digging went on. The children ran around the hut. Napasio sat back on her heels after a while, and Namor's mother came forward and tapped her shoulder and took over. When Leftie stopped for a few seconds and straightened up, Alan took his place. More villagers had arrived and it was hard to tell who was a follower of the Story and who wasn't. A crowd of sixty or seventy had now gathered round the hut in silence. One policeman stayed with his gun trained on those by the grave, and the other had climbed to a knoll behind the house, the better to see the whole crowd.

Alan hit wood with the digging stick.

A gap-toothed moonfaced woman that Liz recognized from last night—she'd been one of those squeezing the isa through the muslin parcels—took over from Namor's mother, and when she in turn wearied, and stopped for a moment, Liz found herself stepping forward and touching her shoulder.

Liz knelt. The side of the hole sloped and crumbled. It was uneven and about a foot and a half down, the dark wood of the coffin lid was visible. There was a lot of soil to be extracted before the coffin could be lifted out. She leaned forward and hauled up a handful and then another. The damp earth came away easily. She noticed that Usai, who had not stopped at all, was silently crying.

When they had cleared around the coffin—it was so small, a roughly hewn wooden box no more than five feet long—Alan inserted the handle of Napasio's broom under one end and tried to lever it up. After much exertion, one end of the coffin rose a few inches above the lip of the pit and then—a loud appalling crack. The side of the coffin had split. Alan lowered the broom and the coffin tilted; there was a sickening adjustment of its contents. Alan tried to let the coffin back down but now it stuck fast, half in and half out of the hole.

The smell. Napasio lifted her skirt and covered her face. Liz put her hand to her nose—her eyes were burning. An evil stench. A clotted smell of putrefaction. It occurred to her that though she had come from a land of death, filled with frequent human sacrifice—both intended and collateral—she had never seen a body of any kind. She looked down and saw several white maggots squirming out of the split wood and falling into the soil below. People began to move backwards.

Werner removed his baseball cap and held it with his Bible; it left a universal indent round his mousy hair, as if he wore an invisible crown.

Raula shouted at the policeman with the spade to "get involved," but this time when he put one leg over the low fence round the garden, Usai stood up and held out his hand for the spade. The policeman handed it over. Usai dug round the bottom of the coffin for a few minutes, then laid the spade aside and continued with his hands. They bent over—Leftie and Alan and Napasio and Liz and Usai—and lifted it, freed it from the earth. It wasn't heavy but the stench was overpowering. They straightened up but then the vessel began to crumble. The wood, rotten after five months in the damp ground, could not hold together; the bottom fell out. What was left of Kaykay slid back into the hole. Alan still held one side of the coffin, but the rest stood empty handed. Leftie stepped backwards, doubled over, and vomited.

Liz looked into the hole. Maggots writhing whitely. Some flesh, some mud, some bones, some hair.

From twenty or so feet away, Josh Werner sang out in his confident baritone, "Jesus bids us shine with a pure clear light." Other members of his congregation were gathered with him now—Watna and his wife, a few others Liz didn't know the names of—and they joined in.

"Like a little candle burning in the night."

Belef had not looked at the coffin. She had not reacted when it came apart but had continued staring into the middle distance. Upon hearing the hymn, though, she jumped up and began running towards Josh Werner. Everything happened very quickly. Suddenly the two policemen were on her, wrestling her to the ground. One of the policemen knelt on her back and was screaming at her to stay still. Usai ran over and pulled the policeman off his mother, shouting, "Stop!" And Josh Werner kept on singing—by himself now: "In this world of darkness"—and Usai wrestled with the policeman. He yanked the policeman's knife from the sheath on his belt and got free of him. He wheeled around to face Josh, his reverend. The man who'd brought him to the light.

"Stop it! You stop now!"

Josh looked at him with shock. His brow bunched close, but he kept singing as loud as he could, as if he were singing before God himself. "So we must shine. You in your small corner and I in mine."

Usai ran at Josh, his knife raised. A shot rang out, unimpeded; it sounded like a small bomb.

Usai bent double, staggered a few feet, and fell on his front on a patch of bare, baked earth. The wound on his back blossomed through the white Britney Spears T-shirt, seeping and spreading until it was a pool around him, shaped like an island, cut off from the world.

CHAPTER 34

For the whole journey back, Liz felt both light and heavy; she was floating mentally, and yet at the same time she could hardly lift her limbs. She drank the wine and watched the movies and couldn't take anything in. When she let herself remember she saw Belef stretched across her real son's dead body, she heard again the inhuman howling. She saw again the terrible expression in Belef's eyes when she raised her head from the body and looked straight at her. There was such accusation in it, and such rage.

After days of travel she reached the country of her birth, and a BBC driver stood at the carousel with the long version of her name scrawled on a board. She let him lift her bag and steer her to the car. In Ballyglass, the house was empty and she took the key from the hollow stone at the foot of the bird table. In her parents' bathroom cabinet she found Judith's zopiclone and swallowed two and crept up to her room and slept for fourteen hours.

When she woke the room was dark and she had no idea where she was. For that second of unknowingness, she felt the liberty of being nothing and no one and nowhere, just potential unrealized, the self before it creeps down into the world to be born—and then she rushed back into her body, into her memories, into this bed and house and town. The bite on her neck itched again. Her heel hurt. She was there and here. Carrying the wounds of there and the weight of here. How small the body felt for what it had to hold; memory and experience and pain. How continually one must fold and trim the soul.

The two policemen pulled Belef off the body, turned the body over.

Already Usai was a corpse, an empty container. The black eyes stared up at the sky and saw nothing at all. There is an argument (she had argued it herself, as an optimistic student) that if people only saw and knew death like this, up close—the corpse, the container—they would not be so keen to make corpses of each other. There was a way to negotiate with the dead, to hear them. But then there is the ancient law—an eye for an eye, a tooth for a tooth—common to all people at all times. Belef had looked at her like that. Like the only conclusion to this was more death.

Liz lay there now in the dark and thought she had spent her lifetime studying the differences, how one tribe does this, another that—and all the time there was no difference, not really, just tiny variations on a theme of great suffering, great loss.

Naspasio had held Belef and Leftie had held Belef and she had held Naspasio and Paolo had held her and—

She lifted her arm out from under the duvet and stroked it with the fingers of her other hand. She remembered the feeling of being held, of holding, of being part of a chain. What divides us is as nothing to what joins us. She would not stop at the eyes. She would journey out beyond the reef of her body and into open sea. The period of watching was over; she knew that as a fact within her. A change had come. But what? And what came next? She would be kind. She would learn to love the world. She would try. As if for the first time, she felt the grief inherent in all things, in all relations, in all love. She thought about her mother and wanted to see her, and sat up and turned the light on.

She found Alison standing at the sink, rinsing glasses.

"You were out for the count."

Liz walked up to her sister and embraced her for a long time. After resisting for a second, Alison allowed herself to be held.

For hours they talked past each other, both so caught up in their own stories, but it still felt comforting to get the details out, to expel the poison.

"And the man McFadden said to him, 'You killed five people that day, you made five people into nothing, but I wish to God you'd killed me too.'

He said, 'I wish you'd come down to my house afterwards and just shot me there on the doorstep. It would have been easier.'"

"I left money for her, for Belef. I left about eighty dollars and thirty pounds under a stone inside her hut. I didn't know what else to do. Margo said it had happened and it was a tragedy but it had happened now. And it wasn't our fault. It wasn't anyone's fault. But maybe the fault was all of us, was everyone."

"I was daydreaming this afternoon about what if Stephen hadn't done it. What if he just hadn't gone with them, if he had turned back, or been sick, or just ran away."

"She'd already lost one child, her daughter, and now she'd lost two. You could see the life go out of her. She just slumped down to the grass over her son's body. She just lay there."

"And Stephen said to McFadden, very quietly, 'You know I killed myself that day too.' He said, 'I made myself into nothing.' He said he'd killed himself that day but he didn't. He didn't do that."

In her father's many-desked study there was an e-mail from Paolo. Because she found the errors in his written English charming and not exasperating, she knew that she was probably in love or something like it. He wanted her to come to London, but she already felt the death of Usai as something that had spoiled everything that happened, that had infected her feelings for Paolo, and she didn't know if they could—or should—get round it. It was easier to forget the awful thing and move on, not looking back. But then she felt that she was always doing that, was always skipping out, and finally she replied and wrote that she hadn't been able to stop thinking about it either, and that she missed him too, and if she could she'd come to London.

By eight o'clock everybody had stopped pottering about; all three Donnelly children were reunited in the dark lounge. Alison and Liz lay top to toe on the sofa, and Spencer was on his back on the rug, holding his straight legs an inch off the ground, then raising them another inch, dropping them an inch. An empty bottle of wine stood on the coffee table.

It had been years since they'd sat around like this and talked. They listened as Alison told them how she couldn't love and she couldn't hate; she'd lost all feeling. But these, being borrowed words, were not quite true, and when Liz reached out a hand for her she started crying.

"Oh honey," Liz started.

"No, no, it's all right."

She blew her nose. They sat in silence awhile, watching the skipping flames of the gas fire.

Spencer said, "It's not very complicated, is it? You don't kill people."

"That's such a simplistic thing to—" began Liz.

But Alison forced a lot of noisy air into her lungs and said, "No, he's right. He's right."

Spencer sprang up and lifted the empty bottle.

"I'll get another."

When he had left the room, Alison said, quietly, to Liz, "I didn't want him to touch me anymore. It was more than that, really. When he touched me I wanted to scream. If he brushed against me in the hotel room or when he'd reach his hand across the table, I just wanted to be far away from him. I was talking to him but I felt like I was shouting from a great distance away, you know? I thought it would get better. But it didn't. It hasn't."

The curtains were open and outside the large sky was full of stars— exit wounds or promises of some greater light behind the black. An orange glow sat over Ballyglass in the distance. There came the low rumble of the cattle grid and boxes of light scrolled across the far wall, across the mantelpiece of Moorcroft vases and Royal Doulton plates and Lalique dancers. Their parents were back.

"It's like a morgue in here," said Kenneth, as he entered. "You not turn on the lights?"

Alison sat up and said, "The kids are upstairs asleep."

"Doesn't mean you can't turn the lights on."

"No, I'm just warning you they're here."

"Fine. How was Guinea?"

"Papua New Guinea."

Judith turned on the lights. Kenneth carried bags from the Murnaghan Outlet. Liz felt as if she hadn't been anywhere at all. Spencer sat up. He said, "Someone was shot dead."

"In Guinea?"

"Papua New Guinea. Actually I wasn't in PNG but an island off it. New Ulster. I told you."

"And someone was shot there?" Judith asked, pulling the curtains.

"A home from home," Kenneth said.

"What'd you buy?" Alison asked, setting her wineglass on a coaster and standing up.

Liz and her mother stood in the kitchen. Liz washed and her mother dried.

"Where?"

"One tumor of six centimeters, right by the bowel. They're worried it might perforate it."

"But they can treat it."

"Well, they can give me more chemo, but you know, the last time the tumors didn't get any smaller."

"I know but—but they stopped growing."

"For a while."

Kenneth and Spencer sat in the living room a few feet away. Kenneth scanned the sports pages of the *Daily Telegraph* and Spencer typed another e-mail to Trisha, telling her everything would be all right, that it would be better now, that now it was out in the open they could at least decide what to do. . . . Kenneth lifted the remote control and turned the television on.

Spencer's phone buzzed. A text from Ian. Do you love her?

Spencer replied with a simple Yes and turned his phone off.

A little later the women moved to the conservatory. The men stayed watching rugby in the lounge. The rhythms of Ulster life as Liz had always known them. Alison turned to her mother and sister and tried to find a story that would fit.

"All his stuff is still in Mickey's room, in boxes, not that he has much. I told him not to be unpacking it."

"But the wedding, all the presents!" Judith said.

And Liz could not suppress an infuriated sigh. What fetish gods the Donnellys were! They'd stay in a marriage so as not to waste the cargo of a fondue set.

"I just mean: people gave things in good faith," said Judith in a wounded tone that left Liz a little ashamed.

"I wrote him a letter and left it on the kitchen table. I said that I didn't want the children—I didn't want to have to tell the children, you know, about any of it. The way it is now sure they can find anything online. They'll be reading all them comments and stories about him. I couldn't bear them to know him as one thing, as their father, and then learn he was this other thing. This monster."

Atlantic padded in and Liz scooped her up. Alison wrinkled up her nose and leaned away.

"You know I've never liked dogs."

Spencer appeared in the doorway, filling it.

"I've news too."

Judith stood up.

"Well, let's all go into the lounge," she said. "I'm sure your father will want to be involved in this."

Spencer sat on the sofa. He placed his fingertips together.

"This is difficult to say—"

"Son, if it helps," Judith began, "I think we know what you're about to—"

"You do?"

"You've been keeping a secret—"

"What—"

"It's OK," Judith began. "Lots of people nowadays are that way. Alison told us—"

Kenneth interrupted, confident, like a local newscaster reeling off some tolerant facts that had been going round the town these last few years: "Sheila Byrne's son Alistair is gay, and Carol Allen's son is gay, and Margaret Costelloe's daughter's a real lesbian—but I could have told you that when she was six. And do you know what Sheila says 'gay' stands for?"

"What are you talking—" Spencer began, but Kenneth would not be waylaid.

"Good as you," he said, nodding brightly. "Good as you."

"I never said that he was gay," Alison shouted. She was getting up, getting ready to leave the room, but Spencer held onto her arm.

"What the fuck are you—"

"Yes, you did," Kenneth said. "And mind your language, son, in this house."

Spencer laughed. "Er, I'm not gay. I've been having a relationship with Trisha."

"Our Patricia?"

"From the office. For a long time."

Only Liz wasn't surprised. She stood up.

"Shall I make tea?"

She sat on the sofa beside Alison, flicking through pictures of New Ulster on her laptop: everything so small and clean and bright and two-dimensional. Alison wanted to know which one was the dead one. Spencer came in, still looking at the screen of his phone and Liz clicked Belef's face closed. When Spencer turned to them, his face wore a look of definite joy.

"They're getting divorced."

"Really?"

"So he says."

"Is he angry?"

"Yeah."

"With you?"

"Yeah."

Their parents went to bed, Spencer left—to find Trisha, they supposed—and Alison and Liz sat on in the living room.

"Shall I get another bottle of wine?"

"Take a bottle of the Shiraz from the garage. He has a box of it behind the running machine."

When Liz came back, Alison had made a nest for herself with cushions on the rug in front of the gas fire.

"Here, set mine here."

Liz placed the glass of wine on the slate hearth, and sat down beside her little sister. They sipped and sat and stared at the gas fire for a second—the uniform buttery flames budding, unlocking, disappearing.

"Are you going back to him?"

Alison shrugged.

"I don't know how people forgive."

"Me neither."

"All marriages have difficult patches."

Alison looked at her.

"I'm just repeating what people say. What do I know?"

"Do you remember how Mum and Dad used to fight the bit out?" asked Alison. "She moved out that time even."

A little frisson erupted in the air around Liz's head.

"She went to the flat above the office," said Alison, still feeling around, Liz thought, to check if she had privileged information, if she knew a story Liz was never told.

"I remember."

Liz stared into the fire. How regular the buds of flame were. The secret to being perfectly dull. Repetition, unchanging, the same shade and shape.

"Do you think there was someone else involved?"

"I don't know."

"But she came back for you," Alison said, and there was a broken sob in her voice. One of the ways Liz knew that Alison was the favorite, that Alison was the child preferred by both her parents, was because of this incident. They had never talked about it for this reason.

"Well, she came back for Spencer," Liz corrected. "Remember how he wouldn't go. How crazy he was, holding onto Dad's leg and screaming. He could only have been four."

"So she took you. I was third choice obviously."

Liz looked at her sister. How could something so apparent never have occurred to her? She had never considered how the episode looked to Alison.

"Ally, she took me because she thought you'd look after Spencer. She didn't think I was capable of doing it, of being motherly."

"That's not what you think."

"It's what I *know*."

"No, no, she didn't want me."

"That's not true. It was because she didn't trust me not to fight with Kenneth, and she didn't think I could look after Spence. Even though I was two years older than you."

Alison sat and clenched and unclenched her jaw, just like Kenneth did when he was brooding on something.

"I was sure it was because . . . I thought she didn't want me."

"Oh Al. You've been reading between the wrong lines."

A little tilting and resettling of the world and its contents. Did Alison settle for men who didn't deserve her because she felt at some basic level that her mother had rejected her? Did Liz refuse to grow up because she felt her mother had told her once that she was unsuited to motherhood and responsibility? And what if neither of those things were the case? Or what if both were? They stared into the fire.

There was a movement behind the glass door. A white nightgown sloped into the kitchen.

"You two still up? I've terrible reflux. I've been trying to sleep sitting up. But I'm going to take these zopiclone."

Their mother, she of the variously interpreted motives, filled a glass of water.

"Do you remember, Mum," ventured Liz, "when you moved out of the house in Coolreaghs?"

Alison sat up straight and both daughters now realized they were eyeing their mother very intently, like two people in a dock before a judge.

"When we moved *here*?"

"No, when *you* moved out," said Alison impatiently. "When you and Dad were fighting loads."

Their mother turned off the tap and came into the living room.

"Now, what made you think of that?"

"We were just talking," said Alison casually, but her jaw was still set like Kenneth's.

Judith sat on the edge of the sofa. It was clearer in her nightgown how thin the cancer had left her legs, how distended it had left her stomach. Looking at her, Liz was suddenly regretful of their present interrogation but Alison was set on the single track, not able to stop or turn.

"Why did you take Liz with you?" she asked.

"Well, Spencer wouldn't go."

"You took me because you thought I'd fight with Dad, didn't you? And because you didn't think I'd look after Spencer."

Judith looked at her eldest daughter.

"No. I can't remember exactly, but—"

"You took her because you didn't want me," Alison said.

"No! I wanted to take all three of you. I can't remember the specifics now! I think you'd locked yourself in the bathroom after Spencer had his fit, and Ken was holding onto him, and he was sobbing. And Liz wanted to go. She'd got into the car and lain down in the back seat. Your dad was hurt, I think, that you wanted to go—"

Judith adjusted her nightgown around her stomach, and swallowed the tablet from her fist.

"It was a difficult time, every family has difficult . . . God, have you two been sitting here thinking up reasons to hate me!"

"No!"

"Not that at all."

Her mother had tears in her eyes, and Liz felt some hardness that she hadn't even been aware of in her crumble. She looked at Alison; she was staring at her mum with a kind of boundless childish hunger.

Upstairs, Liz sat on the bed and looked out at the scattering of stars, the dark fields, the light from the corner of Sidney's farmyard. It felt stuffy and she opened the window and felt a new coolness sweep over her face. The flowery brocaded curtain shifted very slightly, almost imperceptibly, swayed by the little breeze she'd brought into the closed room.

ACKNOWLEDGMENTS

For their patience, insight, and careful suggestions, many thanks to Natasha Fairweather and Paul Slovak. For his trust and enthusiasm, many thanks to Nick Pearson.

Thanks also to the John Simon Guggenheim Memorial Foundation for a fellowship that aided the completion of this novel, even if the fellowship was to write a nonfiction book about poetry. (I'm on it.)

While some of the occurrences in the narrative are based on real events, all the characters are imaginary. I read and took prompts from many books on Northern Ireland and on cargo cults, including Susan McKay's *Northern Protestants: An Unsettled People*; Peter Taylor's *Loyalists*; *Lost Lives: The Stories of the Men, Women and Children who Died as a Result of the Northern Ireland Troubles* by David McKittrick, Seamus Kelters, Brian Feeney, Chris Thornton, and David McVea; Peter Lawrence's *Road Belong Cargo: A Study of the Cargo Movement in the Southern Madang District, New Guinea* and his *Gods, Ghosts and Men in Melanesia*; David Attenborough's *Quest in Paradise*; Peter Worsley's *The Trumpet Shall Sound: A Study of "Cargo" Cults in Melanesia*. I borrowed a few details—such as the names of Belef's spirit children—from Andrew Lattas's anthropological study *Cultures of Secrecy: Reinventing Race in Bush Kaliai Cargo Cults*.

Thanks also to Jon Moorhouse and Dave Saraga, wherever they are, with whom I first traveled to Melanesia almost twenty years ago.

As always, thanks to Zadie for everything.